LEFT FOR DEAD

ALSO BY SEAN PARNELL

NONFICTION

OUTLAW PLATOON

FICTION

MAN OF WAR
ALL OUT WAR
ONE TRUE PATRIOT

LEFT FOR DEAD

A NOVEL

SEAN PARNELL

WILLIAM MORROW
An Imprint of HarperCollinsPublishers

HarperCollins books may be purchased for educational, business, or sales promotional use. For information, please email the Special Markets Department at SPsales@harpercollins.com.

FIRST EDITION

Library of Congress Cataloging-in-Publication Data

Names: Parnell, Sean, 1981- author.
Title: Left for dead : a novel / Sean Parnell.
Description: First Edition. | New York, NY : William Morrow, an imprint of
    HarperCollinsPublishers, [2021] | Series: Eric Steele series ; vol 4 |
Summary: "Special Operative Eric Steele battles a renegade group of
    bioterrorists armed with a devastating virus in the fourth pulse-pounding
    military thriller from the New York Times bestselling author of Outlaw
    Platoon"— Provided by publisher.
Identifiers: LCCN 2021032634 (print) | LCCN 2021032635 (ebook) | ISBN
    9780062986610 (hardcover) | ISBN 9780062986627 | ISBN
    9780062986634 (ebook)
Subjects: GSAFD: Suspense fiction.
Classification: LCC PS3616.A762 L44 2021 (print) | LCC PS3616.A762
    (ebook) | DDC 813/.6—dc23
LC record available at https://lccn.loc.gov/2021032634
LC ebook record available at https://lccn.loc.gov/2021032635

ISBN 978-0-06-298661-0

21 22 23 24 25 LSC 10 9 8 7 6 5 4 3 2 1

FOR MY CHILDREN

LEFT FOR DEAD

ACT I

CHAPTER 1

ZHAGANTU, CHINA

The helicopters arrived at midnight, and the men they carried killed everyone they met.

There were three of the machines, black and hulking but sleek as sharks, all emblazoned with the red stars of the Chinese Communist Party's People's Liberation Army. They were Harbin Z-20s, heavily armed, capable of three hundred knots airspeed at treetop level and each hauling a dozen assaulters. They looked much like U.S. Army UH-60 Black Hawks, but they were not cheap knockoffs. Their rotor systems had been expertly cloned from a crashed American stealth helicopter, gifted to Beijing by the Pakistanis after U.S. Navy SEALs had terminated Osama bin Laden.

The Harbin Z-20s were very quiet. No one heard them coming at Toqui 13, the most secret biological warfare laboratory in all of China.

The lab was a Level V facility drilled into the summit of a wind-scarred butte that resembled Devils Tower in Wyoming.

It was located in the absolute nowhere of the north central Chinese badlands, ten kilometers from the Mongolian border. You couldn't just stumble upon it, and if you did you'd be shot on the spot and no one would find your corpse. Toqui 13, whose name meant "Spearhead" in Mandarin, had been built to harvest only one thing: a genetically enhanced corona virus called Gantu-62 that could kill a Notre Dame linebacker in fifteen minutes.

Dr. Ai Liang, a full colonel in the People's Army, was the laboratory's director, and up until recently she'd been fervently dedicated to the Chinese Communist Party. The daughter of a distinguished couple of the Cultural Revolution, she'd already become a star of the Chinese Communist Youth League at age sixteen and had graduated with honors from Changchun University of Science and Technology while simultaneously pursuing her military career. Mao Zedong was her God.

But three weeks ago something had happened that had flipped a switch in Dr. Liang's head. Her research assistant, Second Lieutenant Chang Wu—a handsome young man with a lovely wife and three precious girls in Shanghai—had slipped on a spill of lubricant from an air compressor and had smashed the glass of an incubator with his elbow. The shards had sliced open his Military Oriented Protective Posture suit, as well as his flesh.

Lieutenant Wu instantly knew what was going to happen, and so did his mentor. Together, they had tested Gantu-62 on laboratory animals—first mice, then rabbits, and finally rhesus macaque monkeys. The viral storm had swept through Wu's bloodstream in minutes, and his immunological response was explosive. It was like an Ebola reaction in hyper speed. Helpless and horrified, Dr. Liang had watched the poor boy wretch up his own intestines, drown in his own blood, and choke to death on the laboratory floor.

Two days prior to this evening, she had finally emerged from three weeks in quarantine isolation, where she'd examined her life and its purpose and had wept until she had no tears left. She had firmly concluded that there should be no Level V biowarfare laboratories, or anything like Gantu-62, *anywhere* in the world.

Tonight she was going to shut the whole damn thing down. . . .

The numerical designation of all such facilities is a reference to how many segregated floors there are. Level I, at the very bottom of Toqui 13, held the effluent decontamination systems. Above that on Level II was the research lab with inflatable seal doors, autoclaves, petri dish germ farms, and breathing hoses into which lab workers plugged their MOPP helmets. Next came Level III—the serious business floor—with buffer corridors, steel double-entrance doors, incubators for "arms-only" handling of samples, electron microscopes, more breathing hoses, and reverse suction pumps to keep the air pressure at less than one atmosphere.

Level III was where they carefully deposited the already deadly, naturally occurring viruses being farmed on Level II and genetically enhanced them to be fifty times more lethal. If you ripped a hole in your PPE on Level III—as Wang Chu had done—they took your corpse right down to the giant incinerator below the blending tank under Level I and sent a very nice note and the Medal of Loyalty and Integrity to your mother.

Levels IV and V were all about reprocessing air, with HEPA filters, exhaust fans, and breathing air reservoirs—two whole floors just to keep everyone alive. And finally at the top was the last level, which didn't count numerically, containing the lab's administrative offices, cafeteria, sleeping quarters, one small amphitheater, and outside past the entrance, a helicopter landing pad.

It was a large facility shaped like a giant steel travel mug sunk into the excavated rock of the butte, with only the top floor and its camouflaged roof exposed. To get there, you had to fly west from Beijing to Hohhot on a PLA aircraft, then ride a blacked-out government bus all the way to Baotou and turn north for Bayan Obo. From that point on, the primitive mountain roads tortured your spine for another sixty kilometers until you reached the alpine tram that took you up to one of the most dangerous buildings on earth. But you only had to do that twice—once to arrive and once to leave. Deployments were a year long. There was no leave time. It was like working at an outpost on Mars.

Now Dr. Liang—outwardly composed though her stomach churned and her eyes were ringed with exhaustion—took her place at the amphitheater's podium to start her emergency briefing. She was an attractive woman in her early forties, petite and toned from the lab's daily tai chi sessions and the yoga that relieved the stress. She had long dark hair swirled up into a bun, hazel eyes, a small nose, white teeth and wore fashionable purple glasses. She was also very pale, but everyone who worked at Toqui 13 was pale.

"I must apologize to all of you for waking you up," she began as she clutched a set of phony PLA directives that she'd forged on her own computer. "However, we have received urgent orders with which we must all comply."

She looked at the twenty-three wide-eyed faces staring back at her. Almost everyone was dressed in PLA track pants and T-shirts because she'd rousted them from their beds. Six of them were women and none of them was older than thirty-one. They were lab technicians, analysts, biomedical experts, and maintenance personnel, and all were patriots and dedicated Party members. The colonel-doctor had dressed in her brown camouflage Military Medical Team uniform to emphasize that her words were blessed by officialdom.

"You are all aware of the unfortunate fate of Lieutenant Chu," she continued, "which has been reviewed by the Committee for State Security. The Party has now deemed Toqui 13 as a domestic risk beyond acceptability." She was lying. She didn't dare tell them the truth because she knew that soon they'd all be interrogated, and if any of them were suspected of conspiring with her treachery, they'd spend the rest of their days in a reeducation camp with the Uyghurs in Xinjiang province. "Therefore, I am very sorry to say . . . tonight we are closing down this laboratory."

Her minions gasped, as if a surge of electricity had coursed through their amphitheater seats. They looked at one another, then back at Liang. One of them clutched an ornate chess set to her bosom and another clamped his own mouth with both hands.

"Yes." Dr. Liang nodded with a mournful expression. "It is a terrible blow, yet it is true. I know this is difficult, and you've all done spectacular work here, but the needs of the Party . . ."

She glanced over their heads past the heavy tempered glass entrance doors. Outside on the landing pad four internal security guards were pacing languidly back and forth. They were armed only with Type 77B pistols. No one ever threatened Toqui 13.

"You have one hour to pack your personal effects, and you will leave everything else behind. We will assemble outside at the tram and begin our journey back to Beijing." She smiled—a nurturing expression, especially for a colonel. Her plan was to be the last one to leave, after she first descended below Level I, poured all over the floor the thirty liters of generator fuel she'd been secretly hoarding, sliced through the high-pressure oxygen hoses, fired up the incinerator, and opened its doors. "Just five minutes for questions, please, and then we must hurry."

A young man raised a trembling hand. He'd been Lieutenant Wang Chu's best friend at Toqui 13 and his heart was still broken.

"Colonel Liang," he began in a quaking tone, "with respect, why can we not first complete the application analysis for weaponization? After all, it is nearly . . ."

Dr. Liang raised a hand to shush him because she'd noticed something strange outside. A thrumming vibration was shivering the entrance glass and she saw a red-orange glow flooding the tarmac apron. The guards were looking up at the sky, and stepping back, and two of their fur hats fluttered off their heads.

A helicopter appeared. It was one of those brand-new Harbin Z-20s she'd seen on the PLA's internal video news network. There was very little dust and debris at the top of Toqui 13's private mountain, so there wasn't the usual brownout caused by these big machines. All at once her heart sank like a stone through dark honey as she realized headquarters had dispatched some sort of military contingent without advising her, which was never a good sign. Moreover, her treachery would soon be exposed. It could all end with her summary execution this very night.

But the helicopter didn't actually land. Its big fat wheels hovered a meter off the deck. Liang's audience followed her gaze and turned to watch as the cargo door slid open and figures began jumping onto the tarmac in the glow of the aircraft's tactical lights. Strangely, they were not regular troops. They were wearing sophisticated black MOPP suits and helmets, with oxygen hoses and their own compact air supplies on their backs. Their faceplates were tinted, and above each was a pinpoint spotlight. They looked like spacemen, except they were all carrying QBZ-95 bullpup assault rifles in 5.8 × 42 mm, and the barrels were fixed with large thick tubes that resembled . . . suppressors.

"*Tien Tahng*"—God in heaven—Ai Liang whispered as they shot the first guard in the chest and he slammed backward into the entrance doors. Then they spun on the other three, who were trying to draw their pistols, but the assaulters' muzzles flashed and their silenced weapons clacked and the guards screamed and collapsed.

"Run!" Liang yelled as she saw the spacemen stepping over the twitching corpses and stomping toward the entrance doors. There were six of them, no, eight or nine, and there seemed to be more helicopters now and her young laboratory comrades leaped up from their upholstered seats and started howling and scrambling in every direction, like a movie audience fleeing a theater fire. The front doors flew open and the killers walked into Toqui 13 with the cold temerity of bored executioners, and started mowing everyone down.

Submachine guns spat silenced fire, severed fingers spun through the air, brain matter splattered the white tile ceiling like gray scrambled eggs. Bullets ricocheted off the metal rims of amphitheater seat backs, but there weren't many of those misplaced shots and as she turned to run, Dr. Liang had the fleeting thought that these bastards were expert killers.

A thundering sound and vibration came from above her as she sprinted across the theater, thinking she might be able to make it out the rear entrance doors, though she had no idea where she'd go after that. Then the landing gear of another helo crunched down on the roof and a second later the ceiling burst open with a flash and a *whump* that slammed her backward onto the floor. She saw the girl with the chess set, Mingyu, a sweet young thing from Nanjing, go sprinting by her on the right just as one of the spacemen zipped to the linoleum on an assault rope, grabbed Mingyu by her ponytail, spun her around, and shot her point-blank in the forehead with a pistol.

Liang had nowhere else to go. She jumped to her feet and rushed Mingyu's killer, and as she hit top speed she left the floor and slammed him in the spine with her boot. He crashed to his face and his helmet bounced but she didn't see or hear any of that because she rolled and kept on running for the glass exit doors at the far side, and as they got closer and closer, amid a torrent of screams and choked gunfire that sounded like a dozen mad-men hammering a dead piano, the doors burst open and another five spacemen came stomping inside. Two of them were carrying satchel charges that looked like the thermite bombs she'd once seen at the EOD school at Kaohsiung, and one of them was haul-ing a gleaming metallic box the size of a large picnic cooler.

She knew immediately what it was: a lead-lined, temperature-controlled, vacuum-sealed system for transporting biowarfare weapons . . . like Gantu-62.

They gunned down Ju-Long, the young master sergeant in charge of the lab's pneumatics, then turned their weapons on her. She ducked and jinked hard to the right as bullets whip-cracked past her ears, and she charged through the door to her office, slammed the dead bolt on the other side, and flew across the room without stopping to catch her ragged breath. The previ-ous director of Toqui 13, the man who'd designed it, had devised an escape hatch for his office. Liang had always thought he was a bit paranoid and had never bothered to inspect it. But now she found it there at the back of her closet, a small door with a twist handle that she could barely see because all of her boots and extra uniforms were piled up inside. She whipped those things over her shoulders in a ferocious blur as the killers pounded outside on her door and opened fire on the lock, and she ripped the escape door open, grabbed the top of the frame, launched her feet through the hole, and crashed to the floor of the buffer corridor on Level V.

She expected a hand grenade to follow her, then realized these men were there to steal something volatile and deadly and wouldn't risk using explosives, but they would surely kill her as soon as they could. She felt blood running down the inside of her trousers from some sort of wound, the adrenaline flooded her veins like *baijiu* hard liquor, and she swooned and felt like she was going to vomit, but she raced for the corridor stairs as the sweat flung from her brow.

Thank God there were no elevators at Toqui 13—no one could head her off. Access to all levels was via steel stairwells that could never fail, and that was also why all the workers had such strong legs. But those legs hadn't saved them from bullets, and with the fresh coppery stench of her own blood in her nostrils, Dr. Liang charged down the stairs.

The lights went out. She fumbled for her cell phone to use its flashlight and found it had bounced out of her fatigue pocket, but that barely slowed her pace because she'd loped those stairs a thousand times. She heard clanging in the darkness above her, sledgehammers smashing the door locks on Level III. Her breaths spewed from her lungs as she passed every level and kept on going until she reached the very bottom and the final door to the effluent systems, and below that, the giant incinerator.

It was pitch-black. She fell down that last short set of steel stairs. She crawled on her torn hands and bruised knees along one cold stone wall. There was still the smell of incinerated flesh in the subterranean cave, but she managed to hold her bile down and felt her way to the expulsion hatch that was opened only for rare occurrences, such as extracting virus culture remnants after a 300-degree Celsius burn, or the charred remains of a loyal comrade like Lieutenant Chu.

She had the only key to that hatch. Her hands were shaking uncontrollably as her slick fingers flipped through the key ring that was still on her garrison belt and she found the right one out of twenty. The lock opened after eighteen seconds of coaxing, twisting, and praying, and she hauled on the hatch. A blast of icy air smacked her face, and she saw a long black tube, and at the very end in the distance, starlight.

A minute later, she was lying on her back outside on a forty-five-degree cliff face of slippery rock, a third of the way down the butte with nothing but blackness below. It was freezing cold and the wind was threatening to whip her right off the mountain.

She looked up, where the fat wasp shapes of three murderous helicopters were winging away into the midnight sky, and the crown of her once precious Toqui 13 exploded in a thundering fireball, and the top of the mountain was engulfed in raging flames.

CHAPTER 2

Eric Steele fell ninety-seven feet and slammed into the side of a mountain. It was a vertical rock wall of black cosmic granite, and the only reason it didn't kill him was that he'd belayed himself with a two-hundred-foot length of 12mm thick Petzl Vector climbing rope. Still, he bounced off the wall like a whiplashed marionette, shattered his MBITR radio, lost his hip pouch of Dutch V40 minigrenades, and it was only by pure miracle that his pelvis didn't crack in half.

Holy mother of God . . .

It was nearly impossible to quietly hammer a rock-climbing piton into a cliff face, even with a custom rubber mallet, so he'd jammed a hex nut anchor into a crevice, linked a titanium carabiner to its steel cable, clipped the black rope into the carabiner and had kept on climbing upward. He'd been at it for more than two hours, repeating that process over and over, and had made it past the thousand-foot mark with fewer than another five hundred to go, when he'd put pressure on what looked like—at least on this freezing moonless midnight—a nice strong toehold.

Negative.

Now he was swinging in the wind with fifty-four pounds of gear on his back, including an FN P90 submachine gun, two extra fifty-round magazines of 5.7 × 28 mm ammunition, a Sig Sauer P226 MK25 suppressed pistol with three extra fifteen-round mags, two combat knives, a tourniquet, a mini water bladder, a rear plate carrier, black Mammut mountaineering boots, tac gloves, MICH helmet, night-vision goggles, and a hip harness of carabiners, ropes, pitons, hex nuts, rappel guides, and now . . . *no* freaking radio, or frags.

He was praying that the hex nut currently holding the rope would last just a bit longer, while the stretched nylon cable *thwanged* in the wind and yanked his climbing harness so far up into his crotch that he thought he might be a candidate for the Vienna Boys Choir.

He hung there for a moment, catching his ragged breath, arms drooping while he mentally diffused the kind of pain that came with smacking yourself into a concrete wall at the speed of a motocross bike. He looked down at the gleaming sliver of the Argeş river where it wound through a forested valley far below, then up the other side to the top of a mirroring peak, and the pink granite fortress that was, of all things, Dracula's Castle.

That's right. This was the spot in Romania that those Millennial Crude jokers had chosen for their new hacker hideout and cyber mayhem spree, a nice little bombproof structure still five hundred feet above Steele's head, with a spectacular view of the former mountaintop citadel of Vlad the Impaler. Made sense to

Steele, and gave him all the more reason to kill every last one of them.

He had many other reasons, of course, beginning with the deaths of three of his Program comrades at the hands of Lila Kalidi, a vicious female assassin who collected the ears of her victims. Kalidi had been contracted by Dmitry "Snipe" Kreesak, the leader of Millennial Crude, who in turn worked for Russia's Federal Security Bureau. Millennial Crude had also battled with the Program's own cyber warfare guru, Ralphy Persko, and while both sides had suffered casualties, nobody held a grudge. Steele's friends were dead, but so was Lila Kalidi. He himself had killed her at close range. So he'd figured "all's fair in love and war" and was prepared to let it go.

That is, until Crude really lived up to its name.

A month ago, the Russian FSB had decided to take out a Russian defector to the United States, Naftali Ostrovsky, who was making too much noise about Vladimir Putin's sexual peccadilloes to American media outlets in Boston. An FSB agent had slipped into the United States and poisoned Ostrovky's tea with polonium, which had put him on a ventilator in the ICU at Massachusetts General Hospital. But Ostrovsky wasn't dying fast enough for the Kremlin.

Millennial Crude was called in, and from their remote headquarters in the Moscow suburb of Kapotnya, they'd shut down all the electrical power to Mass. General for two full hours, including the backup generators. Aside from Ostrovky, who'd expired in ten minutes, four other innocent patients on ventilators had died, plus three newborn infants in incubators.

Steele might not even have known about all this if not for

Ralphy Persko. The Program had been disbanded by order of President Rockford, but Ralphy had a private obsession with Millennial Crude and had kept on tracking their activities. When he told Steele about their attack on Mass. General, the news about the helpless babies boiled Steele's blood.

Steele knew there'd be no Program support or equipment for a hit on Millennial Crude, so he and his currently unemployed keeper, Dalton "Blade" Goodhill, had turned to an old CIA special tactics hand, Thorn McHugh, who happened to be as wealthy as Mark Cuban. The three men had met one night in East Potomac Park in Washington, D.C., and after hearing Steele's and Goodhill's pitch, McHugh had simply walked away. The next day a FedEx letter had arrived on Steele's doorstep at Neville Island, Pennsylvania. It contained a black American Express card in Steele's name—no limit.

After the Boston slaughter, the Russians had decided that Millennial Crude should relocate for a while till the whole thing blew over. Romania seemed the perfect spot: lots of remote mountains and less-than-curious villagers. The country had been a Soviet satellite for decades, but even after Gorbachev nothing much had changed. You could buy just about anything with oligarch money in Bucharest, including a modular ceramic tactical operations center shaped like a giant igloo, with double thick tempered glass doors, sidebar living quarters, a Jamie Oliver kitchen, minigymnasium, banks of 8Pack OrionX personal computers and satellite uplinks, and all of it delivered by contracted heavy-lift helos and assembled by FSB engineers. The nine bodyguards were Russian private military contractors from Grupa Vagnera, who slept outside in a trailer and never entered the dome.

Ralphy Persko knew all this because ever since the Program

had stood down, he was incredibly bored and had lots of time on his hands. He hadn't asked Steele for one penny for the intel. Nevertheless, Steele intended to add a fat tip for Ralphy to the Thorn McHugh budget.

Steele finally stopped swinging at the end of his rope, reached over and grabbed the main line, and pulled himself back to the vertical wall. The granite was slimy and slippery as hell and he didn't have crampons on his boots, but he'd file that memo for later—if there was ever going to be a "later." He spread his black-clad legs wide, found what seemed like two load-bearing toeholds, reached for a couple of fingertip ledges, and started inching his way back up the cliff face like Spider-Man—just much slower, and more cautiously, and extremely bruised.

It took another hour setting belay hexes, paying out rope, inching upward and sweating in the icy night, and then he was peering over an onyx shelf at that salmon-colored dome, straight ahead on a summit clearing among a copse of Romanian pines. The moon had just popped up from behind a charcoal fur ball of clouds and it was so high and bright in the indigo sky that he wasn't even going to need the NVGs mounted on top of his helmet. He slithered on his stomach over to the left behind a long coffin-like slab of granite, took one long pull from his hydration bladder, and started quietly shedding gear—the rock-climbing hardware, ropes, harness, and carabiners. He came to his knees, slung the P90 subgun over his back, pulled the P226 from his thigh holster, screwed on the Knights Armament silencer, and press checked the handgun. He wished he still had his radio so he could tell Goodhill he'd made it to the top. And oh yes, the grenades; he wished he still had those too.

Oh, well, FIDO . . . fuck it, drive on . . .

He rose and moved forward at a hunched, graceful glide, especially for a large muscular man wearing mountaineering boots. The slab of granite on his left had a twin on the right, forming a roofless corridor, and suddenly at the end of it a figure stepped into view. It was one of the Russian sentries, a tall man wearing a Spetsnaz camouflage smock, black tactical pants, a fur hat, and slinging a Romanian AK-47 with its peculiar folding stock. He was lighting up a smoke and his back was turned to Steele.

For a moment, as he floated closer, Steele felt a twinge of remorse.

Dude's just a gun for hire, probably doesn't even know what he's doing here, or who these people are he's protecting. . . . Maybe he's got a wife, little kids, a faithful dog. . . . Maybe even a little old mamushka back in Moscow or Saint Petersburg. . . .

Steele shot him in the back of the skull.

He stepped over the bleeding corpse and kept on going, and at that moment he crossed the mental bridge over what he internally called his "red river." You could conduct surveillance of a target, or any sort of long-range recon mission, and withdraw without reaching that next laser-focused level if you did no harm. But once you'd taken that first life it was like everything collapsed into a very narrow tunnel, at the end of which appeared each of your mortal opponents, and there were only two lives at a time, yours and theirs, and only one would survive. His red river wasn't a pretty feature, but every true warrior had one, and once you crossed it you had to be totally on your game, or die.

The dome grew larger. It was late at night but he could see a soft red glow suffusing the interior like the combat bulbs in a warship's combat information center, and it was no surprise that these Millennial Crude cyber thugs would still be up working because they wreaked havoc all over the world in multiple time zones. Steele headed straight for the entrance, a set of double doors in inch-thick Perspex with vertical brass handles, which he knew wouldn't be locked because there was no point in having a close protection contingent outside if they had to first get a key or permission to come inside and save your ass.

Then all at once two more Russians appeared, on the far right and far left of the dome, each hustling, as if the demise of their fallen comrade had triggered some sort of biosensor alarm. Steele, moving with his arms locked out front in an isosceles two-handed grip on the P226, shot the man on the right in the face, then swung left in a weird lunge like a bowler's pitch, and with only his right hand still gripping the pistol, shot the left man in the right knee. The bullet kicked his legs out from under him, and as his nose smacked the ground Steele put another one in the top of his skull. Both AKs clattered as they fell, but that didn't matter because he was already at the door, holstering his pistol and swinging the P90 subgun around.

The Fabrique Nationale P90 is a strange-looking weapon. It is short, lightweight, constructed of polymer, and looks like a backward black hatchet where you tuck the blade under your arm, the bullets spit from the end of the handle, and you grip it by two black donuts welded to the bottom. The magazine sits on the top of the receiver, and the empty shells spray out the bottom like an M240B machine gun. The bullets are nasty-looking things that resemble brass spikes on a leather punk collar.

When Steele came through the front doors—and locked them from the inside, using a steel carabiner on the interior handles— the hackers who turned from their work stations saw something reminiscent of Arnold Schwarzenegger's alien nemesis in

Predator. There were four of them seated at two separate work-stations, right and left, in front of their superspeed OrionX PCs, and because Millennial Crude was ecumenical, the men were Italian, Iranian, Norwegian, and Greek. Between the two sta-tions stood Dmitry Kreesak himself, in skinny black jeans and a billowy pink shirt with his thick hair gelled back above his Hugo Boss glasses. "Snipe" seemed to be enveloped in a cloud of smoke, which made sense, since the atmosphere reeked of cannabis.

For a moment everyone froze. Then Steele spoke across the room to Snipe, in perfect Russian.

"Pravda, mudak? Bol'nitza?" Really, asshole? A hospital?

At that point the jig was up. The hackers might have had beefy Russian sentries as babysitters, but they were short on faith and had Romanian Model 2000 pistols clipped under their desks. The four young men—all with greasy hair and questionable hygiene—tried to deploy the guns but were dead before they could bring them to bear as Steele buzzed each pair with twenty rounds from the P90, shattering their bones and exploding the $30,000 computers behind them. Since the P90 magazine held fifty rounds, that left him with ten for Snipe.

The young Russian mastermind—who Steele might have pit-ied for his horrible upbringing by an absent father and prostitute mom, if the kid hadn't turned into a heartless motherfucker—yelled something incoherent, came up with a Romanian Model 98 fully automatic "Dracula" pistol, and fumbled with it in clumsy panic as Steele advanced on him, switched his selector to single fire, and methodically stitched him from his crotch to the bridge of his glasses until the P90 ran dry. Snipe collapsed in a mist of arterial blood, and at that moment, his professional partner and occasional paramour, Kendo, showed up.

She was a beautiful Korean young woman, multilingual, brilliant, techno-talented and devoid of a soul. Her moniker reflected her particular talents with the *jingum,* the long sword similar to the Japanese katana, and she exploded out of some recess in the dome, wearing a red bathrobe, jangling silver bracelets and silver sandals, with her long black hair flying wildly and her *jingum* whipping at Steele like a scythe.

He dropped the empty P90, and it swung to his back on its strap. He reached into a left calf scabbard and came up with a Gerber Mark II 6.5-inch combat knife, which made Kendo's perfect smile gleam because that toothpick was nothing compared to her razor-sharp three-and-a-half-foot blade, which she was raising over her head when Steele unholstered his P226 again and shot her twice in the chest.

"Just teasin'," Steele said to her corpse as it bounced on the floor. "Thought I'd give you your moment."

At that point the six surviving Russian bodyguards were desperately trying to get in the front door, but Steele's carabiner was holding firm, and their efforts to shatter the bulletproof glass did nothing more than spider it and cloud their view.

At the back of the dome, a small young man appeared from one of the sleeping quarters with his hands raised high, shaking like a fawn on an interstate highway. He was babbling in French, which happened to be one of Steele's languages.

"*Ne tirez pas! Ne tirez pas!*" He begged the black-clad killer not to shoot.

"*Mains sur le mur.*" Hands on the wall, Steele said, and the young man spun around and slammed his palms to the curving plaster.

Steele asked him about an emergency rear exit. The French

hacker thrust his chin at a restroom door and said it was through there. Steele thanked him and shot him in the back of each hand with the pistol, which made the young man scream as he slid to his knees, leaving bloody handprints and scarlet trails.

"If you can't be a good example, at least be a vivid warning," Steele said to him in French as he left.

Ralphy had acquired overheads from a buddy at a commercial satellite reconnaissance firm, so Steele knew exactly where to go, and it wasn't back to the cliff face. The Millennial Crude hackers—now all dead but one, who wouldn't be keyboarding anytime soon—had been delivered to their perch by helo, while their Russian bodyguards hoofed it up and down a long slim trail through the sloping forests on the north side of the peak. Steele popped his NVGs down over his eyes because the towering firs would obscure the moon, and took off at a dead run downhill.

It was like playing some ultralevel of Halo 5, with everything bouncing in grainy green, gunfire banging behind him as the furious Russians gave chase, and tracers starting to zip past his head and chunk off pieces of trees. His boots pounded on the slick track and kicked up stones, but he only ran faster, and he holstered the Sig and reloaded the P90 on the move. He was wearing a lightweight square of RMA Armament Level IV body armor in back, because that's where he always took the most incoming after a job was over, and sure enough an AK-47 round *wanged* off the plate and vibrated up through his skull. He knew the trail was exactly 1,234 meters of twisting snake path, but he wasn't counting his strides, and in eight minutes he burst from the trees, slid on his ass down a muddy slope, and started sprinting north along the pebbly bank of the Argeş river.

Fifteen seconds later the Russians also burst from the forest behind him, but now he was out in the open and an easy target, so he spun on the run and emptied half a magazine of 5.7 × 28 mm at them, which screamed like a buzz saw and sent them slamming onto their faces.

For a moment as he ran Steele had the fleeting thought, *I need more gym time*. His heart was hammering, his breaths spewing, and he yanked the balaclava down away from his mouth. Then he had another thought, more urgent and ominous. *This is exactly how it happened to Dad*. His father, Hank, who Steele had discovered was also an Alpha operator, had ended his career this way, being chased by Russians in Siberia. In just one more klick Steele would break out on the banks of an enormous lake, the Lacul Vidraru, and either Dalton Goodhill would be there with the boat, or he'd be dead and on fire, just like Hank Steele's extractor, which was why his son had never seen him again.

There was one more low-hanging copse of trees up ahead as the Argeş straightened out, a canopy of teasing black arms and fingers, and through that Steele thought he could see the silhouette of Goodhill's Riva Rivale 52 speedboat. Its black-green hull was rocking on the lake as the wind kicked up whitecaps, and it was slewing around, and Steele thought he heard the twin engines revving, which meant that Goodhill could hear the gunfire and sensed he was about to arrive.

Steele tore off his MICH helmet and the NVGs with it, and ripped off the balaclava. He couldn't swim with that stuff on his head, and none of it was government property anyway. He ripped open his Velcro plate carrier and dumped that on the run as well, betting that the Russians couldn't hit him in the same spot again. But they sure as hell were trying. Bullets snapped in the air overhead and on both flanks and sparked off rocks along the bank, and without turning he tucked the P90 upside down and backward over his left shoulder and gave them another wild burst.

He tossed the subgun last, hit the ice-cold water like an Olympic swimmer, and started cranking hand over hand and with both boots kicking. The boat was about fifty meters out but it looked like a mile and he'd never swum so hard in his life. The Russians pounded onto the bank and started firing like maniacs just as Steele reached the stern ladder, hauled himself aboard, and crashed facedown on the engine cover pad behind the radar post. He saw Goodhill—now sporting a bristly red beard and a watch cap and looking like Zorba the Greek—as he cranked the throttle, spun the wheel, and the twin MAN diesels roared to life, and Steele almost slid off the boat into the churning water.

Goodhill raised one hand sky high, clutching something that looked like a Claymore mine clacker. Steele flipped onto his back to watch the shore, where the Russian AK barrels were spitting those ugly yellow starfish bursts, and then all six of them were gone in a blinding flash as eight kilos of Semtex detonated under their boots.

Steele cranked his head back and looked at Goodhill upside down.

"Nice touch," he rasped over the roar of the engines.

Goodhill turned from his wheel and grinned.

"I thought you'd like it, kid."

CHAPTER 3

President John Rockford wasn't much of a shot, but he was certainly sincere.

Golf was supposed to be the preferred game of diplomats, statesmen, and business tycoons, which made sense, since it was nice and quiet and you could have yourself a laid-back conversation about something unremarkable, like nuclear disarmament or the Russian invasion of Ukraine. But Rockford, when he didn't feel like talking business, always chose the trap and skeet range at the presidential weekend retreat. You could jam your earplugs in, blast away with a high-priced, over-under, twelve-gauge shotgun, and enjoy the fact that everyone around you was temporarily deaf.

It surprised his staff that he rarely shattered a clay pigeon, since he had such an extensive army record and a chestful of ribbons— "fruit salad" as service members called the rows of medals—and had also once helmed the CIA. But first and foremost, Rockford had been a tank commander, not a rifleman or a sniper. With a rifle he had trouble with a paper target at 25 meters, but with an M1A1 Abrams main battle tank, he could take out a Russian T82 at 4,000 meters while bouncing across the Iraqi dunes at 60 mph.

Thankfully, the shotgun sprayed out lead in a wide cone so he couldn't completely embarrass himself.

Anyway, he cherished this particular shotgun much more than the sport. It was a Benelli U 828 in beautifully grained satin walnut furniture and a nickel-plated receiver with leafwork engraving. It had been bequeathed to Rockford by his now deceased friend and mentor, former president and commander in chief, Denton Cole. And the thing that made it priceless—in a sentimental rather than bluebook-value sense—were the initials *DC* carved into the walnut stock, which Cole had done himself with a pocketknife, right there at Camp David.

Six months prior to his death from brain cancer, President Cole had taken his then vice president, John Rockford, for a long walk in the woods around the presidential retreat. He was carrying the Benelli over one shoulder like an old-time minuteman as they strolled, and he'd handed it over to Rockford and grinned wryly as he tapped the deeply furrowed letters.

"You probably think these are my initials, John, but they're not. They're a reminder that in Washington, *Dee Cee*, sometimes you have to shoot a goddamn congressman to get anything done."

They'd laughed about that, of course, but it wasn't funny anymore. Cole had died, and Rockford—who'd never dreamed in his life of being vice president of the country he loved, let alone president in a ridiculous twist of mortal fate—had inherited the mantle that no man in his right mind would want. He'd been a career army officer, rising to the rank of full bird colonel, and had been close to pinning on his first general's star when Cole's predecessor had ordered him over to Langley as acting director, CIA. After that he'd figured on retiring gracefully from both the army and government, when presidential candidate Denton Cole had called him to ultimate service as VP. If you were a patriot, you just didn't say no to something like that.

He'd loved working for Denton Cole. The man had been supremely honest and honorable, sort of like Harry Truman. A straight shooter, which was more than Rockford could say about himself out here on the range.

"Pull," he muttered. The target machine in the dugout *thwanged* and an orange clay disk went spinning up into the overcast sky like a flying saucer. Rockford did as his sometimes firearms coach had taught him—relax, breathe, lead and squeeze—and the Benelli kicked him in the shoulder and the clay disk shattered into dust.

He heard some light applause. It was the first lady, sitting nearby on a bench, wearing a pair of teal Rosies Workwear coveralls and Foster Grant sunglasses. She grinned at her husband and went back to reading her paperback. She was a former fashion model, yet she had two master's degrees, spoke five languages, and could look stunning in a burlap sack and clown shoes.

Rockford grunted "pull" again, a clay pigeon flew, he missed it completely, and it went sailing out over the berm at the far side of the skeet range and bounced somewhere in the grass. He cursed, broke the shotgun open, the empty shells popped out, and he started reloading from his belt pouch. He glanced over at one of his Secret Service agents who was standing nearby in a dark blue windbreaker, stone-faced.

"You wanna try it, Jack?"

The agent turned to the president and smiled. "Can I use my sidearm, sir?"

"No. You'll probably hit it, twice, goddamn show-off."

The agent grinned more broadly and went back to scanning the perimeter.

The exchange reminded Rockford of another gunman, the one who'd coached him so that at least he could hit something once in a blue moon. Eric Steele. Now there was a shooter, cool as ice, never a wince in his rock-jawed face or a flinch in those weird green eyes. When Rockford was still VP, long before Denton Cole's death, he'd once asked Steele to take him out to Thorn McHugh's property in the Virginia boonies, where McHugh had bequeathed a thousand acres to the Program for whatever kind of training the Alphas had in mind.

Steele had instructed Rockford in shotgun basics, with the patience and calm demeanor of a yoga guru, and after an hour he'd managed to knock over a few of the ten steel plates that were mounted on hinges atop a raised horizontal log about twenty-five meters away. When his shoulder had started to ache from the shotgun's recoil, he'd taken a break and asked Steele to show him what he could do. Steele had drawn his handgun from his waistband and knocked over all ten plates so fast that it sounded like a jackhammer hitting a xylophone.

Thinking about all of that again now made Rockford frown with a shudder of guilt. Eric Steele had saved his life, along with most of his cabinet and nearly every major foreign head of state, while they were all mourning the passing of President Cole at Washington's National Cathedral. And the really shameful thing was that very few people knew anything about it. But Rockford knew, and shortly after that near conflagration, he'd shut down the Program. He'd had no choice about it really. The highly classified intelligence and special operations unit, which had been successfully kept under wraps since shortly after World War II, was starting to suffer from leaks and cracks in its figurative foundation. But putting a wrecking ball to it had still made him feel like an ungrateful sap.

The Program was the secret lifeblood of so many true patriots, the kind of people he'd served with in combat who'd give their lives and fortunes for you with barely a second thought. Eric Steele was one of those people, and now he'd put that dedicated warrior and all of his Program brothers and sisters out to pasture.

"You sure know how to say thank you, Rockford," he muttered to himself, then he yelled "pull," blasted one clay pigeon out of the sky, yelled it again, and shattered the second one before it got ten feet from the dugout. He handed the shotgun to Jack. He knew when to quit.

Rockford turned, gave the first lady a wink and a cock of his chin, and she smiled and got up to join him. They often liked to walk through Camp David's woods, where they could chat in something like semiprivacy, even though there were always agents with guns close by. It was about half a mile's stroll of fresh air and lush greenery from the range to Aspen Lodge, the presidential cabin, but Rockford and Lisa could make it last an hour.

They didn't get very far. A golf cart appeared on the tree-lined roadway, zooming toward them with purpose. At the wheel was Ted Lansky, Rockford's chief of staff and his former director of clandestine services over at CIA. Lansky was a husky, big-shouldered man who'd quit smoking his beloved pipe decades ago, but he still clutched an old briar in his teeth like a pacifier and rarely removed it except to stab it at someone like a rapier. Jack, the head of Rockford's Secret Service detail, got between the president and the braking cart. Lansky hopped out and snapped at him.

"You think I'm gonna run over the boss, Jack?"

"No, sir, but you might have a stroke and lose control of the wheel."

"You gunslingers are all friggin' dark," Lansky said, then blushed a shade and said "sorry, ma'am" to the first lady. She grinned. Fashion models were accustomed to hearing much worse.

"Mr. President," Lansky said, "'fraid I have to run you back up to the Big House." He used the sobriquet for the lodge devised by President Eisenhower's staff. "White House routed a call from China."

"Just what I need to ruin our weekend," Rockford growled. "A colloquy with those pirates."

"It's not official, sir. Not from Beijing."

"Oh?"

"Do you want me to come up later, John?" Mrs. Rockford was starting to pull away from where she'd hooked her husband's elbow.

"No, Lisa." He patted her hand. "We'll all ride up there together." He turned back to Lansky. "What's it about, Ted? Any idea?"

"Well, fellow claims he's a party insider. Says he's on the run, doesn't have much time, and he'll talk only to you."

The president helped Lisa into the back of the cart and climbed in beside her, while Jack went around to the front passenger side and Lansky reclaimed the wheel. A black armored Suburban appeared from the other side of the skeet range, tinted windows rolled down and black M4 barrels jutting discreetly at the sky.

"So why'd they put him through, Ted?" Rockford asked as Lansky started driving back up into the woods. All sorts of crackpots called the White House every week demanding to talk to the president.

"He gave them a Langley asset code, sir," Lansky said. "And he said if they didn't let him talk to you, they'd be responsible for starting World War Three."

CHAPTER 4

THE BIG HOUSE, CAMP DAVID

To the sailors, leathernecks, and Marine One helicopter pilots who served at the presidential weekend retreat, the sprawling patch of remote wooded real estate in northern Maryland was known as Naval Support Facility Thurmont. They didn't call it Camp David, and it certainly wasn't Shangri-la, as President Franklin Roosevelt had first named it. It was a land-locked naval base, and one of the most prestigious postings in the seaborne service.

Every one of the sailors, security detachment marines, navy chefs, firemen, Seabees, riflemen, and helicopter crews was hand selected, and after their tour of duty at Thurmont, which almost invariably included at least one handshake with the president, each would receive the Presidential Service Badge. That was something that didn't go unnoticed by your chain of command and would forever pop up in your 201 file, raise an eyebrow, and cause some lieutenant commander to nod and mutter, "This swabbie's shipshape. Good to go for my crew."

Bud Garland had served as a young ensign assigned to NSF

Thurmont back when John F. Kennedy was president. Kennedy, a decorated navy hero of World War II who'd commanded a doomed patrol torpedo boat called PT 109, always had a place in his heart for sailors and had spotted young Bud taking out the trash one day behind the Aspen Lodge. The dashing president had stunned the young squid by engaging him in half an hour of banter about poop decks, flag signals, and nuclear submarines while Soviet ambassador Anatoly Dobrynin waited for Kennedy in the Birch Lodge and steamed. Bud Garland had been thunderstruck by that encounter, which inspired him to remain in the navy, where he'd ultimately risen to the rank of admiral.

Admiral Bud Garland's only daughter, Katie, had in turn been awed by her father's remarkable record of service and had followed his lead. She'd served multiple tours aboard aircraft carriers and missile boats as a naval officer, had then attained a master's and Ph.D. from the Harvard Kennedy School, and had been plucked from a think tank to serve as President John Rockford's national security advisor. She was forty-two, relatively young for such a lofty position, and with her wide, seemingly permanent smile and Jackie Kennedy hairdo, she looked like a housewife from that old politically incorrect TV show *Father Knows Best*. But she was hard as nails.

The Aspen Lodge, formerly called The Bear's Den by its first resident, Franklin Roosevelt, is the centerpiece of NSF Thurmont. It's a modest rustic structure where presidents have been resting their weary heads since 1942, with plenty of raw stone and knotty pine, a big kitchen, great room, four bedrooms, five fireplaces, a swimming pool built by Richard Nixon out front on its three-acre patch, a small three-hole golf course out back, and an underground bomb shelter that's deep enough so that a suitcase nuke can wipe out the lodge and the president can still pop back out, smoking a cigar.

Outside are two terraces, one lower, one higher, of interlocking flagstone, where barbecues are held and Scrabble played. Inside, the large central great room is decorated with Adirondack-style chairs and sofas upholstered in homely grandma prints, and large picture windows that look out on lush green panoramas in summer and crisp winter whiteness at the back half of the year.

Katie Garland, who despite the informalities at Camp David always wore dark suits that resembled her naval uniforms, was pacing back and forth across the great room, chewing on a pencil and stabbing it down into a notebook at every turn of her carpet track. She believed that if you worked for a president there was no such thing as time off, no matter how long your run lasted. Presidents were like brain surgeons, always on call, even if they were technically "on vacation," and she thought of herself as the surgeon's apprentice, which she essentially was.

The front door to the Big House banged open as Rockford pounded into the room like the movie character Shrek, making the crystal coffee cups rattle in their saucers where the navy stewards had set them on the table in front of the long couch, upon hearing the CIC was on his way back from skeet. Lansky followed on his heels, while Mrs. Rockford peeled away like an outside wing woman in a fighter plane formation and headed for the master suite, and Jack pulled the door closed and stayed on guard right outside.

"What's the skinny, Kate?" Rockford shrugged off his shooting jacket and tossed it onto a worn armchair where Ronald Regan had once liked to sit and kick his cowboy boots up on the coffee table.

"Mr. Lansky briefed you, Mr. President?"

"He did."

"Then you know as much as I do, sir. He wouldn't give us a name. Just called himself Casino. Must be an intel handle of some sort, though we don't yet know who gave it to him."

Garland pointed to an old-style dial telephone that had been set out for the president on an end table beside the couch. It was fire-engine red, a relic from the Cold War days, and had once served as the emergency line between Kennedy and Nikita Khrushchev. The telephone's current residence was actually up at the Laurel Lodge, the building reserved for official meetings and staff functions a thousand feet northwest through the woods, but Garland had had the phone unplugged and brought down to Aspen because it still functioned off of a landline. She didn't trust cell phones, even if they were encrypted and secured by the NSA.

"How many other leakers are going to be on this call, Kate?" the president asked.

"Just us, sir."

Rockford smirked. "You two ever leak on me, I'm going to take you down to the skeet range, and you ain't gonna need your coats."

Garland smiled, Lansky grunted, and Rockford crashed down on the end of the couch and dropped his big palm on the handset. Garland and Lansky walked across the room to another old wall-mounted telephone—an ugly pink model that had once been called the Trimline—stood shoulder to shoulder, and when Rockford nodded and picked up his handset, they did as well. They shared it between their ears while Lansky covered up the mouthpiece.

"This is President Rockford."

There was a long pause and an intake of breath, as if the person on the other end couldn't believe it. But then a low male voice with a Chinese accent tinted by British boarding school tones thanked the president for his time.

"I am grateful for your compliance, Mr. President."

"I haven't complied with anything yet. Who are you?"

"I am known as Casino, sir. I do have a name, but it would not be wise yet to share it."

Rockford thought the guy sounded shaky, and also like one of those expensive tailors he'd occasionally used in Hong Kong.

"Then state your case, Mr. Casino." Rockford looked across the room at Garland and Lansky and rolled his eyes.

"Mr. President, I do not have much time, as I was forced to wait for a long period until your underlings could find you."

Rockford said nothing. Lansky's face turned a bit red and Katie Garland smirked. She let Lansky hold the Trimline phone by himself and took notes in shorthand with her pencil. The voice carried on.

"Until very recently, Mr. President, I was a full-fledged member of the Chinese Communist Party's National Congress, as well as the Central Military Commission. I have since fled Beijing, and I am currently in hiding. I did so because I have information of utmost importance that must be acted upon very quickly."

"Then you'd better spill the beans."

"Excuse me?"

"Tell me what you know."

"I know that you have China's secretary general in a panic, Mr. President. I know that you instituted trade policies that are costing the Party its base of support, as the Chinese people see how flimsy is their alleged utopian government. I know that the chairman's effort to deprive you of access to the South China Sea has been exposed and that you have warned him unequivocally not to proceed. I know that the CCP has never encountered an American president who cannot be bent to their will, or bribed, or frightened."

"Then you know a lot indeed, Mr. Casino. What else?"

Rockford covered the mouthpiece of the red phone and mouthed to Katie Garland, *Are you recording this?* She smiled and held up a small "clicker" that looked like a Bluetooth camera trigger. It was a remote-control device for recording everything that happened in the room, as well as all telephone transmissions, hardwired or not. Rockford rarely used the system, as he was convinced that such things always caused the downfalls of kings. But today he was grateful they had it.

"What else, Mr. President?" The man's voice now sounded almost smug, as if Rockford were the only one on earth who couldn't see what was going on. "The chairman sees no other avenue now but to draw the United States into total war. He is fully prepared for millions of casualties, while he believes you are not. It will happen soon. It will happen in ways you cannot imagine."

Rockford's jaw went a little bit slack, then tightened into ripples under his temples as his anger grew. His ire wasn't a result of being threatened; rather it was a reaction to truth. Indeed, the Chinese would accept millions of deaths in order to dominate the world, while the United States had grown so soft that even with a war still going on in Afghanistan, a single American casualty caused hands to wring as if the Twin Towers in New York had fallen again.

"Do you have details of these plans, Mr. Casino?"

"I do, Mr. President, and I will turn them over to you when I am convinced that in turn, you can save my life. As they say in your cinema, don't call us, we'll call you."

And the line went dead.

Rockford sat there for a moment, rotating the red phone receiver in his hand, as if wondering if it still had JFK's handprints on it. Then he looked over at Garland and Lansky, who'd hung theirs back up on the wall.

"Kate, call over to CIA and get the director over here for a chat. Whoever gave Casino his code name is probably his handler, and I'll bet that handler's got a cubicle at Langley. Just a hunch."

"Yes, Mr. President." She wasn't going to argue that speculation. Rockford had run that shop long enough himself and knew all their tactics, techniques, and procedures.

"Ted, see if NSA's got anything on the source," Rockford said to Lansky. The National Security Agency at Fort Meade monitored all traffic coming in and out of NSF Thurmont. "I doubt they'll be able to track it down, 'cause it was probably some sort of computer call strained through Tor, but it can't hurt to ask." The president meant the Onion Router, a method of disguising computer transmissions and IP addresses. Just the fact that he knew such things always impressed his subordinates.

"Yes, sir, will do," Lansky said.

Rockford got up from the couch and wandered over to the big picture window that looked out over the lower-level terrace and the kidney-shaped swimming pool. Lisa was sitting out there in the sun at one of the small tea tables, twirling her hair with a finger and reading her book. He shoved his big hands in the pockets of his shooting trousers, a baggy pair of 511s, and found two full shotgun shells, which he pulled out and rolled in his fingers like worry beads.

Maybe this guy Casino was full of crap, or maybe he was real, but one thing Rockford knew for certain. A war with China would be the sort of nightmare that JFK had always feared with the old Soviet Union. Kennedy had managed to avoid it and had saved the country, and probably the entire Earth, from utter devastation. But Rockford had always suspected that what Kennedy did might have been the very thing that had cost the young president his life.

It didn't matter. He looked at his beautiful wife and imagined her disappearing in a white-hot cloud of nuclear ash. He'd have to do the very same thing as Kennedy too.

"And, Lansky, when you're done with that call," Rockford said over his shoulder, "you're fired."

Lansky snapped his head up from his cell phone. Katie Garland spun around from where she was just ringing off with the CIA, looked bug-eyed at Lansky, and then at the president's back.

"I want you to revive the Program, Ted. And I want you to go over to Q Street and run it. I need eyes and ears I can trust, of which there are few. Get me Alphas back out on the streets overseas, and find me someone to replace you over at 1600. Tell whoever you select that it's temporary, maybe a year."

"Yes, sir," Lanksy said in something of a hoarse whisper. He'd suffered a heart-pounding shot of adrenaline and needed a moment to recover.

"And, Ted," Rockford said, "one more thing."

"Mr. President?"

"Find me Eric Steele."

CHAPTER 5

In the best-case scenario, Eric Steele expected to be arrested. In the worst case, it wasn't going to surprise him if he disappeared.

Everything that he and Goodhill had done overseas had been extralegal, a lawyerly term that, despite its sound, meant way outside the law. They'd used private funds donated by a former government intelligence officer to purloin targeting information and reconnaissance via the computer hacking talents of yet a third former covert employee. Then, they'd acquired lethal gear and munitions and had crossed multiple international lines to assault and terminate multinational individuals, including Russian intelligence assets, without sanction by any sort of official U.S. government body.

Never mind that the targets were murderous bastards who'd relished slaughtering both innocents and enemies. Steele knew that he and Goodhill were probably screwed.

From the sprawling lake called Lacul Vidraru in Romania,

the two former Program operators had flown to Croatia, but not aboard any sort of commercial aircraft. Five kilometers north of where Steele had plunged into the icy water and swum to the boat, Goodhill had throttled back the racing Riva Rivale to five knots as a helicopter appeared from the midnight sky. It was a silver Russian Mi-8 cargo helicopter, emblazoned just below the cockpit with a large cartoon of the Looney Tunes Road Runner cracking a whip, and it was being piloted by Allie "Whirly" (no known last name), a hotshot blond helo master who'd flown contract jobs for the Program, but was now back to shuttling for oil rigs and timber firms all over the world.

With his body aching bones to toes, Steele had climbed up into the hovering helo via a slim rope ladder deployed by Allie, and then Goodhill had grabbed the rungs himself, just after killing the speedboat's engines—after all, a renegade fast boat like that could hurt somebody. From there they'd flown to Split, a lovely little palm-lined airport on the shores of the Black Sea in Croatia where, just before deplaning on the tarmac, Goodhill had shaved off his beard with an electric razor and Allie had grabbed the back of Steele's head with her pilot-gloved hand and tongue kissed him long and deeply. That was just to remind him about their brief but very steamy affair some years back at Bagram Airfield in Afghanistan, and that a return to that romance was always on the table.

Steele had gotten the message with a sloppy grin. Goodhill had rolled his eyes.

They were standing just inside the modest airport terminal hall, dressed once again in civvies supplied by Allie, when Steele turned to Goodhill.

"Okay, boss man, what's the plan?"

Goodhill raised a finger toward the ceiling.

"Look up, kid."

The airport sign, SPLIT, was hanging from a pair of chains.

"Okay, I get it. We're breaking up here."

"Correct," Goodhill said. "Not that it's gonna make a difference."

"Right," Steele agreed. "Probably won't even make it through Customs."

"Customs? Probably won't make it down the jetway at Dulles."

Neither of them thought they'd arrive back to the States without serious consequences. In fact, the schedule manager at the Austrian Airlines counter just a few meters behind them was a CIA asset who'd already been informed, by way of NSA intercepts relayed through Langley, that the FSB satcom link between Moscow and Transylvania was going crazy, and to be on the lookout for freelancing operators of a certain type.

Well, Steele and Goodhill were definitely those types. One looked like John Krasinski, that actor on the Jack Ryan TV series, but harder and without the beard. The other looked like Robert Duvall and Ed Harris had birthed an angry muscular child, with a telltale parachute riser scar running down from behind his right ear. The desk manager texted Paris station on an encrypted iPhone. Paris called Virginia, and it took all of fifty-two seconds for the CIA's Directorate of Analysis to call Ted Lansky at the White House and ask, very politely, "Um, sir? Aren't these guys your former Program boys?"

So Steele and Goodhill grabbed different flights back to Dulles. But they knew it wouldn't matter. The jig was most likely up.

By the time Steele got to Dulles it was high noon, six hours behind Europe, and he'd been traveling nonstop for twenty hours and was pretty raw. He had no luggage, just a backpack so he wouldn't look completely suspect, plus his civilian passport, a slim wallet with some phony pocket litter, the Amex card supplied by Thorn McHugh, and a couple of hundred euros. The sun was shining through the Boeing's windows and painting the tarmac's shimmering fumes, and he took his time deplaning and strolling down the long jetway, and had a short-lived fantasy that nothing at all might happen here.

He didn't even make it to passport control. Two very large men were waiting for him at the gate, dressed in identical black suits and matching Oakley sunglasses, though slightly different Macy's ties. They didn't say a word to him. He didn't speak to them either. One of them took the lead, Steele fell in behind him, and the second muscle picked up the rear. But Steele had no illusions there were only two of them. He had a reputation. There were probably six more security on the flanks, dressed in Hawaiian shirts or college football jerseys, packing Tasers in touristy butt packs. They wouldn't draw firearms here inside Dulles, but if they had to, they'd give him enough voltage to lower his IQ.

The point man nodded at two cops flanking a restricted exit door to the tarmac. The cops nodded back and he pushed the emergency bar, but the alarm had already been disabled by arrangement. They all trotted down a gangway into the blazing light, and Steele thought about how it was barely spring but that season always rushed by.

I just love Washington summers . . . not. Well, maybe I'll spend this one someplace balmy, like Devil's Island . . . and the next one . . . and the one after that.

Two large black Suburbans were waiting on the sticky tarmac, with heat waves rising up and blurring their wheel wells. Steele's leading goon opened the rear door of the first one, Steele slipped inside into the air-conditioned gloom, and the door slammed hard and the locks banged home. There was an inch-thick Plexiglas divider between him and the driver, and he squinted at the profile of the driver's passenger. It was Miles Turner, an African American former Special Forces officer the size of a linebacker, with five combat tours and two bronze stars in his 201 file. Turner was the former chief of security for the Program, and Steele hadn't seen him in nearly nine months.

"Hey, Miles," Steele said. "Glad to see you got yourself another gig."

"Shut up, Eric," Turner said without turning his head.

That didn't bode well for a jolly afternoon, but Steele just raised an eyebrow, slunk back in the seat, and took the opportunity to doze. He figured if they were heading somewhere like the Central Detention Facility in Southeast Washington, D.C., it would take at least an hour in midday traffic. But after a while, a large pothole bounced him awake, and he saw they weren't headed toward D Street at all. They were cruising along Q Street Northwest, past Hank's Oyster Bar, a place where he and Meg Harden had mooned over one another on multiple occasions before he'd screwed that up, and heading toward . . . *No, that can't be.*

Sure enough, they took a left between Sixteenth and Seventeenth Streets, and descended into an underground garage, right past a very obvious sign that said CLOSED UNTIL FURTHER NOTICE. It was the garage that had serviced the Program's new headquarters, before the whole thing had been forced to shut down. Charles, the Bermuda-born, English-accented, and well-armed parking attendant, wasn't there anymore, nor was there another vehicle anywhere.

The Suburbans parked in the dusty darkness. Steele's door

opened and he got out. The rear door of the second Suburban opened and Goodhill exited, stretching as if he'd enjoyed a gourmet meal and a delicious nap.

"What time'd you get in?" Steele asked him.

"'Bout three hours before you. Spent it in that tank playing Tetris."

"Very productive."

"I pinged you on Instagram with something," Goodhill said. "Didn't see it?"

"Nope. What was it?"

"Recipe for New Orleans Creole gumbo."

"Nah, I'm a northern boy."

"Yankee trash."

"All right, wiseasses," Miles Turner snarled. "Let's move."

Turner headed up the ramp to the street, with Steele and Goodhill trailing behind, followed by the muscle who'd greeted both men at the airport. The Surburban drivers, who were just as large, joined in to further discourage the fresh arrivals from bolting. Outside on the street the troop turned left, and Turner pulled a key from his belt and opened a set of large glass doors beneath a sign that still said GRACELAND IMPORT EXPORTS.

"Is this like *Law and Order*?" Steele said as he went inside. "Where they take the perps back to the scene of the crime?"

Goodhill shot a finger eastward.

"The scene of the crime's that way, kid, about six thousand klicks."

"You two really think you're funny, don't ya?" Turner sneered.

"We wanted to be comedians," Steele said, "but our humor died from Covid-19."

"Stand in front of the camera."

Merry, the comely young blond Program receptionist who'd once sat there behind the substantial desk beneath a Robert Salmon maritime painting, had been replaced by an electronic eyeball on a tripod. Steele and Goodhill took up side-by-side positions in front of the lens. After a moment the large steel elevator behind them hissed open, and they all squeezed inside like seven beefy men in a meat locker. When the door opened onto the second floor, the submarine chamber meant for security, with all its bells and whistles and electronic locks, was no longer there. The Program was dead and there was nothing there to defend.

Both Steele's and Goodhill's tendency to confront stress with flippant banter dissipated quickly when they saw the mess that had once been the Program's tactical operations center. When the organization had first been forced to move from its secret location at the White House—after having been ensconced there since just after World War II—no one had thought those accommodations would ever be matched by real estate anywhere else. Yet Mike Pitts, then the Program's director of operations, had wheeled and dealed and nagged for a substantial slice of the black budget. The TOC had been turned into something out of a Hollywood set designer's imagination: slate floors with tunneled power lines, lush carpets, workstations with pneumatic VariDesks, a monster eight-paneled digital display, four compartmentalized "tanks" off the main floor for ultrasecret analysis work, a gourmet kitchen, a security armory, perfect climate control, and a fully secure compartmented information facility, or SCIF.

But now Pitts was dead, and Steele thought that the vision before him was serving as a metaphor for his former commander's tragic demise. Almost a year had passed since "Snipe" and Millennial Crude had hacked into the Program's control systems and trashed the whole place, and it looked like the government had just surrendered, walked out and locked the doors. All the servers were burned out, but the computers still sat there, gathering dust. The big multisectional flat screen on the northern wall had spider cracks down the glass display, because when the Russians had hijacked the feed, one of Ralphy Persko's geeks had gotten so fed up she'd hurled a coffee tumbler at it. Everything was musty and damp, because Snipe's finale had included turning the overhead sprinklers on full force. The faux mahogany walls were stained, and so was the expensive carpet. It was sad to look at, and it stank.

"Get the hell in here."

Steele and Goodhill turned to see Ted Lansky, the president's chief of staff, standing inside the ruined SCIF at the head of the once perfectly polished conference table. But he wasn't just standing, he was pacing, with his suit jacket off, white shirtsleeves rolled up, tie loose and flipped over one shoulder, and that ever-present pipe jammed in his teeth.

The two men walked in, Miles Turner yanked the door closed behind them, and Lansky glared at them and opened fire.

"Fucking Title 18 U.S. Code 922!" He pulled his pipe from his mouth and jabbed it across the room like a German Luger. "'It shall be unlawful for *any* person, except a licensed manufacturer or dealer, to ship or transport *any* firearm or ammunition in interstate or foreign commerce.'" He was holding a sheaf of papers, obviously compiled by some sort of prosecuting attorney, and he tossed the first one up in the air and went on. "Title 18 U.S. Code 1952, interstate and foreign travel in aid of racketeering

enterprises! 'Whoever travels in foreign commerce with intent
to commit *any* crime of violence, and if death results, shall be
imprisoned for any term of years, or for *life*.'"

He flung that document up in the air as well, where it spun
to the floor like one of those helicopter seeds from a fir tree, and
then he dropped the papers and slammed both palms on the
table.

"Are you two out of your freaking minds? Do you have any
goddamn idea what's been going on since you pulled off your little payback play in Romania? Did you even, for one seminormal
minute in your very minuscule minds, consider how this might
affect the president, and national security?"

Steele and Goodhill stood there ramrod stiff like a couple of
plebes at West Point. They knew Lansky well enough to understand when he wasn't really asking a question.

"The only reason Rockford's been able to claim to the Russian
ambassador that he knew *absofuckinglutely* nothing about this, is
because he didn't." Lansky stuck his pipe back in his teeth and
pounded the table with a fist. "And the *only* reason he's been able
to say with a straight face that there's no such thing as the Program, which the Russians apparently knew everything about, is
that the goddamn thing no longer exists!"

"Well, sir," Goodhill ventured, "then it looks like we took appropriate and completely deniable action, at precisely the right
time."

Lansky cocked his head, lowered himself into a dusty plush
chair, and said very quietly, "You know, Goodhill, I can have you
disappeared. I can have frigging Alcatraz opened up again, just
for you and your half-cocked trigger boy here."

"Yes, sir." Goodhill chose to not respond anymore, and Lansky turned on Steele, using his pipe stem as a gun barrel again.

"There's only one reason you're not going to some Supermax as a toilet boy, Steele. The president is currently dealing with an international issue—not of your making, for once. The Red Chinese are cranking their games to a lethal level. He wants the Program revived."

Steele and Goodhill both raised their chins at that, but they didn't dare look at one another or speak.

"He not only wants it revived," Lansky went on, "but he wants it done yesterday, and you're both going to do it. That means us finding the budget, rehiring personnel if we can, recovering Alphas from whatever they're doing, or training up new ones, etcetera ad nauseam." Lansky reached to the table and picked up the pile of law codes again. "You don't have to volunteer, of course. The choice is, you can spend the whole weekend talking to some very ambitious FBI agents, who've already been inquiring about your travel habits, or you can play ball. Are we clear?"

"Sir." Steele raised a finger like a schoolboy. "You keep saying 'us.'"

"I'm going to be running the new Program myself, for one year. And you two clowns are going to work for me. Good enough?"

That was a shocker to both men, but they were smart enough to save their feelings about Lansky taking the helm for later, and in private. Or so Goodhill thought until Steele opened his mouth.

"All right, sir, but then I have one question," Steele said while Goodhill glared at him sideways and wished he could cut out his tongue. "If the Program had still been up and running, would you have sanctioned our hit on Millennial Crude? Because if not, to be honest, I don't think I'll be able to work for you."

Goodhill mentally face palmed himself. Lansky turned another shade of scarlet.

"Both of you be here at 0700 tomorrow, ready to work your asses off," he fumed. "Now get the hell out of my TOC. And if you fuck this up, I'll turn you over to the Russians myself."

CHAPTER 6

Ralphy Persko still lived in Crestwood, halfway between Silver Spring, Maryland, and Washington's National Mall.

He still occupied the top-floor flat of a classic old brownstone on Sixteenth Street NW, and ever since he'd been involuntarily retired as the Program's top geek and computer genius, his landlord, Mrs. Jepson, had been much more pleased with his tenancy. There were no more late-night comings and goings of his strange friends, except for his cherub-faced roommate, Frankie, and thank the Lord no helicopter had ever landed on the roof again. And while Ralphy's cover story about losing his job as a digital librarian at the Smithsonian surely engendered Mrs. Jepson's sympathy, at least he was still paying the rent.

Mrs. Jepson had no idea, of course, that the pudgy, curly-haired lad who often helped her take out the recycling was in fact a national hero. And Ralphy would never have called himself that, even though he'd received a Presidential Medal of Freedom, as well as the National Intelligence Medal for Valor, alongside

Frankie, Eric Steele, and Dalton "Blade" Goodhill, right there in the White House, in a quiet evening ceremony attended by no one but the president and his immediate staff. After the event, their medals and accompanying certificates had all been retrieved, with apologies, and locked in a safe. Then the four of them had gone over to Lost Society in northern D.C., stuffed themselves with thick sirloins, gotten drunk, and split up.

Ralphy hadn't done very much since then, and neither had Frankie. They both lived on their government separation allowances for a while, took on odd jobs doing computer coding over the net, and Ralphy pursued his flight simulator hobby with desultory lack of enthusiasm. He suffered from a form of PTSD, though he wouldn't have termed it that.

Intelligence analysts and computer geeks weren't supposed to be kinetic-action types, but in the waning weeks of the Program, Ralphy had been sucked into the dark vortex of special operations, and not of his own volition. Eric Steele needed him, and you didn't say "no" to a guy like Stalker Seven, who could inject you with a call to duty using nothing more than a look. During the course of Ralphy's "voluntary assist," three Program Alphas had been horrifically murdered by that international terrorist Lila Kalidi, and he was only thankful that he hadn't discovered their corpses himself, because Kalidi took ears for souvenirs. Then she'd tried to murder Steele as well, and somehow Ralphy had wound up with Steele and that semihuman pit bull, Dalton Goodhill, aboard a helicopter insanely piloted by that former Apache tank-killer flygirl, Allie Whirly, and had nearly puked his heart out along with his guts.

And finally, like the culmination of a bad acid trip—something that Ralphy had actually experienced, because Frankie believed that mind expansion might be the key to neurological thought transference—he and Eric Steele had defused a massive load of Semtex in the bowels of the National Cathedral, and he still often woke in the middle of the night, his trembling fingers trying to decide which wire to cut, and his curly mop drenched in sweat.

Frankie would fetch him a cold beer and pet him for a while till he fell back asleep. She was sweet, but she knew he was damaged.

Ralphy and Steele hadn't seen each other for months. Like battle buddies who'd endured something together that they couldn't speak of to anyone else, they still texted on occasion with short phrases like "Just checking in" and "How's it going?" just to show that each still cared. But aside from Steele's recent request for some overhead surveillance of Romania, the Program was gone, Steele was probably working security on an oil rig or bodyguarding some billionaire, and Ralphy was thinking about opening a vape shop with Frankie somewhere—like maybe a place without political turmoil, riots, deadly diseases, and social justice warriors who'd go after your job if you used a horribly offensive term like "gal." He was thinking it might have to be OCONUS (Outside the Continental United States), like the Caribbean isle of Grenada, and all of these current musings and broodings made the knock on his door very late this night the last thing he expected to hear.

Eric Steele could be quiet as a hunting cat, so tonight he'd arrived at Ralphy's door after jacking open the downstairs entrance and taking the four flights with barely a boot sole whisper. He rapped his knuckles on the door five times, waited half a minute because he knew Ralphy would be fetching his Glock, then rapped again and stood back. The peephole popped, the four locks pinged and clacked, and then Ralphy was standing there in the weirdest getup, clutching his handgun down by one leg, wearing sandals, shorts, a *Top Gun* T-shirt, and with a full jet pilot's oxygen mask, hose, and red jet jockey helmet on his head, sun visor up and his big eyes blinking.

"Think you might be taking this virus mask thing a little far, Ralphy?" Steele said.

Ralphy's answer through the rubber mask sounded like somebody talking with a cardboard box on his head.

"Steele. What the heck are you doing here?"

"Happy to see you too." Steele stepped inside and closed the door. "Thanks for inviting me in, Dr. Who."

Ralphy took a step back and unsnapped the O2 mask, which fell away to one side like a hotshot fighter jock's. "I'm not wearing it for that. I was in the middle of a simulation."

Steele looked over at the center of Ralphy's living room. The big couch he remembered was gone, and so was the coffee table where Ralphy had set up a computer dedicated to flight simulation, with a high-end joystick and a pair of rudder pedals under the table. Now there was an actual full cockpit there, like something Ralphy had bought on eBay from a video arcade. He'd clearly enhanced the flight panel and head-up display with his own monitor, programming, and controls, and Steele could even hear a set of surround sound speakers burping out jet engine noises and the tinny voices of other players who were probably thousands of miles away.

"I hope you guys are raiding an Iranian nuclear reactor," Steele said. "The Israelis need a break."

Ralphy put the gun down on a side table, pulled off the helmet and tucked it under his arm. "Really, Steele, I'm glad to see you, but you never show up just for a beer."

"I'm that transparent, huh?"

"Yup."

"Well, I wanted to thank you for the recon."

"No sweat, dude."

"Where'd you get the overheads? Commercial satellite firm?"

"Planet Labs."

"Not bad, though a couple of features were off, maybe PL's behind on real time."

"Uh-huh." Ralphy was still waiting.

"By the way," Steele said. "Rumor is, Snipe and his crew have retired . . ."

"What *is* it, dude?"

"The Program's being revived."

Ralphy just stood there and blinked while thousands of thoughts and flickering images flashed through his mind like an old film strip on fast-forward, backward. Frankie, who'd been reading in bed, had heard Steele arrive and had just wiggled into an oversize Mickey Mouse nightshirt. She stumbled out of the bedroom on the right and held onto the doorjamb with both hands, her bug-eyed expression matching Ralphy's. Steele smiled down at her. With her petite figure, floral tattoos, ankle bracelet, full lips, and huge hairdo of ringed black curls, she looked like a hippie throwback from Woodstock. She also had a large and wickedly fast brain, and she adored Ralphy, which in Steele's eyes made her pure platinum.

"Seven, did I just hear you say what I thought you said I heard?"

"Hi, Frankie." Steele's smile held as he realized that Frankie's shock and perhaps pleasure at the news had twisted her tongue. "Want to rewind and try that again?"

"Did I just hear you say the Program's coming back?"

"That's what you heard."

Frankie looked at Ralphy, who returned her gaze as they both chewed their lips and read each other's minds. The last time Frankie had seen Steele at the apartment, he'd just stumbled inside, after having pulled Lila Kalidi's stiletto out of his back. Frankie'd had no choice but to clean the awful wound and sew him up, so she had a few nightmares of her own, and at the moment seeing him again caused her an olfactory sense memory of his blood all over the floor.

"Tell us more, Steele," Ralphy said hoarsely.

"There's nothing much more. President's chief of staff, Ted Lansky, will be taking Mike Pitts's old job, at least for now. Me and Goodhill are tasked with reassembling assets, so I figured I'd start right here."

"What's the compensation?" Frankie asked, always the practical participant.

"Not sure yet," Steele said. "Probably standard G-12 package." He looked around the apartment, past Ralphy's simulator, and saw that the formerly active high-powered computer banks that had always hummed and whizzed on their long worktable before were mostly swathed in dust covers. "I'm sure you two love what you're doing these days, but you know, for the sake of nostalgia . . ."

Frankie slipped an arm around Ralphy's waist and pulled him close.

"I'm not sure, Seven. Ya know, Ralphy's a little damaged from all that stuff. . . ."

Ralphy looked at her. He'd never heard her say anything like that before.

"We're all damaged," Steele said. "And this is cute, kids, but

I need answers right now." He looked at his watch, as if he were about to click a lap button.

"Okay, we're in," Frankie said quickly.

"We are?" Ralphy asked her.

"Good," Steele said. "We're going to start the revamp tomorrow, but you two stand by for another day till I call you for in-processing." He looked directly at Ralphy. "Meantime, I need you to do me a favor."

"Sure."

"I need you to recon any unusual activity in China over the past two weeks. Look mostly for anything of military preparations in nature, like troop movements, tanks, planes, warships, and so forth. But also scan for anything more unusual that still might be relevant, like shifting large numbers of vehicles or personnel. It might even be something off the mark, like moving five thousand Uyghur prisoners, or something kinetic, like a thermal plume. And do it fast. Got it?"

Steele turned, pulled the door open, and stepped into the hall.

"Seven, wait," Ralphy called after him. "How am I supposed to do all that?"

Steele smirked. "Hack into the National Geospatial Intelligence Agency, dude."

He closed the door hard, the locks all pinged, and Ralphy shook his head slowly and muttered, "How come every time he asks me for a favor, it always starts with a crime?"

CHAPTER 7

LOWER MONGOLIA, CHINA

It snowed when Colonel Ai Liang finally crawled across the Mongolian border.

Of course it did. Her luck had been running that way.

She was soaking wet, her lips were blue, and her teeth were chattering like a monkey mimicking his observers in a zoo. The blood still oozed from her waist wound, where the bullet had pierced her tunic from the rear, ripped through her flesh, and exited the front. It had coagulated somewhat in the cold, but every time she raised her right arm, it tore again and gushed as she grimaced. The breaths poured from her lungs in runnels from her small nose and steamed her glasses. She had to swipe at them often with her other sleeve so she could see.

She'd fallen down the lower half of Toqui 13's mountain, even though she'd tried to climb down carefully. The slope was just too steep and slippery, with hardly any handholds, and every rock she tried to grab was like an oiled saddle pommel, and every brittle branch cracked off and sliced her palms until they bled. Then she tried to do it on her rump, like a child too small and scared to take the stairs, but she only rolled and scraped and tumbled. When she finally hit the bottom, she lay there panting for twenty minutes, until she was fairly sure she hadn't broken anything.

She struggled to her feet and walked. The sky above was black as coal with purple clouds scudding in the wind, but enough stars winking here and there for her to find the Little Dipper and the North Star, and she staggered that way, wondering why the bastards who'd murdered her friends and comrades hadn't come back around to hunt her down and kill her. Maybe they assumed she'd died with all the rest, incinerated in their thermite inferno, but it was strange that they hadn't double checked. She would have, in their place. She was a scientist, but a soldier as well, and very thorough.

It didn't make her happy to be right. She'd just come upon a wide rushing river and knelt there on the bank, washing her aching hands and slurping freezing water from her trembling cupped palm, when she heard the helicopter. One of those killers had clearly been chastised when he reported that she'd fled into the lower levels of the lab, and no one had seen her after that, eye to eye, dead or alive.

The rotors pulsed the air as they grew louder. The machine was winging in from the north, straight above the rushing rapids of the river, and she panicked as her eyes flicked right and left, finding only low scrub, gnarled trees stripped bare by the wind, and nowhere to hide from its searchlights or their guns. Those Harbin Z-20s were state-of-the-art helos, with Forward Looking Infrared, and in less than another minute they'd spot the image of her overheated body and shoot her into shreds.

She tore her glasses off, stuffed them in her pocket, sucked as much air as she could, held her breath, and flung herself straight down into the roiling black water. Her hands scrambled for a hold on something at the bottom, weeds and underwater brambles, and she twisted them around her forearms and wouldn't let them go as the roaring rapids pummeled her and flailed her boots behind her. She'd been a fine swimmer once at the military academy. Back then when she was young she could swim the whole Olympic pool, end to end and back again, fully submerged with just one breath. She counted fifteen seconds, then thirty, then a minute, while her lungs burned and screamed for mercy and she held it even longer, and then had nothing left.

She exploded from the surface, spewing silt and water from her mouth and gasping, and she rolled onto her back and bugged her blurry stinging eyes at the heavens. But it was gone. Nothing there. Silence, except for the wind. She weakly flopped her arms and legs, swam over to the bank, crawled up through the mud on hands and knees, and wept.

She staggered north again, for hours, her sodden uniform so heavy on her small form it felt like chain mail armor. Everything she'd ever done in her life came back to her in visions—her youthful loves, her Party dedication, her hopes and dreams and foolish plans, all so meaningless here and now, where she knew she was going to die soon if she didn't find some shelter. But maybe . . . maybe . . . if she could only cross the border . . .

And there it was, a long line of gleaming barbed razor wire, left to right across a high black berm, silhouetted against a thick foamy sky of gray fog. She stumbled up that long shallow rise and had no choice except to fling herself across the ripping shards of steel. She tore herself free on the other side, bleeding from fresh rents everywhere.

And then the snow came, heavy and hard, curtains of swirling flakes that blinded her. She was instantly coated in a sheet-white shroud, and wiping her glasses did nothing now. She stumbled onward, for no reason, with no direction, her bones growing more brittle by the minute, drained of hope as she fell to her knees, and at last, surrendered.

Her glasses had fallen in the snow. She heard something, raised her head and blinked at a shape in the raging storm. A horse. No, that couldn't be. A huge horse, black as onyx. It snorted and came near her, and sitting in its ornate saddle was the figure of a man. No, not just a man. A Mongol warrior. He was huge and heavy with furs, black boots in the stirrups, a peaked Mongol cap, gleaming eyes, and a drooping pirate's mustache. A long rifle was strapped across his back and some sort of scimitar was gripped in his right glove, while his left hand twisted the reins.

She placed her frozen hands onto her knees and pushed herself erect. She would stand up, straight and defiant for her own execution. At least that little bit of honor.

But the Mongol didn't kill her, or utter a word. He reached down, gripped the front of her uniform tunic in one massive hand, lifted her off the ground like nothing more than a rag doll, and swung her legs behind him onto the horse as she grunted, speechless.

And they rode off into the blizzard.

CHAPTER 8

Mike Pitts had blown his own brains out because he'd been black-mailed by Millennial Crude, forced to betray the Program and his country, and had therefore been responsible for the deaths of three of his best Alpha operators. When his quartermaster, Penny Amdursky, had heard the terrible news, she'd quit government service and gone back to school.

Penny had begun her federal career in the army as an infantry S-4, a logistical expert who handled the influx and outflow of war-fighting matériel, such as uniforms, gear, weapons, and ammunition. Working that job for the Ranger regiment, she'd then been selected to do the same task for Delta at Fort Bragg, which meant she had a security clearance higher than God's. From there, Pitts had recruited her for an ultrasecret special operations outfit based out of the White House, and she'd thought she'd died and gone to heaven. She'd loved working for Mike Pitts, and his death had shaken her faith and crushed her spirit. With the Program dissolved, she'd decided to pursue her second passion, design management and communications, at Georgetown University.

But three days ago, she'd received a call from the former Program's top operator, Stalker Seven, aka Eric Steele. Getting a summons to service from an Alpha like Steele was akin to a locker room towel boy getting a call from Tom Brady. She was a hair's breadth away from finishing her master's degree. She decided her matriculation could wait.

Now she was standing in the middle of the once brand-new, then completely trashed, and soon-to-be-new-again Program headquarters space on Q Street NW, wearing a pair of paint-splattered overalls. At five foot three she was petite and infantry lithe, with short black hair like minx fur and a pair of thick spectacles the army called "BCGs"—birth control glasses—which made her look like a female version of Harry Potter. To the right of Penny stood Steele, Dalton Goodhill, and Ted Lansky. To her left stood Mike Pitts's former adjutant, Betsy Roth, a tall blond woman with fashionable glasses and a pornographic vocabulary, who had also just been rerecruited, and Miles Turner, who still had no idea why he'd agreed to rejoin this frigging circus.

They were watching a team of security-cleared maintenance workers seconded over from the Pentagon as they rolled the once faux mahogany walls with thick white paint. Simultaneously, another crew was installing seashell-colored carpet, and yet another was dragging in white Herman Miller workstations, matching Lino office chairs, white Alienware Aurora R11 computers and monitors, and ergonomic VariDesks, also in matching cream cheese hues.

"It's all kind of white," Steele said.

"Extremely white," said Dalton Goodhill.

"Virginal white," said Betsy Roth. "Not that I'd know."

"You don't think this theme's a little too bright, S?" Ted Lansky growled to Penny. Everyone called her S, for S-4, a play on James Bond's famous quartermaster, Q.

"Internal corporate psychometric studies indicate a degree of higher productivity with a lighter shade environment," Penny said. But then she glanced up at Miles Turner, who'd taken a judgmental posture, arms folded as he examined the transformative decor. "Does this trigger any sort of privilege thing for you, Miles?"

"Don't care if it's purple," the African American security chief said. "Just tell me you're not ordering matching firearms."

"Only a couple Accuracy International Arctic Warfare sniper rifles," Penny said. "For winter work. The rest of the pieces are camo or standard black."

"Okay," Miles said. "I'm down with that."

"You're eating a big chunk of my budget for this, Amdursky," Lansky said to Penny.

"Sir, creamy and dreamy is the same price as dark and dreary. I checked."

"Uh-huh," Lansky grunted, then turned to Steele and Goodhill. "Seven, Blade, my office. And you too, Turner."

He turned and marched to the kitchen/break room. He had no office yet, and the SCIF at the other side of the TOC was being remodeled by Penny's worker bees. They'd already pulled out the classic old conference table and were replacing it with an Alibaba marble white and silver slab, with pop-up microphone modules and matching chairs. The kitchen was being repainted by a young man and woman. Lansky said, "You two Jackson

Pollocks take a break," and they fled. He leaned back against the stove and looked at Steele, Goodhill, and Turner.

"Brief me on recruiting status."

Goodhill jerked a thumb at Turner and said to Lansky, "Is he cleared for this, sir?"

"I'm cleared for rumor, *sport*," Turner hissed down at Goodhill. He was half a head taller than Steele, who was six foot two and four inches taller than Goodhill.

"Miles is going to run your assessment and selection," Lansky said to Steele and Goodhill, "then he'll turn them over to you two for OTC." He meant the operator training course. "I want you two flexible for now."

"Can you handle that, Miles?" Steele said.

"Don't worry," said Turner. "I'll have 'em wishing they were back in Pineland." He meant the North Carolina woods where officer candidates for army Special Forces were weeded out during the infamous Q-Course.

"We're thinking we'll want a completely separate assessment and training track for keepers," Goodhill said to Lansky, meaning the handlers like him who were attached to each Alpha.

"And we'd like to bring back Shane Wiley," Steele said. Wiley was an older yet very experienced keeper. He'd handled Collins Austin, who'd been murdered by Lila Kalidi. Her death had taken a toll on Wiley, and he'd almost quit the Program, just before it died the first time.

"Think he's up to it?" Lansky said.

"None better," said Goodhill, who rarely complimented anyone. "They've got him instructing over at the Farm."

"I'll make a call to CIA." Lansky stuck his dry pipe in his

trouser pocket, pulled a small notebook from inside his blazer, and made a note with a pen.

"We need a TDA," Steele said. He meant a Table of Distributions and Allowances denoting personnel, ranks, tasks, and corresponding budgets.

Lansky looked at him and smirked. "I'm bringing Mrs. Darnstein back in here. She's already working it."

"Oh, joy." Steele rolled his eyes. Mrs. Darnstein had been the Program comptroller, an elderly, razor-sharp accountant who questioned every receipt, right down to the costs of number two pencils. "She'll want us offering McDonald's minimum wage, no holiday bonus."

"Embrace the suck," Lansky said. Then he looked at the kitchen doorway, where Ralphy Persko had appeared, with Frankie hovering behind him. They were wearing matching Southern Breeze Graphics T-shirts that said GLOCK, PAPER, SCISSORS. CHOOSE WISELY. Lansky pulled his pipe back out and jabbed it at them. "Get in here, geeks."

"Did you two clear yet?" Steele said to them. He'd sent Ralphy and Frankie to an outside security contractor for revetting, which included the mind-numbing 136-page questionnaire for national security positions, new fingerprinting, and family background checks.

"Yeah," Ralphy said. "They did everything but an anal probe."

"Too bad," Turner grunted. "Goodhill likes that." He and Goodhill exchanged grins. They were warming to each other again.

"Before you two kids get any deeper into this," Lansky said to Ralphy and Frankie, "I know you've been doing the horizontal tango. You've been civilians for a while so I'm not going to go full pope on you, but if I see any PDAs around here, I'll cut your hands off." He meant public displays of affection. Ralphy and Frankie just blinked and nodded. "Now give us whatever Steele asked you for."

"Um, well, sir . . ." Ralphy began with a stutter, then opened his big brain valve. "We ran high alt and nap surveillance on every major CCP potential target, but we didn't get anything weird on overheads or signatures, including the usual troop or naval flows in the South China Sea. But we did get one kinky hit on a large thermal plume, just south of the lower Mongolian border. Looks like some sort of facility went up, burned for two days, and spectral analysis picked up coolant and chemical bursts, like maybe from a lab."

"How the hell did you get all that before you were cleared?" Lansky said.

Ralphy said nothing. Frankie looked at the floor and chewed her lip.

"Okay, never mind. Go tell Penny you two need stations online ASAP, then lock in your firewalls and work it some more."

"Yessir," the geeks echoed and disappeared.

Something buzzed inside Lansky's blazer. He took out a cell phone, answered it, said "Right now?" and put it away. He looked at Steele, who was wearing torn jeans, running shoes, and a wrinkled white shirt rolled up at the sleeves. "Is that all you have to wear?"

"Here?" Steele said. "Yes, sir. Why?"

"All right, get your ass downstairs. There's a car waiting for you. And tell them your fucked-up sense of fashion wasn't cleared by me."

CHAPTER 9

The big fat royal blue armored Suburban wasn't exactly an Uber. Its front fenders were flying the American and presidential flags, its windows were tinted like a pair of Oakley tactical sunglasses, and its fuselage gleamed in the sun like a brand-new bullet. Out front, a pair of Metro D.C. motorcycle cops sat on their gurgling Harleys, boots on the pavement, staring straight ahead. Behind the Suburban a matching armored Expedition follow car hummed like an impatient panther.

Steele stood there on the sidewalk, hands in the pockets of his ratty jeans, figuring the convoy belonged to some White House staffer who'd stopped for a pee or a latte from the nearby Starbucks. Then the Suburban's passenger window rolled down, a low female voice said, "You expecting an engraved invitation, Mr. Steele?" and he realized this was his ride. He stepped off the curb, the window closed, and a Secret Service agent appeared from the other side of the SUV and looked him over with a judgmental squint.

"You carrying?" the agent asked.

"Just a tape measure," Steele said, "but it's dull."

"Do I need to pat you down?"

"Only if you miss your gig with the TSA."

The agent smirked and pulled the door open.

Steele had never met National Security Advisor Katie Garland in person, but he'd seen her perfectly put-together persona many times on TV and knew her by reputation. She never shied away from the gotcha journalists on all the major networks, and no matter how hard they pushed her, she always remained calm, quick tongued, and icy. She had a smile that reminded him of those wild African desert dogs he'd seen in Namibia, who always looked so friendly until they ripped some creature's throat out.

Garland waved him into the gloomy cool cabin. He slid onto the plush leather seat, the door closed with a whisper, the shotgun rider remounted, and they started to roll.

"I see we pulled you away from respectable labors," she said as she looked him over. She was wearing a dark suit, a starched pearl blouse, a presidential seal lapel pin, and a modest crucifix.

"Sorry about the attire, ma'am," Steele said.

"No biggie." She waved slim fingers with short buffed nails, no color. "The president's hosting a luncheon at the Four Seasons for the French PM, but don't fret about the duds. From what I've heard, he likes you. Hasn't told me why."

She pressed a button on the console between them and spoke to the driver on the other side of the Plexiglas partition.

"Julius, inform Hammer's detail we're en route," she said, using the Secret Service code word for Rockford, "but since our guest is maintaining *very* casual cover, I suggest we rendezvous in the galley."

"Yes, ma'am," the driver's piped-in voice replied.

"And step on it," Garland added. "Those frogs hate waiting for food."

As far as hotel restaurants go, Bourbon Steak at the Four Seasons is fairly spectacular. The twenty-foot teakwood ceiling features suspended, circular, hatbox-shaped Malaysian lanterns, cream brocade curtains frame the enormous plate glass windows, and the polished bumper-pool-size tables are surrounded by richly upholstered mid-century chairs. It's a fine spot for a modest presidential VIP luncheon, effected by moving only a few furniture pieces around, and the spectral hues from sunset yellow to beaver fur brown make the atmosphere welcoming and warm.

The kitchen, on the other hand—much like the engine room of a spectacular cruise ship that guests never see—is steamy, greasy, noisy, and hotter than Hades. Pots bang like cymbals, flames spit and hiss, and the chefs, sous chefs, and waiters curse one another in a stressed-out Babel of tongues, especially when spoiling the meal of some high-flying ambassador can get your ass fired, without references.

Steele stood there inside the gourmet melee with Katie Garland, who was dabbing her neck with a handkerchief because they'd already started to sweat. They'd come in through the rear entrance past two flinty-eyed Secret Service agents—whenever POTUS was around no access was left unguarded—and as they waited on a linoleum patch in front of a long, stainless steel food pickup divider, behind which were the sauté, fry, and grill station stoves, the galley cooks ignored them because they had no idea what was about to transpire. Then the double entrance doors flew open like an Old West saloon, President Rockford strode in with

four agents, and the entire staff went dead silent and stiff as a
family of lemurs when a lion bursts from the jungle.

"Carry on, people!" Rockford boomed with a smile and waved
his arms. They all returned to work, but with one eye cocked for
potential disaster.

"Eric," the president said as he thrust out a meaty hand. He
was perfectly pressed, as always, in a dark suit and regimental tie.
Steele hesitated for a moment but Rockford said, "Don't give me
that elbow crap. I get tested every day," and Steele grinned and
they shook hands, hard.

Like his predecessor, Denton Cole, John Rockford had always
treated Steele with great respect for his Alpha status, and a degree of paternal affection. The feelings were mutual for Steele,
and despite the great difference in status, they'd dealt with each
other on an even keel. When Steele had gone off on a rogue
mission to Russia, trying to unearth the fate of his long missing father, Hank, Rockford had risked his political fortunes and
sent in Delta to rescue Eric. In turn, Steele had risked his life to
keep President Rockford from being blown to kingdom come by
Lila Kalidi. Essentially they were battle buddies, and there is no
stronger bond.

Rockford stuck his hands in his suit pockets while his agents
eyed the cooks and their flashing Ginsu knives.

"I left that Frenchy mooning over Mrs. Rockford," he said.
"But I can't take too long."

"The floor is yours, sir," Steele said.

Rockford looked over at the cooks, assessed their physical features, and in dead fluent Spanish said, *"Amigos, por favor, danos cinco
minutos. Cuándo terminemos, si lo desean, firmaré sus delantales."*

He asked them for five minutes' privacy, with a promise to afterward autograph their aprons, and the stunned cooks dropped their knives and disappeared.

"Had a Guatemalan girlfriend in college." The president winked at Steele. "So, down to brass tacks. Lansky briefed you on my Chinese walk-in?" He used the pejorative term for a volunteer spy who walks into an embassy uninvited, offering all sorts of raw intelligence. In this case he was referencing the phone call at Camp David.

"He did, sir."

"Well, I never trust walk-ins," the president said.

"Ditto, sir," said Steele.

"So, this guy, who calls himself Casino, claims the CCP is planning a big move against our assets out there. Might be true, might not be. I called over to Tina Harcourt and had her run it down." He meant the newly appointed director of CIA. "She tells me they once had an agent inside CCP called Casino, but that gentleman was blown and is currently taking a dirt nap."

Steele was surprised to hear the president use street slang for a dead man, then remembered he'd once been a hard-charging armor officer who admired George Patton.

"Lansky also pinged me just before you got here, Eric," the president went on. "Says you've got something else on China."

"Yes, sir. It's some sort of facility near the southern Mongolian border. Might be a secret laboratory, went up in smoke."

"Think it's a coincidence?"

"I generally don't believe in such things, Mr. President."

"Me either." Rockford rubbed his jaw for a moment. "Listen, I like Harcourt and I trust her. However, we're still weeding out leakers and political holdovers at Langley, which is why I called on you, and why I tasked Ted with standing the Program up again. I want you to take point on this, Eric. I've got more faith in you and a crew of hard-core Alphas than I do in an army of CIA analysts and NSA eavesdroppers. Go after it. Can I count on you?"

"I think you know you can, sir."

"Good." Then Rockford reached out and gripped Steele's shoulder, which surprised him and made Katie Garland and the president's agents flinch. "That's the first part of why I wanted to see you. The second part is about your father."

Steele just stood there, but he felt something turn over in his guts. Rockford had mentioned his father only once before and he had no idea what was coming.

"This country betrayed that man," Rockford said, and his blue eyes gleamed with rare emotion. "I'm not going to make excuses for what was done to your father. He was nothing but a patriot, and we abandoned him, turned on him, left him to the wolves. I want you to find Hank Steele. I want you to find him, tell him the president gave his word that we'll do our best to make up for all of it, and bring him home. And if he wants to tell me to go pound sand, he can do it to my face in the White House. The only consequences will be a medal, twenty years of back pay, and a big fat bonus. Are we clear?"

Steele had trouble finding his voice, but he smiled and said, "Which do you want me to do first, sir?"

Rockford grinned. "The Chinese thing."

"Roger that."

"Keep me posted through Lansky, but if you've got something outside of channels, go directly through Kate here." Rockford turned to Garland. "Are we good, Kate?"

She smiled her wild dog smile. "I'll give him my cell, Mr. President."

"Outstanding." Rockford looked at his watch. "Okay, I gotta go pretend I like foie gras." He turned to leave, but a Secret Service agent leaned over and spoke in his ear.

"Oh yeah, I forgot," the president said. "Bring the cooks back in here first, and get me a felt pen."

Rockford always kept his word.

CHAPTER 10

The sun was draining into the pewter waters of the Potomac when Steele and Goodhill finally left Q Street. It was a warm sun, a shimmering umber sun, and its light lanced through the marble columns of the Lincoln Memorial and glittered off the glass at the Smithsonian Air and Space Museum. It was a beautiful becalming thing to see, nature in all its celestial glory, waving its comforting curtain across the heart of America's seat of government.

But neither man noticed, or cared.

Miles Turner had tasked one of his armed drivers to get them to wherever they were going. Steele's coveted sidearm, the Colt 1911 bequeathed to him by his father, which he'd retooled for 9 mm ammunition, was still nestled inside a custom steel box with a thumbprint biosensor lock, in turn welded under the seat of his emerald-green 1967 GTO, which in turn was still parked in a long-term underground lot in Rosslyn, Virginia. He no longer had an apartment in D.C., so he was staying temporarily at the Holiday Inn.

Goodhill's cut-down Remington 870 in 20 gauge—a nasty, short little thing with a custom shoulder rig that *thwanged* whenever Blade drew the shotgun from under his jacket—was also locked in a steel box, but ensconced in the closet of one of his female admirers, with whom he was temporarily crashing in Crystal City.

The men had not discussed getting a place together, nor would they. Keepers and Alphas were way too ornery and similar to share a kitchen and bathroom.

"We're not going to get this damn thing spun up for months," Steele murmured. He was staring out the SUV's right-side passenger window.

"We don't need it all spun up right now," Goodhill said. He was across the wide seat from Steele, squinting out the opposite window. "We just need a few good tier-one door kickers that can operate on the down low, way down range. The rest of the admin crap'll catch up."

"Down low. Then we're talking SF, Delta, maybe some ISA if we can steal them from the DIA. Or maybe some special tactics people from Langley, if they haven't gone soft."

"No SEALs, huh?" Goodhill asked.

"SEALs don't do subtle. Undercover to them means three hookers at the same time in a Bangkok brothel."

Goodhill laughed at that. Then he leaned forward and said to Turner's assigned driver, "Hey, you're not a squid, are ya?"

"No, sir. I was air force, Green Hornets, Twentieth Special Ops Squadron."

"Cool. Wouldn't want to offend." Goodhill sat back again, looked at Steele, and said, "Hey, how about checking out some air force PJs or STS guys? Pretty well rounded."

"PJs as Alphas? Their motto's 'That Others May Live.'"

"Oh, yeah, no good. We need shooters, not priests."

"And we need some female prospects too," Steele said.

"I know some girls on a roller derby team who could probably kick my ass." Goodhill smirked at the thought. "And I'd probably like it."

"You're not going to last in this PC environment, Blade," Steele said.

"Kid, you're just jealous of my clear-eyed worldview."

They were quiet for a minute as the driver took them straight down Fourteenth Street toward Franklin Square. In a few more blocks the White House and the Ellipse would appear off of Steele's starboard flank, and already he could see more Metro PD activity on the streets, because the evening ruckus in Lafayette Square had become a regular thing. Still, Washington had remained fairly civilized, with only a few shops boarded up, as opposed to Manhattan, where Fifth Avenue still looked like a scene out of *Escape from New York*.

"Looks like Lansky wants to totally reghost everything," Steele said.

"Yep, and everybody too. Shame that Max Sands has to die," Goodhill said, meaning Steele's cover as a sales rep with Graceland Import Exports.

"Ditto John Booth," Steele said in reference to Goodhill's previous cover, "but to be honest, that name always gave me the creeps with the whole Lincoln's assassin thing."

"I didn't choose it. Computer did. And just so you know, the only true love of my life was a beautiful black girl from Atlanta."

Steele turned and looked at Goodhill's shiny shaved bullet

head, busted nose, and bulldog jaw. Goodhill cocked his chin down, confirming what Steele thought he'd just heard.

"You know, Dalton," Steele said, "I'm seeing you in a whole new light."

"It's the light just before the fucking darkness, so don't get too excited."

"Where do you gentlemen want to be dropped?" the driver asked.

"Constitution Ave.," Steele said. "I'll stroll the rest of the way and you can drop my gorilla off in Crystal."

"Roger."

Another half minute passed while they thought.

"I don't much like the HQ name change either," Goodhill said.

"Yeah. From Cutlass Main, to Sawtooth? I think Lansky's got a comic book writer on the payroll."

"Let's get Ralphy to tell him Sawtooth's being used by a JSOC unit or something."

"Good idea. Then we can choose something more respectable, like Toothpick Forward."

Goodhill laughed heartily at that and slapped Steele's knee as the driver stopped and Steele opened his door.

"Watch your six," Steele said as he slid from the SUV. "There's gonna be some pissed-off Russians on the hunt very shortly."

"I got Kevlar skin, kid. You watch yours."

Steele shut the door and started walking west on Constitution Avenue as the SUV rolled away, and right away he sunk into a brood. The president's tasking hadn't fazed him, because he'd been down that road many times before. The Program had been as close to the fictitious Impossible Mission Force as anything could be, and would be again, and like all the other Alphas selected, he was highly trained and cursed with an obsessive need to succeed. If it couldn't be done, he'd do it. If it couldn't be found, he'd find it. Plus, his love of country and calling to a higher duty were emotions that ran just under his skin and could quickly be activated. John Rockford knew that. Rockford knew that if he tasked Steele with a mission, he'd nail it or die trying.

But that wasn't it. It was the other part, about his father. It was about the discovery a year before that Hank Steele had once been an Alpha too. He'd walked out of his son's life when Eric was nine years old, and had never come back, and there wasn't a damn thing you could do to repair such pain. Sure, the president could declare Hank a national hero. Sure, Eric might be able to find his father out there somewhere, and they might have a reunion and be able to sit down and share a cigar and a beer and, eventually, laugh over similar war stories, or stare off together at the stars while they swallowed their past. But nothing could fix the years of loneliness that Susan Steele had endured, or the fact that Eric had forced himself to assume the role of "man of the house," a common phenomenon with fatherless boys, and never completely reparable.

The president had ordered him to go find his father and bring him home. He wasn't sure that he wanted to anymore.

Lost in his musings, Steele realized that he'd already cut southwest past the Lincoln Memorial and was approaching the Arlington bridge. Letting his mind lapse like that, instead of remaining split-brained and alert to all threats, was not a good trait for an Alpha.

You're slipping, mister, losing your mojo. . . . Might have to ask Goodhill and Turner to burn your ass and tune you up again, like some green FNG.

He entered the bridge span, between the two bookend statues called *Valor* and *Sacrifice,* each of an enormous steed being ridden by Mars, the god of war. Beyond that he could see the rolling green hills of Arlington National Cemetery and its thousands of white marble teeth, the graves of men and women like him, too many of whom he'd known personally, and still quietly mourned. And even though he wasn't going to visit them today, it felt somehow disrespectful to be dressed as he was, like a sloppy handyman, but he pressed on and braved the next train of thought he'd been resisting all day.

Meg Harden. They'd worked together at the Program, she as a brilliant intel analyst with a talent for martial arts, while he was the sharp end of the spear. They'd kept their love affair secret, until no one was pretending not to know anymore, and then he'd rolled her into his list of suspects when it was clear that the outfit had a mole. In fact he'd nearly killed her, which had definitely put a wrinkle in their relationship.

For a long time after that, Meg had refused to see him. It took a lot of coaxing for her to relent and forgive him, and they'd taken up where they'd left off. But it hadn't stuck. Meg had stopped thirsting for action and wanted a normal life. Steele only wanted to find his next target. He hadn't seen her for months.

I should just take up with Allie Whirly. All she wants is regular head-banging sex. We could run helicopter hunting trips for wannabee Rambos in Alaska. . . .

For a moment, that seemed appealing.

Problem was, he still loved Meg, and always would.

He'd crossed the bridge, turned right and was heading north, and he could see the Marine Corps Memorial up ahead. It was a magnificent sculpted reproduction of Joe Rosenthal's famous photo of the Marines raising the flag on Mount Suribachi at Iwo Jima in 1945. The image always stirred his soul and reminded him of his beloved grandfather, a World War II leatherneck who'd fought at Guadalcanal. Grandpa never spoke of that battle. The real heroes rarely did.

There were hardly any tourists about the wide circle embracing the statue. But hanging back in the tree line, Steele saw five questionable-looking dudes. They were all dressed in black, with matching facemasks, which wasn't that unusual. Except a couple were wearing backpacks with the grips of short baseball bats sticking out. And they all had spray paint cans in their hands. They were staring at the memorial and grunting in low tones, and he assessed they were up to no good.

He knew he should just walk on by. He didn't. An old photo of his grandpa appeared behind his eyes—skinny, filthy jungle fatigues, dangling M1 carbine, steel pot helmet, thousand-yard stare, and very proud. He strolled up behind the five men and quietly joined the pack, looking over their heads, as if they might be a crew of innocent bird-watchers and he just wanted to see a falcon too.

"Pretty magnificent, isn't it?" Steele said.

The five men started and turned. They hadn't heard him approach. Few folks ever did.

"What the fuck's so magnificent, asshole?" one of them said.

Steele kept his gaze on the statue, with an admiring smile on his lips as he slipped off his Oakleys and tucked them into his shirt pocket, as if just wanting to see the statue more clearly.

"My granddad fought with those guys," he said as his peripheral senses assessed.

Big one on the right, muscle guy, slow, left one's faster, two outliers on the flanks are hangers-on, last one's the danger, knife-wielder . . .

The men faced him fully now, in a semicircle, their eyes above their black masks squinting and pleased to find prey.

"Then your granddaddy was a fucking fascist, wasn't he, white boy?" the muscle guy said, which was amusing, because all of them were Caucasians.

"Actually, he was a *genuine* antifascist, not like you Antifa scum," Steele said. "I assume you're gonna tag that with yellow, since it's the color of cowards."

The muscle guy said "Fuck *you*" and thrust out a meaty paw to shove him. It never landed. Steele jinked to the left, trapped the guy's right wrist in a vise grip, yanked him off balance, reached over that arm with his left and elbowed his assailant's jaw so hard that it cracked out loud and he went down like a prizefighter clanged by George Foreman. After that, the rest of it was a blur, and Steele was a tornado.

The second bat wielder drew a Louisville slugger from his backpack. Steele chested him like a locomotive, Krav Maga style, trapping the bat arm with his left elbow. Then he smashed the guy's nose with a wicked palm strike, grabbed the hair on top of his head, yanked him over his motorcycle boots, and kneed him full force in the groin. That guy went down wailing, and with blood gushing over his teeth, and now the bat was Steele's.

He backhand smacked it into one outlier's forehead, which made a sound like a meat mallet on a rib eye steak, then he gripped the bat two-handed as the fourth dude lunged at him, and he hit one out of the park into his solar plexus. The blow lifted him clear off his feet and he went down on his back, his legs and arms twitching in the air like a cockroach.

The fifth Antifa, as Steele had assessed, came up with a long knife and dropped into an amateur gangbanger stance.

Steele hopped backward, dropped the bat, crooked his finger, and said, "I'm your Huckleberry," hoping Val Kilmer wouldn't mind being plagiarized. The knife boy took the bait, yelled an unintelligible curse, and lunged. Steele shattered his right knee with a whipping roundhouse kick, eagle-clawed his hand, took the knife away as he screamed, and whipped it like a boomerang into the trees.

He was painting all their weeping faces red with one of their spray paint cans when he heard a panting voice behind him order, "Drop it!"

He turned to find two trembling park rangers, a young man and a woman, both pointing Tasers at his chest.

"You're under arrest," the female ranger spat.

Steele released the can, raised his hands, smiled, and said, "Well, it's been that kind of a day."

CHAPTER 11

ULAANBADRAKH, MONGOLIA

Colonel Doctor Ai Liang lay half dead in a Mongolian village yurt, but she wasn't gone just yet. She had lost a lot of blood, had a raging fever, and was dangerously dehydrated, yet she was hanging on in the care of her determined nomadic hosts, who would view it as a great dishonor if their guest did not survive.

Her rescuer, Gengi Phon, was the elder of this nameless collection of conical huts squatting on a snow-swept plain in the wilds southwest of Ulaanbadrakh. A strapping horseman of forty-two, Gengi was also an expert smuggler who regarded the southern border with China as a mere suggestion, and ranged freely back and forth for collections of Chinese spices, purloined firearms, ammunition, and jewels he snatched from errant hikers. He was a hard man descended from four centuries of cavalry warriors, but he had his own set of private honorable rules.

The horseback trek from the border had ranged across nearly forty kilometers of relentless blizzard. The Chinese woman, in her torn, soaked, and bloody leopard spot uniform, had at some point fainted and slumped against the fur pelts warming Gengi's massive back. He'd slung her arms around his neck and roped her wrists together so she wouldn't fall off. Her breaths were weak, and once when he stopped to check, so was her heart. He'd forced cold water into her gullet from a camel skin bladder, and rode on.

The village was composed of six yurts the Mongolians called *gers*. They were circular, shaped like giant Hershey's Kisses, with wooden beam skeletons cocooned in roped canvas and furs, and openings in their sloping peaked roofs for a single-pipe chimney. They were warm inside from mixed peat and woodstove fires, while frozen outside and coated in gleaming ice. Each had a single, ornate, bright green, amber, or chartreuse wooden door, but there were no televisions or telephones. At night the *gers* were lit by oil lanterns. The Mongols' emergency flashlights were squeeze-powered Russian models and the precious few batteries they owned were used for their old-style Chinese transistor radios. Gengi's heavily blanketed horse stood outside in the snow, next to a Russian Ural motorcycle that wasn't a recreational toy.

"She must not expire," Gengi said to his wife as they stood side by side in the *ger,* watching the Chinese woman breathe. They were speaking Khalkha, a Mongolian dialect unlike any other on earth, which could be written in Cyrillic but also in a Mongolian script that looked very much like cave drawings.

"She will not die in our home, husband," his wife replied. She was raven haired, with sweeping Asian eyes and wide cheek-bones, and swathed in bear furs and also a long scarlet skirt, with thick boots roped like Roman sandals. "I have just fed her soup and she is holding it down."

"She appears lost to this world to me," Gengi grunted. He pulled a three-legged stool close to the wooden pallet bed upon which Liang was snuggled beneath two layers of camel hide, and sat down. His great mustache was gleaming wet from the condensed steam of his nose, and his long thick hair was roped at the back of his great skull into something he had no idea the Americans called a man bun. He touched Liang's forehead with calloused red fingers that looked like overcooked sausages.

"The woman is fevered," he said.

"It will break," said his wife. "I have prayed for it."

"You have prayed for it? Why?"

"We shall not be shamed. And besides, the ground outside is too hard for a grave."

Just then, Colonel Liang stirred and fluttered her eyes. Above her, through her blurry vision, she saw a conical starfish of wooden beams laced with billowing canvas, below which hung a small cloud of smoke and steam. She glanced to the left and saw two long wooden pallet beds, like the one she felt under her spine. She glanced to the right and saw a low table made from some sort of crate. Upon it was a steaming iron pot, next to a pile of bloody white strips of cloth. Her drenched uniform hung from a wooden pole above her neatly ordered boots, like a soldier's burial plot, and she realized she was naked beneath a pile of animal fur. The snippets of her rescue in the snow came flooding back from her frozen memory, and a large male face loomed above her like something from the tales of Fu Manchu.

"*Huan ying lai dao shi jie*," the man's bass voice said in fluent Mandarin. Welcome to the world.

Liang blinked and she tried to speak, yet nothing came out but a croak. Then a woman's face appeared, a ladle touched her lips, and something that tasted like syrupy ramen warmed her throat.

"*Xiè xie*," Liang managed. Thank you.

"I am Gengi Phon," said the man. "You are in my village in Mongolia. Who are you? Why did you flee, and why are you wounded?"

Dr. Liang's tongue was still thick. She looked at the woman, whose eyes were nearly black, yet kind. The woman smiled, showing gold-tipped teeth, and she ladled more liquid into Liang's mouth and it soothed her clutched throat.

"I am a colonel in the Chinese army," Dr. Liang rasped. "I am the commander of a secret . . . facility. We were attacked by troops . . . I don't know who. Everyone was killed . . ."

"But you," Gengi said.

"Yes." Beneath the furs, Liang carefully explored her skin. It was hot, even to her own touch, and the flesh of her waist wound was swathed in a slimy pâté that felt like some sort of animal blubber, perhaps seal.

"These troops," Gengi said, "were Chinese?" His breath smelled like harsh tobacco and onions.

"They arrived in helicopters, but I do not know."

Gengi's leathery face lifted away and back, as if he'd just realized that his guest was contagious with something.

"These men. Do they know that you survived?"

"I . . . I believe that they do." Liang wasn't going to lie.

Gengi looked at his wife. The woman shrugged, and then glanced sideways at Gengi's three rifles, which were resting across a fixture made from the antlers of elk-like Mongolian red deer. The rifles were bolt-action British Lee-Enfields in heavy .303 caliber, but no match for modern firearms.

The door to the *ger* creaked open, a blast of frigid wind swirled into the hut along with lances of snow-bright light, and a large young man covered in snow-crusted fur stepped inside. Twenty minutes before, Gengi had stepped outside and blown a summoning blast on his ram's horn. The young man was his son. Gengi stood up and went to him. He was the image of his father, though slimmer at nineteen, and his mustache wasn't yet as full or menacing. Gengi spoke to him in Khalkha.

"Ganbaatar," he said. The name meant "steel hero." "You must ride to Zuunbayan."

"It is sixty kilometers, father." The young man's eyes narrowed. "The snow is growing."

"As are you, my son." Gengi's massive hand gripped his son's shoulder. "Take your rifle, water, food, and a second horse, Uli's horse. Bring the man from Tibet, the monk they call Tenzin, the one who worked with the American spies." He leaned closer, and spoke lower, even though he was certain the Chinese woman would not understand.

"Bring him quickly, Ganbaatar, before she dies."

CHAPTER 12

"Were you born a dumbass? Or did you have to go to school for that?"

That was about all that Dalton "Blade" Goodhill had said to Steele when his Alpha called him from the processing room at Arlington County Jail.

Steele had been allowed the single requisite call to an attorney, but having recovered from his momentary lapse in professional judgment at the Marine Corps Memorial, he'd quickly realized that if Ted Lansky discovered what he'd done, his newly re-freshed Program career could be terminated at birth. Somehow, his stupidity had to be kept under wraps. So he'd called Goodhill instead, told him briefly what had happened, then cringed as Goodhill cursed him and clicked off.

For once he was happy with cell phone technology because his keeper had no handset to smash.

The park rangers, having witnessed Steele's decimation of the Antifa thugs, knew they didn't have much of a federal case and had turned him over to Arlington County sheriffs and relayed what they'd seen. He'd politely offered them his wrists for the cuffs, hadn't made a fuss, and one of the EMTs who'd arrived in an ambulance had looked at the carnage and snorted, "What? You're gonna book this dude for defending himself from *five* of these assholes?" No charges were going to stick, but he still had to be processed.

The jail was nice, for a prison facility. It was a modern, multi-story, clean cement structure on Court Street, where the interior cells were raised behind a blue balustrade catwalk, above a central recreation area of blue and beige tiles and neat tables bolted to the floor for bitching and cards. The cells were cinder block, freshly painted and disinfected, with the usual open toilets, small sinks, beds as hard as the warden, and single-slat windows with no view except the next-door police precinct's walls.

Steele had been questioned briefly by a bored deputy, finger-printed, and locked in a holding cell. Unfortunately, his timing sucked, because he had no new cover yet and all of his pocket litter, including his Pennsylvania driver's license, said Eric Steele. His fingerprints, however, had long ago been ghosted out of the federal record, so these fresh ones weren't going to return a single match. Very soon now, these folks were going to get very suspicious, so while he bided his time he was hoping that Goodhill would come up with a solution, and fast.

The solution arrived that night at 10:21 P.M., in the form of a sound, a light tapping along the internal catwalk outside. Steele was sitting on his bunk, still wearing his civilian attire and pondering his life choices, when a figure appeared outside his cell.

Steele had met Thorn McHugh only once before, in the dark in a park. The man was something of a ghost himself, one of those old-world spooks from days gone by, but he'd heard enough whispers about McHugh's past and recognized his stature and form. The man standing there had a slight smile playing on his wind-weathered lips, below a pair of gold spectacles and a green fedora. He was wearing a dark blue corduroy jacket with leather elbow patches, twill trousers, brown cordovans, and a tie. His cane was mahogany classic, with a right-angle polished grip instead of a curve, and Steele imagined it could be twisted off to reveal a rapier blade.

"I had hoped for a less formal reunion," said McHugh. He was somewhere in his seventies, but his voice was much younger and had a Yalie lilt that was nearly British.

"Thank you for coming, sir." Steele rose to his feet. "I apologize for any inconvenience."

"Oh, it's no bother, my boy." McHugh jutted the tip of his cane through the bars at Steele's shirt and asked, "Is that blood yours?"

"No." Steele felt embarrassed.

"Fortuitous. Then you shan't need attention." McHugh turned his head to someone in the corridor and nodded. A jailhouse deputy stepped into view, unlocked the cell door, and slid it open. "Come," McHugh said to Steele. "The county sheriff is a friend, but I'd prefer not to dally and try her patience."

Outprocessing was short and painless. The sheriff's officers behind the front desk barely said a word—someone had made a call. They handed Steele a large ziplock plastic bag with his Rolex Submariner, a few quarters, wallet, and cash, had him sign a form for recovery of his possessions, nodded at McHugh, and went back to watching their monitor screens. Ever since child predator Jeffrey Epstein had died mysteriously in his Manhattan cell, with the blame being laid on his "goons," prison guards all over the country had kept their eyes peeled and their coffee caffeinated.

McHugh opened the main entrance door, swept a polite "after you" hand for Steele, and they strolled out onto the street. Arlington was quiet this late on a weeknight. There weren't any statues around to tag or burn. They walked north on Courthouse Road. It was chilly, and Steele was tired, hungry, and secretly ashamed. But McHugh took his elbow, squeezed it slightly, as if to say "It's all right. We've all screwed the pooch once in a while," and he kept his fingers there as they walked.

"You know what they say about old spies, my boy?" he said.

"No, sir. What do they say?"

"Nothing." McHugh smiled as he tapped his cane on the sidewalk. "No one is supposed to know who they are."

Steele smiled as well but kept silent. He sensed he was going to learn something.

"I was much like you as a younger agent. Fraught with emotion on occasion. They turn you into a certain kind of chap, then expect you to freeze that persona when something unexpected, and unrelated to your mission, all at once rears its ugly head."

"I should know better by now," Steele said. "I can usually control it."

McHugh squeezed his elbow again.

"It's not an admonition. My father was with the OSS during the war. Parachuted into France, on more than one occasion. I followed in his footsteps, as you did in yours."

Steele looked over at McHugh's expression, which was slightly bemused, but he was keeping his old eagle eyes on the path.

"Yes, I knew him." McHugh nodded once as they walked. "I was with the Company, as we called it back then, for many years.

One of my mentors at Langley, who shall not be named, invited me on a fishing trip in Chesapeake Bay. There were, of course, no fishing poles, and no fish. He explained to me that a select few of the old guard believed that Langley had become too large, unwieldy, and unsecure. He revealed another, much smaller agency where he thought I'd be more suited to serve. We shan't say its name, shall we?"

"No, sir."

"Yes, and that's where I met one of the finest operators I'd ever known." McHugh winked at Steele. "Aside from my own father, naturally."

Steele felt the flush rising up through his throat. Thorn McHugh had worked with Hank Steele. A hundred questions instantly popped into his mind, but he held his peace.

"By the way," McHugh said, "I heard you received a postcard from him."

"I did." Steele had no idea how McHugh could possibly know that.

"Might I ask where it came from?"

"The picture on the front was of Bali."

"Ahh, the tropics." McHugh smiled. "So he's probably somewhere in the Alps." Then he transitioned to fluent French. "*Tu crois qu'on a une queue?*" Do you think we have a tail?

"*Je n'ai pas vu ça,*" Steele replied. Not that I've seen.

"Three long years in Saigon," McHugh said in English again, as if by way of explanation for his French. "I was in Hue in '68, when the bullets were pirouetting through the embassy and we were burning all of our files. Hence, the leg." Then he rapped his cane on his right lower leg and it made a knocking sound—wood on wood. "I ran a network of joes from Tibet. Later on, I also handled an asset, deep inside the CCP. We called him Casino, but that man is unfortunately dead. The fellow who called Camp David is an imposter."

"The president told me that this morning," Steele said.

"I know."

This man runs deep, Steele thought. *Very deep.*

"He's also tasked me with this Chinese threat," Steele added.

"I know that as well."

It was so matter-of-fact that it didn't invite discussion. They passed the Bayou Bakery, which was closed but still exuding scents of chocolate croissants that made Steele's stomach growl, but they pressed on and turned left on Clarendon.

"Tell me, my boy," McHugh said. "How often do you find yourself wanting to quit?"

"Often," Steele said. McHugh wasn't the kind of man one lied to.

"Good, then you've got a healthy mind. It's the ones who can't envision a normal life who become dangerous to themselves, and to others."

They were approaching the Court House Metro station when McHugh slowed, stopped, and turned to Eric. He was tall and their eyes nearly met.

"You shall need to be thoroughly ghosted again, my boy. This lovely old town of mine is, shall we say, crawling with Beijing operatives. Close all of your bank accounts, dispense with your civilian friends, put things to bed with Ms. Harden. And I'm afraid that lovely GTO must be garaged. Endure something horrible, for now, like a Prius. I realize that it's not easy, nowadays, what with Facebook, Instagram, Twitter, and so forth." He pronounced it Twitt-ahh. "You must indulge such practices, of course, otherwise you shan't appear real, but only in a very sophomoric manner. And your keeper must do the same. We must build you both anew."

Steele was stunned by McHugh's use of the personal plural pronoun. He was still in the game. He was somehow still with the Program, but at a level above the clouds. And he also realized that the man hadn't yet spoken his name out loud, or Goodhill's. McHugh released his arm and began heading for the Metro station stairwell. Then he turned and came back.

"Ah, one more thing," he said with a smile. "You're too, shall we say . . . pretty. Grow an unruly beard, get yourself a pair of brown contact lenses, and a scar."

"A scar?" Steele said.

"Why, yes. Use a carpet knife. They're only five bucks at Home Depot."

And then he was gone.

CHAPTER 13

ROSSLYN, VIRGINIA

It was raining like a biblical warning to Noah when Steele drove out to the firing range.

He'd texted Goodhill with an all clear, told him he'd be taking the day for "assigned tasks," and checked out of the Holiday Inn, where he'd barely slept, despite knocking off three mini-bottles of Jack from the fridge. Outside on the street, the sky was bruised purple and spitting torrents onto parked cars, mailboxes, and the wind-warped umbrellas and soaked galoshes of the fortunately still employed. It matched his mood, and he recalled the infantry complaint of his brothers from the 10th Mountain Division: "If it ain't rainin', we ain't trainin'."

Fair enough. Let's get some . . .

He walked two blocks and extracted the GTO from a nearby long-term garage, but seeing the sleek emerald-green machine made his chest ache. In the evening he was going to drive it up north to his house on Neville Island outside Pittsburgh, lock it up tight under a cotton cocoon in his garage, and forget about it—if he could.

The idea of driving some hybrid turd like a Prius made him cringe, yet he'd taken Thorn McHugh's suggestion as an order. He decided he'd lease one, rather than buy it, but he'd still feel like a traitor. Pennsylvania was fossil fuel country, and he was a hard-core Pittsburgh homeboy.

The GTO had an after-market CD player installed. He cranked up Guster's "Come Downstairs and Say Hello," and wound for an hour through the green Virginia hills, sipping a large Starbucks Americano as the wipers punished the windshield. There were shooters who eschewed caffeine because it could make you trembly, but Steele never did. An operator might be sharing an espresso with an informant in Algiers one minute, and the next minute wind up in a gun battle.

Train the way you fight. . . .

At the back half of the Program's operator training course, Alphas honed their firearms and hand-to-hand skills in business suits, ski suits, track suits, boots sunk in mud, waist deep in rushing rivers, handcuffed, blindfolded, and even buck naked. If you were ready for anything, nothing would be a surprise.

Speaking of which, sin of mortal sins, he was way too short on range time. Once, back in Afghanistan, when he was a master sergeant in Special Forces and considering a tryout for Delta, he'd sat on a shell-pocked hill in Jalalabad with a B-Squadron operator known only as Hulk, who'd imparted some wisdom about success in the Unit. "If you're not spending four hours a day on the range, somebody's gonna ask you why, and you better have a damn good answer."

So, he was going out to the thousand-acre patch of remote training area that had been gifted to the Program, on the QT, by none other than Thorn McHugh. He told himself again that he needed the tune-up. Then he admitted to himself that was a lie. Meg had reluctantly agreed to see him at her place in Falls Church. He was just stalling.

Whatever, dude.

He turned in off the main road between a pair of old oaks and drove up a long muddy lane for a mile. The Program had spent a cool 200K on a full-perimeter sensor system that locked onto any trespasser's cell, or a vehicle's license plate, much like E-ZPass monitors. It was probably deactivated, and Ralphy hadn't yet cranked it up again, but if somebody knew he was there, who cared?

He parked, donned a black slicker and a Steelers ball cap, pulled his father's 1911 from the box, tucked it into his jeans, took a canvas Whole Foods shopping bag from the trunk, and locked up. The rain was pinging off the car and the rocks scattered around the shooting bench area. He walked right past the three layers of steel target setups and into the woods.

Every such Program outdoor range—there were three, located East Coast, middle America, and West Coast—had a secret cache of weapons and ammunition. You had to memorize exactly where they were, or you'd find yourself stomping around through the brush like a lost Cub Scout. He didn't have a set of Ranger beads, the rosary-like string you used to keep count of your paces, but he figured he could manage. He knew his pace count was 62 for every 100 meters. He took out his cell, tapped the compass icon, stomped 300 meters northwest through the brambles at 342 degrees, shifted to 67 degrees northeast for another 125 meters and stopped. The rain picked up even more.

Go ahead, God, piss on me . . .

Not cool. He'd have to make up for that one Sunday in church. He couldn't remember the last time he'd been in a church. Oh, wait, it was the National Cathedral, when he was praying Ralphy wouldn't blow them both up, along with everyone else on-site.

The cache was buried under a big boulder that could only be moved by muscle. He felt like Sisyphus as he rolled it away, found the handle, and pulled up a rectangular patch of phony moss glued to a steel hatch. Under that was another safe-weight door with a manual digital lock. He punched in his old code and was thankful it still worked.

The cache was deceptively large, about the size of a big man's iron coffin, and set into a concrete cocoon—no one could steal it without a backhoe and a crane. All the long arms and pistols were encased in weatherproof custom ziplock bags and clipped horizontally to the walls. None had trigger locks. The ammunition was ordered in the center well, in standard military green metal boxes, calibers and volumes marked in yellow.

He selected an FN SCAR 16S, a 5.56 mm assault carbine with a 17.44-inch barrel and gas piston system, currently in use by USSOCOM. It had dark flat earth-colored furniture and pop-up adjustable sights. He didn't pull any sort of reflex sight from the box.

Next up was a Remington 870 TAC 14 shotgun in 12 gauge, the Marine Magnum version with nickel plating and a black polymer stock that looked like a club. He didn't like fancier shotguns. You weren't likely to find one of those lying somewhere on the battlefield. Both long arms were already affixed with tactical slings.

He didn't choose any of the pistols. He had his father's Colt.

He pulled a can of 5.56 mm, one of 9 mm, stuffed his slicker pockets with shotgun shells, slung a pair of Peltor ear protectors around his neck, closed up the cache, and hauled it all back to the range.

He killed targets in the rain for an hour, moving smoothly, quickly, faster each time. He didn't have a tactical vest, so the extra mags went into the rear pockets of his jeans, though nothing ever hit the mud but his smoking empty shell casings. He started at the bench with the FN, took down ten steel round targets using double taps on the initial advance, transitioned to the Remington, blew down five more, transitioned to the pistol, and finished off the third wave. The guns banged hard, even in the pouring rain, and the water in the air blended with the nostril-flaring smoke as the explosions concussed his skull and the rounds pinged steel and he moved like a fluid robot and fired without thinking anything at all. It was like meditating in a lightning storm, and he did it again, and again, and again, without stopping for a break or a sip from his now cold-as-snake-piss coffee.

Finally, he was out of ammo.

"Try doing *that*, Keanu, when the rounds are inbound," he said out loud.

Then he felt a little conceited. Truth be told, Keanu Reeves was actually a very fine shot and had taken some prizes in three-gun matches. A shooter from Hollywood was rare. Hats off.

He didn't clean the hot firearms. He'd have to come back for that. There was preening gear in the cache but no overhead shelter, so he just wiped the FN and the shotgun down, locked everything up, and rolled the boulder back. After that he went back and picked up every single gleaming shell from the mud, stuffed them into the Whole Foods bag, looked around once more, as if inspecting a crime scene, turned to walk to his car, and froze.

Dalton Goodhill was blocking his way. He was standing between Steele and the GTO at about ten paces. The raindrops were pinging off his bald head, which looked like a dinged-up beige bowling ball, but like most infantry-trained veterans he no longer had any rain flinch. A pair of Snoopy goggles were around his thick neck, his black leather jacket was open over a white T-shirt, and he was wearing leather chaps and square-toed boots. Steele saw the gleam of his cut-down shotgun under the jacket.

"Ralphy's got the sensors up," Goodhill said.

Steele nodded. That's how Goodhill knew he was there. He peered over his shoulder past the GTO.

"Where's the bike?"

Goodhill rotated a thumb toward the access road.

"Back there."

Steele realized he still had the Peltors on. That's why he hadn't heard the bike. He took them off.

"You rode your motorcycle in the rain?" he said. "You may be crazy."

Goodhill ignored the Billy Joel reference and said, "Well, I am my brother's keeper."

Steele's shoulders relaxed. Goodhill had come because he was concerned, though he'd never say that.

"Thanks for sending McHugh," Steele said.

"Better than some slimeball ambulance chaser."

"I assume you know his status with the Program."

"I do."

Steele wondered if he'd ever really know who was who in this Alice in Wonderland game.

"You still pissed?" he asked his keeper.

"Oh, yes. Never been in a fight myself, never trashed a bar, never been brought up on charges. Motherfuckingteresa, ya know." Goodhill grinned.

Steele did too.

"Guess I don't have to ask who won," Goodhill said, meaning Steele's street fight from the night before.

"The Marine Corps."

"Semper Fi." Goodhill looked Steele over. "You all right, kid?"

"Yes."

"And all tuned up, trigger-wise?"

"On target."

"Good. What's next on today's agenda?"

"Meg."

"Okay, see ya later for adult beverages. You'll need some inebriation."

Goodhill turned and walked back through the puddles to his bike. Steele got into the GTO, cranked up Guster again, and left.

An hour later he was sitting in the car in the underground parking garage beneath Meg Harden's apartment building in Falls Church. He was staring at his cell, just about to text her and say he was there, when all at once every app on his phone disappeared. He still had his government-issued iPhone clone and had forgotten it wasn't under his control. Ralphy was relinking the TOC comms. The screen went black, red letters appeared that said SAWTOOTH COMM CHECK, then those disappeared and everything else came back.

Pretty soon now, Flash messages would be coming his way. Game on.

He sat back and exhaled a sigh. Meg Harden. The only woman

with whom he'd ever considered making a lifelong run. He saw her as he had the very first time, with her raven-black hair, crystal-blue eyes, a set of small dimples that gave her a cheerleader visage but belied her petite muscled form and martial arts skills. He heard her again, whispering things in his ear that daughters of generals weren't supposed to say, even in the throes of passion. He saw her naked, flushed, breathless and sated, sitting on his lap on the couch in her apartment. He saw her happy, furious, courageous, and scared. He saw her on her knees in the underground chapel at the National Cathedral, her eyes streaming as he pointed a pistol at her face.

It was never going to work. They both knew it, though they'd certainly tried like hell. This wasn't a game in which lovers thrived. But still, this was going to be hard.

Just do it . . .

He locked the 1911 in the box, got out of the car, went into the lobby, and stabbed the ringer for her apartment. She didn't ask who was there. She just buzzed him in and he took the stairs, as always. When he got to the top he was breathing hard, but not from the climb. He walked down the pristine carpeted hallway where her doorway loomed at the end.

He was reaching for the bell button when the door opened. He looked at her beautiful face, and then glanced down where her small hand was resting on her belly.

She was seven months pregnant.

N O   A C K N O W L E D G E D   L O C A T I O N

EYES ONLY

SAP (Alphas/Support/Off Stations - FLASH)

From: SAWTOOTH MAIN

To: All CONUS PAX

Subj: Duty Recall

Source: Staff Ops/Duty Officer

Confidence: N/A

IMMEDIATE, all CONUS PAX, inc ALPHAS,
KEEPERS, SUPPORT, TECH, SEC PERS,
ARMORERS, A&S INSTRUCTORS: Report

SAWTOOTH 0730 hrs EST for Retrofit, all transport modes cleared. Emphasis, No Exceptions.

STATUS: DEFCON Yellow.

Operational window: Immediate Execute

CHAPTER 15

MAPUTO, MOZAMBIQUE

When the deep dark blues of the Indian Ocean sweep toward the southeastern coast of Africa, they turn into the warm, glistening, emerald waves of Delagoa Bay.

Cargo ships, great and small, tossed by the storms of a merciless sea, lean toward Maputo with their crews smiling at the rails, anxious to explore, drink, and dance in a city that on casual inspection resembles Miami. Host to a million souls, Maputo is Portuguese in its colonial splendor, yet wholly native in its scents and hues.

It has five-star hotels and poverty-line slums, magnificent churches and legalized brothels, upscale rock-and-roll bars and seedy dives where tourists can be stripped of their wallets and still fall into bed, drunk and happy. The teeming markets are piled with fresh fruit and fish. The girls in Maputo are mahogany skinned and beautiful. The men are the same, and often muscular from hauling crates at the seaside docks.

You can have the time of your life in Maputo, but it's suggested that you take note of Mozambique's national flag. It is green, black, and yellow, with a red triangle in the hoist, inside which you'll find an AK-47 with a bayonet, crossed over a farmer's hoe, both laid upon an open book, and all superimposed over a Marxist star. It is the flag of FRELIMO, the Mozambique Liberation Front.

These people are not to be toyed with.

It was only seven in the morning when Maputo's pilot station at Buoy 6 first noted the ship bearing down on the main cargo terminals. The station, a small floating barge with a black hull, a white-and-green superstructure, and an "aquarium" on top, was in the command of a former deep-sea fisherman, Abdul Magide, who dispensed pilots from the buoy to incoming ships to guide them through the Xefina channel, which had a comfortable draft of 13.7 meters.

Peering through his binoculars as he sipped black coffee and chewed a French roll, Magide was troubled, because the captain of the ship that was rapidly filling his lenses hadn't replied to his radio calls. He'd tried in Portuguese, then a Bantu dialect, Emakhuwa, and finally in English. Nothing.

This ship was not some lightweight fishing scow that perhaps had a rum-soaked crew who might be stirred by an air horn. It was a four-hundred-foot container vessel with a gleaming forest-green hull, a three-story white superstructure and bridge at the stern, and double rows of Maersk and Zim containers neatly ordered on the sunken deck all the way to the bow. Block print white lettering on the ship's port flank said OCEAN AFRICA, a reputable shipping firm. It should have been slowing to three nautical knots in preparation for one of Magide's forty-ton bollard pull tugs to come alongside. It was not. It was churning up white foam behind its propellers and steaming as if it was a competitive yacht.

The ship was nearly due east of Buoy 6 at a hundred meters when Magide reached up and yanked three sharp blasts on his horn. Then it careened right by him, without a single visible crewman on deck. It was flying a Liberian flag. The name on its stern was *Windhoek*.

Magide punched his emergency siren as two of his pilots rushed up the ladders into his aquarium and peered out the slanted windows, cursing in Portuguese. Then he called the boys at Buoy 11 and told them to get the hell out of the way. Then he called the harbormaster and breathlessly told him to warn everyone at the cargo terminals just past the Xefina channel.

It was way too late.

The ship kept coming. It was not slowing down.

There are no wooden wharves at the Maputo cargo terminals. Ships cut power and are gently nudged alongside a series of off-load landside gunwales protected by giant rubber tires, where hundreds of dockworkers man container cranes and refueling hoses. It's backbreaking, sweat-dripping labor under the African sun and is as risky as deck crew work on an aircraft carrier. When the harbormaster's sirens went off, they raised their heads from their slithering chains and steel cables, saw the *Windhoek* bearing down, and scattered like insects from an anthill fire.

Screeching like a banshee cutting steel with a chain saw, the *Windhoek*'s bow sliced into the terminals at twenty degrees, sending tires spinning up into the air, flipping two dockside trucks onto their sides, and taking out six blue plastic latrines. Four of its forward containers broke from their stanchions, one bucked off the port side and crashed into the water, and as the bow splintered the quay, it burst through a gas-powered generator and started a fire. Then, with the lancing prow jammed in the freshly cleaved scar, the engines slammed the fuselage broadside into the docks, where it shuddered and bucked and moaned, with the props still turning, until they encountered an upright steel submerged stanchion, and shattered halfway down to the nubs.

The *hee-haw* sound of fire engines loomed. . . .

Rod Kruvalt took the call at Maputo's central police station, headquarters of the PRM, the Police of the Republic of Mozambique. Captain of the municipal SWAT team, Kruvalt was well respected and a semicelebrity. The son of a Rhodesian mercenary and black African mother, he had wiry blond curls, yet a distinctly African face and hazel eyes. He also had a wry sense of humor, but no one around him dared reference his racial mix, because they were never quite sure how he'd take it.

After a long stint in the Rhodesian army, Kruvalt had hunted poachers all over Africa, with the occasional ISIL fighter dropped by accident. He was under six feet, with soccer legs, rugby biceps, and brilliant white teeth chipped in the front by a pair of brass knuckles, though the man who'd used them on him was dead.

Kruvalt listened to the gasping harbormaster, who was babbling in Portuguese, hung up, and stomped down the stairwell into the SWAT team's break room. Six of his men were in there, dressed in their field gray tactical uniforms and enjoying a breakfast of scrambled eggs. They were looking forward to a day of rappelling training at an abandoned building down by the Mercado Janete market, and their guns and ropes and gear were piled on the floor at their feet. Kruvalt barked at them in his South African English accent.

"Drop your cocks and grab your socks, mates. We're off."

They arrived at the dockside twenty minutes later aboard a green Patriot3 Elevated Tactics armored SWAT truck with POLICIA stamped on the side and a heavy assault ladder mounted on the roof. The truck bounced over coiled cables and stopped twenty meters back from the ship, which was shuddering and banging against the quay's remaining tire array like an epileptic whale. Kruvalt got out and stared up at the monster while his men tumbled out and pulled on American "Fritz" helmets, donned Israeli load-bearing vests, and checked over their worn AK-47s. Kruvalt had a shorter Krinkov, but it was also in 7.62 mm because he preferred that everyone used the same ammunition. He also had a Sig Sauer P226 in a thigh holster—a personal choice.

He turned and saw a line of crookedly parked regular Maputo police cars and their shouting cops, keeping curious onlookers back from the scene. Then a small sweating man in a Nehru suit and glasses rushed up to him—the harbormaster, Ingo Ferreti.

"Captain," he gasped to Kruvalt in English. "We do not know what this is!"

"Well, it's a bloody ship, Ingo."

"I know, I know, but she would not stop."

"That's sort of clear, don't you think?"

"Yes, yes, but we don't know why. Perhaps she was taken by pirates, Captain. Perhaps she has hostages aboard!"

"We're about to find out." Kruvalt pressed a SWAT-gloved hand into Ferreti's chest and cocked his chin back over his shoulder. "Now go tell those PRM uniforms to get everyone the fuck out of here. This thing might blow up."

Ferreti needed no further encouraging. He took off at a stumbling run, waving his arms and yelling.

Kruvalt turned to his men, who had formed a semicircle and were squinting at their captain through steamed-up SWAT goggles.

"All right, mates. Let's do this line astern, pick your shots, and watch for anyone popping from hatches." He pointed at the largest man in the team. "Charlie, if I go down, stomp right bloody over me and kill them all. Got it?"

"Right, sir."

Kruvalt climbed up the truck's side ladder, with his men in short order behind him. Atop the Bearcat, he punched a pneumatic actuator, and the wide black assault ramp whined and rose and extended over the end of the dock, vibrating in the air above the undulating deck of the ship. He poised out there at the lip of the ramp, looked behind him at his men, nodded, and one after the other, they jumped.

Twenty minutes later, the ship's engines coughed and murmured and fell eerily silent. Then Kruvalt and his men appeared at the gunwales, helped one another climb back up onto the Bearcat's ramp, and reversed down its fuselage ladder to the ground, where they tore off their helmets and slurped great draughts from their water bladders.

Kruvalt found Ingo Ferreti crouching behind a fire truck, where the firemen were still hosing down the remains of the smoking generator. Ferreti stood up. His hands were trembling and he was lighting one cigarette with the butt of another. Kruvalt snatched both from his surprised mouth and crushed them out under his SWAT boot. There was too much fuel around.

"Well, Captain?" Ferreti whined. "Well?"

"There wasn't a fucking soul aboard, Ingo," Kruvalt said. "It's a ghost ship."

CHAPTER 16

Rod Kruvalt headed west from Maputo to Siteki, late in the afternoon.

He'd left his team at dockside to supervise the PRM cops and cordon off the *Windhoek,* where the dead ship was now gently bumping the ravaged pier in the swells of a rising tide. Ferreti had given him a lift back to the station at Avenue Kim Il Sung, chattering his frets all the way, whereupon Kruvalt had squeezed Ingo's bony shoulder and promised he'd solve the mystery. He knew that soon he'd have to have a conversation with the chief of SERNIC, the National Criminal Investigation Service, but for the moment there was only one man he wanted to see.

He changed from his SWAT gear into khaki bush shorts and a safari shirt, stuck his Sig in a waistband holster, got into his truck, and drove.

Kruvalt cherished his old 1993 Land Rover Defender 110 Spectre. He kept its spearmint-green skin in perfect condition. It had a 5.7L rebuilt Chevrolet engine, thirty-seven-inch Maxxis

Trepador tires, a puma hood, fire and ice steps, and a powerful winch. It was a four-door beast and long for a bush car, but he could stuff a couple of handcuffed perps in the back, or if need be, a corpse.

The way to Siteki was fifty kilometers, but Kruvalt didn't mind the drive. Once he crossed the Matola River and wound through the sprawling huts of Boane, the EN2 byway emptied out, and he spooled up "Mama Cass," as he'd named the truck—he was a diehard The Mamas and the Papas fan—and cruised through the rolling green hills, past steaming palms and the perfectly thatched huts of villages where the women sauntered with impossible loads on their kerchiefed heads. As his CD player pumped out "California Dreamin'" he turned left through Siteki, downshifted, and climbed south into the Lebombo mountains toward Mabuda Farms, whose name meant "Place of Dreams."

The farms were a magnificent tourist enclave, with quaint pastel-colored guesthouses, bird sanctuaries, hiking trails, a swimming pool, and wonderful native food. George Wheelwright worked there occasionally as a horseback riding guide, which Kruvalt thought strange for an older man who'd clearly once been a soldier or mercenary of some sort, but Rod asked few questions. He knew many men like George, who spoke very little, knew so much, and kept their pasts to themselves.

At Mabuda, the stable manager told him that George had gone home for the day, so Kruvalt turned the Land Rover due east again, onto a narrow dirt road, and climbed higher, much higher, up to one of the highest green peaks of the Lebombo in Mozambique.

Twenty minutes later, he honked the Land Rover's horn as he pulled up and stopped outside Wheelwright's teakwood cottage.

It was in fine condition, especially considering the assaults of hard sun and pelting rains on the peak, but Wheelwright had built it himself, and he was an orderly man with talented hands. The screen door creaked open and Wheelwright stepped out onto his front porch.

He was tall, yet still muscular, with thick bristling gray hair, a sharp nose and square jaw, like that legendary old American actor Lee Marvin. He wore a white African collarless dashiki, old blue jeans, and leather sandals, and he was smoking a pipe.

Kruvalt got out of the Land Rover and offered a casual salute. Wheelwright smiled with closed lips.

"You should have called first, Rod," he said in a voice that sounded like sandpaper on rusty iron. "I would've cooked you a rhino fillet."

"I tried to, mate, but the line was busy."

They both grinned widely. Wheelwright didn't own a phone.

Wheelwright turned and went back into the house. Kruvalt followed. They'd dropped the niceties long ago. They'd first met six years before, when Kruvalt had arrested George after a bar fight in Maputo. Three young stevedores had thought they could roll the old American for his cash, and Wheelwright had knocked them out cold. Kruvalt had torn up the charge sheet and let him go, and they'd been fast friends ever since.

"Clara or Preta?" Wheelwright asked. They were the pale and dark versions of Laurentina beer.

"Preta, mate."

Kruvalt sat down in a rattan chair in Wheelwright's salon, on one side of a glass-topped coffee table made of candlenut wood. He looked at the whitewashed walls, which had no photographs of any kind, only a few framed watercolors painted for George by the kids at Mabuda Farms. Wheelwright came back from his small seaside kitchen with the iced bottles and sat down across from him in another rattan chair. They clinked the bottles and swigged. George set his pipe in an ashtray made of polished morganite, and the smoke curled toward the thick-beamed ceiling.

"So, what's the skinny, copper?" Wheelwright said. "It's a long way up here for a beer."

Kruvalt leaned forward and told George the story of the *Windhoek,* from the first alarm at HQ, to the moment he'd driven out of town. By the time he was done, Wheelwright was squinting over Kruvalt's head, streaming pipe smoke from his weather-scarred lips, and he'd put down his beer.

"A ghost ship, you say," he said. "Nobody aboard. Like something out of the Bermuda Triangle."

"That's correct."

"And you didn't find anything on it that might be a clue?"

"Just this," Kruvalt said. He reached into his bush shirt pocket, and placed a gleaming brass empty shell casing on the glass.

Wheelwright picked it up, turned it over, and looked at the base where the primer was gone.

"You expect me to know what this is?" he said.

"If anyone does, you do, mate."

"Not sure the compliment's warranted."

"Take a guess."

"It's Chinese."

Kruvalt cocked an eyebrow. "State your case."

"Seven six two by thirty-nine. Head stamp, eighty-one over seventy-one." Wheelwright shrugged, as if such knowledge were common. "That's a Norinco lot, PLA issue, probably at least twenty years old. Did you see any bullet strikes anywhere on board?"

"Nothing at first glance, but we were only aboard for twenty minutes," Kruvalt said. "We're going back. I'd like you to go with us, George."

Wheelwright dropped the shell on the table, as if it were infected with something contagious, and sat back in his chair.

"Why me, Rod?"

"I think it's obvious, mate. You've already made this little trip worthwhile. My guess is you'll save me straining my brain."

"Well, we wouldn't want that." Wheelwright smiled. "It's already weak."

Kruvalt ignored the quip. "Consider it?"

"Consider. Not promise."

"Bloody fair enough."

Kruvalt downed the rest of his Preta, rose from his chair as Wheelwright did the same, and they shook hands.

"I'll fetch you tomorrow at ten," he said.

"I might be busy with the horses."

"Eleven, then." He wasn't going to be dissuaded.

"Might be available. Might not."

"We'll see," Kruvalt said, and he walked out to his Land Rover and drove away.

Wheelwright didn't follow him to wave goodbye. Instead, he pursed his lips, sighed, and walked out of the salon, through his small kitchen, and out onto his seaside veranda. He'd made it out of bamboo, and at night when the wind blew hard, it whistled and moaned. He stood with his hands in his jeans pockets, with his straight-stemmed pipe clutched in his teeth, squinting into the distance and far away at the glittering buildings of Maputo and the sea.

In a heavy mortar ammunition crate beneath the floorboards of his house, he had some items of equipment that he only used when he was certain he was alone. One of them was a Celestron Ultima 100 spotting scope. It was a very substantial instrument with 66x magnification power and a field of view of fifty-two feet at a thousand meters. He thought about fetching it from the crate, mounting it on its tripod, and taking a look at the pier where the *Windhoek* lay in its berth, but he changed his mind. He wasn't going to see much from here.

He'd have to go down there with Rod in the morning. He owed him and he couldn't say no.

He turned to walk back into the house, then looked at the dusty old mirror he'd hung on the wall of the veranda. It was there because he liked shaving outside with a ceramic bowl and a straight razor, an old habit from days in the field gone by.

He took a long hard look at the man in the glass. But he didn't see George Wheelwright.

The man he saw was Hank Steele.

ACT II

CHAPTER 17

MANCHURIA, CHINA

The fortress of the Swords of Qing was in the northwest wilds of Manchuria, and so far from the lives and loves of Shenyang that only the wheeling hawks knew it was there.

Shenyang was the provincial capital of Liaoning, a sprawling metropolis of twenty-three million souls, which still held the ancient Qing dynasty's great Mukden Palace, now merely a disgraceful museum. But if you traveled far west of the city, across many kilometers of winding roads where the suburbs disappeared and the bamboo villages sprouted near Chifeng, and if you dared ride northwest into the much higher mountains from whose peaks you could see Dariganga deep inside Mongolia, that's where the last of the Qings had chosen to make his stand.

Zaifeng, the forty-year-old commander of the Swords of Qing, had built the fortress in the lee of twin forested summits, between which a rushing ten-foot-wide waterfall tumbled through a paddlewheel electric generator. His headquarters building was

an exact replica of the Dazheng Hall of Mukden Palace, a magnificent octagon of bloodred walls, matching exterior columns,
a double capped sloping roof of terra-cotta tiles and green jade,
and golden dragons perched and slithering everywhere. From the
wings of this *zŏng bù,* his men had constructed a ten-foot-high
perimeter wall of granite stone that circled a pitch the size of a
football field.

In the middle of this courtyard sat three Harbin Z-20 assault
helicopters, covered by artillery camouflage netting and so many
additional woven leaves that not even a Keyhole satellite could
have picked them out. The helos were the same ones that Zaifeng's men, following his orders to the letter, had used to slaughter every living soul at the Level V laboratory called Toqui 13.

But Zaifeng did not think he was a killer.

He thought he was an emperor.

Born in the squalid sewers of Shanghai, his mother, Wang Li,
was an affable whore who worked the two-star hotels along Nanjing Road, riding male tourists on their lice-infested beds and
leaving them breathless and stripped of their yen. Wang Li had,
in turn, learned her trade at the feet of her own mother, Wang
Jing, an imperial Chinese consort who'd screwed half of the Japanese high command while they occupied Manchuria during
World War II.

They were beautiful, brazen, clever women, and Zaifeng was
the product of their quiet power.

Zaifeng was the epitomical latchkey child, often left to his
own devices while his mother bedded foreigners for clothing and
food. He was small-statured but quick, often bullied, but resil-
ient. He was brilliant, yet eschewed school for Shaolin kung fu,
and whenever truant, which was often, ran betting chits for older

gang boys and broke fingers for grateful pimps when their johns refused to pay for desultory fellatios. He had thick unruly black hair like a Manga character, penetrating eyes, a small scarred nose, and a smile that could mean either mirth or murder. If Zaifeng had been wronged and stepped into the street carrying his Wushu *bo,* the long wooden staff of the Shaolin warrior, the whole street cleared.

Zaifeng's grandmother, Wang Jing, died when the boy was sixteen. It was then that he finally asked his mother, Wang Li, about the origin of their names. After all, Wang Li meant "beautiful monarch" and Wang Jing meant "quiet monarch." It seemed a bit haughty for whores.

"Your grandmother," Wang Li said as Zaifeng carried the old woman's still warm ashes in an earthenware urn, "was the consort of Aisin Gioro Puyi, the last emperor of the Qing dynasty of our beloved China. I am his bastard child, and you are his bastard grandson. You were named after Emperor Puyi's father, Zaifeng."

Zaifeng didn't believe his mother, not for a very long time. But while completing three dreary years in the People's Liberation Army as a special forces close-combat instructor, he found himself studying the history of his supposed ancestry, even though he thought the tale of lineage was a fantasy. His alleged grandfather, Emperor Puyi, had been a virtual prisoner of the Japanese in "Manchu" until 1945. Then, after the war when the Chinese Communists had taken over, both Puyi and his brother, Pujie, had spent a horrific decade in a reeducation prison, the Fushun War Criminals Management Centre.

Puyi had died a stateless pauper. The Chinese Communist Party had decimated Imperial China's last great dynasty, and the family's fortune and honor.

There was no concrete evidence of this ancestral connection, except for one thing. Zaifeng's mother kept a bequeathed keepsake from his grandmother, a thick lock of hair in a small glass box, allegedly cut from the end of Emperor Puyi's queue, the traditional braided Qing ponytail. Zaifeng took the hair, and along with his own blood, had them tested by a DNA laboratory.

The results shocked him and rocked his world. Now he had that string of laboratory test result numbers, which no one but he understood, tattooed on the inside of one muscled forearm.

Puyi was *not* the last emperor of China.

He was.

Inside his headquarters, the *zŏng bù*, he sat at a massive fifteenth-century desk stolen from the Forbidden City in Beijing, which he regarded as his birthright rather than theft. Much of the surrounding decor in the large conical interior space was antique Chinese furniture, some purloined and some purchased, while heat was provided by a huge iron woodstove that flickered and spit from the center of the polished teak floor. But Zaifeng himself was not a traditionalist in terms of fashion. He wore an up-collared black leather motocross jacket, black tactical trousers and boots, and the only nod to his regal heritage was a crimson turtleneck underneath the jacket, with small crossed swords and a golden dragon embroidered below his throat.

Zaifeng was writing in a leather notebook of parchment pages with a pheasant quill pen and inkwell. He never used computers, ever. Without looking up, he queried a young man standing before his desk at parade rest.

"Do you have a body count, Po?"

"We estimate eighty-two, *Xian Sheng*," Po said, using the formality of "sir." He had the form of an Olympic gymnast and was dressed in similar fashion to Zaifeng, but there was also a snow-dusted villager's burlap wrap thrown about his shoulders. Whenever outside in the fortress courtyard, all the men camouflaged themselves against prying eyes in the sky.

"You estimate?" Zaifeng stopped writing and looked up at Po, who held the rank of first lieutenant with the Swords of Qing. That was the highest rank Zaifeng allowed his officers. Loftier promotions fomented dangerous ambitions.

"The action took place very quickly, *Xian Sheng*. Miko did his best to count."

"But no one escaped?"

"No one."

"You are sure?"

"No one, *Xian Sheng*. They were shark-infested waters."

"*Tai hao le.*" Excellent.

Outside the headquarters' thick double doors the baritone sound of a brass gong thrummed the wood. Zaifeng nodded at Po, who turned and snapped, "Come." The doors swung open and one of Po's long-range scouts entered and bowed. He wore a thick brown quilted jacket over a traditional *yi* tunic and hemp *shang* skirt, above high leather boots encrusted in snow. He removed a fur hat coated in ice and advanced, though not too far.

"Make your report, Feng," Po said.

"*Xian Sheng*," the scout said to Zaifeng. "The woman is alive."

Zaifeng's mouth turned down. "You are certain? The one who escaped from the laboratory."

"I am certain, sir."

"Where is she?"

"She is being cared for by a Mongol smuggler, in a village southwest of Ulaanbadrakh."

"What is your proof, Feng?" Po challenged his scout.

"Sir, I witnessed the woman outside of a *ger*. She fit the description provided by Bao, who pursued her into the laboratory sub levels."

"And that is all?" Zaifeng asked.

"No, *Xian Sheng*." Feng reached into his tunic and showed his commanders a pair of long-range Zeiss binoculars, camouflaged white. "Her PLA uniform was also drying on a line."

Zaifeng nodded with a tight smile. "I am impressed, Feng. How did you infil and exfil?"

Feng returned his commander's smile. "Leather personnel carriers, *Xian Sheng*."

Now all three men smiled. The slang expression meant "boots."

"Excellent soldiering," Zaifeng said. "Go warm yourself, feed yourself, and offer blessings to Buddha."

Feng bowed again and withdrew. When he was gone and the doors closed, Zaifeng tapped his quill on his ledger.

"Assemble C-Squadron," he said to Po. "It is far, so prepare the horses."

"Yes, *Xian Sheng*," Po said. "What are your orders?"

"My orders are to kill her. And everyone in that village."

With his headquarters empty again, Zaifeng rose from his desk, removed a large iron key from a drawer, walked through a small maze of walnut wood Qing dynasty Fushouyi armchairs and a Hongmu recliner, and opened a lock in the floor. He pulled on a large square hatch and descended a narrow, curving stone stairway, illuminated by small electric bulbs. He was thoughtful as he carefully picked his way down, as the stairs were slick with moisture.

His ledger had revealed some concerns regarding Swords of Qing income and expenses. For the moment they were fine in terms of arms, ammunition, and nourishment, but helicopter fuel was expensive, and one could never neglect soldiers' salaries, no matter how loyal they were. His acquisitions team would have to move on Shanghai once again, perhaps liberate funds from a bank, or barter with the warlords on Nanjing Road for payment in exchange for muscling extortions. But that would be no problem. The warlords were all his childhood friends.

Yet aside from all that, so far his plan was proceeding. Gantu-62 was highly effective. The Americans were already repositioning some naval assets near the South China Sea. If he could effect a clash of titans between the Chinese Communist Party and the United States, the entire world would be grateful when the CCP was no more, and the Qings ruled again.

He reached the bottom of the stairwell and entered a large, freezing stone cavern. The stone walls dripped with icy rivulets, which an electric heater off in one corner hardly seemed to be curing at all. But this wasn't a place of creature comforts.

Chained to the far wall by his wrists was a slumping figure. The slight bony man was heavily clothed in a quilted tunic, pantaloons, and fur boots, yet still he shivered in waves, and when he raised his pale face to look at Zaifeng, his black-rimmed glasses were fogged by the ragged breaths curling up from his wide nostrils. Zaifeng walked to a rickety wooden table in the center of the cavern, turned the switch on an electric teapot, and smiled at the poor fellow.

"You won't be here for very much longer, Mr. Casino," he said. "But I need you to make one more telephone call."

CHAPTER 18

Miles Turner was not actually a sadist, but he could have played one on TV.

He was a very large man with legs like a leopard that had mated with a giraffe, so his strides were incredibly powerful and long, and the three men and one woman who were trying to keep up as he tramped through the woods, vaulted over old stone walls, hurdled fallen tree trunks, and barreled through thickets of thorn were at this point praying he'd have a massive coronary and die.

Their eyes stung with sweat that poured from under their boonie hats. Their shoulders were bleeding where the straps of their fifty-pound rucks had rubbed them raw. Their lungs were burning as they panted steam into the frigid night air, and all of the blisters inside their old-style cordovan jump boots had burst, soaking their matted socks in plasma.

He'd issued them leather boots because they hurt more. The man was the progeny of the Marquis de Sade. They didn't know his name, if he had one. He only referred to himself by the initials M.T. One of them had breathlessly grunted behind his back that "empty" was an apt description of his soul. Unfortunately, he didn't look like he was going to expire anytime soon.

In the past, the Program's assessment and selection phase had begun at a remote patch of Fort Bragg called the Salt Pit, where prospective candidates were pitted against USASOC special operators to test their mettle in land navigation, weaponry, physical endurance, and hand-to-hand combat. The environment was secure, and the army types had no idea who these "OGA" (Other Governmental Agency) civilians actually were, but Ted Lansky had since decided that even Bragg wasn't airtight enough. The entire A&S would now be conducted at Thorn McHugh's donated patch of a thousand acres, where the only prying eyes belonged to raccoons and deer.

Miles had begun with ten candidates, selected by Lansky and Betsy Roth from classified 201 files, all of them college-educated, multilingual combat veterans with multiple tours who looked ripe for an offer of "something new." They were Army Rangers, Special Forces, and Air Force Special Tactics stars, and all had been vetted many times over so that, at least for the moment, deep background investigations and psychometric exams wouldn't be necessary, until the group was pared down to a select few.

Their first test had occurred at the firing range, where Eric Steele and Dalton Goodhill sat them all down and gave them an over-the-top OPSEC briefing.

"This program does not exist," Steele said. "If you're accepted for the operator training course—'bout as likely at the Cleveland Browns winning the Super Bowl—neither will *you*. It is not an OGA. It is not part of the Beltway's alphabet soup. If by some miracle you do move on to OTC, your current units of record will officially TDY you to someplace OCONUS no one's ever heard of, and from there you'll disappear, never to be heard from again. Are we clear so far?"

The ten candidates nodded, but one of them raised a finger. At that point Goodhill growled.

"No friggin' questions, people. There's not a goddamn thing you need to know. Going forward, you will not speculate, discuss, inquire, or conjecture, not with any of us, *or* each other. Furthermore, you will *not,* under any circumstances, answer any questions posed to you without first asking for 'Condition X.'" (He used air quotes.) "If one of us grants that condition, *then* you can talk. But first, let's see if you can hack it through twenty-one days of hell. Feel me?"

They'd all seen some gnarly cadre, but this bald bulldog called "Blade" was like a colder version of Mr. Freeze. And, of course, they had no idea he was lying. The A&S would only last five sleepless days and nights, though it would feel like a month.

Steele and Goodhill had then put them through their paces with M9 handguns, M4 rifles, M249 SAWs, shotguns, hand grenades, and LAW rockets, nonstop for nine hours. Half deaf, smoke-blinded, and powder burned, Stalker Seven and Blade had promptly failed them all. However, after defaming their performance and feigning disappointment, the Program duo had "reluctantly" allowed them to carry on.

For a "break," Steele had then given them a six-mile land nav exercise, timed, out and back. He issued them one map, gave them five minutes to study it, took it back, and said, "Bring me the red pennant on a pole. And don't forget the log." It was a 150-pound tree trunk.

After that, Ted Lansky had sent in an Israeli contractor named

Yigal Arbiv, one of the IDF's top experts in the Gidon system of Krav Maga (penny-pinching Mrs. Darnstein objected but was overruled). Arbiv was a bullet-headed man built like a beer cask with Popeye arms, and when he was done, one Ranger had a broken elbow, an air force guy had been choked out and quit, four more had failed—for real—and the remaining quartet were those now chasing after Miles Turner, and half wishing Arbiv had knocked them out too.

They'd begun the current phase running a country road at dawn. After seven fast miles of sole-slapping tarmac, Miles had taken them off into the woods. He didn't appear to have any sort of map or GPS device and they had no idea where he was going— maybe he didn't either, but it didn't seem to matter. He'd given them two five-minute breaks, forbade them from sitting because he said they'd never get up, let them wolf a KIND Bar and slurp water, and pressed on. It was freezing. Their bodies steamed like cavalry horses. A cold high moon stabbed through the towering pines, but all they saw was M.T.'s massive back, into which they were tempted to put a bullet from their sweat-slickened M4s.

"Y'all still with me?" Miles called from the point as he crashed through the woods.

"Roger, sir." That was the woman, a twenty-seven-year-old operator from the air force's 820th Base Defense Group at Moody.

"Outstanding. You just hit thirty miles."

"What percentage is that, sir?" one of the surviving Rangers asked.

"None a ya goddamn business, troop," Miles snapped.

Two miles after that, they broke from the woods into a wide clearing of dew-soaked grass. Off in one corner sat a blacked-out Suburban, with the late Collins Austin's former keeper, Shane

Wiley, at the wheel. Penny "S" Amdursky sat in the passenger seat, taking notes on a manifest, with Steele and Goodhill in the back. They were all drinking coffee from a Dunkin' Donuts Box O' Joe.

"Well bust my buttons, he's still got all four," Shane Wiley said as they watched Turner position his sweating candidates at the corners of a large grassy rectangle, and then had them extract tactical lights from their ammo vests and point them up at the sky.

"What if one of them had broken an ankle or something back there?" Penny asked.

"Then the poor bastards'd be carrying that dude or dudette," Goodhill said.

"Oh gosh." Penny was very happy to be an admin type sitting in a cozy car. "What happens next?"

"More torment," Steele said.

The feathery black tips of the surrounding pines began to flutter, the *thwops* of incoming rotor blades loomed, and a black helicopter appeared. It was a contracted UH-1 Huey with no tail numbers, piloted by Allie Whirly. Miles Turner's grateful candidates tore off their boonie hats, stuffed them in pockets, and basked in the rotor wash cooling their brows. Allie set the helo down, Miles hustled his flock into the open cargo bay, jumped in after them, and the helo pulled pitch and roared away.

"Where they going now?" Penny called above the thunder.

"Nowhere." Steele smirked.

Inside the Huey, the enervated prospects had slumped to the floor and were already shedding their rucks and making sure their M4s were on safe, barrel down. Turner sat across from them, back to the cockpit, his expression unreadable as Allie banked the big bird and winged out over the woods. The cargo door was open, the wind was a blessed thing, and wherever they were headed to next, at least they wouldn't be walking.

Shane Wiley rolled down the Suburban's window and lit a cigarette. He was getting on in years, going fully gray, slimmer than ever before, and had almost quit the business after the loss of his beloved Alpha, Collins Austin. Langley had hired him as a training contractor over at Camp Peary, the CIA's basic training facility otherwise known as the Farm, but his heart wasn't in it. Then Lansky had called.

Now, breathing the chilled mountain air and once again in the company of like-minded special operators, he felt happy to be there, like he'd finally come home. Sure, he was tired after nearly four decades of hard-driving missions, but he said to himself, *Just thank the lords of war, old man. You can sleep when you're dead.*

Two minutes later, Allie's lumbering Huey swept back into the clearing and set down. Miles Turner jumped out first, followed by his four candidates as they grunted and stumbled and tried to sling their M4s and get their rucks back on, and chased after him back into the woods.

"What happened?" Penny gasped. "Is something wrong with the bird?"

"Nope," Shane said.

"Just part of the assessment," Steele called from the back. "See how much shit they can take."

"You mean they're not really going anywhere?"

"Sure they are," Shane said. "Another eighteen miles on foot."

"Oh my gosh. You people are *awful.*"

"Life's a bitch." Dalton grunted and grinned.

"And then you get Covid," Shane said. He field-stripped his

cigarette, tossed the shreds in the wet grass, rolled up his window, and drove off into the woods.

Twelve hours later, the four candidates were naked except for their underwear, freezing and shivering in a slimy prison cell on the outskirts of Lynchburg, Virginia, and being water tortured and bitch slapped by men who appeared to be police officers but would definitely not have passed muster with the Patrolmen's Benevolent Association.

After their fifty-mile ruck hump—the last leg of which included pushing a Vietnam-era Willys Jeep laden with four thousand rounds of ammunition up a two-hundred-foot hill, and then fording a neck-deep rushing river—the candidates had arrived at a camouflaged trailer in the woods. They were ordered to dump their gear and weapons, shed their filthy utilities, wash up, dress in civilian clothes off a rack, and hustle back outside. The female prospect from the air force, known as Slick, had stripped naked along with the Ranger and the two SF men, and no one had even glanced at her. They hadn't slept in fifty-two hours. That kind of exhaustion murders libidos.

Outside the trailer, as dusk loomed, they slurped ice-cold coffee and ate putrid Spam from cans as Steele briefed them on their next task, a mission to the city of Lynchburg. At the Grand Hotel on Main Street, a Russian FSB agent named Katrina Rostoff was holed up in a suite, with a four-ounce flask of the deadly nerve agent Novichok in her possession, which she was about to pass to an unknown assassin. They'd have to gain access to the suite, recover the nerve agent from Rostoff, and try not to kill her, or themselves, in the process. Shortly after Steele's briefing, a driver from Turner's security detail drove them to Lynchburg in a blacked-out panel van.

The infiltration phase went pretty well.

Each candidate had a twenty-dollar bill in the pocket of their off-the-rack jeans. Slick had the driver stop at the Lynchburg Community Market, where she bought a chocolate birthday cake in a white cardboard gift box and had "Happy Birthday Kat" scripted on the icing. Inside the hotel's lush lobby, she burst into tears when the receptionist lady—in accordance with hotel policy—wouldn't give her Katrina Rostoff's room number (impressive, since Slick's only dramatic acting prior to that had been in a high school production of *Our Town*). Slick showed the woman the cake and begged to be allowed to surprise her "beloved sister." It worked. She hurried to the elevator bank with the box, her three coconspirators slipped into the lobby from a side door, and they all rode up to the seventh floor.

The exfiltration phase was a disaster.

Slick rang the room bell while her mates stacked up out of sight. When the door cracked open, they hurled themselves at it, broke the security chain, rushed the woman inside, and tried to pin her down to the couch. However, Katrina Rostoff was actually Ted Lansky's adjutant, Betsy Roth, who happened to have a brown belt in Brazilian jujitsu, also enjoyed method acting, and was wearing a red silk Japanese robe with embroidered arachnids. Betsy screamed like a banshee, hurled lamps and ashtrays at her assailants, and cursed them in howling fake Russian. Six policemen were there in a flash, cuffing the four Program candidates while Betsy smirked and sipped wine.

They weren't really policemen, of course, though they looked the part with their Lynchburg PD uniforms, badges, and guns. They were contractors from a private military company called The Cauldron, owned and operated by a former Marine Force Recon captain named Kevin McMahon and his former NCOIC, Liam Flatley. In the final phase of their Marine Corps service, McMahon and Flatley had run the unit's Survival Evasion Resistance and Escape school. They knew how to break hearts and minds.

The "police station" was also a mock-up, a repurposed white brick warehouse on the far side of the railroad tracks between the Public Works Complex and Memorial Avenue. But the candidates never saw the exterior, because they were hooded like falcons and thrown into a phony paddy wagon outside the Lynchburg Grand, then dragged from the wagon at midnight, whereupon the fun began.

McMahon screamed in their faces. The range of his pornographic lexicon was impressive. Flatley preferred to use his hands and SWAT boots. Neither man was large, but they could both summon cold dead eyes and had the kinds of arms that develop from constantly twisting things. The other four "policemen" delivered various implements of discomfort to their team leaders, like servants at a Hellboy cocktail party.

In the basement of the building, which could have doubled for a dissident prison in Tehran or a Mississippi county jail, the four Program hopefuls had their handcuffs and hoods removed and were frisked and stripped to their skivvies. Their wrists were then bound in front with thick hemp, and they were left alone. Soon thereafter, the Ranger decided that this process was going to go on all night, so he might as well sit.

"Who the fuck said you could sit?"

McMahon stormed into the cell. Flatley appeared with a fire hose and blasted all four into the stone dungeon walls until their skins were raw and they were gasping for air. Then the other four "cops" appeared and helped rope the quartet's wrists to meat hooks embedded in the ceiling, so that only the balls of their bare feet touched the floor.

"Who the hell are you people?" McMahon growled as he weaved between the stretched-out glistening bodies, slapping a truncheon against his thigh. "I want names!"

"Dopey," the Ranger said with a sneer.

"Grumpy," said one of the Special Forces NCOs.

"Sleepy," said the other.

"Cinderella," said Slick. "Snow White was a bitch."

Flatley hit them with the fire hose again, which made them spin like weathervanes in a hurricane. Then he dropped the hose, walked into the cell, pulled a stun gun from his duty belt, and said, "We don't fucking tolerate disrespect," and zapped each candidate in the ass, with a good long generous jolt.

No one screamed. No one begged for mercy. However, Miles Turner, who was watching the proceedings on a monitor in a control room upstairs, along with Steele, Goodhill, Shane Wiley, and Penny (who mostly covered her eyes), wasn't overly impressed. After all, these people were airborne and air assault qualified and each had at least one bronze star with a "V" device for valor. Steele, on the other hand, noted the performances of McMahon and Flatley. He thought they might make good Program candidates themselves.

McMahon summoned his four cop subordinates. They appeared in the dungeon cell carrying beer tubs full of ice water. Flatley bound the prisoners' ankles and submerged their dangling feet in the tubs. McMahon would have preferred to just water-board them, but that was now an indictable offense. Both men, when not working contracts for the U.S. government in an effort to develop the finest special warriors, were actually doting fathers and loving husbands. Here, they were demons.

"I'm gonna ask you again," McMahon screamed. "Who the fuck are you people?"

The Ranger began singing Creedence Clearwater Revival's "Fortunate Son." The other three joined in. McMahon and Flatley exchanged nods, both inserted earplugs in their ears, then Flatley tapped an app on his cell phone and the dungeon exploded with the most horrific music blasting from giant recessed speakers— the entire Barbra Streisand album *Walls*.

Variations on this theme carried on for another five hours. None of the candidates broke or offered more than phony cartoon character names, though they were clearly spent. As dawn was breaking, Steele told McMahon and Flatley to cut them down, toss in some dry towels, and deliver the first one to him in the interrogation room. It was a battleship-gray space, with a metal table in the center below one bare lightbulb, a single chair, a sur-veillance camera high in one corner, and nothing else.

Steele waited there until Flatley delivered Slick. She had a big towel around her shoulders, her wrists were bloody raw, she was trembling from the cold, lack of nourishment, and the pain rack-ing her body, yet her posture was defiant. He noted her thick, short blond hair, stubborn nose, and hard green eyes. An experienced keeper could turn this girl into an Alpha, he thought. Dress her up right, and no one would have any idea.

"Sit," he said.

She did, in the chair facing the table, but she didn't lean on the table or slump. She just looked up at him.

"You did well, Slick. But I'm afraid you didn't pass."

She didn't react. Not a flinch.

"It was the hotel phase, where you failed to recover the Novichok." Steele leaned his hands on the table and looked down at her. "So, let's do an after-action review. Tell me where you think you went wrong."

Slick took a breath and was about to speak. Then she hesitated, and smiled ever so slightly.

"I am requesting Condition X, sir," she said.

Steele smiled as well.

In the monitor room, where Shane Wiley was staring at the camera feed and listening to every word, his eyes glistened as he turned to Miles Turner and Dalton Goodhill and said, "She's mine."

CHAPTER 19

National Security Advisor Katie Garland hurried from the White House press room when an aide whispered in her ear.

She was reluctant to leave because the press briefings were often the highlight of her high-stress days. The entertainment was the president's press secretary, Stacy McAvoy, a slim blond young woman with a Shirley Temple demeanor and a mind like a bear trap. A reporter from CNN had just asked Stacy, for the umpteenth time, why President Rockford insisted that the mullahs in Tehran were still a worldwide terrorist threat. In turn, with her kindergarten teacher smile, Stacy had asked him which Ivy League journalism school he'd failed to graduate from.

Garland and her aide, Wesley Fenster, pushed through the press room door and into the West Wing, a warren of surprisingly small offices and cubicles, with cream-white walls displaying classic American artwork of tall ships and uniformed patriots, and polished doorways and moldings of dark chestnut. Everything from mouse pads to coffee mugs, pewter urns full of M&M's and paper-wrapped snacks, was emblazoned with the presidential seal, and while the tops of the wooden desks were neatly ordered, they were covered with so many government reference books and stacks of paper the place looked like a printing company. Thick folders containing intelligence assessments, many stamped TOP SECRET, were closely guarded by busy hands, and the low-intensity atmosphere of telephone voices and primly suited personnel holding tête-à-têtes resembled a Wall Street trading floor, but with manners.

"The president's got an incoming call," Wesley said to Garland as she clipped along on her modest heels and he tried to keep up. "They're holding it in the Watch Room, NSA's back tracing."

"Origin?" Garland said and then smiled at the president's acting chief of staff, Tony Hinds, a tall handsome man, formerly the CIA's chief of station in Kenya. "Hi, Tony."

"Katie." Hinds nodded as he hustled by in the opposite direction.

"China," Wesley whispered.

Garland stopped beside the double desk station just outside the oval office and looked at Wesley.

"Is it *that* source?" She wasn't about to say "Casino" out loud.

"Yes, ma'am."

Garland turned to the president's Oval Office gatekeeper, a twenty-seven-year-old baby-faced aide who was still getting carded at the local D.C. bars, though she rarely had time to go out.

"Maggie, where's the boss?"

"Down in the Sit room, ma'am. Waiting for you."

"And where's VPOTUS?" She meant the vice president.

"He's at the cave today," Maggie said. The vice president sometimes worked out of a secret location in Washington, just to keep America's enemies guessing.

Garland touched Wesley's suit jacket.

"I'll see you after, Wes. You know how the boss feels about tourists."

"You bet, ma'am." Her aide took no offense. Rockford didn't like a lot of onlookers around, probably a habit from his old days at Langley.

Garland headed for the wide carpeted stairwell that led down to the Situation Room, taking the steps in long strides, with her action folder tucked under one arm. Jack, the president's lead Secret Service agent, was manning the large mahogany door.

"Where is he, Jack? Big tank, little tank?" She meant the large National Security Council conference room, or the smaller side conference office where the president took his most secure calls.

"Not sure, ma'am," Jack said as he pulled the door open. "But he's not in a Superman tube, that's for sure."

In addition to the larger secure conference centers, there were also circular glass individual tubes, like old-style phone booths, with encrypted handsets inside.

"They should have made those damned things bigger," Garland said. "Can't put a whale in a tuna can." She jabbed a finger at Jack's face as she went on through. "Don't tell him I said that."

The Situation Room, a full floor below the West Wing, was not a single boardroom-type space but a five-thousand-square-foot complex of ultra–high tech duty stations, secure computers, flat-screen monitors lining the walls, and encrypted communications modules, all manned and womaned by an around-the-clock staff of strictly apolitical officers, equally apportioned from the intelligence community, Homeland Security, and Department of Defense. Central to that were three large conference rooms, the walls lined with active countersurveillance equipment, with dual flat screens at the head of each long polished wooden table, surrounded by plush black leather chairs. From each of these rooms the president and his staff could reach out to nearly two thousand similar facilities worldwide, domestic or international, and from his CIC seat at the head, the president could carry on a friendly convo with the Italian PM about cuisine, or go full secure for a *Fail Safe* chat with the British PM about nuclear war.

The original Situation Room had been installed on the orders of John F. Kennedy in 1961, just after the debacle of the Bay of Pigs. In 2007, President Bush had commenced four months of new construction, resulting in the most sophisticated such facility anywhere on earth. The times they were a changin'.

Garland turned her cell phone over to a duty officer—even the national security advisor had to follow the rules—then she stopped in the master conference suite and looked around. Tony Hinds had taken his reserved seat near the head of the table, but the only other person there was a uniformed naval aide, a female lieutenant commander. Hinds looked up from his thick briefing folder, shrugged, and shot a thumb toward the side door, which led to the "little tank" deeper inside.

Garland walked over. It was strange that the president hadn't wanted his own chief of staff in attendance, but his quirks were usually for a reason. She passed into a small hallway, took an immediate right, and found the president sitting at the small desk inside the square room, before a circular table with only four chairs. It was no more impressive than the office of a midlevel corporation's head of HR, except for the gleaming bank of secure communications gear that faced the president like a jet cockpit display. Rockford's suit jacket was slung across the back of his chair. His blue tie was perfectly knotted, but his cuffs were rolled up and his blond hair looked finger combed.

At the table sat Tina Harcourt, director of CIA. She had curly shoulder-length brown hair, glasses that looked like fashion rejects from 1965, thin eyebrows, a thin nose, thin lips, and no makeup, giving her the aura of a Missouri small-town librarian. That physical impression had stood her well as a field agent, first in Islamabad, then Ankara and later, Mosul, where her nonofficial cover was as a USAID distributions clerk. No one had doubted her. She looked far too cold and prim to be anything else.

"Hi, Katie." Harcourt smiled, which raised her demeanor from frosty to lukewarm.

"Director." Garland nodded.

"Get in here, Katie." The president flapped his hand at her. "We don't want to lose this guy."

Garland shut the door behind her back and remained standing, though she propped her action folder open on her hip and clicked a pen.

"You ready?" President Rockford said to Harcourt.

"Yes, sir." The director had a pen poised as well.

"Stroke of luck," Rockford said to Garland. "Tina was down here on another matter."

Then he glanced over at the left-hand wall, which was mostly taken up by a large square window that looked out onto the master conference suite. Tony Hinds was in there, along with the naval officer and some other folks who were gathering for a security update on Southeast Asia, which was going to be chaired by Harcourt. The president spun around, pressed a button on a rear console, and the window instantly fogged over, like frosted glass. Garland had never seen that before. She pulled her chin in and blinked.

"Any sufficiently advanced technology is indistinguishable from magic," the president quoted with an impish grin.

"Arthur C. Clarke," Garland said. "But it's still weird."

"Here we go." Rockford punched a speaker button on his yellow-framed encrypted handset. The sound of static filled the room. "This is President Rockford."

"Mr. President." It was the same thin voice and Hong Kong accent that he'd heard at Camp David, or at least seemed to be. NSA would run a voice print on both versions and compare. "I am thankful for your courtesy."

"We are thankful for your information, mister . . ."

"Casino."

"Yes." Rockford looked at Tina Harcourt. Her expression gave away nothing. "So, where are we?"

"We are at a critical juncture, Mr. President. I will need, as we discussed, protection and shelter now."

"I understood that the last time. . . . But in exchange for something a bit more substantial, my friend."

"First, I will give you my coordinates." The man calling himself Casino read off two sets of numbers, latitudes and longitudes. Garland jotted them down.

"We've got that, Mr. Casino," the president said.

"I have, in my possession," the thin voice went on, "a classified cable from the Chinese Communist Party containing two crucial bits of intelligence. One is that the CCP has already tested a new extremely deadly biowarfare weapon, somewhere in the world, and found it to be one hundred percent effective."

He said nothing else for a moment. Tina Harcourt shrugged at Rockford. If any such thing had happened, she was pretty damn sure she'd know about it.

"And the other bit?" Rockford said.

"Two, that the CCP will employ this weapon against large American naval assets, perhaps in multiple locations around the world, their objective being to render Taiwan unprotected against invasion. I suggest that you do not leave these assets vulnerable. I will reveal further details to you, along with this cable for verification, when I am in your hands." He paused to take a breath, but it sounded almost like a tremor. "Find me. I am waiting."

The line went dead. No more static. Garland immediately tore off a page of her action notebook, left the room, and came back without it. She found the president on his feet and stomping around behind his too-small desk like an angry cat with its spine curled.

"So now we're playing friggin' hide and go seek? The CCP's supposedly worked up a super biowarfare weapon, because their Covid-19 disaster wasn't fucked-up enough. . . . Apologies for my language, ladies . . . And they've tested it somewhere, but that hasn't popped up on anyone's radar? Really?"

"We've had absolutely nothing about any biowarfare incident, sir," Harcourt said. "I'd know if we did."

"And I would *too*," Rockford sputtered. "Would've been in the PDB." He meant the presidential daily briefing. "And now this cat's claiming they're ready to go to war over Taiwan, and they're going to use their super-duper killer bug to take out our naval defense line? Christ, it sounds like some spoof on Austin Powers."

Katie Garland wanted to say, *That would make it a spoof on a spoof, sir,* but she didn't.

"The only thing this guy didn't claim," Rockford added, "was that Xi Jinping's demanding *one billion dollars.*" He said that last part like Doctor Evil, then shook his big head and jammed his hands in his pants pockets.

"Do you think this Casino's legitimate, Director?" Katie Garland asked Harcourt.

"No. That asset was run long ago by one of our senior handlers, who's now retired," Harcourt said. "From what we know, the real Casino's cover was blown and he was executed. Beijing doesn't take kindly to moles."

"Yeah? Who says, Tina?" Rockford posed. "Could've been an old-school deception op, right? Suppose Casino was actually a double agent, feeding us tailored intel. Then they faked blowing his cover, and faked taking him out of the game. So, we think he's dead, but in fact he's a secret Chinese national hero, 'cause he plied us with bullshit for years. Meanwhile, he's still deep inside the committee, but this time he's turned for *real.*"

"Jesus." Tina Harcourt blinked at the president. "You're still better at this than I am."

"I'm just older and cynical and twisted is all," Rockford said.

There was a knock on the door. Garland opened it and the navy lieutenant commander was standing there with a secure tablet in a yellow frame. Rockford waved her inside.

"Spill it, Commander."

"Mr. President," she said. "Those coordinates are two hundred kilometers east of Taiwan, at a small atoll off of Miyako-jima."

"What's on that atoll?"

"Nothing that we know of, sir."

"See, Tina? Hide and go seek!" Rockford jammed a big finger at Harcourt, as if the whole thing was CIA's fault. He turned back to the naval officer. "Where's the Roosevelt strike group currently?"

"Hawaii, Mr. President. At Pearl."

Rockford chewed his lip while he considered that for a moment and said, "Get me CINCPAC." He meant the commander of the Pacific fleet. "And tell Tony Hinds out there to call a Joint Chiefs conference for nine tonight, right here."

"Yes, Mr. President." The officer closed the door.

Rockford crashed back down in his chair. Tina Harcourt rose from hers.

"Mr. President, I'd like to postpone this Southeast Asia review and get back over to Langley. I want to poll station chiefs for anything on this alleged bio incident."

"Good idea," he said. "Come back here tonight for the Joint Chiefs thing."

"Will do."

Harcourt nodded at Katie Garland and went out. Katie closed the door again behind her. She could never tell if Harcourt didn't like her, or just didn't care for humans in general.

"Katie, when we're done here in a moment," Rockford said, "use one of the tubes and brief that kid from the kitchen."

"Yes, sir." She knew he meant Eric Steele, but he wasn't going to make any overt reference to the Program or Alphas, even in the most secure bunker on earth. "You're thinking about moving all of our heavy assets out of Pearl, aren't you?"

"That's right," he said.

"I agree." Garland nodded. "They'll be safer in open water."

"Maybe." Rockford picked up a dark blue pencil embossed with the presidential seal, tapped the eraser against his teeth, and exhaled a long sigh. "But remember the USS *Lexington,* Katie. She survived the attack on Pearl Harbor, and was sunk at the Battle of the Coral Sea."

CHAPTER 20

ULAANBADRAKH, MONGOLIA

Colonel Doctor Ai Liang awakened from her third straight night without fevered dreams or delirium, and was somewhat amazed to be still alive.

She knew that she'd dipped her toes in the River of Styx, and it was only because of the unselfish ministrations of Gengi Phon and Mistra, his wife, that she lived at all. Mistra had patiently fed her ramen, with a spoon carved from camel bone, and had broken her fever by swathing her in piles of suffocating furs until the sweat burst from her brow, at which point Mistra had cooled her again with finger strokes of snow, scooped from a ceramic bowl. How the woman had healed her bullet wound, Ai Liang had no idea, but when at last the slimy pâté was peeled from her waist, the flesh underneath was pink, and closed up, and sealed.

The Chinese had some magical medicines, but apparently whatever the Mongols had was from another world.

Gengi Phon himself was one of the most frightening characters Ai Liang had ever seen. He was enormous, with eyes like burning stones, a great drooping mustache, and a bun of thick black hair like a Japanese sumo wrestler. She had no idea why he'd bothered to rescue her at the border, until she'd eased from her fevers and began to know Mistra. Though the woman had skin like leather, eyes like a leopardess, and gold-rimmed teeth, Gengi's wife was so kind and tender that she could not have been with a man who did not have a generous heart. That's how Ai Liang knew that Gengi Phon was good.

Over the past few days, she'd risen from her bed in the *ger,* was able to dress in Mongol burlap and boots, and had actually been outside. The fresh air was marvelous, despite the cold, and the landscape swathed in white was magnificent. She'd looked at her PLA uniform, where Mistra had hung it outside on a line after mending the bullet holes and washing away the blood. She had the fleeting thought that maybe she should burn that camouflaged costume of her dreaded past in Gengi's fire, and be done with all of that forever.

She felt safe here, although defecting to the Americans would be even safer. Yet perhaps she would stay, if Gengi Phon and Mistra would have her.

Their son, Ganbaatar, seemed a good boy. He was the much younger and slimmer version of his father, though it was easy to see what he'd soon become. Ganbaatar didn't speak Mandarin like his father, and Ai Liang had no knowledge of Khalkha, so all of their interplays were nods and smiles. But Ganbaatar was rarely there, as his tasks for the village, such as selling pelts or precious goods that Gengi Phon seemed to acquire somewhere, took the boy far away. On one of those journeys, early after Ai Liang's rescue, he'd gone off to a place called Zuunbayan, and returned with the Tibetan monk called Tenzin.

Ai Liang didn't know why. Tenzin was unlike any monk she'd ever seen or met. He spoke many languages, including English and German, often to himself, as if he were practicing. He was bald like a monk, but he wore a Russian fur hat with earflaps, a leather jacket, and blue jeans. He chain-smoked. He cursed under his breath. He hummed prayers to Buddha, in between asking her, even while she could still barely speak, what she was doing there, and how, exactly, she'd come to be wounded, and who were the mercenaries or soldiers who'd done this to her and her comrades, and had destroyed the laboratory. It made no sense that the CCP should do such a thing, he said. What was in that lab? That question he'd nearly shouted, as if he were interrogating her, and had been taught to do so by someone else—it was surely not something he'd learned at a holy monastery like Shaolin.

Then he'd disappeared, mumbling about being so foolish and forgetful, and had borrowed a horse and ridden off. Ai Liang wondered if in fact she had dreamed the entire appearance of Tenzin.

This morning she was sitting on the hard wooden edge of her bed, dunking torn chunks of sesame flatbread that seemed very much like *shao bing* into a bowl of Mistra's wonderful soup. Gengi Phon had left very early, and Mistra was outside hanging her wash. It was a clear cold day, the sun made the canvas cap of the *ger* glow as it rippled in the wind, and Gengi's fire roared and crackled in his potbellied stove, with most of the sweet-scented smoke curling skyward through the roof's apex hole.

The door to the *ger* suddenly flung wide open and Ai Liang jolted and nearly spilled her soup. The monk Tenzin filled the doorway, with his fur hat, jacket, and jeans encrusted with snow, as well as his black cowboy Roper boots. He was carrying a large leather satchel, and he pulled the door closed, yanked off his cap to reveal his shiny bald pate all pink from the cold, and exclaimed, "Yooreekah!"

Ai Liang had no idea what this expression meant, or that it was Tenzin's version of "eureka," Greek for "I've found it!" She watched him as he gingerly placed the satchel on the hard dirt floor, then tore off his fur mittens and rushed to the stove to warm his frozen fingers. Atop the iron belly was a ceramic teakettle. He poured himself a draught in a steel mug, pulled a small pewter flask from his pocket, added a pinch of some kind of clear alcohol, sipped and said, *"Ahhh, mama de niunai,"* which meant "Ahh, mommy's milk" in Mandarin.

Tenzin grabbed a three-legged stool and placed it to one side of Ai Liang's feet, facing her bed. Then he fetched his leather satchel, sat on the stool, put his steaming teacup on the floor, placed the satchel on the bed, and carefully unbuckled the straps, as if it contained some ancient artifact lifted from a museum. And indeed, when he removed the contents, it looked like some kind of electronic relic from the previous century. But Ai Liang recognized it right away, because she'd studied such things at military school. It was an olive-green, American military, long-range, multiband radio, with a collapsed whip antenna and some sort of keying device that folded down from its face beside a mechanical frequency dial.

"It is beautiful, Colonel, is it not?" Tenzin exclaimed in Mandarin as he rubbed his hands together.

"It is very . . . interesting, Tenzin," she agreed. "Where is this from?"

"Oh, about 1985, as I recall."

"No, not when. Where?"

Tenzin pulled a pack of Dubliss Black Mongolian cigarettes

from his pocket and lit one up with an old American Zippo. He opened a hatch in the back of the radio set and inserted some sort of large square battery. Then he rubbed a thumb and one finger together, flicked a toggle switch, turning the transmitter on, and slowly spun its frequency dial, as if he were cracking a safe. A small red activity bulb glowed, and he looked like he might pee from excitement.

"It was gifted to me by an American spy," he said, "many, many years ago. That's when they still cared about Tibet, before those filthy Chinese flooded the American markets with their cheap coffeemakers and dildos, the fuckers." He seemed not to realize, or care, that Ai Liang was herself Chinese as he slipped a pair of ancient earphones from a canvas pouch attached to the radio and pulled them onto his ears. "Listen to that!" he shouted in English and shot a finger at the ceiling. "Fucker works!" Then he went right back to Mandarin. "Anyway, this man from the CIA supplied us with guns and equipment and money. Then the shit hit the paper fan, the ring was blown, and most of us were caught by the Commies. Some even died, but not me. My handler had to haul ass. However, he swore to me that he'd always be out there, listening somewhere. Now we shall see, won't we?"

Ai Liang blinked at Tenzin's profile as he worked on the radio set. He looked like one of those old World War II operators summoning a British airdrop, but he was so damned weird she still wasn't sure he was real.

"Tenzin," she said in a measured tone, as if talking to a mental patient. "May I ask, how do you know this man is even still alive?"

"That motherfucker?" Tenzin waved his cigarette hand in the air. "He had his leg blown off at the Battle of Hue, then fought his way out on the back of a rickshaw with a .45 pistol in each hand. Believe you me, he's *alive*."

Ai Liang didn't say anything else. She watched as Tenzin took off his wristwatch, an old Breitling special forces model circa 1984. As he lay the watch down beside the radio, she saw that its worn black rubber band was stamped with the letters of the English alphabet, plus ten Arabic numerals, and beside each one were the corresponding dots and dashes of the old Morse code. Then he took out an iPhone, thumbed the side switch, and said, in English, "Siri, you *twit*, what's my current GPS location?" When the metallic voice responded with the lats and longs, he grinned like a child. Then he removed a book from the radio pouch, along with a pencil, flipped to a random page and began circling words, one after the other throughout the text. Ai Liang noted that the book was a well-worn paperback copy of F. Scott Fitzgerald's *Tender Is the Night*.

"Tenzin, what exactly are you doing?" she asked.

"Saving your sweet ass, Colonel," he said as he kept on circling. "Book code. Old school. I have a copy, he has a copy. We keep them till the day we die. If I wanna send him a message, or the other way around, I choose a page, relay the page number, then create the message using words from that page, and each one gets a number, depending on where it is on the page. Get it?"

"No."

"Fuck it. Doesn't matter." Tenzin pulled down the Morse code keypad, looked at his notes, and started tapping away.

"Tenzin," Liang said. "Did you even know your handler's real name?"

"Of course not." He was concentrating intently now. "Called himself Hua Chang Mao."

Liang thought about that. *Hua Chang Mao.* Her English was close to fluent from all of her academic studies, but she could think of no English equivalent to "spear of the flower" . . . except for perhaps . . . thorn.

Tenzin tapped away on his Morse code key for an hour. It seemed to Ai Liang that he was repeating his message, over and over again. He smoked nearly half a pack of those foul Dubliss Blacks during that time and kept asking Ai Liang for more tea. Mistra came back into the *ger* and saw the monk hunched and pecking furiously like some wild tech nerd. She and Ai Liang exchanged smirks and shrugs, and Mistra retreated to the far nook that served as her kitchen and started chopping ingredients for curried lamb stew.

Then Gengi Phon barreled into the *ger.* He was dusted with fresh snow, carrying his old Enfield rife, and demanding to know why his son, Ganbaatar, wasn't there. Tenzin stopped tapping because the Mongol's presence demanded full focus. One never knew with these kinds of men.

The door opened again soon after and Ganbaatar stepped inside. He too was slathered in snow, yet his demeanor was calm. He was also slinging a rifle, and he slipped its strap from the shoulder of his camel fur jacket, propped it on the floor rack next to his father's, and removed his conical Mongol hat.

"You are very late," Gengi Phon said to his son. "It does not take an extra day to return from selling hogs in Khangi."

"It does, Father, if you have seen what I have seen."

"Tell me."

They were speaking Khalkha. Ai Liang did not understand, but Tenzin did and had turned from his radio, all ears.

"A man, father, in the hills by the south river." Ganbaatar swept his long arm toward somewhere southwest, outside. "He thought he was hidden, but I saw a gleam from something he had and I tied Uli's horse and climbed closer. He was watching our village, with the kind of spyglass you do not buy even in Ulaanbaatar. He had a weapon as well, nothing like our rifles. I saw it, Father."

Gengi Phon nodded, slowly, then blew a long breath through clenched teeth. "Precious boy," he said as he reached out, squeezed his son's shoulder, then looked at his own boots, where the melting snow was puddling his earthen floor. He chewed his lip as Ai Liang flicked her eyes from Gengi to Mistra, who was now standing close by with her camel bone spoon. Their faces were telling a story, and it wasn't a happy fairy tale.

Gengi Phon turned to Tenzin.

"Call your gods, monk. Call them quickly. These men are coming. They will come soon."

CHAPTER 21

The *Windhoek* was still dead in the water, silent and mysterious, its irons creaking as it gently bumped against the splintered quay, offering no clue as to the fate of its crew. But Rod Kruvalt knew that the abandoned vessel had a ghostly tale to tell, and George Wheelwright might just be his ship whisperer.

Kruvalt had shown up at Wheelwright's mountaintop house the morning after their chat. It was just after sunrise when his big Maxxis tires crunched on the gravel, a presumptive act, given that his American friend had begged off until at least late morning, with no promise to come along then either. Yet George ambled out of the house, barefoot, in baggy red boxers and a half-open chambray shirt, gray hair askew, and smirked.

"Ambush technique, huh, Rod?"

"That's right, mate," Kruvalt said. "Hit 'em at dawn, before they can melt away into the jungle."

"All right, you dirty merc. You win."

Now they were winding back down through the hills toward

Maputo in Kruvalt's green Defender, with Wheelwright more properly dressed in an epauletted bush shirt, jeans, and French desert boots, no socks. Kruvalt was in his SWAT utilities, The Mamas and the Papas were crooning "Monday, Monday" from his CD player, and he had all the windows open to the sweet humid African air. They were sipping black coffee that Kruvalt had brought along from Café Acacia, because he knew George liked it. Wheelwright was smoking his pipe, and they didn't say much.

It wasn't the first time that Kruvalt had asked his mysterious friend for assistance. Over the past eight years there'd been some occasions when the PRM's homicide division was stumped and the detectives had turned to SWAT Captain Kruvalt, mostly because they knew he had a background in mayhem. On one such instance, Kruvalt, stumped over a case himself, had consulted with Wheelwright.

"I just can't figure it, mate. They've got this gangbanger bloke, drug dealer type, shot in an alley behind the Southern Sun Hotel. Point-blank, big caliber, close range in the chest, but no friggin' exit wound and no bloody bullet."

"Who were his clients?"

"Street trash. The usual."

"Who were his suppliers?"

"Russians, or so the detective constable reckons."

Wheelwright had thought about that for a moment, and then said, "Ice."

"Excuse me?"

"It's an old Chechen technique. Twenty-gauge shotgun, cut down, with blank ammunition. The ice slugs are made in a mold, like Popsicles. You just have to keep them in a cooler till right before the hit. Then you chamber a blank, drop a slug in the barrel

end, like a musket, and it's goodbye Charlie. No bullet, no ballistics to trace. Betcha that shotgun's in the drink somewhere."

Kruvalt had been stunned. "George, you're a bloody genius.
Medical examiner said the only thing he found was powder
burns and water."

"Nah, I just read a lot of Agatha Christie."

Right. Kruvalt reckoned there was a lot more to Wheelwright
than that, but he'd worked the jungles and slums all across the
continent for most of his adult life and knew when to ask, and
ask not. Africa was still the land of diamond smugglers and ivory
poachers, warlords and slaves, the wealthy and the destitute,
clashing in violent surges. In the course of one day, you could run
across a village of missionaries slaughtered by ISIS fighters, and
before sunset come across the same Islamist maniacs slaughtered
in turn by French special forces. It was still a place where soldiers
of fortune came to live and let die, and sometimes disappear.
George Wheelwright certainly seemed like one of those types,
but friendships between men of their particular talents could be
ruined by too many questions.

Yet after a couple of more cases about which Kruvalt had asked
Wheelwright for his opinion, and had again received the sort of
responses that only a widely experienced professional could prof-
fer, he'd quietly inquired about the man's background. He still
had his photo and fingerprints from the barroom brawl arrest, as
well as the charge sheet with a few personal details. He ran him
through INTERPOL and EUROPOL, and had a SWAT team
support geek check all social media and the internet. Nothing. It
was as if George had been born the previous decade and hadn't
gotten around yet to carving the scars that all hard men leave in
their wake. But he decided not to dig any further, because his

inquiries might set something in motion that could do George harm, so instead he asked him point-blank.

"So, what's your background, mate? Throw us a bone."

"Special forces. Don't make me lie past that."

"Figured as much. You retire, or get the boot?"

"Neither. Sometimes you get left for dead, and it's better that way."

"All right, mate. As long as you're not wanted for murder. . . . Are ya?"

"No, but I'm wanted for breaking a few hearts, worldwide."

George had made that remark without a smile, and Kruvalt had decided to just let it go. . . .

They arrived at the docks, where a cordon of PRM uniforms were still keeping onlookers away from the *Windhoek,* backed up by eight of Kruvalt's SWAT team, but the assault truck was gone, and a wooden gangway with rope handrails now lay from the tarmac to the ship's gunwales. Port activity was returning to normal, with the tipped-over vehicles righted back on their tires, the latrines back in place, and a new gas generator sending power to pneumatic bolt drivers that hissed in the air down the quay. The early sun was already steaming the port, the harbinger of a hot day, yet what Kruvalt noticed was its glint off the zoom camera lenses of a couple of guys in the crowd of gathering civilians. Word of the ghost ship had gotten around.

He parked the Defender inside the cordon, pulled a flexible mask of black mesh material over his head and around his throat, and handed one to Wheelwright.

"You skittish about the plague?" George said.

"No. The reporters."

Wheelwright nodded, but instead pulled his bandanna on and

over his nose, then fetched a pair of Ray-Bans from his pocket and donned them.

"Is this Lone Ranger enough for you, Tonto?"

"Who's that?" Kruvalt asked.

"Never mind."

They got out of the truck. Wheelwright left his pipe in the ashtray. Ingo Ferreti hurried over from somewhere, fiddling with an unlit cigarette in his pudgy fingers. He was trailed by a fat black man in a seersucker suit, a chief inspector from SERNIC called Boondo, who didn't have much use for SWAT types.

"First one's the harbormaster," Kruvalt muttered. "Second one's a dick."

"Not his given name, I'm guessing," said Wheelwright.

"Correct."

"Good morning, Captain!" Ingo was almost doing a jig. "This should be exciting."

"Hello, Ingo."

Boondo pushed past Ferreti, puffing his slabby chest out. There were food stains on his parrot tie.

"I'm going aboard with you, Kruvalt."

"Your call, Inspector." Kruvalt shrugged. "But my boys think there might be a bomb in the engine room. We're taking the sapper with us. Is your life insurance paid up?"

Boondo thought about that for a moment, chewed his big lip, looked at the ship, then said to Kruvalt, "All right, we'll wait for your all clear."

"Seems wise."

"Captain," Ingo said. "We spoke to the gentlemen at Ocean Africa. There were eighty-two men on the manifest."

"Distress calls?" Kruvalt asked. "Lifeboats?"

"No." Ingo looked up at George Wheelwright and grinned. "And who is this masked stranger?"

"My maritime clairvoyant," Kruvalt said. "He reads the minds of empty ships."

"Oh."

Kruvalt cocked his chin at Wheelwright and they headed toward the gangplank as his SWAT team members gathered around. He selected four of them and said, "Masks on, gloves on. Don't touch anything but the hatch handles. James, take the boys below and sweep the crew quarters and the engine room. Me and my advisor here'll do the bridge and the deck aft of the superstructure. I don't reckon there's any ordnance aboard, but watch for trip wires anyhow. Right?"

With Kruvalt in the lead, the six men walked up the plank, hopped down onto the swaying steel deck, and split up. The vessel looked very clean, almost new, with its cargo containers neatly ordered and the white and orange lifeboats still hanging from the davits. There was none of the detritus you'd find on a deck from high winds or crashing waves, such as broken stays, loose cables, or twisted rails, so there'd been no storm. He and Wheelwright climbed up a set of steel stairs and entered the bridge and the pilothouse. The empty captain's chair was perched before a semicircular plotting table, with some maps and charts, an open pack of Camels, and a glass ashtray full of butts. The navigator's and comm guy's stations looked just as neat and unremarkable.

"It's like they just bloody disappeared," Kruvalt said.

"Beam me up, Scotty," Wheelwright remarked.

The two men walked through the bridge and climbed down another ladder to the stern deck. With the forward decks of the ship crowded with cargo, this was the spot where the crew would relax, take in some sun, play cards, smoke, tell lies about women, and complain. There were a couple of saltwater fishing rods jammed into rail holders and a few beach chairs, but nothing else. The only curious thing was a fire hose, snaking across the deck and still locked to a valve on the superstructure, and the deck was wet, but that could have been from rain.

Then Wheelwright spotted something and strode across the deck to a large engine exhaust pipe. It was two feet wide, curved like a tuba and jutted up from the engine room below. He peered at a trio of punctures in its metal skin and ran his fingers over them. Kruvalt joined him there.

"Bullet holes, mate?" he said.

"That's right."

Kruvalt touched the holes too. "Could be they had weapons aboard, for pirates or sharks. Maybe somebody got drunk and had an A.D." He meant accidental discharge.

"With a Chinese AK-47 and restricted PLA ammo?" Wheelwright said. "Possible, I guess." He pulled a pen from Kruvalt's tunic pocket, pushed the tip into all three holes, one after the other, then put it back and looked past Kruvalt to the ship's stern. "That railing's at thirty meters. Even if fired from there, these punctures would be perfectly round. But they're not, Rod, they're oblong."

"So?"

"They passed through something first. Something that made them tumble."

Then James popped up from a belowdecks hatch. He was sweating in his SWAT gear and couldn't bear wearing his mask anymore, so he pulled it down.

"Whatcha got, Jimmy?" Kruvalt asked him.

"Nothing in the engine room, boss. And the crew bunks look like they just up and left, without even taking a bloody tooth-brush. Books, girlie mags, Nintendos, and all their clothes in the racks. No cell phones. Not one."

Kruvalt turned to Wheelwright.

"What's your guess, George?"

Wheelwright thought about that for a moment.

"Hijack," he said. "Either they're all being held for ransom somewhere, and Ocean Africa's going to have to pay a boatload of money, or it's something else and they're all dead."

"Not all of them, boss," James said. He was holding up his ra-dio handset. "You just got a call from the coast guard. An Inter-ceptor picked up a survivor."

"No shite, James? Where?"

"'Bout two hundred nautical miles due east, in open water. And they said you'd better haul ass, 'cause he's barely alive."

CHAPTER 22

THE INDIAN OCEAN

The police of the Republic of Mozambique in Maputo didn't have their own helicopter, and neither did the SWAT team, which had pretty much blown its vehicle budget on the Patriot3 assault truck. But Captain Rod Kruvalt did have friends, many of whom he'd made in Rhodesia or South Africa, the kinds of men with a narrow range of particular skills, little hope of retirement pensions, and unquenchable thirsts for adrenaline.

A few of those men were currently working for Dyck Advisory Group, a private military company based in South Africa that had a stable of French Gazelle assault helicopters, M134 Miniguns, lots of ammunition and semidemented pilots and crews. They were very busy providing air-to-ground support for Mozambique marines engaged in a fight for their lives against Islamic State warriors way up north in Cabo Delgado. But such men also needed a break once in a while from the killing fields, and one crew was staying, along with their camouflage-painted, no-tail-number Gazelle, at the Radisson Blu Hotel, which happened to have a landing pad on the roof.

The PRM did have a police launch, but a two-hundred-mile boat trip out to the coast guard's Interceptor would have taken all day, and Kruvalt was anxious to speak to the *Wondhoek*'s lone survivor while the man still breathed. So he'd called over to the Radisson and had the pool boys track down pilot Jacob Farley, who was already half in the bag on a lounge chair while he listened to Crystal Axis singing "Killing in the Name" through earbuds—the reason he hadn't answered his cell phone.

"Me and my mate need a lift, Jake," Kruvalt said.

"Fuck off, Rodney. It's my down day."

"I know this very willing young lady, works at Coconuts Live, has all the attributes you favor, and loves flyboys."

"Fucker. Who's paying the fuel charge, and where to?"

"I am, from the kitty. And it's about two hundred nauts, due east. You just drop us off on a coast guard scow and go back to the pool, with Rita's telephone number."

"You know that's at the far end of my range, right, Rodney?"

"I know you owe me your ass, Jacob."

"Fucker. Meet me on the roof."

"Are you sober, mate?"

Farley laughed. "I haven't flown sober in years."

It was a beautiful day for a low-level flight from Maputo toward Madagascar. The waters below started out teal and gecko green, then darkened to a deeper royal blue, with the occasional white spouts from whales and the silver glints of flying fish wings. Farley flew the Gazelle from the left seat. He was barefoot, still wearing his swim trunks and a Hawaiian shirt of psychedelic palms. Kruvalt sat in the right seat, with Wheelwright in the cramped rear, sitting on the bench amid a vibrating mess of spent shell casings, porn magazines, sweat-stinking "sterile" uniform parts, and a pair of Merrell mountain boots that appeared to be caked in dried blood.

The Aérospatiale Gazelle model SA 342K has a cruising speed of 264 kilometers per hour, so they spotted the coast guard French-made HSI 32 Interceptor after about an hour and twenty minutes. It was a sleek-looking fast attack craft thirty-two meters in length, with all sorts of radar and antenna arrays atop a high wheelhouse with 360-degree windows. The boat's crew, at least those who weren't on the bridge, were milling about in their blue and gray camouflage uniforms on the forward deck, which was the only spot where Farley could deposit his guests, since the small stern ramp was occupied by a bright orange Zodiac. Farley already had the coast guard's frequency up on his headset, and he called the bridge.

"Afternoon, mate. PRM taxi here dropping off some trash. Be a sport and pull down those whips for a minute so I don't slice the ends off, over."

Two coast guard crewmen appeared atop the bridge and man-handled a pair of high whip antennas into seaward curves, and Farley carefully brought the Gazelle into a hover just inside the pointy bow. He threw a snappy salute and a "get out" thumb at Kruvalt, who stuffed a scrap of paper with Rita's scribbled number on it into Farley's shirt, then opened the clamshell door on his side and slipped down to the skid in the rotor wash. Wheelwright shoved his tiny cargo door open on the opposite side, barely squeezed through, and they both dangled from their respective skids for a moment, nodded at one another, and dropped to the deck. Farley banked away and was gone in a flash.

With the Gazelle departed it got instantly quiet, except for the circling gulls. The Interceptor was sea anchored and rolling in gentle waves that licked at its navy-gray hull. Kruvalt and Wheelwright got to their feet and looked at the boat's forward superstructure, which leaned away toward the stern in a slant. A slim black man was sitting on a foam mattress on the deck, leaning back against the bulkhead, flanked on both sides by seven members of the crew, one of whom was holding a white umbrella to shield him from the sun, while another, probably a navy corpsman, was painting his sunburned face and lips with an oily salve. To the right on the deck was a bright orange life ring with WINDHOEK stenciled on it.

Kruvalt and Wheelwright walked over, and a young ensign rose from a squat. Rod shook his hand.

"Kruvalt, captain, PRM SWAT."

"Ensign Borges," the young officer said, then nodded at Wheelwright as well.

"What's his status?" Kruvalt asked.

"Not good. Nigerian kid, messman on his ship. We think he was in the water for two days."

"Sole survivor?"

"Thus far, sir."

Kruvalt nodded and moved in as the naval crewmen made space. He squatted next to the Nigerian sailor, and Wheelwright mirrored him on the other side. The young man's face was terribly swollen, his eyes were gleaming slits, and the skin of his arms was peeling away like burned crepe paper. He wore only a dirty yellow singlet and shorts. His legs were covered by a lightweight space blanket that gleamed in the sun.

"Hullo, son," Kruvalt said.

The sailor seemed to stir from delirium, looked at him and whispered, "More water," in Nigerian-accented English. One of the sailors handed Kruvalt a plastic bottle and he tipped a gentle stream into the man's mouth.

"What happened out there?"

"It was nighttime. . . . We were running from Ambovombe to Maputo." The man's weak voice was gurgling and he leaned his head back and closed his swollen eyes. "A big helicopter came . . . white . . . United Nations. Landed on the stern. Spacemen got out."

"Spacemen?" Wheelwright said.

"Five, or six . . . they had guns, and something like . . . a milk can."

Wheelwright looked at Kruvalt, who shrugged and said, "Then what, mate?"

"They called for the captain . . . he came down from the bridge with some others. They talked for a little . . . I did not hear what."

"Where were you?" Wheelwright asked.

"In the galley . . . I saw it from the porthole. They shot him . . ." The sailor coughed, a liquid sound from his heaving lungs.

Kruvalt touched his sunburned shoulder, but just barely and only to let him know he was still there, and said, "Take your time, mate."

"It was terrible, terrible . . . They made the rest of the crew come to the stern . . . everyone but me. They sprayed them with something from the milk can . . . it made them scream and choke and the blood came from their noses and eyes . . . They shot the ones who tried to escape."

Wheelwright and Kruvalt locked eyes, then Kruvalt asked the sailor, "Why not you?"

"I jumped. I took the life ring."

"From where?"

"Topside . . . all the way up."

Wheelwright lifted the edge of the space blanket and looked at the sailor's legs. They were broken. He laid it back down.

"Then what?" Kruvalt said.

"I don't know. She was still running, but slow. . . . I heard more screams but no more gunshots. . . . And then the bodies splashing, all of them."

"Which bodies?" Wheelwright said.

"The whole crew."

The sailor's eyes were still closed, but tears spilled from the swollen corners and ran down his crimson burned cheeks. Kruvalt touched his trembling hand where it lay on his lap.

"Where are they?" he said, but he was looking up at the ensign, who raised his palms and shook his head.

"All gone," the sailor said.

"Where?"

"Sharks."

A couple of the navy crewmen were covering their mouths with their fingers as they listened.

"Why didn't the sharks get you?" Wheelwright asked.

"I don't know. We were more than eighty. . . . Maybe their bellies were full."

Then the young sailor shuddered and stopped talking. Kruvalt

touched his curly hair and then the corpsman nudged him aside
so he could check the man's neck pulse. Kruvalt and Wheelwright got up and Kruvalt took the ensign's elbow and the three
walked over toward the bow.

"What do you make of it, Borges?"

"Not a clue, but he told us the same story, twice. And now,
to you."

"And there was nothing else in the water?" Wheelwright asked.

"Just one more thing." Borges called over to one of his sailors,
who bent and opened a plastic cooler that looked like a blue-and-
white picnic beer chest. He came over to the trio and held up a
large plastic ziplock bag.

Inside was a gnawed-off hand.

CHAPTER 23

"Eric, that is one fugly car."

Steele turned and looked at his mother. Susan Steele never used language like that, even when the profanity was camouflaged by contractions. She stood there next to him on his gravel driveway, arms folded, chewing one stem of a pair of purple Vogue sunglasses as she regarded the vehicle.

"Not really, Mom. It's just a Toyota."

She turned her head, dipped her chin, and peered at him from under her brunette bangs. She was tall, still trim, and had just arrived from her new real estate job where she'd managed an open house all day long and had nailed the sale. She was wearing ankle boots, blue jeans, a pink roll-neck sweater, and a light leather jacket. She felt about dresses the way her son felt about ties.

"Eric. It's a hybrid."

"Yeah, that's right. It's a Camry."

"That color is something like a prostitute's nail polish."

"*Mom.*" Steele smiled at that, but he also blushed. "It gets great mileage."

Susan cocked her head, as if she hadn't heard what she'd heard.

"Did you say . . . mileage?"

"Well, yeah." He glanced over his mother's head at her lease, a white Jeep Wrangler Sahara. Thank God the days of his childhood were long gone when his mom had worked two jobs, back-to-back, just to keep them alive, and sometimes a third on weekends. But he had a different discomfiting thought.

Jesus. My mother's cooler than I am.

"I've been in those things," Susan said as she pulled a face at the glossy red Toyota. "The engines don't make any noise. You can't even tell when they're on."

"Well, I'm sort of past the Fast and Furious stage. . . ." His voice trailed off.

Susan moved to him, reached up and touched his forehead.

"Are you all right?"

"Of course." He snorted unconvincingly and pulled her hand away.

"Where's your car, Eric. Your *real* car."

"It's right in there." He pointed at his double-door garage.

"There's a corpse in the trunk, isn't there . . ."

"No!" He laughed, squeezed her shoulder and kissed her forehead.

"There's something wrong with you," she said. "Nobody with a GTO drives something like this. It's just not . . ."

"Let's go eat, Mom."

He took her elbow and they walked to the front door, which looked like a classic chestnut piece from the Craftsman era, but was actually a Krieger level-four blast door. Steele had built the first version of his house with his own hands, a conversion project from an old warehouse owned by Dravo Corp, the former manufacturer of World War II invasion landing craft. That iteration of his island fortress, in the middle of the Ohio River just northwest of Pittsburgh, had been burned down to charcoal briquettes in a "dispute" with a team of Russian terrorists. During the ensuing running gun battle, Steele's first GTO had also bitten the dust, and his mom, who was visiting at the time, had almost died as well. As often as possible, he tried not to think about that.

But now Version 2.0 of Schloss Steele was complete, and better and more secure than the first. The reinforced concrete walls had been shipped in from the same manufacturer of the T-walls used in Afghanistan, but here they were stuccoed white for a friendlier appearance. The windows were double-paned ballistic glass, with fashionable jet-gray steel frames, and the exterior had a perimeter of invisible cameras and sensors, a complex array designed by Ralphy Persko himself. Once again, Steele had constructed a safe room inside with a closed-circuit air supply, but now that bunker had a steel hatch in the floor, through which you could drop to a hundred-meter illuminated escape tunnel that broke out into the woods. He'd also rebuilt the armory, adding six M72 Light Anti-Armor Weapons to the inventory, because the last time he'd found himself up against determined shooters using M249 Squad Automatic Weapons.

Most of the remaining interior appeared "normal," with a sprawling open-floor-plan living area, a white brick fireplace (the chimney cap could be remotely slammed shut), four nice bedrooms with baths upstairs (each had a skylight and a concealed drop-down ladder, so they could be used as sniper perches), and furnishings by Raymour & Flanigan (nicer than IKEA; not as pricey as Stickley Audi & Co.). Steele had hired a Pittsburgh designer to create the kitchen, which featured stainless steel appliances and a central preparation and dining slab of white-and-gray speckled granite. He didn't spend much time cooking, so that was mostly for his mother—or maybe for some future spouse, who wasn't likely to appear in any near year.

Inside the house, Steele touched a button on something that looked like a thermostat on the wall. The cover flipped up, he palmed a reader, and the low *thunk* of pneumatic door and window locks sliding into their barrels reverberated throughout the house. The box beeped and an app on his cell came alive, displaying the shifting images from six different cameras. He glanced at it, put it back in his jeans hip pocket, and snapped the alarm cover down. His mom had already gone into the kitchen and dropped her big purse on the granite.

"Okay, sport." She rubbed her hands together. "What are we making?"

"It's already done, Mom." Steele walked over to his BlueStar forty-eight-inch range, an appliance made in Reading, Pennsylvania, because he tried hard not to buy anything manufactured in China. He donned a quilted red oven glove and pulled open the door. "Couple of sirloins, baked potatoes, sautéed asparagus. Good?"

"Excellent! I knew I smelled something good, but didn't want to presume."

"Choose your wine, Madame," Steele said as he plated the food and delivered it to the granite strip.

His mom walked over to a slim wooden wine rack beside the Sub-Zero refrigerator and twisted some bottles to inspect the labels.

"What's Egri Bikavér?"

"It's Hungarian, very robust. You'll like it."

"Is that the name of the winery?"

"No. It means 'bull's blood.'"

"Matches the day I had. That client was so stubborn I almost had to kill him to get him to sign."

She found a corkscrew in a drawer, sliced the wine bottle collar, dragged the cork out, waved the bottle through the air rather than letting it settle to breathe, and poured two hefty glasses. They sat down on stools across from each other, clinked to "cheers," sipped the wine, and tucked into the food.

"You're growing a beard," Susan said as she chewed demurely and looked at her son. "I like it, but I haven't seen you do that since Afghanistan, and only then in pictures."

"Well, somebody suggested it'd make me look a little less . . . aggressive," Steele lied.

"Liar. Some girl likes you scruffy. Is it Meg?"

Steele stiffened internally, but showed nothing on his face and kept on chewing.

"Nope."

"I don't know, son." Susan sipped her wine and inspected his eyes. "A beard, a Toyota hybrid. It's all very Woodstock. Are you planning on opening a weed shop?"

Steele grinned at that but kept on chewing his food. At least his mother had quickly gotten away from the subject of Meg Harden.

"So, speaking of Meg Harden," she said. "Have you seen her at all lately?"

Steele swallowed a piece of meat, drank a good slug of the Egri, and said, "Well, actually . . ."

And then he was right back there on Meg's balcony in Falls Church, where they'd stood together just a few days before. They were looking south toward the glistening waters and greenery of Lake Barcroft, though neither of them was seeing the scenery, and Steele was aware that off to his left and eastward, the white spindle of the Washington Monument jabbed at his temple as if to say, *Keep in mind who you are.*

"I seriously considered ending it, Eric," Meg had said.

He knew she didn't mean her life. She meant the baby. He looked over at her perfect profile, her sleek small nose and crystal-blue eyes, and that mink-black hair that often swept his face when they were breathing each other's breaths. She was wearing one of his old dress shirts, the one with the blue pinstripes, sleeves rolled up—he wondered for a moment if she'd done that on purpose—and a pair of black leggings and sandals. Her body was still as athletic as ever, with the only evidence of her pregnancy a large bump, as if she'd tucked a soccer ball under the shirt.

"Why didn't you tell me?" he said.

"We're not married, Eric. It wasn't a mutual decision. It was mine."

She was right. He'd had his chance to change all that and had chosen the mission first.

"We could change all that," he said.

Meg turned her face and smiled, but in a way that someone regards an alcoholic when he promises, for the twentieth time, to quit. She slid her small hand along the balcony's balustrade and covered his larger one, but she didn't squeeze.

"He's going to be our son," she said, "but we're not going to be a family. I've been working as a consultant for Homeland Security, right from here, and it's going to stay that way. No more crazy adventures for Meg. And you've got to do what you do. So, he might know you as someone who cares about him, if you want, but no more than that. I'm not going to be one of those special operations widows who gets a house and a mortgage from Tunnels to Towers."

He couldn't really speak after that. It all stuck in his throat. The Program had just come off life support. He was back in the game, and he wasn't going to pretend he'd quit if he didn't mean it, or want it. So instead he reached out, pulled her close, kissed her hair and held her while they gazed at the sunlight fading away.

"I'm going to see the Program JAG," he said quietly. "Have the beneficiaries changed on my will."

"Don't die for us," Meg whispered. "Live, if you can. So he can meet you, and you can meet him. . . ."

Steele returned to the moment. His mother had put her fork down and was staring at him. Then he told her the story, and everything that had been said. Susan listened, then pushed her plate away, leaned back, and focused on her wine instead. She turned the balloon glass and looked at the swirling bull's blood.

"I spent an awful lot of years blaming your father for lots of things, Eric," she said. "But I knew who he was when I married him, and I knew what might happen, and I did it anyway. Love has no logic. Love has no cure. I was just like hundreds of other wives, of fighter pilots, spies, and SEALs. And now, may God forgive us, there are so many women in combat, and their husbands and kids are just like me, and you." She smiled, but it didn't touch her eyes. "Remind me what that postcard said."

"It had palm trees on it," Steele said quietly. "He wrote on the back. 'Wish you were here. I love you. I hope someday that you will understand. HS.'"

Susan Steele nodded. "If that's all that you ever get from your father, it will have to be enough. I've moved on, and you should too."

He saw that her eyes were glistening, and knew that none of that was possible, or true. She reached across the granite and touched his hand.

"Don't marry Meg, Eric," she said. "But don't be like Hank, either. Be a father to your son, and I'll be his grandma too."

Steele's mother left not long after that. They pretended to enjoy a dessert of coffee ice cream, walnuts, and chocolate syrup, but the clouds of the past and the present hung low in the house, and at last she grinned and teased him some more about his car, and hugged him and left.

He locked everything up, set the sensors and alarms, went down from the kitchen interior stairwell to the garage, and looked at his gleaming GTO. But he didn't stay long because it made him feel like Batman after having his wings clipped, so he switched off the light and went back upstairs to his bedroom suite and the bathroom.

He looked at himself in the mirror, at his burgeoning scruffy beard, and he opened the medicine cabinet, removed the new box of tinted contact lenses, and worked them into his eyeballs. His jade-green eyes were gone, obscured by mud brown. He reached for the carpet cutter he'd bought at Home Depot, then decided against it and put it back.

He leaned across the sink, closer to the mirror, and with his left fingers he stretched the flesh of his left cheek. Then he pulled a Benchmade folding blade from his jeans pocket, and flicked it open.

"If you're gonna have a knife scar," he said to himself. "Use a fucking knife."

CHAPTER 24

EYES ONLY

SAP (Alphas/Support/Off Stations - FLASH)

From: SAWTOOTH MAIN

To: All CONUS PAX

Subj: Muster

Source: Staff Ops/Duty Officer

Confidence: High

All CONUS PAX, inc ALPHAS, KEEPERS, SUPPORT, TECH,
SEC PERS, ARMORERS, OTC INSTRUCTORS, AIR:

TOTAL RECALL

Emphasis, No Exceptions.

STATUS: DEFCON Amber.

Operational window: Immediate Execute

Steele barreled through the double glass doors on the ground floor of Sawtooth Main, and already he wasn't happy.

At two o'clock in the morning, the Program-encrypted app had flashed and buzzed on his government iPhone clone, right in the middle of a dream about Meg when things were still hot and heavy. He'd jumped out of bed, only to discover that his self-inflicted cheek wound had bled right through the bandage and all over his brand-new MyPillow, so that went into the garbage. From there he'd hopped in a cold shower, toweled off, replaced the bloody bandage with two butterflies and a long wide Band-Aid, gotten dressed and armed, grabbed a travel mug of coffee and a stale croissant, and had driven all night down to D.C. in that fugly car.

In the Program's underground parking lot, the formerly officious uniformed attendant with the Bermuda accent, Charles—who kept a MAC-10 submachine gun in his cash drawer—had nearly remarked on Steele's amusing mode of conveyance but saw his expression and thought better of it. Steele, wearing Redwing oxfords, jeans, a white dress shirt, dark blue blazer, and Oakley sunglasses, stomped up the ramp to the sidewalk, then stopped short and frowned at the new nameplate above the building's doors. GRACELAND IMPORT EXPORTS had been replaced by SCHMIDT & HEARTHSTONE, LLC.

Seriously? What are we, a freakin' furniture store now?

Inside the lobby, the white leather sofas had been subsumed by a muddy Naugahyde set from Price Busters, and on the north wall the Robert Salmon painting of a merchant schooner had surrendered to a cheap canvas print of a Hunter Wood. But at least the big desk was still there, and to Steele's surprise, so was Merry. The comely, blonde, twenty-something girl had apparently found no better employment between Program iterations, and since it was easier to vet someone who'd already been through the clearance ringer, they'd put her back into play again.

"Nice to see you again, Merry," he said as he walked up to the desk.

"Sir?" She clearly didn't recognize him with the beard.

"Formerly Max Sands." His smile was unconvincing, and the Band-Aid array didn't help.

"Oh." She pointed at the tripod with the electronic eyeball on top. "Retina scan, please."

He took off his Oakleys and bent his left eye to the Cyclops, but Merry's computer made a sound like a belching frog, and he remembered he still had his brown contacts in. "Dammit," he muttered as he peeled his eyelid back with his right hand, reached into his eyeball with his left digit and thumb, and Merry flinched as he plucked the contact out and the reader made the appropriate *ding*. But then she was staring at a bearded man who had one luminous green eye, one mud brown, a freshly bandaged face wound, and looked half like the former Stalker Seven and half like something from *The Terminator*.

"Um, I think I should call someone—" she started to say.

"Merry, I'm low on caffeine, I just drove four hours in a shitty car, and I'm having some PTS issues today."

"I'm sorry, but you know, it's standard procedure."

He started to lean across the counter. She gulped and pressed a button under her desk, and across the lobby, the elevator door opened.

"Thank you," Steele said. "Wise choice."

He emerged on the second floor onto Sawtooth Main and a hive of buzzing activity. Everything was blinding white, but the main screen across the floor was up and running, with all eight of its modules occupied by an interactive map of central Asia. Ralphy, Frankie, and four other newly recruited geeks were all at their stations at two banks of computers on the left quadrant, while a mirror quadrant on the right was occupied by four intel analysts and two comms people. They were all wearing casual civilian clothes, headsets that made them look like customer support at a credit card call center, and each station had a small flagpole and tags marked with things like PSYOPS, COVER, CRYPTO, and PERSEC, so you wouldn't have to always ask who was who. Penny Amdursky had her own station with a tag that said simply S, and Miles Turner's security goons—all former special operators—watched the proceedings from four corners, wearing blazers concealing Glock 19s and hammerless backup .38s. Steele saw Mrs. Darnstein, wearing a frumpy flowered dress, her white hair all crazy and a pair of big glasses hanging from a beaded chain, bending over Ralphy's station and wagging a finger at him. "*Never* order from Staples, Mr. Persko. We can get these things *much* cheaper through the GSA."

"What the hell happened to you now, kid?"

Steele turned to Dalton Goodhill, who'd emerged from the kitchen carrying two mugs of coffee and handed him one. He was wearing his motorcycle jacket, open in front, with his short shotgun gleaming under his armpit.

"I was ordered to foil FR." Steele took his coffee and sipped.

"You think a scar and a beard's gonna do it?" Goodhill sneered. "You should have let Kalidi cut off your ear. And what's with the cat's eyes?"

"Don't start."

"Okay, but your modeling career's in the shitter. So what did Garland say?"

"POTUS got another call from Casino. Told us to stand by for a possible extract, but there was nothing actionable yet."

"Well, there sure as hell is now."

A recessed speaker crackled from somewhere and Ted Lansky's voice boomed, "SCIF. *Now.*"

Steele and Goodhill walked over to the Sensitive Compartmented Information Facility, followed closely by Ralphy, who hustled with a laptop across the floor. The seal on the pneumatic door hissed, Betsy Roth pulled it open from the inside, and the three men walked in to find more blinding decor. The long white marble conference table slab was surrounded by matching leather task chairs, and at the far end sat Ted Lansky at the "helm," looking like he'd been up all night, which was probably true. His tie was flipped over one shoulder, his sleeves were rolled up, and his dry pipe was stuck in his teeth, which he'd never bothered to whiten even after thirty years of tobacco, coffee, and wine.

Steele quickly assessed the participants. Penny Amdursky was seated on the far-left side of the table near Lansky, which meant that whatever was coming would require gear. Next to her was Miles Turner, which revealed nothing, because security was always part of the game. Next to Turner was Allie Whirly, which meant someone would be flying somewhere—Steele's stinging eyes stopped right there for a second because Allie was wearing an unzipped A-2 flight jacket that looked like a butter soft Bloomingdale's version, and underneath that, a very snug, horizontally striped, blue and white top. Past her was Shane Wiley, a keeper without a trained Alpha as yet, so that was curious. Betsy was cruising the room, dropping Eyes Only briefing packets with diagonal red tape seals in front of each chair.

"Looks like an aircraft carrier for UFOs," Goodhill said about the white marble table slab.

"Shut up and sit, Blade," Lansky said as he perused a thick briefing book.

"Top of the morning to you too, sir," Goodhill muttered.

Betsy Roth shut the door, punched a keypad lock, a bolt chunked home, and the shades rolled down over the double-paned glass walls, obscuring the conference room from the rest of the TOC floor. Steele, Goodhill, and Persko took their seats across from their comrades.

"You three open your packets," Lansky said. He was still reading something and didn't look up. "You've all got new covers and legends."

Ralphy's eyes went wide and he whispered to Steele, "I've never had a cover. Why do I need a cover? I like my name."

Steele found Betsy leaning over his left shoulder.

"Yours is Matthew Schneider," she said. She was wearing some kind of heady perfume.

"Schneider?" Steele pulled his chin back. "What the hell kind of name is that?"

"It doesn't matter," Betsy whispered in his ear. "I'd screw you even if it was Gooseberry." She looked up to see Allie glaring at her across the table, blew her a kiss, and said, "And you too, flygirl. I'm ecumenical."

"*Schneider,*" Goodhill snickered.

"Laugh it up, Blade," Betsy said to him. "Yours is Samuel Katz."

"All right, people," Lansky said as he closed his briefing book. "Listen up." He clicked a smart tablet in front of him and its mirror image appeared on a large flat screen behind his head. It was an interactive map of north-central China and the Mongolian border, and wherever he tapped on his tablet a glowing red marker appeared on the map. "Approximately two weeks back, we think a CCP level four or five biowarfare research lab was destroyed right here. Persko spotted it first, NRO confirmed, then a KH-11 Keyhole was tasked. Found a smoking hole in a mountaintop. All the alphabets thought it was an accident." He meant the various intelligence agencies around the Beltway. He looked up at his audience. "With me so far?"

They all made affirmative noises. Allie Whirly touched Steele's shoe under the table with her boot, pointed at his cheek, and cocked her head. He mimed a shaving mishap and focused back on Lansky.

"Right after that," the director went on, "an alleged Chinese informant reached out to the White House, claiming that the CCP is about to draw us into a war."

"Oh no," Penny Amdursky whispered.

"Don't get your panties in a wad yet, S," Lansky said. "There's more."

And the political correctness award goes to . . . not you, Steele warned Lansky in his head.

"A few days ago, this source made contact again and claimed to be ready to share concrete intel on his claim, but only if we'd pick him up . . . here." Lansky tapped his tablet again, and the map on the wall switched to a view of a small atoll off of Miyako-jima, two hundred kilometers east of Taiwan. "However, last night, SEAL Delivery Vehicle Team One deployed from a sub out there, reconned the atoll, and found NAFT."

"What's NAFT?" Ralphy whispered to Steele.

Lansky heard him and said, "Not a fucking thing. Just crabs. And finally, also last night, we received hot intel that in fact that Level Five lab in China was *not* destroyed in a mishap, but was subjected to a helicopter-borne assault. All laboratory personnel were killed except one, and that person has found shelter . . . here." He tapped the tablet again, and the wall screen switched to lower Mongolia. "She's a full bird colonel in the CCP and she's being protected by some very accommodating Mongol villagers. We don't know who wants her dead, but if we don't get to her first, she will be."

Lansky looked up from his tablet at the team members there in his SCIF, but he was seeing the previous evening's late-night rendezvous with Thorn McHugh, on the grounds of the Army Navy Country Club. McHugh had called the meet, and Lansky had found him sitting on a bench in the dark, wearing a smart fedora, a trench coat, and holding a worn paperback copy of an F. Scott Fitzgerald novel. But he knew he wasn't going to get a lecture about American literature. Old spies used old ways.

"I received a transmission from a very old and trusted source," McHugh had said as Lansky sat down.

"Using what method? Morse code?" Lansky had quipped, then was jabbed by such a hard glare from McHugh that he thought, *Jesus. That's probably true.*

"Belay the flippancy, Theodore. This is serious business," McHugh had said. He opened the book, showed Lansky a page with many words circled in pencil, then closed it again. "We have some very precious human cargo, who may prove to be the most valuable Beijing defector of your lifetime, requesting rescue and recovery, posthaste."

Then McHugh had gone on to lay out the details, including the precise location in the lats and longs relayed by Tenzin, and he added that should the monk wish to come along too, Lansky should ensure that happened as well.

None of this was relayed by McHugh in the form of a suggestion or request. Only a small slice of the Program's multimillion-dollar budget was formally linked, under heavy classification and cover, to the DoD, and only that so Mrs. Darnstein and Penny Amdursky could utilize government resources. The rest was completely ghosted from all federal records and supplied by wealthy persons unknown. Thorn McHugh was the point man for those silent patriots, as well as the informal chairman of Cemetery Whisper, an organization of like-minded, former intelligence officers worldwide. If McHugh "suggested" a mission, he'd already consulted with someone high above Lansky's pay grade, perhaps even the president himself.

Lansky had quickly understood the importance of what McHugh was telling him, and had promised to fire off an urgent flash.

"Yes, very good." Thorn had patted his knee, taken his book and his cane, and said as he left, "Make the eggbeaters whirl. . . ."

Then Lansky was back in the SCIF, his flashback having lasted mere seconds.

"All right, people. Assets," he said and looked at Allie Whirly. "Let's start with you. What've we got for transport left over at Langley AFB?"

"Um, just a Little Bird, sir." She meant an MD 500 light assault and reconnaissance helicopter. "The Gulfstream's gone."

"Well, beg something from the air force, and a crew. If they give you a hard time, call NSA Garland's aide and have her twist some nuts." Lansky looked next at Miles Turner. "What's our status on Alphas?"

"We've accepted two so far," Miles said. "But they just started OTC. An SF team sergeant from Third Group and an air force shooter."

"Is that the Moody chick?" Lansky asked.

"I thought she was pretty nice," Betsy Roth offered.

"Moody *Air Force Base*, genius," Lansky snapped at his adjutant. Betsy blushed.

"No frickin' way are they ready," Dalton Goodhill growled. "That SF dude's shaky on urban cover. . . ."

"Slick is ready," Shane Wiley said about his prospective new Alpha. "She's good in the woods, good on the street, and blooded.

Everybody makes fun of those air force Base Defense Squadron types, but she took down a motorcycle bomber at Kandahar with a 249 from the top of an MRAP, and when it jammed, she got down and finished off his partner with her M9."

"I like her," Lansky said. "Take her. But we need one more besides Steele, in case he gets KIA'd." He said that without apology or emotion, then looked back at Miles and said, "You're on."

"Damn." Miles shook his head. He'd promised his wife that he'd never again deploy and he murmured, "I was gonna stay married this time."

Lansky turned to Penny Amdursky.

"S, what you got for support out there? Let's say if our FOB's somewhere in range of the target, like Vladivostok."

"Sir, all of our safe houses and slicks were shut down." Penny raised her palms like a helpless-looking emoji. "When it looked permanent, Mrs. D had sort of a liquidation sale. We haven't reconstituted yet. I don't have any assets out there."

"I do," Steele said.

"Reliable?" Lansky asked him.

"Yeah, but pricey."

"Okay," Lansky said, and then to Goodhill, "Watch his spending."

"I'll keep my hand in his pocket," Goodhill said.

"I knew it." Miles grinned at Blade, who shot him the bird.

"All right, people," Lansky said. "You're going to work this problem all day, and you're going to launch tonight. Persko, I want you sucking intel from all sources so Stalker Seven and his crew don't wind up in the shit. Betsy, go through State, lie your ass off, and get me clearances for cargo from Russia to Ulaanbaatar. I'll handle the Mongolian airspace. Clear?"

They all mumbled rogers and yessirs, and Lansky turned to Steele.

"You're point on this mission. Got anything to say?"

"No, sir," Steele said. "Show up, kill the bad guys, rescue the damsel in distress. What could possibly go wrong?"

CHAPTER 26

ANKILILOAKA, MADAGASCAR

He was a very small boy, in a very large jungle.

He was called Fanamby, which meant "challenger" in the Merina dialect of Malagasy, the national language of Madagascar, and he'd been so named by his father and mother because he'd barely survived his birth.

At nine years old, Fanamby was not much larger than a fully grown bamboo lemur, a koala-like primate found only in the rain forests of their tropical island off the coast of eastern Africa. Fanamby was fascinated by the elusive, cocoa-colored furry creatures, and he and his best friend, Tombovelo, would often shed their pink buttoned shirts and leather sandals, and in only their blue shorts, stalk the creatures through the dripping canopies and shadows of the enormous baobab trees. The boys loved the cuddly jungle mammals, they had similar large, gleaming dark eyes, and the lemurs laughed at them while they looked down at the boys from dizzying heights and chewed their bamboo shoots.

Fanamby's mother, Lanitra, spent her mornings hiking for

miles with a plastic yellow jerrican to fetch fresh water from pools of rain—their small village of thatched huts had no wells or pipes or faucets. Lanitra and her sisters spent the afternoons weaving colorful scarves from harvested silkworms, which they sold in Ankililoaka to the tourists from Europe, who always loved the simple people for two days or so and then went home. Fanamby's father, Haja, was a constable with the La Gendarmerie Nationale, and Fanamby was very proud of him in his dark green tunic with his shiny badge and his French képi policeman's cap. Lanitra and Haja were poor, but they loved each other very much, and that made Fanamby a happy boy.

Fanamby would venture alone, and often very far, into the jungles of the vast Parc National Mikea, to bring a full basket of wild silkworm cocoons to his mother, which she called "living gold." Sometimes he would meet Tombovelo, who also collected cocoons for his mother, and they would hike all the way through the forests, ten miles, to the emerald waters of the African sea. By sunset, Fanamby would be very tired, and would struggle back up the long grassy hill to their village west of the thunder ridge with his burden.

But today, he wasn't dawdling on his way home for his dinner of stewed zebu beef, fat rice, and lasary tomato and onion salad.

Today, he was running.

"Why do you run, Fanamby?" Haja had come home to the village for dinner and was sitting beside Lanitra on a three-legged stool. "Was it a lion?" He grinned at his son, who had dropped his basket of gray-white cocoons and was bending over, gripping his small knees and breathless. There were no lions in Madagascar.

"No, Father, no," Fanamby gasped. "It was a whale."

Lanitra looked up from where she was sitting cross-legged on a straw mat with her three sisters. They were spinning silk from the sticky cocoons with bamboo rods that they turned in their brown palms.

"A whale? Do not spin tales to your father, boy."

"I am not lying, Mama." Fanamby's dark eyes were very wide and his small face glistened with sweat. He pointed back at the edge of the jungle far below their hill, where the farmers' bony white-and-black cattle were nosing at the shoots and grass. "It is so big!" He stretched his little arms as wide as he could. "It is white and just like the whales we saw when Uncle Andry once took us out in his fishing boat."

His father frowned and got up from his stool. His son had been taught to never lie. He picked up a metal tin cup and poured some water from Lanitra's jerrican and made Fanamby drink.

"Slow down, Fanamby," he said. "How could a whale be in the jungle?"

"I do not know, Father." Fanamby slurped and then gripped the cup in his trembling hands. "But it is there, in the small valley between the tallest baobabs, covered by many leaves, and I was frightened and I threw a stone at it."

"Did it move?"

"Don't be silly, Haja," Lanitra said to her husband while her sisters grinned and shook their heads.

"It did not move, Father," Fanamby said, "but it made a sound."

"What sound?"

"A sound like when we play Kudoda and the stones fall in the metal bowl."

Haja thought about that for a moment. A whale. A whale with a skin like a Kudoda bowl. It made no sense, but Fanamby never lied.

"Show me," he said, and Fanamby turned and started right off back down the hill, and his father followed.

"Haja!" Lanitra called. "You are working!"

Haja touched the revolver on his hip and called back to her over his shoulder. "I am investigating, woman. That is my work."

Even though Fanamby was exhausted, he was only nine, and the village children of that age—and everywhere else in fact—have reserves of strength that have long left their elders. It was hard for Haja to keep up with his little boy and he kept calling out to him to slow down. At last he had to order him to stop while he caught up and took his small hand.

"Father, we must hurry," Fanamby said. "The whale might get away."

"He will not get away, son." Haja was still wondering what this creature might be, or how it had found its way so deep in the jungle from the sea. But he supposed such things were possible. The typhoons could wash many strange things ashore and deeper inland than one could imagine. "And if it does, then perhaps it was only sleeping."

"Yes, yes, but let's hurry!"

Fanamby pulled away again, and Haja quick-marched after him into the jungle. It was already growing dark and he wished he'd thought to bring his large policeman's flashlight. The night owls were cooing, the ring-tailed lemurs were howling in the trees, and an ominous roll of thunder fluttered the high canopies of leaves beneath glimpses of angry charcoal clouds.

They tramped across the rotting floor of fallen tapia and Bismarck palms, with Haja swinging his muscled arms to strike away clinging vines, and Fanamby hopping over clusters of Darwin's orchids as their silky white petals spun to the ground behind his sandaled feet. And then they were rising up through the brush, along a steepening slippery grade, where at the top Haja could see the crowns of the baobab, like the wigs of sinful dancers, silhouetted against the sky. They broke out onto a ridgeline where the jungle thinned, and breathless from that last climb, they both looked down.

It was there, below, in the lush moist valley, which was filling with evening shadows. And indeed it looked like a giant white whale. Its bloated body was the size of the missionary school bus in Ankililoaka, and its thick tail was as long as that and more. It had a pair of large gleaming glassy eyes above a bulbous black nose, and fat black protrusions below its belly that certainly looked like fins to Fanamby. It had been covered with a blanket of what looked like a fisherman's net woven with palm fronds, but there'd been a furious storm from the sea just one day before, and the winds had swept most of it away. There were strange black markings on the body just behind its gills.

"You see, Father?" Fanamby was practically hopping up and down as he gripped Haja's uniform pant leg. "You *see*?"

"Yes, my son. And I am proud of you, and pleased that you did not lie." Haja pulled Fanamby close and gently tousled his wiry hair. "But it is not a whale." He opened a leather pouch on his belt and unholstered a walkie-talkie. "It is a helicopter."

CHAPTER 27

Hank Steele only emerged from his alias, George Wheelwright, when he was completely alone.

Even then, it would have been hard to discern. His voice didn't change. He wore the same clothes. Their culinary tastes were identical. As George, he'd smoked the same pipe for eight years in Africa, as he had for a decade as Rick Granger in Ho Chi Minh City, and before that as Marshal Fenault in French Polynesia.

All of those covers had been provided by members of Cemetery Whisper, the ghostly group of veteran spies and special operators of loosely allied nations, who cared for one another once they were burned. A desperate man or woman, somewhere in the world on the run, would find salvation in a fresh passport, supporting papers and funds, usually in a graveyard dead drop, and there they would bury their pasts. After that, they could only confess who they really were to themselves. Those were the rules of redemption.

Hank spoke fluent Russian, French, and Vietnamese, but

George would never reveal those skills because they were the sorts of clues that could expose a man's trail. Hank was an expert in firearms, ballistics, explosives, and unusual modes of transportation. George knew a lot about these things as well, but ostensibly only from books. Hank had a second-degree black belt in Tang Soo Do, the Korean martial art that combines tae kwon do, subak, and Chinese kung fu. George knew how to handle himself, but mostly from back-alley brawls as a kid in Connecticut. Hank eschewed cell phones, smartphones, tablets, and computers of any type, because they were the nemeses of any man who didn't want to be found. George also eschewed such devices, but because he was sure they caused cancer.

They both liked animals. They both liked kids. They both had secrets, but who didn't?

There had only been one great love of Hank's life. He never expected to find that kind of love again, nor did he try. George occasionally flirted with the ladies, but only because they thought him attractive, and such innocent encounters reminded his true self, Hank Steele, that he was still alive.

If anyone wanted to see the real Hank Steele, it would happen as it did on this balmy evening at his house on the hill, when George Wheelwright opened his hollowed-out copy of a novel called *Winter* by Len Deighton. There in the carved-out space between the pages was an old black-and-white photo of Hank Steele in his U.S. Army Special Forces dress greens, with Susan Steele as his beautiful young wife, and their eight-year-old son, Eric—all of them grinning, all of them happy, and none of them imagining that very soon after, the three would never be together again. . . .

Hank heard a horse on the narrow road that rose up from

Mabuda Farms. He looked once more at the old photograph, placed it back in the hardcover book, and the book went back on his shelf of old classics and tomes. Then he listened to hear if the horse would pass by or whether its hooves would crunch on his perimeter of seashells and stones. A moment later, they made that sound, and he got up from his rattan chair and went out on his front porch. The teakwood slats creaked loudly under his feet. He'd built them that way on purpose, just as the samurais built their homes.

"*Boa noite,* George." A young girl greeted him in Portuguese from the spotted mare's saddle. She was twelve and pretty with beaded hair.

"*Boa noite*, Carlota." George walked over and stroked the horse's nose. He was still wearing his jeans and bush shirt from his excursion with Kruvalt, but no shoes. Carlota was one of the girls who worked with him at the stables.

"I have for you a telephone." She grinned with very white teeth and dimples. She liked practicing her English with George. She handed him an open flip phone that he recognized as one from Mabuda Farms's front office. It was a little slick because she'd been clutching it for the entire mile's ride.

"Wheelwright," he said into the phone.

"Carlota told me her whole life story, mate." It was Kruvalt, with a smile in his voice.

"She's a lovely girl and will be Mozambique's beauty queen someday." Wheelwright smiled up at Carlota, and she giggled and blushed. "But you made her ride up here for a reason."

"I did in-bloody-deed," Kruvalt said and his voice turned darker. "That fat fuck Boondo from SERNIC got a call from the Gendarmerie in Antananarivo."

"Madagascar?"

"That's right. Seems some constable and his kid from Ankil-iloaka were out tramping about in the Parc National Mikea. Know where that is?"

"Southwest, on the sea."

"Spot on. Guess what they found."

"Don't make me guess, Rod. Carlota's waiting." He'd walked a few feet away, and he glanced back up at her and winked. She blushed again.

"A bloody big white helicopter, George. A fucking Mi-8, in fact, dumped in a cut in the jungle with a camouflage net and all. Kid only spotted it 'cause they had a blowout last week and the wind must've stripped her cover."

"Are we surprised, Rodney?" Hank instantly pictured the big Russian-made flying machine with its bulbous body, twin turbines, and long tail boom.

"Fuck no."

"Did it have markings on it?"

"Big black letters. U.N. I told those gendarmes to set up a perimeter and stay the hell away from it until someone from infectious diseases sniffs its arse."

"You know what this means, right?" Hank said.

"It means that poor bastard from the *Windhoek* wasn't hallucinating, or lying."

"Where's he now?"

"In the morgue."

"And where's that hand, Rodney?"

"In the freezer beside him."

"Keep it there, Rod. And I think you should put a twenty-four-seven guard shift on it."

"Already done."

Hank thought for a moment and said, "Somebody's got to take a look at that hand. Somebody else."

"Got any ideas, mate?"

"Yes, I do."

"All right. Let me know whenever you want to come clean. I'm all ears."

Hank Steele nodded at the cell phone. "Soon," was all he said, and he flipped it closed.

He walked into the house, found some red apples in his kitchen fruit basket, and brought two outside, one for Carlota and one for the mare. The horse devoured hers with her domino-size teeth and big lips, while Carlota frowned at her apple and said, "George, no candy?"

"No, sweetheart," he said. "They're bad for that beautiful smile." He handed her back the flip phone as she giggled and rode away.

Hank stood for a while, watching the girl and her horse until they became small figurines in the wind-stroked grass on the long hill down to Mabuda Farms, and then disappeared. He saw a cluster of flickers in the darkening valley where Chino was making fires to cook for the guests outside, and above him the sky was purple and pink and the black silhouettes of bat hawks wheeled. He would be sad to leave this place, but he knew it was time.

He'd been hungry when one of Kruvalt's men had driven him back from Maputo. Now he only wanted a drink and a smoke. He went into the house and came out with his pipe, a leather pouch of tobacco, an imported bottle of Dewar's, and a cup made from a cow hoof, no ice. There was a chair on the front porch that he'd made from bamboo poles and cowhide, and next to that a table made from a Bugarubu drum, and he sat down, leaned back, lit up his pipe, and sipped.

The Program. That's where his life had turned. . . .

Before that, he'd been just another team sergeant in a 7th Special Forces Group Operational Detachment Alpha. Sure, he was proud to be one of the "quiet professionals," and his 201 file had swelled with overseas missions and citations, but he'd felt no more special than any other green beret. After all, his father had fought as a Marine in the Pacific. He couldn't beat that and he didn't try.

Young SF NCOs had a tendency to marry the first girl who'd have them, given their long stints away. Jolana was a Czech beauty who didn't know any better. She'd weep whenever he left her, which was often, and they'd had a young daughter, Marla. The divorce was plain and simple, typical for Fort Bragg. That place was replete with young mothers who quickly got wise and then married lawyers or accountants. Then Marla had grown up and had her own child, so Hank now had a granddaughter. He wondered who she was and what had become of her.

He was nothing to her. He wished he'd been more.

He'd fallen much harder for Susan Gannon, a tall, patient, beautiful nurse who could have been a fashion model. Being married to Susan was a blessing each day, even though he was living a lie. He still wore his Special Forces uniform, but that was just cover. By the time they met, he'd already been in the Program for years. Together they had a son, Eric, whom they both adored, and whom Hank thought of as his redemption for all the dark things he'd done for his country.

"Might I buy a green beanie a refill?"

He heard that voice again, that semi-British Yalie twang, in some bar on Bragg whose name he'd forgotten. The man was older, debonair, with a sly smile and a cane. Soon after that, Hank had volunteered for something that had no official name. And then came the missions, one after another, to places so dangerous that few men ever returned. And finally, Russia, and he hadn't returned either.

Camp Number 722. A terrorist training camp whose candidates Hank was supposed to kill, and where he'd discovered at the very last minute that all the trainees were children. That's where he'd drawn the line and that's where his country had burned him. The Russians had sent him to Lubyanka, where the KGB had tortured and tried to turn him, and failed, and eventually a colonel named Putin had, with ill-disguised pleasure, told him that the U.S. government had convicted him in absentia of treason. Then it was five more years in a hellhole called Black Dolphin prison, until he'd finally dug his way out and escaped.

But he couldn't go home. Ever. If he did, Susan and Eric would find themselves the targets of hatred and disdain forever, like the wife and children of Lee Harvey Oswald. He still loved them, terribly, as much as he had on the last day he saw them. But he'd sworn to keep them safe. They were his final mission.

Yet just a year or so before, he'd heard from another member of Cemetery Whisper, a burned Russian Spetsnaz named Vitaly Chak, who'd told him that Eric had run a renegade solo mission to southern Russia and had tried to find him. That's why he'd sent that postcard. He knew it would hurt, but sometimes a man had to reach out from the grave.

This thing with the *Windhoek* was churning in his guts. Something told him it wasn't a one-off. A Chinese PLA rifle bullet? Men in "spacesuits"? One biowarfare plague had already nearly destroyed humanity, and he suspected this hit was something similar and could potentially be much worse. He knew that his son was an Alpha, and he knew that he had to see him. But Hank Steele wasn't the sort of man who lied to himself. It was partially about the *Windhoek* and what was going on, and more than partially, because time was going too fast and he needed that one last chance.

He had no idea how or why this had happened, but in his head he heard Bob Dylan's prescient tune, "Simple Twist of Fate."

He'd finished two brimming slugs of Scotch, but he didn't remotely feel it. He got up with his pipe, went into the house to his study at the very back, flicked on a battery lamp, and rolled up the black-and-orange Sankara rug from the floor. He removed three floorboards, then lifted the heavy mortar ammunition crate by its rope handles from the musky darkness below.

He locked the study door. He opened the crate. Inside, next to his Celestron spotting scope and a Vietnam-era French MAT-49 submachine gun, was the old black-and-green, Ten-Tec Century 21 transceiver, along with a set of C-47 pilot headphones and a telegraph key mounted on a polished wooden board. He set them all out on his scarred candlenut desk, then removed a large ashtray sitting on the top of a fruit box next to the desk. Inside was a small gas generator. He started it up and plugged in the radio set.

He sat down in his curved-back rattan desk chair and looked at the telegraph key. He wouldn't need a Morse code chart, because every number and letter was carved into his brain. But he would need one more thing.

He got up and went back to the mortar crate and took out a book.

It was a very old copy of F. Scott Fitzgerald's classic *Tender Is the Night*.

CHAPTER 28

The Program's Gulfstream G650 transcontinental jet had been decommissioned and sold off to an Arab sheik from Dubai, but the air force version sitting on the tarmac looked very much like it, and would certainly do. It wasn't easy to recover and reassemble assets after so much time, and the support staff at Q Street, particularly Penny Amdursky, felt like they'd held a garage sale and were now trying to track down the neighbors who'd bought all their toys.

But it paid to have friends in high places. One call from Katie Garland over to the air force chief of staff at the Pentagon, and lo and behold, they had a jet.

Also, for some inexplicable reason, perhaps owing to a bureaucratic glitch, all the contents of the Program's team room—on the second floor in the back of a hangar belonging to Air Combat Command's 1st Fighter Wing—were still there. All the weapons and tactical gear were still in the armory. No one had touched any of the Alpha lockers, including those of the deceased, which traditionally remained undisturbed forever, like the cocoons of sailors buried at sea. And while the palm print and retina readers outside the team room's half-ton iron door had been dormant for nearly a year, Ralphy Persko had blinked them alive from Q Street with thirty keystrokes and a prayer.

Steele arrived at Langley with his small quick reaction force in two of Miles's security Suburbans. The composition of this QRF was unusual in that Alphas generally operated as singletons with only a keeper nearby. In this case, the mission required some redundancy, plus additional firepower, so he had Dalton Goodhill along, then brand-new Slick, who hadn't even received her OTC tab yet (technically, those completing the operator training course were awarded only virtual tabs, because there were no uniforms on which to wear them), her keeper Shane Wiley (having lost Collins Austin to the female assassin Lila Kalidi he was regretting now that he'd put Slick up for this), and Miles Turner, who wasn't an Alpha at all. Allie Whirly was also along, but she had no role on the manifest and would be there just in case someone needed to steal an aircraft downrange. Ralphy's computer had spit out a name for the mission, Purple Rain, which was random and could in no way be connected to China or Mongolia, because that's how the algorithm was designed.

This time Steele remembered to pluck out his brown contact lens before plugging his eyeball into the retina reader, and when the door lock clicked and they hauled it open, he squeezed the lens back in and Allie said, "The green eyes are so much prettier."

"Maybe, but I'm Matthew Schneider now, and I believe that's sexual harassment."

"I'd harass you all night long, Mr. Schneider." She grinned a wolfish grin.

Inside the team room, Steele walked past the Alpha lockers and tried to ignore the engraved nameplates of Jonathan Raines, Collins Austin, and Martin Farro, which were now essentially metallic tombs containing personal effects that no one would ever touch—a Program tradition. He punched the digital locks on the Steelwater safes containing long guns and heavy weapons, and turned around to summon Slick, whose real name was Melody Spintrap (for which she'd been thoroughly bullied in middle school), and was now Stalker Eleven. Next to her stood Miles, wearing an expression that said he hadn't signed up for this, and behind them Dalton Goodhill and Shane Wiley.

Miles and Slick joined Steele and they started selecting firepower. Steele, a firm believer in cross-pollination, decided they should all be using the same ammo, so the men pulled HK416s with Aimpoint CompM4 red dot sights from the racks, and Slick chose an M249 Squad Automatic Weapon para version with a collapsible tube stock and an ACOG sight. They drew long black duffels from the lockers and packed up the guns, lots of empty magazines, and three drums for Slick's light machine gun, but then Steele locked the safes.

"What about handguns and LBVs?" Miles said. "And comms."

"And maybe some grenades, boss?" Slick said to Steele. "Some ammo?"

"We'll get all that from the supplier downrange," Steele said. "And the parachutes."

"Parachutes?" Slick's blond eyebrows rose. "Um, you know I've only done static line, right? No HALO or HAHO." She meant the two variations of special operations high altitude parachuting.

"No sweat. We'll be keeping it simple," Steele said. "LALO."

"What's that?"

"Low altitude, low opening. Static line, no reserves."

"Oh." Slick swallowed and looked up at Miles.

"Don't say I didn't warn ya," he said.

"You three look like the Mod Squad," Shane Wiley commented from where he, Goodhill, and Allie were standing side by side.

"Yup," Allie agreed. "Linc, Pete, and Julie."

"Who's that?" Slick asked.

"Never mind," Goodhill said. "You're too young."

They took the duffels, locked up the team room, and headed back out to the tarmac.

The two pilots and a crew chief were waiting outside the Gulfstream. All three had previously worked for the Program and had returned to air force assignments, but Ted Lansky had yanked them back with a signed presidential order, for which refusal was not an option. Steele recognized them as the same ones he'd once hijacked for his unauthorized trip to find his father in Russia. The chief pilot looked up at Steele's bearded face and squinted.

"You look kind of familiar."

"Yeah, I was once an uncooperative passenger, but I'm all better now."

"Oh, shit . . . You're not still carrying that hand cannon, are you?"

Steele smiled and pulled open his leather bomber jacket. His father's 1911 was right there in a hip holster. The pilot shook his head.

"That's why I never liked grunts." He cocked his chin at his crew, and the three climbed aboard their jet.

The Gulfstream's gleaming white fuselage began to glow with a strange red and blue oscillation, and Steele and his team turned and squinted down toward the end of the airstrip. A convoy of dark vehicles was cruising rapidly closer and Steele realized that all of the base's air activity had stopped. They looked like government, and as they neared he heard fender flags whipping and saw motorcycle outriders.

"What the hell's this now," Miles said. "I'm up-to-date on child support, so it can't be that."

The convoy made a long loop to the right, across the wide runway, then came back and stopped in a semicircle, cupping the Gulfstream from about seventy meters away. There were two motorcycle cops on Harleys, a black Suburban, the presidential Beast, another Suburban, a tactical truck, and two more bike riders. Steele figured this might be National Security Advisor Garland again, perhaps bearing some last-ditch "attaboy" message, but the Beast's front passenger door opened and the president's lead Secret Service agent came around and crossed the tarmac.

"Evening," said Jack. "You're Steele, right?"

"For you guys, yes."

"You carrying?"

Steele opened his jacket, unholstered his handgun, handed it over to Dalton Goodhill, and said, "Nope."

"Good," Jack said. "Let's take a walk."

He and Steele crossed the tarmac, heading toward the Beast as more Secret Service agents appeared. A rear door opened, Katie Garland got out, then Ted Lansky, and finally President Rockford himself. Steele heard Allie Whirly behind him whistling low in amazement and then Goodhill hissing at her, "Flygirl, shut up."

John Rockford shook Steele's hand. He was dressed for some sort of occasion, wearing his signature woolen navy-blue coat, dark suit, white shirt, and scarlet tie. Before he could say anything the whine of heavy jet engines loomed, and they all turned to watch Air Force One floating down from the evening sky, and its tires touched the tarmac without even a squeal and its engines reversed, then faded away. Rockford smiled at Steele and gestured over his shoulder at the Gulfstream.

"Mine's bigger than yours," he said.

"No argument there, Mr. President."

"What happened to you?" Katie Garland, buttoned up against the cold in a trench coat, was looking at Steele's eyes, bandage, and beard.

"My old face is on too many servers, ma'am." He wasn't going to be flippant with the national security advisor. "We're going for a few changes."

"Oh, I see," she said, though it was clear she was no fan of scruffiness.

"Steele," the president said, "Ted briefed me on something a short while ago. I know you're about to launch, but I told him you needed to know." Rockford cocked his large head at Lansky, who stepped forward and seemed to be chewing his pipe stem, as if he were about to convey bad news.

"Okay, Stalker Seven," Lansky said. Even if the president was using Steele's name in an open forum, he wasn't going to. "Here it is, and I'm going to keep it short because the president has to go. Earlier this evening, the man with the cane received another encrypted radio message, but from Africa this time."

Steele knew he meant Thorn McHugh, who'd supplied the intel about Colonel Liang and apparently still had such an extensive network of informants that it would have made Julian Assange jealous.

"This message was long, detailed, and came from Mozambique," Lansky went on. "In short, the sender relayed that someone hit a cargo ship out there and killed the entire crew of eighty-two, except for one survivor, who's no longer surviving. Sender thinks a biowarfare agent was used, that the Chinese are involved, and believes he has proof."

"All right, sir," Steele said. He wasn't sure what Lansky was getting at, since that wouldn't affect his pending mission. "Sounds like it might be connected to this PLA laboratory director we're about to go snatch, but—" He stopped talking because the president had put his hand on his shoulder.

"The sender's your father, Eric."

Steele felt all the blood drain from his face. It usually took a lot to spike his adrenaline and his heart rate, but he felt his pulse pounding in his neck and a weird sort of squeal in his ears. He hadn't heard that sound since the last time a grenade had detonated too close.

"Yes. And?" That was all he said to Lansky, because he didn't feel able to say more. His teeth were grinding, his mind reeling. He was trying to remain professional about this.

"He wants to see you," Lansky said.

Tell him I'm busy, banged through Steele's head. *Tell him he's twenty-five fucking years too late.* But he didn't say anything like that. He said nothing.

And then he felt the president's gloved hand on the back of his neck, and he was walking Steele away from everyone else, another ten meters out on the tarmac, so they could be alone. The only sound on the wind was the low rumble of the Harleys and the distant turbines of Air Force One somewhere down the field. The president turned him around. His thick blond hair was fluttering in the breeze and his blue eyes were gleaming.

"Listen, son," he said. "There's a shitstorm brewing between us and Beijing, and I've got to know if it's real. I need you to go get that Chinese colonel and keep her alive. And then I need you to get her to Taiwan while I figure out if I have to crank up the entire Pacific Fleet and throw the toggles on a bunch of nuclear Tomahawks from safe to armed. . . . Now I know this is all kind of hard, but it's a to-be-or-not-to-be moment, slings and arrows and all that Will Shakespeare shit. *Comprendé?*"

"Yes, Mr. President." There was no hesitation in Steele's voice. Presidents had that effect on him.

"Good. Now go get her, and bring her down to their special ops base at Pingtung. And if your dad actually shows up, try not to be an asshole. You're gonna be a father yourself soon."

Steele stared at his commander in chief, and blinked.

"Yeah, I'm the president." Rockford smirked. "I know stuff. And besides, everyone's kid thinks their dad's a moron at one time or another. Trust me, yours will too." The president looked at his watch. "Now let's get the hell out of here. I've got a midnight rally in Tucson, and you've got serious business."

"Safe travels, sir," Steele said.

"Good luck," said Rockford.

They shook hands, hard, and held it for a moment. Then they both about-faced and walked off in opposite directions, like duelers, except they didn't turn around at ten paces and shoot.

CHAPTER 29

The Crystal Tiger casino was the last place Eric Steele wanted to be after a thirteen-hour flight, a refueling stop in Anchorage, a fifteen-hour time differential, head-banging turbulence, no decent food, and no sleep. But Steele wasn't calling the shots. The man doing that was Oren Belmont, an arms dealer whose services Steele had engaged in various global hotspots, and who he also suspected of being more than eccentric, perhaps even nuts.

Belmont was somewhere in his early thirties—no one really knew because he had four different passports with conflicting dates of birth—and was half French, half Israeli, and had gained his firearms expertise from service first in the French Foreign Legion and then the Israel Defense Forces paratroops. He spoke French, Hebrew, English, German, and Russian, all with near native accents. He had girlfriends in multiple countries, dressed like a metrosexual magazine editor from Manhattan, wore outrageously expensive watches, and could tell you when the temperature of a Château Latour claret wasn't quite right, or kill you at twenty meters with a throwing knife.

His sole proprietor firm, Triple-S (Special Services Solutions), supplied much more than guns and ammunition. He seemed able to get his hands on just about anything, from Ducati motorcycles to Draeger SCUBA gear, from miniature Dry Combat Submersible submarines to DJI surveillance drones and Little Bird helicopters. Once, when Steele had found himself pursued and outnumbered in Mali by a murder squad from Islamic State, he'd called Belmont, who'd somehow made an Arava special operations aircraft land in a field and perform a rapid exfil turnaround.

Belmont's services were pricey, but he'd never gouged Steele or failed to deliver. He also had few qualms about selling to anyone, except for the ISIS types.

"I *know* I'm a death dealer, *mon ami,*" Belmont had once said to Steele over drinks in Sarajevo, "but I'll betcha the dude who sold spears and shields to the Spartans was stocking the Persians with the very same shit. Anyway, I don't sell to those motherfucking haji beheaders. Man's gotta sleep at night, right?"

Belmont knew Steele was arriving in Vladivostok with a crew, but he didn't ask why and he didn't ask who. He'd sent Steele a text in French via WhatsApp.

"*Casino Tigre De Cristal. Viens seul. Et essaye de ne pas t'habiller comme un clochard.*" Crystal Tiger Casino. Come alone. And try not to dress like a bum.

The Gulfstream had landed in Vladivostok, a port city at the southeastern tip of Russia, and Steele's "new" face made it through passport control without ringing alarms, so he stopped inwardly cursing McHugh. Comparisons are often made between Vladivostok and San Francisco, both of which border on oceans, have impressive suspension bridges, high hills of quaint stone flats, great fishing wharfs, and crowds of Chinese tourists. But Steele and his team were too spent to appreciate anything touristic. They locked their guns in the jet's cargo hold, took their backpacks, and headed for the Lotte Hotel, and hopefully, a nap.

After everyone had gone to their rooms, Steele searched the lobby for a bellhop his size, handed him four hundred euros, and said, in fluent Russian, "*Tovarich,* I don't have time to go shopping. Would you be so kind as to find me some appropriate clothes for a nightclub? Same fit as you, and keep the change."

An hour later, he was dressed to kill.

The Crystal Tiger was located on a remote patch of property twenty kilometers from the city. It was a sprawling entertainment and gambling complex, with upscale nightclubs, gaming rooms, an outdoor IMAX-size video screen across which beautiful Russian girls pranced in bikinis, and towering crystal columns bracing the high entrance doors. He walked in wearing a black velvet jacket over a cream silk shirt, charcoal twill slacks, and black loafers. The lobby was as large as the MGM Grand's in Las Vegas, and the pulsating music shivering the chandeliers was Grace singing "You Don't Own Me."

He knew where he'd find Oren Belmont, so he headed straight for the baccarat room. Sure enough, Belmont was perched, alone, at a kidney-shaped table, smoking a Balkan Sobranie and ogling the busty blond dealer instead of his mountain of chips. He had jelled brown hair, long sharp eyebrows, wily dark eyes, a square jaw, and a paratrooper's lithe physique. He was wearing a buttery black leather blazer over a chartreuse silk shirt and black trousers. He looked like a panther toying with a lamb.

"Nice threads, dude." Belmont smirked as Steele took a seat.

"Glad you approve."

Belmont peered at Steele's face. "But that beard and the scab make you look like a fucked-up kibbutznik. Are we calling you Shlomo now?"

"Matthew will be fine."

"Way too New Testament, but whatever." Belmont took a drag off his Sobranie, which Steele realized was camouflaged weed, filled his pockets with chips, and pushed a tip stack across to the dealer. Then he squeezed her fingers and said, in Russian, "I'll pick you up Saturday night, baby. Wear something that'd make mama faint."

The blond girl giggled, Belmont leaned across the table, tongue kissed her, and said to Steele, "*Allons-y.*"

They walked into the Crystal Tiger's main nightclub. The decor was red and black, and it was packed to the gills with patrons and bar girls weaving among the tables. At the close end was a stage with gleaming stripper poles around which tall Russian beauties snaked and twitched, their seminude bodies painted in purple tiger stripes. As they made their way to the bar at the back, Belmont slung an arm around Steele's shoulder and whispered close to his ear.

"How many are you, dude, and what's on the menu?" He had marijuana breath.

"Three kinetics, including me. I need water for the squirt guns, firecrackers, vests, radios, static line chutes, and a plane."

"That's all?" Belmont laughed. "And you're flush for that?"

Steele opened his jacket and showed him a thick stack of euros. They were all five hundreds.

"That's the deposit," he said. "I'll wire the rest."

"You're my moneyball, *bay-bee.*" Belmont slapped Steele's butt. "If I wasn't straight, I'd do you."

"You'd do me anyway, ass hat, if the price was right."

"True." Belmont snickered.

"So why'd you drag me all the way out here?" Steele said.

"To make sure you're clean, no tail." Belmont winked at a young man sitting at the bar, who Steele recognized as his taxi driver.

"You're such a trusting soul," he said.

"*Toi aussi.* That's why we're both still alive."

Belmont pushed into the bar and ordered two large vodkas, neat. Steele waved his off, so the arms dealer shrugged, downed both drinks, saw Steele's expression, and said, "Dude, I *always* drink and drive!"

Ten minutes later they were doing 140 kilometers per hour in a green-and-black Audi R8 V10 Spyder convertible, which would have made Steele long for his GTO, except Belmont had the top down and it was midnight and freezing. Belmont had pulled on a leather Snoopy helmet and goggles, and with the unbuckled earflaps whipping in the wind and his white teeth lit by the dashboard, he looked completely insane, while Steele was hatless and felt like he was freefalling in Antarctica. The car's speakers were blasting out Lil Pump's "Gucci Gang," the Lazurnaya Ulitsa coastal "highway" was no wider than a Virginia driveway, and the only good things about the ride were that it would be short, they couldn't make vapid small talk over the wind, and if Belmont flipped it, Steele wouldn't feel a damned thing.

Traffic thickened at the eastern outskirts of the city, so Belmont had to slow down, and as they cruised through the winding streets toward Milionka he pushed up his goggles and said, "You dig her?"

"It's a very fine car, Oren."

"She's the shit!" Belmont banged the steering wheel.

Steele had taken out his cell and texted Goodhill at the hotel, telling him to roust Miles and Allie, leave Shane and Slick behind as emergency backup, track him on his locator app, and meet at his end point. Milionka was a crusty old neighborhood of crooked red brick buildings that had once been Vladivostok's most dangerous district, replete with whorehouses, drug dens, and ruthless Chinese gang lords. Now it was a trendy cluster of cafés, hip clothing shops, and street minstrels, but at night it seemed to revert to its former sleazy status, like a municipal vampire. Belmont parked the Spyder in front of a brownstone with an iron-barred cigar shop at the bottom under a big sign in Russian that said DIM-I-ZERKALA—Smoke and Mirrors.

Goodhill, Miles, and Allie were standing in front of the shop, their breaths making blue clouds in the air. Belmont lit up another joint as he and Steele got out of the car, and he smirked at the new arrivals and said, "Is that all you got, Bro? An old dude, a brutha, and a barrista?"

Steele rolled his eyes and said to his crew, "This is our friend Oren."

"Can I kill him now?" Goodhill growled.

"Can I hold him while you kill him?" Miles said to Goodhill.

"I'm a pilot, asshole," Allie said to Belmont.

Belmont laughed and said to Steele, "I like them. Let's go."

He clicked a button on his car keys, disabling the shop's alarms, and they went inside. It looked like the kind of smoke bar you'd find on Newbury Street in Boston, with puffy leather couches, ceramic ashtrays, and pistol-size butane lighters. All the walls were lined with glass cigar cases. Belmont walked to the one at the back, pressed another button, and the case split open in the middle and both halves rolled away to reveal an old-style European elevator with an iron grate door.

He waved everyone in, but the lift didn't go up, or down. The whole thing spun around 180 degrees, and they were facing an armory four times the size of the cigar store.

"*So,* Steely? Is this cool, or what?" Belmont cooed as he pirouetted into his secret stash. "Oops, my bad . . . I mean *Matthew.*"

Steele was staring at wall racks of firearms, stacks of ammunition, RPGs, grenades, metal shelves full of load-bearing equipment, helmets, uniforms, parachute rigs, MBITR radios, drones, and electronic gear even he couldn't identify. It would have been highly unusual to find such a thing in the States, unless it was a prop house in Hollywood, but the firearms laws in Russia made it nearly impossible to buy a BB gun.

He whistled and said, "How the hell . . . ?"

"Hey, dude, I *know* people," Belmont said. Strangely, there was an old-fashioned leather barber's chair in the middle of the space, and he plopped down into it, kicked the footstool up, flipped down an armrest panel with a smart tablet on it, and said, "*Yallah,* let's shop!" He came up with a laser pointer, spun the chair like a naval antiaircraft gunner, and started firing it at pieces of equipment.

"*Drei Schützen.*" Three shooters, he sang out in German and swung to the left. "Let's go for the Marom Dolphin load-bearing vests, right over there. And the helmets. Don't forget the helmets!"

He spun to the right. "NVD PVS-14 night-vision goggles, monocular, right up there. Nice and light, right? And you can grab those T-10 chutes over there. The T-11s suck."

Goodhill, Turner, and Allie tried to keep up as they yanked items from shelves and made a pile on the floor.

"See those radios up there?" Belmont spun to the left and tipped back. "Tadiran PNR-1000 UHFs and headsets, and right under those you got Glock combat knives in *wicked* black." He spun fully around, making Steele jump back, and squealed, "Weee! Let's go with a couple dozen Dutch V40 mini-frags, right there in that box, and you can grab those Sig Sauer P226s, thigh rigs, and mags." He spun once again full circle while he sucked a long drag off his blunt. "Take the generic water bladders. Why splurge? And there's some cold weather shit over there. It's Salewa, Italian stuff, alpine boots and jackets and gloves. Oh!" He spun one last time and said, "And a thousand rounds of ammo, cool? On the house, whatever mix gets you off."

Belmont was high as a kite and bubbly with joy. He stopped the chair, hammered on his tablet for half a minute, threw his hands up high, and said, "Forty thousand euros. But for *you, Matthew*, the family discount. Thirty-five thousand, a steal! That doesn't include the airplane, though. You did say you needed one, *n'est pas?*"

"Right," Steele said, though he was thinking about the costs and how Mrs. Darnstein was going to take his head off. "A jump plane, long range, low altitude."

"Where's the X, dude?"

"Southern Mongolia."

"*Merde*, it's still fucking freezing down there. Okay, I'll have my boys stuff all this shit on your jet, and get you a humanitarian assistance clearance through to Irkutsk and Ulaanbaatar. Meanwhile, I'll see what the Mongols have." He spun to Allie Whirly. "Can you fly a Russian cargo plane, hot stuff?"

"I can fly a bathtub if it's got propellers," she said.

"I'll *bet* you can, baby." He grinned at her.

Steele's cell buzzed in his jacket pocket. He walked away to a corner of the armory while his crew started packing up the gear. It was Ralphy, calling through an encrypted app hidden under a Tetris icon.

"Speak," Steele said.

"Mr. Schneider, we just got a real time overhead from sky eyes. Your unfriendlies just crossed the border. Good news is, they're on horseback, but you still might wanna hustle up."

"How many?"

"Um, that's the bad news . . . Sixteen."

"Thanks."

Steele clicked off. He walked back over to Belmont, where Goodhill, Turner, and Allie had gathered around the barber chair and were all looking at him.

"We're going to need more ammo," he said. "And rockets."

CHAPTER 30

In the Dazheng Hall of the Swords of Qing, Zaifeng was down on his knees.

He had just completed an hour of Tao Lu practice with his *bo*, spinning, whirling, and catching the Chinese rattan staff in dizzying blurs, then blocking, lunging, and stabbing at imaginary enemies, all of whom fell and were slain with a driving blow. He wore only cuffed black Shaolin pantaloons and quilted shoes, and his muscular back gleamed with sweat, a sprawling tattoo of crossed swords over a golden dragon, and the pink welts of scars from a life of knives.

Now he was resting in a meditative pose, his calves folded beneath his thighs, his buttocks resting on his upturned soles. In the frigid air of his *zŏng bù*, steam from his skin fogged the air as he knelt, eyes closed, before a small golden Buddha embraced by a ring of flickering candles. He was not a religious man, but he believed in karma, the blood of his forefathers, and dynastic destiny.

Zaifeng's lieutenant, Po, had entered the headquarters hall and stood there in silence, waiting. He knew his commander would speak when he sensed his presence.

"What do you have for me, Po?" Zaifeng's voice was like a cougar's breath.

"The squadron has crossed the border, *Xian Sheng*. They are five hours from the target."

"Good. What else?"

"A transmission from Scarlet."

Zaifeng opened his eyes. The Swords of Qing had a female agent in the United States, a Chinese American working as an analyst for the CIA at Langley. She had a top secret clearance and always passed her polygraphs because she claimed, quite honestly, that she had no affinity for the Communist Chinese.

"What did she say?"

"The ship was found and inspected, as well as the helicopter," said Po. "The Americans believe the Central Committee is involved, and that Taiwan may be their target. The Roosevelt strike group is being dispatched from Pearl."

The granite expression on Zaifeng's face didn't change.

"And what does this mean to you, Po?"

"That the false flag is working."

"Precisely. And?"

"That I suppose . . . we no longer need Casino."

Zaifeng nodded, then raised a hand and flicked his fingers through the mist of his own excretions, which Po understood meant he should go. The lieutenant turned and left, quietly closing the thick entrance door.

Zaifeng rose, picked up his *bo*, and slipped off his formless black shoes. It was very cold in the hall yet he hadn't ignited his stove, but he often trained half naked in the snow, so this chill inside was nothing. He walked to the dungeon hatch, pulled it open, and descended the dark stone stairwell.

The man they called Casino was still in the dreary cavern and chained to the glistening stone wall. Yet his bonds had been slackened because he'd been cooperative—in fact, inventive with his whispered pleas to the American president—so draining his already failing body of strength would have been unnecessarily cruel. He was still the enemy, of course, and a traitor to the Chinese people, but the Swords of Qing were not animals.

Zaifeng appeared at the foot of the stone stairwell, framed in the yellow glow of its string of small bulbs. He walked toward his prisoner, tapping his *bo* on the slick rock floor and unmoved that its temperature was peeling the skin from his soles.

Casino raised his head. He had black bristles now across his slackened jaw and his eyes were rimmed with exhaustion, resembling a raccoon's. For the first time since having him captured and brought to the fortress, Zaifeng called him by his real name.

"Chan Myung," he said. "Did they give you a meal today?"

"Yes, Your Highness," the prisoner whispered, then coughed. The lieutenant called Po had told him to always address Zaifeng that way.

"Good. And I have news for you. Your tasks are complete, and you preformed them well."

Chan Myung sat a bit more erect on his stool. His feet were roped to its legs and his thighs shivered.

"I did the best that I could," he said.

"Yes." Zaifeng began to walk back and forth across Chan Myung's vision, tapping his *bo* on the floor, and the prisoner followed him with his bloodshot eyes, as if watching a pacing tiger. "And now, I feel that you deserve a full explanation."

"I would only want freedom, nothing more."

Zaifeng stopped and looked at him. "You will be liberated very shortly." He resumed pacing. "I feel it important that the Communist Party understands. And as we all know from our schooling, the education of the masses begins with a single pupil . . . like the very first plant one waters in a farmer's field, which then spreads its seeds across the land."

"You will be releasing me back to the Party?"

"Let us say that your message shall soon be delivered . . . and so will mine. When the Americans believe that the People's Liberation Army has destroyed one of their aircraft carriers, with all aboard, Beijing shall hear us, loud and clear." Zaifeng stopped moving and faced his prisoner, gripping the *bo* like a Roman centurion as he gazed at the dripping ceiling. "At any rate, Chan Myung, hear this. My grandfather was the last great emperor of China. He was imprisoned by the imperialist Japanese, made impotent as they raped Nanking, then collared like a dog and made their puppet in Manchu. And what happened, Chan Myung, when again we enjoyed liberation? When he should have regained the throne of the Forbidden City? You and your kind came along."

"But, Your Highness," Chan Myung stuttered, "I was not born—"

"The Japanese, at least, understood what an emperorship means!" Zaifeng boomed and Chan Myung fell silent. "You did not. You imprisoned him again, humiliated him, *reeducated* him in the foul godless rantings of Mao Zedong. We were made to wear dunce caps, confess our sins, stripped of our livelihoods, our honor flayed from us along with our skins!"

Zaifeng inhaled a long breath and exhaled steam from his lungs. He grew quiet again and went on.

"Yes, the Japanese raped Nanking, but you Communist thieves rape the world. In place of a glorious dynasty, you are now a kingdom of corporations. Where once every man was freethinking, you have turned us into submissive fools. Your Party tells us how we may think, what we must say, what books we may read, which of us must be silenced, who must be stripped of their livelihoods for ill thoughts and expressions, and who shall be rewarded for cowardly compliance."

Zaifeng lowered his gaze and tipped his *bo* toward Chan Myung, who tried to swallow but couldn't.

"You have stripped us of our cultural greatness, in exchange for making sneakers for Nike and smartphones for Apple, using our precious little girls as slaves."

"I . . . we . . . we can repent, Your Highness," Chan Myung whispered. "We can change—"

"It must end, Chan Myung. We must have honor again." Zaifeng's expression softened. He'd said what he needed Chan Myung to hear. "But I can assure you of this. You will be remembered as a hero to the Chinese people, the free Chinese people, because without you the CCP could never have been overthrown."

It was then that Chan Myung realized that Zaifeng was mad, and that he would never be leaving this place.

"May I ask a question?" He was weeping now.

"Ask."

"Why did you make me give the Americans a false location, so they could rescue me?"

"So that when you did not appear, they would believe that the Party had caught you, and that you were dead."

Chan Myung gathered some courage, his last.

"But you are delusional, Zaifeng! The Americans are soft. Covid wasn't enough to make them go to war with Beijing, and it decimated countries all over the world. What makes you think that this insane plan of yours will work?"

"Faith," said Zaifeng. He squeezed a button in the middle of his *bo,* and a long slim bayonet sprang from its snout like a stiletto.

Chan Myung closed his eyes.

CHAPTER 31

Allie Whirly could fly just about anything, but the Russian Antonov AN-2 was a stubborn *beotch*. It was the world's largest single-engine biplane, looked like an obese Sopwith Camel from World War I, and weighed almost four tons, empty. The passenger cabin, nothing more than a shell of ribbed girders and rattling metal skin, could deliver twelve paratroopers from the left rear cargo door, if none of them were impaled on the bladed tail. You jumped from this airplane only if you were a Soviet Spetsnaz, or crazy.

This one had been gifted to the Mongolian Air Force by the Russians after the Vietnam War, was striped in ugly olive-and-white camouflage, and still had the faded Soviet star on its flanks and patched-up bullet holes. Ten years back it had been sold off to a Mongolian crop duster, which was why Steele had been able to rent it at Chinggis Khaan airport in Ulaanbaatar with a reference from Oren Belmont and six thousand euros in cash. He'd lied and told the proprietor they were only taking it sightseeing.

"At night?" the crop duster had marveled.

"My pilot's snow-blind. She likes the moon."

But there was no moon, nor stars. There was a two-thousand-foot ceiling of thick purple thunderheads and a 40 mph head-wind, and the route to Ulaanbadrakh was a rolling carpet of snow below, from which craggy ice hills popped up without warning. Roaring headlong at five hundred feet above ground and 160 miles per hour, the Antonov rattled like a garbage can in a hurri-cane, and the engine was so loud that in order for someone to hear you, you had to shout in their ear.

Allie was in the cockpit's left seat, left glove on the airplane's old-fashioned yoke, right glove on the center console throttle, wearing her leather flying jacket and the Snoopy helmet and goggles she'd borrowed from Belmont, with no intention of ever bringing them back, if she survived. The cockpit instruments were marked in Cyrillic, but air speed indicators and altimeters looked the same in any language. Shane Wiley hunched in the right seat, wearing a fur hat and leather gauntlets as he stared wide-eyed out the six-paneled frosted-up windshield, regretting his reenlistment. Allie had dubbed him her copilot, even though he hadn't flown anything since training in a Piper J3 as a kid.

"Can you fly this thing?" she'd asked him as they took off.

"Why the hell would I have to?"

"In case I get shot in the face."

"Well, I can probably crash-land it."

"That'll work."

In the rear passenger cabin, which had been stripped of seats long ago, Steele, Slick, and Miles sat boots to rump near the open left door. A black icy wind whipped through its maw and hammered their faces, while their spines were pounded like kettledrums by the bouncing steel floor. They all wore the Italian alpine suits, boots, and gloves they'd taken from Vladivostok, plus balaclavas picked up en route in Irkutsk, but none of that did much for the wind shear. They were rigged with only T-10 main parachutes—no reserves. They'd be jumping from five hundred feet, with no time for emergency procedures. If any of their mains failed, they'd be jelly on toast.

"Two minutes!" Dalton Goodhill yelled and held up two fingers as he crouched near the door. The Antonov wasn't rigged as a jump plane, so there was no steel cable running along the ceiling for their static line hooks. Instead, Goodhill had snapped them to a large steel eyebolt on the floor used for securing a crop dusting tank. He wasn't really sure it would hold.

Steele cranked himself onto his feet, which was a bitch, since he had a 60 lb gear bag clipped to the D rings on the front of his chute harness, with a snake line running from there to the bag's deploy pocket. Making it even more awkward was his H&K 416 strapped across the bag's top and a Russian RPG 26 anti-armor rocket strapped underneath. Goodhill had to grip the front of Steele's harness and help him up, and Steele grabbed a fuselage spar and threw his boots apart like a sailor on the rolling deck of a submarine.

Steele turned and offered a glove to Slick, knowing it would be even harder for her, with the weight of her M249 SAW, yet neither he nor Miles had offered to switch weapons with her till they hit the ground—you just didn't pull that chivalrous crap anymore, especially if a woman was an Alpha. However, lending a hand to a battle buddy was SOP, and so was the shove Miles gave her ass. Then Miles was next, Slick gave him a hand, he banged the top of his helmet on the ceiling, the plane made a hard left bank, and he slammed into that side of the fuselage, grabbed two steel ribs overhead and bellowed "*Goddammit* Whirly!" but no one heard him.

Goodhill, as jumpmaster, jabbed himself in the chest with three fingers and the three waddled toward him and the door. He checked that their yellow static lines were running clean to the hook and that each of his jumpers was properly gripping the slack. Then he grasped the doorjamb with his left hand, Steele's harness with his right to keep him from premature ejection, stuck his big bald dome out the door, and looked down. He was not wearing a hat but only a headset linked to Allie and a pair of goggles, and his cheeks flapped in the roaring wind stream like a cocker spaniel's jowls on a joyride.

Steele tried to orient himself to the ground, but at this speed and altitude the view was nothing but blurred patches of white and black blobs rushing by. He heard Allie cut the engines back, looked to the left at Goodhill and saw him shout something into his boom mic. Then Goodhill shot him a thumbs-up, turned the digit out toward the sky, stepped back into the cabin, and Steele released his static line, palmed both sides of the door, and hurled himself into oblivion.

It was like being smacked in the face by a sheet of ice needles, then his harness jerked him like he was being hanged, his boots whipped up above his nose, and with the snap and flap of unfurling nylon all at once he was suspended in blessed silence. He knew he had no time at all to prepare for landing, so he quickly unclipped the gear bag, and it went sailing away between his boots and bounced at the end of the line. He was racing at the ground at fifteen feet per second and rocketing forward with the wind. He reached up, grabbed the front right riser, and hauled down, and the chute spilled air and spun him around. It didn't help much, but it would all be over in seconds.

Right before he slammed into the snow like a burlap bag of wet cement, he looked over his right shoulder and saw the target. There was the Mongolian village, exactly like the images Ralphy had sent to his phone, with those little *gers* like a bunch of mushrooms covered with white icing, flickering yellow glows coming from their slit windows, and wisps of smoke from their roof holes.

And beyond the village, maybe two klicks past some flat pastures that rose into hills, he saw something like the kind of dust trail you'd see rising from a Humvee convoy in the desert. Except that it wasn't dust, it was snow, and the Humvees were charging horses. And then Mother Earth sledgehammered his spine.

His was on his back in the snow and his chute was trying to drag him back to Ulaanbaatar. He thumbed the righthand Capewell, yanked the pin, and the canopy collapsed. He jumped up, tore off his harness, pulled his Glock blade from his calf scabbard, ran to his gear bag, and started slicing the snake line and straps. He heard an impact and a grunt to his left and knew that was Slick, and to his right Miles plowed face-first into a hill. In half a minute Steele was wearing his LBV full of ammo and grenades, his 416 was slung across his chest, and the RPG 26 was slung across his back. He remembered he didn't have body armor.

Well, Grandpa didn't have any either . . .

Slick ran to him, fully geared up and spewing breath. She was burdened like a turtle under her kit and that M249, but she looked wicked and wild-eyed. Miles appeared, loping through the snow, yanking his 416's charging handle on the run. No one said a word. Steele thrust two fingers toward the village and they took off at a dead run.

The first person Steele saw at the village edge was a short figure in head-to-foot furs, holding what looked like a British Enfield rifle, and running toward him with a crazy grin glowing in the dark. It was Tenzin and he yelled in English, "You motherfuckers are late!" Then, like some apparition from Genghis Khan's hordes, a Mongol warrior in full traditional garb pounded up on a black horse from around the side of a *ger*. It was Gengi Phon, his huge chest bandoliered in ammunition, gripping a rifle in one hand and with a long bow and arrows slung from his back. Then his son, Ganbaatar, appeared on a great white horse from the left, dressed and kitted just like his father, and the horses snorted and reared up and stomped.

"*Jesus*," Slick panted. "Where the hell are we?"

"You're gonna die in a David Lean movie," Miles said.

"Who the heck's that?"

"Never mind."

"*Tovarich*," Steele called to Gengi. "*Govorish po-russki*?" Speak Russian?

"*Da*." Gengi nodded.

"Flank them," Steele said to Gengi, and then to his crew, "Try not to kill the horses. Don't use the rockets unless you have to."

Gengi understood that somehow and said, "Thank you. I like horses." He jerked his steed to the right, Ganbaatar jerked his to the left, and they took off in opposite directions.

"Can you hit anything with that?" Steele jabbed a finger at Tenzin and his World War II rifle.

"I can freaking blow your ear off at a hundred meters and leave your glasses on."

"Good. Find a hill."

Tenzin took off at a run.

Two women rushed from the door of the nearest *ger.* One was a tall Mongol wearing long camel furs, the other a small striking Asian woman wearing incongruous fashionable glasses and dressed in the full uniform of a PLA colonel. *She wants to die like a warrior,* Steele thought. He went to her, gripped her small shoulders, and looked down into her eyes. He'd thrown his stupid brown contacts away and she stared back up at him.

"Colonel Liang?" he said in English.

"Yes, yes." She was breathing hard but looked steady and determined.

He pulled his father's 1911 from his hip holster and pressed it into her trembling hands. "We'll be back," he said. "But if things go wrong, save the last bullet for yourself." He turned to Miles and Slick.

"What's the plan, boss?" Slick said.

"Straight up the middle."

"Wife's gonna be pissed," Miles said.

Steele opened into a run, between the rows of *gers,* with Miles on his right and Slick on his left, pounding through the ankle-deep snow. They broke from the village onto a dipping plain of white with black thorn bushes poking up here and there like porcupine heads, and where the plain rose up into shallow hills, they could already see the horses barreling toward them and hear their hooves and hissing snorts. Then all at once the purple clouds above split, as if Moses had waved his staff, and the moon burst from the sky like a halogen searchlight and they all flipped their NVGs up away from their eyes.

Steele threw a fist in the air, skidded to a stop in a spray of snow, and threw himself prone, with Miles and Slick slamming down ten meters to either side. They shouldered their weapon stocks, flicked their safeties off, took long deep breaths, peered through their Aimpoints and ACOG, and saw a full squadron of black-clad gunmen, heads bent over their horses' whipping manes, getting closer, and closer. . . .

"Wait for it," Steele said in a cold flat tone to his crew. "*Wait for it. . . .*"

At fifty meters out, the cavalry point man jerked upright as a longbow arrow impaled his neck from the right and he flew off his horse. Tenzin's rifle cracked from somewhere, and the second man wailed and collapsed on his steed and the horse kept on galloping and thundered by. The rest of the horsemen opened up, their Chinese QBZ-95 bullpup assault rifles banging out blinding white barrel bursts and gunfire that echoed back from the village like hammers on car fenders.

"Now!" Steele barked and his 416 jerked as he blew one assaulter off his horse on the right, then another on the left, and he heard Slick's M249 spitting bursts and Miles's rifle cranking and spinning out shells in the air. He saw Ganbaatar on his horse, charging from the left into their flanks, whipping some sort of gleaming scimitar above his horse's ears, and it sliced into one man's throat and removed his entire head.

"Up!" Steele yelled.

He jumped up and moved forward at a measured pace, his 416 at his shoulder, firing at everything that showed above the head of a horse. One of the animals went down in the snow, kicking and screaming, but he couldn't think about that now. Slick matched him step for step on the left, firing bursts, switching drums, and on the right Miles saw two of the horsemen had abandoned their saddles and were crouching in the snow trying to pick Steele off. Miles pulled two Dutch grenades from his kit, yanked the pins, fastballed them thirty meters directly between the two, and the double bangs blew them right off their feet.

Steele looked at him and called, "Nice throw."

"U of Maryland baseball," Miles called back.

Then a horse exploded from behind a hill and was on top of Steele before he could fire. Its rider, dressed in full black like a ninja, thrust his rifle down at him and pulled the trigger as Steele jerked hard to the left, grabbed the exploding barrel, and yanked so hard it pulled the rider right off the saddle and into the snow. The ninja rolled, came up and charged him with some sort of long wicked blade. Steele butted his helmet into the man's skull, trapped the knife arm with his left elbow, snapped it as the man screamed, yanked his Glock blade from his scabbard, drove it hilt deep into his sternum, and dropped him dead on his back.

He took a breath, brought his rifle back up, and scanned the carnage. Eight riderless horses were charging around as if they'd burst from a barn fire. Black-clad corpses, a couple skewered by Gengi's arrows, lay grotesquely twisted where they'd fallen, but the rest had retreated back toward the hills and dismounted. They were battling it out with Gengi, Ganbaatar, and Tenzin, who had nothing but bolt-action rifles. Gunfire flashed the snow and banged off the hills. He had to finish those people off or Allie wouldn't be able to land the plane—or worse, they might shoot her down.

At that moment the Antonov showed up, roaring in from the right at a hundred feet high. He saw the open cargo door, with Goodhill kneeling right there, and the lumbering beast strafed the remaining killers as his keeper tossed grenades like he was emptying a basket of apples. Allie yanked the Russian biplane up to the right, Goodhill crashed back inside, and a line of white explosions ripped through the Chinese squad and he heard men moaning while their horses galloped off and disappeared.

Silence. The biplane receded beyond the hills. Slick and Miles started checking corpses to prevent any sudden surprises. Steele heard something behind him and spun around. It was Colonel Liang, led by Tenzin holding her elbow, with Steele's pistol still gripped in her trembling hand. Steele pried it from her gently and jammed it into his holster. Gengi appeared on his horse, and then Ganbaatar. The father's left arm was torn through with a bullet hole, and the son's face was smeared with the blood of a man he'd slain, but they were smiling at each other as if they'd just won a lottery. Steele jammed a fresh mag in his 416, just in case, then Slick and Miles pulled back in, but they kept their weapons trained outboard at the hills.

"Slick," Steele said, and she turned. He pointed to a large flat field off to the left that looked long enough for a landing strip. "Over there. Signal Allie. She'll wag her wings when she sees the flash."

"You bet, boss." Slick pulled a small flashlight from her vest and took off.

Steele looked up at Gengi and said in Russian, "Do you wish to come with us? You, and this young man and your wife."

"Never," Gengi said. "But we are thankful. We will have many horses and rifles now."

"*I'm* coming with you," Tenzin said to Steele. "I'm a fucking dead man here."

"Wise choice," Steele said.

He looked up to see Allie circling the big bird in from the

south. She didn't wag her wings but instead turned hard, set up
her final leg at the far end of the field, cut the engine, and let it
pound down into the snow as Slick sprinted out of the way. The
fat Antonov stopped as its big prop tossed up white clouds. Slick
called Steele through his headset and suggested he might want
to hustle.

Steele reached up to shake Gengi Phon's hand. The man's grip
was like a commercial vise.

"We owe you," Steele said. "We will not forget."

"The righteous owe nothing." Gengi grinned.

Steele cocked his head, and they all headed for the airplane.
Colonel Liang was struggling through the snow and looked paper
white pale. She'd been close to her own death too many times to
believe she'd survive this too.

When they reached the plane, Goodhill leaned from the door
and said to Colonel Liang, "Nice to meet you." He grabbed her
by the front of her uniform and hauled her inside. "Now let's get
the fuck outta here," he said to Steele. "Not sure we got 'em all."

Tenzin climbed in with his rifle. Goodhill took it from him
and hurled it back out in the snow. Allie opened her side cockpit window and yelled back to Steele over the rumbling engine,
"*Honey,* can we please go?"

Steele shoved Miles up into the plane from behind. Miles
turned and dragged Slick after him. Then Goodhill suddenly
jerked his face up over Steele's head and said, "Fuck, I *told* ya."

Steele spun around. A horseman had appeared out of nowhere
and was charging them hell-bent for leather. He was screaming
something and had his Chinese bullpup up, and as the barrel
exploded, Goodhill ducked, the round *wanged* as it pierced the
fuselage an inch from his ear, and Steele drew his father's 1911

and shot the rider twice in the chest. The dead man flew off the horse, somersaulted, and flopped on his back ten feet from Steele's boots. His horse went galloping off around the plane's tail.

Steele exhaled and leaned back against the doorway. Tenzin's face appeared next to his from inside, and then the monk climbed out, walked over to the corpse, peered down at his lifeless eyes and turned him over. He pulled off the man's balaclava and stared at the back of his bare neck. He took off his glove, touched the cold skin, looked up at Steele, and pointed down at a large tattoo.

"These are not Chinese Communists, my friend," he said. "These are the Swords of Qing."

ACT III

CHAPTER 32

"Who the *hell* are the Swords of Qing?"

President John Rockford slapped a top secret file on the conference table in the Situation Room's main tank. It was early evening, he hadn't had dinner yet, and a growling stomach on top of a global emergency was a recipe for a foul mood. He'd tossed his suit jacket over the chair and rolled up his sleeves, and his blond hair looked like he'd combed it with a salad fork.

"Somebody buy me a freaking clue," Rockford snapped to the sixteen pinched faces surrounding the polished oak slab. "Sounds like one of my kid's Xbox games."

"Mr. President," Tina Harcourt said, unfazed by the boss's bite. "We have one source in Hong Kong, with a secondary in Laos, pegging them as a Chinese dissident group. However, they're essentially dormant, and certainly not kinetic." The CIA director glanced at Rockford's file and wondered where his intel was coming from, but she wasn't going to ask in open forum.

"Well they're sure as hell kinetic *now*," Rockford growled. "A whole squad of them just went full Mike Tyson on some of our SpecOps people in Mongolia."

Chairman of the Joint Chiefs General Maxwell Wheeler raised a bushy gray eyebrow. He'd just arrived from the Pentagon and a secure briefing call with the JSOC commander at Bragg. No Delta, SEALs, ISA, or any other top-tier units were currently operating in Mongolia, and if the CIA had any Special Activities Division folks down there, Harcourt would at least have flinched. *Or maybe not,* Wheeler thought. *She's as cold as Kim Jong-un's little sister.*

Wheeler, his four stars gleaming from the army's "new" World War II–style dress uniform, was seated to the president's right, next to National Security Advisor Katie Garland. Beside him sat the chief of Naval Operations, Admiral Harold McCormack, then General Milt Efron, director of the NSA. To the left of the president was his chief of staff, Tony Hinds, then Tina Harcourt, Air Force Chief of Staff General Jennifer Myberg, and finally Homeland Security chief Raphael Gonzalez. At the table's far end sat Dr. Seymour Pressfield, director of the National Reconnaissance Office. The rows of "guest" chairs behind the heavy hitters were occupied by support staff—some uniformed, some not.

Rockford's secretary of defense was away in Riyadh, and on the flat screen behind the president's head the image of Vice President Elmore Carson was being piped in from the cave. He was a slim handsome black man with graying curls and a boyish smile, which gave the weird impression of them all being observed by Barack Obama.

"Mr. President," Admiral McCormack said as he plucked a handkerchief from his black naval blazer and cleaned his gold-

rimmed glasses, "unless NAVSPECWARCOM is keeping something from me, we don't currently have any teams in that AOR."
He meant SEALs operating in the area that included Mongolia,
and he was fishing for more details, which he sensed he wasn't
going to get.

"Nothing green there either, Mr. President," General Wheeler
said, meaning army units of any kind.

Air Force General Myberg didn't bother echoing her colleagues.
None of her special tactics people, including PJs or JTACs, would
be anywhere near Mongolia unless tasked with supporting the
army, navy, or marines.

"So, if I might, Mr. President," Tina Harcourt ventured.
"Which SpecOps people are we talking about?"

Rockford shot her a look that could have withered a Utah cac-
tus. "Contractors," he snarled. "And it's not relevant right now."

He stalled for a moment by rubbing his jaw and perusing
the TS file. This was going to take some finesse. The Program
was still just a rumor inside the intelligence community, and he
wanted it kept that way. There were other black budget units
operating outside the Department of Defense's formal structure,
but he couldn't pretend it was one of those spook crews without
Wheeler nosing around. In order for the Program to remain via-
ble and effective, he had to keep it under wraps while simultaneously revealing its concerns and targets.

Not easy to do, and events were transpiring superfast downrange, in real time.

Mongolia's time zone was EST plus thirteen hours. Eric Steele
had pulled off the rescue of this Chinese colonel, but apparently
he hadn't felt secure about flashing Q Street until he was out of
Mongolian airspace. It had taken some hours for the QRF to

get back to Ulaanbaatar, reboard the Gulfstream, and get out over open water en route to Taiwan. Then Lansky, breathless and practically biting through his pipe stem, had shown up at the White House's back door and personally handed the flash file to the president, who'd then called an emergency meeting of relevant stakeholders.

Shoulda stayed in the army . . . I'd be retired and fly-fishing right now.

Rockford jotted something on a presidential notepad, tore off the page, and handed it to Katie Garland. She glanced at the message.

Brief them, but blind.

Garland folded the note and stuck it in the pocket of her Ann Taylor suit.

"Gentlemen and ladies," she began, then turned to Tina Harcourt. "With your permission, Director."

Harcourt nodded, though she hated being upstaged by political appointees, and Tony Hinds sat back and crossed his arms. He wasn't a fan of Garland, whom he thought had too much of the president's ear, and he looked like a dubious Morgan Freeman.

"As most of you already know," Garland continued, "over the past two weeks, we've had a series of anomalous incidents occurring in that part of the world. First, a Level Five biological research laboratory in northwest China, near the Mongolian border, was destroyed in what appeared to be an accident." She looked at the National Reconnaissance Office director. "Dr. Pressfield?"

"Confirmed, ma'am," said the NRO chief. He was a rumpled bald man who looked like George from the Jerry Seinfeld show.

"Well," Garland said, "it now appears that the accident was

in fact an assault by heliborne troops. The only survivor was the laboratory director, a PLA colonel, who escaped on foot across the border."

"How do we know that?" Admiral McCormack asked. "And who were the assaulters?"

"Patience, Harold," the president said. "The plot thickens." He circled a finger at Katie to continue.

"In the interim," Garland went on, "an apparently unrelated incident occurred in the Indian Ocean off the coast of Mozambique. An African cargo vessel ran ashore, with its entire crew of eighty-two personnel missing and presumed deceased."

"Been tracking that," the chief of Homeland Security muttered. "Thought it was hype."

"That's the drama CNN's been flacking all week, like the Flight 370 thing," General Wheeler said, referencing the 2014 disappearance of a Malaysian airliner that had seemingly dropped off the face of the earth during a flight from Kuala Lumpur to Beijing.

"You need to start watching Newsmax, General," the president said, "instead of that cartoon network."

"Noted, Mr. President." The Joint Chiefs chairman smiled, though he also flushed a bit.

Rockland nodded at Katie Garland, and she carried on.

"Further, the aforementioned contractors have now rescued our Chinese colonel, while being opposed by these anti-Communist Swords of Qing. We now believe the destroyed laboratory was developing a gain-of-function biowarfare agent, and that weapon may now be in the hands of the insurgents, with nefarious intent."

"Excuse me, Kate." Air Force chief Myberg raised a finger. She was a former C-17 pilot with dark red hair and silver wings on her blue dress uniform. "Define gain of function."

"It's a biological warfare development technique," the president broke in. "You take a naturally occurring virus and enhance its lethality, like we used to do with anthrax at Fort Detrick. It's the same thing that happened with that lab in Wuhan and Covid-19." He thanked Garland with a chin dip and turned to the CIA director. "Take it from here, Tina."

"Our speculation—and that's all it is at the moment," Harcourt said, "is that the ghost ship in Africa was used as a test bed, but we're still not sure by whom. Additionally, the president has received direct contact from a singleton source in China, claiming to be an informant inside the Central Committee. This man claims that the Chinese Communist Party is planning an assault on our warships in the South China Sea, which may or may not involve this biowarfare agent."

"Holy Christ," Admiral McCormack whispered.

The conference devolved into sputters as the president's advisors regaled one another with I-told-you-so comments. Vice President Carson tapped on his remote microphone, which snapped heads around, and he said from his flat-screen perch, "*Please*, people. I can't hear when you all do that."

They settled back in their plush chairs, though a couple were loosening ties and pouring themselves water from crystal carafes. A young woman sitting behind Tina Harcourt tentatively touched the CIA director's shoulder and whispered something. Harcourt tapped her CIA fountain pen on the table, making a *ping*ing like sonar.

"If you all would indulge us, please," she said. "My senior Chinese analyst has something to offer."

"Go ahead, young lady," the president said.

"This is Felicia Min." Harcourt turned her chair aside to give her analyst the floor.

The young woman was trembling as she rose from her chair behind Harcourt. She was short and slim, in a pale gray suit and large glasses beneath drop-down black bangs. She clutched a thick file folder over her chest and only made eye contact with the table. Felicia Min was her name, but to Zaifeng and the Swords of Qing, she was "Scarlet."

"Mr. President, and most honored guests," she began in a slight Cantonese accent, "the Swords of Qing are a small group of Chinese nationalists, who believe that the Chinese Communist Party must be overthrown, and that the rule of China must be returned to the rightful descendants of the last emperor of China, Aisin Gioro Puyi."

She was telling the truth about that part. The rest was a lie.

"However, this group of dissidents are, as you would say in English, wannabees. They have no power, no methods of effecting their aims. I have researched them thoroughly for years. It is my belief that this entire effort is in fact a false flag operation by the CCP. Beijing is using these activities, and the Swords of Qing claims, as a carefully designed smoke screen. Their true objective is to confuse us and take us off course."

"All right, Ms. Min," the president said. "So if that's the case, then what do you think is Beijing's plan?"

Felicia Min at last looked directly at someone, in this case the most powerful man in the world.

"Mr. President, they are going to invade Taiwan."

The tank fell silent as a grave. Tina Harcourt nodded at Min, and the young woman bowed and sat down. The president took a long sip of water. He wished it was gin.

"Director," he said to Harcourt, "do you support this theory?"

"Mr. President," Tina said, "I have full faith in our subject matter experts. Her assessment should come as no surprise."

Rockford folded his fingers on the table and stared into nothing as he thought about the implications. No one could deny the red Chinese lust for Taiwan, which they'd regarded as a renegade province ever since Chiang Kai-shek had declared its independence in 1950. Beijing's hatred for Taipei was legendary—it was said that every time Taiwan held military exercises, or "sneezed," the CCP caught a cold and became further enraged. Had the Reds decided to make their move? And if they did, who could stop them but the United States? He raised his head and looked at many pairs of geopolitically experienced eyes.

"All right, people. Better give me sitreps." He jabbed his presidential pen at McCormack. "Admiral?"

"We've got the Roosevelt carrier strike group steaming that way. Her escorts include one guided missile cruiser and five guided missile destroyers, and she's got a full air wing of F-18s and support aircraft aboard. I'll have to check on the sub deployments."

"All right. General Myberg?"

"We can have B-1Bs in the air from Guam on an out-and-back rotation, whenever you say, Mr. President," she said. "And we've got F-35s and F-15s in Japan."

"Very good." He slung his big jaw at General Wheeler. "Max?"

"If the balloon goes up, first in would be 1st Special Forces group out of South Korea," General Wheeler said, "but I can crank up the 82nd and deploy them forward."

"Marine Corps elements?" the president asked.

"South Korea," Admiral McCormack said, "but I'd work up a landing exercise on Taiwan right now, Mr. President, with Taipei's invitation, of course. Show of force."

Rockford nodded. He knew that his military forces were still the finest in the world, and he could have them rocketing toward the South China Sea within twenty-four hours. But they were all playing with fire, and at the moment the only ace in the hole he had was a half resurrected, deep black special operations program, and one hard-core operator named Eric Steele.

"Well, what are your recommendations, people?" he said.

"Satellite recon, sir," said Dr. Pressfield. "Let's move some Keyholes and see what they're doing."

"Skirmish line," said Admiral McCormack. "Let's get a small vessel tripwire in the water off Taiwan's west coast."

"They might not hit from the sea," General Myberg said. "They've got Xi'an Y-20 heavy transport aircraft. They could launch an airborne assault before our first marines step ashore."

"Signals," said General Efron of NSA. "I'll triple our focus on traffic intercepts."

The chairman of the Joint Chiefs had his big arms folded and was looking at the ceiling, as if his comrades were a bunch of timid kickball players on a kindergarten school playground.

"Mr. President," Wheeler said as he puffed up his chestful of medals. "This is all weak-kneed stuff. The best defense is a kick-ass offense. I say we go preemptive. The Chinese have been angling for a fight for decades. I say we give it to them and strike first."

Rockford stabbed Wheeler with an iron gaze from his cool blue eyes.

"Not on your life, General." The president shook his big blond head. "We prepare, move assets, and sop up the intel . . . but we wait. We're not going to pull the trigger first. I didn't take this job to start new wars. I took it to stop them."

CHAPTER 33

It was close to dawn when the Gulfstream's wheels bounced on the landing strip at the southern thumb of Taiwan.

Steele felt like he'd been beaten with a bamboo kendo practice sword. He'd hardly slept on the plane, even after they'd gone feet wet over the Sea of Japan and he'd sent his flash to Ralphy—the point after a mission when he'd usually relax. His joints were aching, his temples pounding, and even his scalp felt like it had been shrunken in a clothes dryer. He actually checked himself over to see if he'd missed a bullet wound, but he was all in one piece and decided it was simply his mind.

You're getting to be like an old skydiver . . . odds are catching up . . .

Something was nagging at him. Something looming in his future. He hated having that kind of internal radar, because it was always on the money.

Everyone else on the jet had slept like an overfed puppy. Colonel Dr. Liang was curled up on one of the seats under a blanket, still in her PLA uniform, though she'd pulled off her combat boots. Goodhill was plugged into something on his earbuds—Travis Tritt crooning "Here's a Quarter (Call Someone Who Cares)"—and snoring. Shane Wiley had slept sitting upright, fingers laced over his stomach like a mummified corpse, while Tenzin perched cross-legged on another seat like a cliché monk. Slick was out cold, wearing her balaclava pulled down over her eyes like a hostage, and Miles Turner was too big for the seats, so he'd stretched out prone on the carpeted floor.

Allie was up forward talking airplane smack with the pilots. Come to think of it, Steele couldn't remember ever seeing her sleep, except for that one time in Bagram after they'd gotten drunk and . . . he struck that image from his mind.

The touchdown on the eight-thousand-foot runway was like somebody driving a Ford F-150 off the half-lowered ramp of a C-130. The landing gear squealed, a coffeepot went flying out of the forward galley, and Dalton "Blade" Goodhill snapped awake, tore off his earbuds, and bellowed, "Jesus H. *Christ.*" Everyone else stirred, groaned, and cursed—in English, Mandarin, and Cantonese—and Goodhill looked across the aisle at Steele and said, "You shoulda shot that flyboy when you had the chance."

"He did it on purpose," Steele said. "Just to bruise my ass."

He looked out his porthole window to see a blacked-out strip. They'd arrived at Pingtung air base, where the independent Republic of China's Airborne Special Service Company—comparable to the U.K.'s SAS or the U.S. Army's Delta—resided behind concrete barriers, concertina wire, and attack dogs, in a no-nonsense restricted headquarters and training facility. Over the course of his career with Special Forces and the Program, Steele had operated with many of the world's top-tier units, but he'd never come face-to-face with these particular badasses. They had a reputation for being among the world's top twenty special operations and counterterror units, including Russia's Spetsnaz or Poland's GROM.

Ted Lansky had allegedly arranged an "invitation" for Steele and his team from the ASSC commander—safe passage, as it were, for allies of the Republic of China, aka Taiwan. But what Steele saw now didn't look like a welcome wagon. All sorts of armored vehicles were circling the aircraft and screeching into stakeout positions, headlights and spotlights blazing. Serious-looking troops, all gunned up, were spilling from their carriages and owning the strip. They were black clad from head to foot, with nothing visible but angry eyes. They looked very much like the Swords of Qing militants that he and his mates had taken down in Mongolia just a few hours before.

Did we take a wrong turn somewhere?

The Gulfstream's navy steward opened the hatchway and deployed the short stairway. A sharp voice in heavily accented English called from outside.

"Come out. Show your hands."

Steele got up, looked around at his blinking compatriots, and said, "No gloves, palms up, one at a time."

He squeezed through the hatch and onto the tarmac. It was humid and still pitch-black outside, though the birds were starting to chirp in the palms just off the runway and tall waves of elephant grass clicked in a thick breeze. He was still wearing his tactical uniform, sticky with sweat, and more than anything he wanted a shower and a nap.

Strange thought, dude, when a sneeze can get you shot.

He took a few steps forward, keeping his hands waist high in plain sight. Squinting in the arc lights, he could see the ASSC commandos holding Taiwanese XT-97 assault rifles, similar to the FN SCAR, but at least with good trigger discipline and no trembling digits. He heard the Gulfstream's engines wind down as his teammates, guests, and the air crew came down and lined up behind him in front of the fuselage.

"Feels like a firing squad," Slick muttered.

"It's cool as long as you signed your last will," Goodhill said.

"Hope they've seen a brother before," said Miles.

"No sweat," said Shane Wiley. "They look like Oprah fans."

Tenzin muttered something in Chinese.

"Silence!" the man with the sharp voice snapped. He looked to Steele like a young squadron commander, but he didn't seem to be the boss.

Then a gleaming dark green jeep pulled up, no top, with its uniformed ROC driver sitting erect as a mannequin. A man climbed out from the other side and walked through the high beams toward Steele.

He was short and wide as a Greco-Roman wrestler, with thick black hair, "unibrow" eyebrows, and a jaw like a German beer stein. He was wearing a sterile black tactical uniform, except for a pair of gold ROC airborne wings over his left pocket, and a nametape in Chinese. He had a large pistol in a thigh rig. He smiled with big teeth and offered Steele a handshake that felt like gripping a ham hock.

"I am told to call you Seven," the man said in baritone, well-studied English.

"You can call me Steele, Commander."

"Very good. I am Colonel Wi Lung Chun, but my English friends call me Panther."

And I'll bet you earned that moniker, Steele thought.

"An honor to meet you, Panther."

"Yes. Where are your weapons?"

"In the cargo hold." Steele poked a thumb back over his shoulder.

"*Sou suo ta men.*" Search them, Panther said to his lieutenant in Mandarin.

Five of the commandos slung their rifles, stomped past Steele, and frisked the nine people behind him, from ankles to crotches, waists, armpits, and hair. He heard Allie titter, "You're turning me on," but he kept his smile inside. The commandos finished and returned to their positions.

"My apologies," Panther said to Steele. "We must be careful in our part of the world."

"No worries," Steele said. "You can search me too if you like."

"I am not worried." Panther smiled. "If you move too fast I will just kill you."

"Fair enough."

Panther waved a ham hand toward Steele's group. "My men will care for your people. Come."

The colonel walked to the jeep, snapped something to the driver, and the young soldier jumped out, saluted, and marched off. Panther climbed into the driver's seat, cocked his big head at Steele, and Steele went around and slid up into the passenger seat. Panther gunned the engine and handed Steele a travel mug emblazoned with ASSC airborne wings.

"Coffee. Black. The way you like it."

Steele didn't ask how he knew that, but he nodded and took a grateful swig as Panther made a screeching U-turn and headed back down the strip. Steele saw a series of low concrete buildings hulking far away in the rising dawn, but Panther soon turned off the strip, trundled along a dirt road between sparkling bulrushes, and headed somewhere north.

It wasn't the first time that Steele had dropped out of the sky in some strange land and been greeted by heavily armed suspicious men. He'd done that often before and knew he had to play it with class and cool. Professionals like this colonel were like jungle animals—if they smelled fear on you, it would ring their alarms. That was the game. He hated it, loved it, was tired of it, craved it, and knew that someday soon, he should quit. That made him think briefly of Meg, and he struck her too from his mind.

They broke from a thick grove of elephant grass and climbed onto a slim dirt lane alongside a muddy green river. The early sun was glistening on the distant waves of the East China Sea, where it flowed south through the Taiwanese strait, just a 140-mile barrier between the island and mainland China. The river beside them was bordered on the far side by rice paddies, where already farmers were bent low, wearing frothy white tunics, baggy pantaloons, and conical hats, harvesting Asia's culinary treasure just as they'd done for eons. It was bucolic, but the vision didn't ease Steele's disquiet.

"I like your Theodore Lansky," Panther said over the engine rumble and the bouncing tires.

"I like him too," Steele said.

"Do you know a man named McHugh?"

"No."

Panther smiled and donned a pair of pilot's Ray-Bans.

"You lie well. Very smooth."

"It's a gift."

They drove a bit farther in silence, then Panther said, "It is not far."

"What's not far, Colonel?"

"The Fo Guang Shan monastery. The place where we go."

"Why are we going there?"

"You have a rendezvous."

Steele didn't have anything on him. Not his 1911, or even a knife. He cast his fate to the wind.

Then he saw it, beyond a bend in the river ahead. The monastery rose from a vast plateau of gentle grasses, a pinkish stone structure of one great castle-like cube in the center, with wings and buttresses on both flanks, all topped by sloping red roofs like the hats of the rice farmers, turned up at the brims. Its walls were blank with only slim window slits like the pupils of cats, as if too much light inside might disturb the monks' meditations.

Panther took the jeep off the riverside path, down through a shallow valley, and up onto a slim paved roadway. It wasn't yet six in the morning, but already there were Taiwanese ranchers clucking at cattle and tapping their rumps with switches, and the bicycles were gathering like flocks of ducklings and an old bus spewed oil smoke. The colonel turned off the roadway again into a wide empty parking lot, where the walls of the monastery loomed high above, like China's Forbidden City.

He stopped the jeep and gestured at a set of stone stairs that rose up in seven stages.

"Up there," he said. "In the garden of Buddhas. I will wait for you here."

Steele got out. He could have taken the stairs two at a time, but he somehow didn't want to take them at all. He saw no one else around, except for one monk in long black robes at the top, who slipped inside an enormous red door. And then he saw the first Buddha, like nothing he'd ever seen before.

It was standing rather than sitting in the traditional sculpted form, and it looked like it was a hundred feet high and weighed thirty tons. It had long fat earlobes drooping to its golden shoulders, its palms extended in welcome, and it smiled down at a great oval below of red brick cobblestones. The great Buddha stood among a copse of lush green trees, and the garden was surrounded, in perfect order, by rows and rows of smaller golden Buddhas, each the size of a man.

Steele had witnessed many wondrous things in the world, but what caught his breath wasn't the spiritual grace or beauty of the deity garden. It was the figure of a man, standing at the other end.

He was tall, gray haired, wearing a safari-type bush jacket and jeans. His back was turned as he looked out over the river valley beyond the garden's south end, and Steele saw he was carrying a silver Zero Halliburton briefcase. This wasn't the first time either that he'd met a stranger somewhere for a drop, and he figured it wouldn't be the last. He checked his surroundings, then walked toward the man and stopped.

Something about him. Something in his form, or maybe the energy buzzing in the air.

He knew it was his father as soon as the man turned and pushed his sunglasses up onto his thick, spiky gray hair. They had the same green eyes. They had the same mouth. Hank walked toward him as Steele's heart pounded in his chest, his fists balled, and he felt like he might pass out, or scream some primitive war cry, or charge him and choke him to death, or hug him and weep. But he was rooted to the spot, frozen like one of the lifeless gold Buddhas. He could barely breathe as his father stopped ten feet away.

Neither of them said a thing for an endless minute as only the birds chirped in the trees. Then Steele, in a voice that sounded to him like the whine of a lost child, said, "Why did you come here?"

Hank put the silver briefcase down next to his African desert boots and said, "To give you a hand."

CHAPTER 34

MANCHURIA, CHINA

A priceless Qing Dynasty vase exploded in a hundred shards on the wall of Zaifeng's *zǒng bù*. It had been a beautiful, white, crackle glaze piece adorned with raised black dragons until Zaifeng had hurled it in a detonation of rage. Now it was merely the shrapnel of history.

"Escaped!" Zaifeng boomed as he paced back and forth in his headquarters. He was dressed again all in black, with only the red of his turtleneck sewn with the Swords of Qing emblem hugging the bulging veins in his neck. His mountain boots boomed on the teakwood. "*How* did you let her escape?"

The scout called Feng shivered where he knelt on the floor. His tactical uniform was stiff with snow and ice crusts, and torn in one shoulder and hip. His wild wet hair was matted with dried blood where a bullet had grazed his skull, and he clutched his fur hat in his lap with raw red hands.

"We were ambushed, *Xian Sheng*." Feng's ragged breaths streamed from his nostrils.

"Ambushed?" Zaifeng stopped pacing and looked across Feng's prostrate form at Po. The lieutenant was standing at attention a good ten paces behind his scout, as if avoiding what could soon be the splatter of Feng's blood. "By *whom*?"

"American commandos, *Xian Sheng*," Feng whispered, ashamed.

"Americans? From where?"

"From the sky. I believe they parachuted. Their airplane attacked us too."

Zaifeng raised his chin. His posture and bunched muscles eased. At the very least, if his men had been defeated in battle, it had been at the hands of worthy adversaries in superior numbers.

"How many of these commandos, Feng?"

Feng swallowed. "Three."

"Three? Did you say *three*?"

"And some Mongols also, *Xian Sheng*," Feng sputtered. "On horseback and—"

"Three Americans and some medieval horsemen?" Zaifeng exploded again, whipping his hand through the air. "You and fifteen of our best men, defeated by a trio of Western dogs? *Pienzeh!*" he shouted. It was not good to be called a liar by Zaifeng.

"They . . . they had many weapons, *Xian Sheng*, and grenades from—"

"Where are the rest of you?"

"Dead." Feng's eyes began to stream. His tears were like mercury rivulets on his frozen face.

"And your horses?"

"Some fell . . . some ran . . ." He didn't dare tell Zaifeng that so many of his horses were now in enemy hands.

Zaifeng fell silent, looked at the ceiling of his *zŏng bù*, then quietly walked past the puddle of melting snow around Feng's knees to his desk. Behind it, in a tall crimson vase, was a double-edged Chinese sword called the *jian* in a lacquered scabbard. He drew the *jian,* swept the blade twice across his thigh as if stropping a straight razor, and walked back toward Feng. Po closed his eyes. He did not want to see this.

"Tell me how you know what you know, Feng," Zaifeng demanded. "Tell me how you saw what you saw. Tell me you are not a liar and a coward, and why I should let you live."

"I was wounded, *Xian Sheng.*" There was no arguing that. The blood was thawing and dripping from Feng's scalp, over his nose and onto his cracked lips. "I crawled to a hill and watched. I heard them speak. They escaped on the airplane with the PLA colonel and others . . ." Yet he saw in Zaifeng's blazing glare that it wasn't enough, and he keened and bent his neck forward. He knew what was coming and began mumbling prayers.

"But you returned on *your* horse, Feng." Zaifeng's breaths were spewing hard. "How did they not see *your* horse?"

"My . . . my horse lies down in the snow when I tell him, *Xian Sheng.*"

Zaifeng blinked, and for a moment he saw the scene. Feng lying there wounded, the sole survivor of this misadventure, with his obedient horse on its side, regarding his master with expectant eyes, awaiting further instructions. He recalled having seen Feng do this trick with his horse before, and remembered laughing. Why would this man lie? Why would he return to the fortress at all, if he knew he was going to die?

"Enough," Zaifeng snapped. "Go."

Feng didn't have to be told twice. He scrambled to his feet, bowed low, then once more as he stumbled backward past Po, out the great door, and ran.

Zaifeng roared in frustration and hurled the *jian* across the room, where it spun through the air, impaled itself in a teakwood wall, and twanged.

He stood stock-still for a full minute, calming his rage. Po hadn't moved from his spot, and Zaifeng could smell his fear. A truly effective commander could never lead his men this way, not with threats of violence, or obedience born of trepidation. They would either follow you out of love, conviction, and loyalty, or not at all.

"Mastering others is strength," he murmured. "Mastering yourself is true power." It was a quote from the ancient Chinese philosopher Lao Tzu, from his *Tao Te Ching, the Book of the Way and Its Virtue.*

He walked to the potbellied stove in the center of his *zŏng bù*, opened the door, and added a dry log to the fire. The flames licked up and haloed his form, then he strode to his dynastic desk and sat down. He opened a drawer and began withdrawing some documents and notebooks, ordering them on his blotter.

"Assemble the men, Po," he said. "Let them feed, then have them uncover the helicopters and ensure they are fueled and checked. Once that is done, have them load the Gantu-62 canister aboard the second helo. That team must be in full protective posture, and most careful. The rest should load weapons, ammunition, and stores, but make sure to use the weight scales so as not to overburden the aircraft. Clear?"

"Yes, *Xian Sheng.*"

"Good. We leave for the island in one hour. Directly, no detours."

Zaifeng had no concerns about flying through CCP-controlled airspace. His pilots were PLA defectors who'd gone missing from their posts a year before. They knew all the frequencies and military codes that could get them safely past air traffic controllers. He gestured at an ornate box that looked like a treasure chest, sitting beside his desk.

"Send someone in half an hour to take this with us."

"Yes, sir," Po said. "But, if I may. We are short of men now for the mission."

"Their deaths served a purpose. Now we will have one empty helicopter to crash into the sea as our decoy."

"But the pilots, *Xian Sheng* . . . They will die."

Zaifeng turned and squinted at his lieutenant. "As did the Kamikaze. Do we not have as much honor as the Japanese?"

"Of course, *Xian Sheng.*" Po saluted and left.

For a while, Zaifeng selected precious objects from his drawers—the flask with the lock of hair from Puyi, some ornate Qing Dynasty emerald and ruby rings, some photographs of his mother and grandmother. Most of the rest were old texts and books, including the famous biography of his grandfather, written by the Scottish diplomat Sir Reginald Fleming Johnston.

When he was done, he closed the chest, walked to the hatch of his dungeon, and went down. He emerged carrying a large olive-green box by its folding handle. It looked like a typewriter case, and he set it in the middle of his *zǒng bù*, knelt for one last prayer before his golden Buddha, and went out.

An hour later, Zaifeng stood in the fortress courtyard. His three Harbin Z-20 helicopters whined in the night and their large main rotors were already turning, whipping ringlets of falling snow through the air. All the men were aboard and he was alone, with a QSZ-92 pistol strapped to his thigh and his *bo* in one hand. He walked to the gate in the fortress's concrete wall and pulled it open. Then he freed all the remaining horses, slapped their slick rumps and drove them through and away.

He took one last look at the waterfall that coursed from the cliff and down through his power wheel, all of it glistening with ice, and then he regarded his *zŏng bù,* its beautiful roof and columns and dragons, and nodded.

He walked to the first helicopter, climbed aboard, and returned the bows of his commandos as they sat, fully geared up, on the benches. Then he moved on into the cockpit and ordered his pilots to leave.

The helos lifted off, and standing behind the pilots, Zaifeng told them to circle the fortress once, and he looked down through the cockpit window at all he'd constructed and loved for so long. Then he told them to make headway and speed.

He didn't look back again as he pulled a remote detonator from his pocket and pressed the trigger, and his *zŏng bù* exploded in a mushroom cloud of smoke and flame and a thousand spinning splinters.

It was no longer the home of the Swords of Qing. He would either be going to his rightful throne in Beijing, or to his death.

CHAPTER 35

Colonel Wi Lung Chun had chosen the far western end of his airstrip for Dr. Ai Liang to conduct her inspection of Hank Steele's gruesome hand.

Just beyond the tarmac was a wide flat plain of six-foot-high elephant grass, where Panther's ASSC commandos practiced their parachute insertions. They always jumped with their sleeves rolled up, and all of their forearms displayed pink wounds from the razor-sharp blades of thick grass. If you didn't have those rite-of-passage scars, you were not ASSC. The parachute landing zone was bordered by razor wire hung with trespass warnings and lies about mines. It was a place far away from prying eyes, where you could quietly and honorably die.

A large mobile chem-bio laboratory had been driven down from the Taiwanese army's 33rd Chemical Troops Group Detection and Decontamination Battalion in Kaohsiung. It was a long, olive-green, heavy-duty truck and trailer, purchased from a firm in Florida called Germfree, and built to Biosafety BSL-3 specifications, with generators, air filtration, and water pumps. The system was foolproof for inspecting mycobacterium tuberculosis, St. Louis encephalitis virus, and Coxiella burnetii, but no one from the 33rd had ever encountered, or heard of, Gantu-62.

Outside the trailer, which was parked at the end of the tarmac, the army chemical corps had set up a large decontamination tent, where six troops in full MOPP IV gear waited with their sweat running into their black plastic boots. It was nearly sundown, but still very warm. Fifty yards removed from that, Panther's commandos had established an armed perimeter where the colonel waited behind a Humvee with Eric Steele and his father, but no one else from Steele's crew. Panther didn't have enough PPE gear on-site for everyone, so his troops and guests had nothing more than standard N95 masks. They were trusting Colonel Dr. Ai Liang, and God.

Dr. Liang was inside the trailer for nearly an hour, during which time Steele and his father stood there six feet apart, occasionally glancing at their watches, regarding the perspiring chembio troops and squinting at the distant sea. Hank smoked his pipe and they hardly exchanged a word, while Panther leaned into his command vehicle and spoke on his Harris radios to general officers in Kaohsiung. In side glances Panther noted the startling physical similarities of the two Americans. He knew they were both special agents of some sort, were father and son, and it didn't take psychic talent to recognize they had family issues. Panther was an expert commando and killer, but he had five kids of his own.

The sound of a pneumatic seal hissed in the evening air, then the steel pressure door of the trailer opened and Dr. Liang emerged. She wore a fully enclosed black helmet with a curved glass faceplate linked to an oxygen hose, a pressurized blue suit, silver gloves, and boots. She locked the door behind her, and as she came down the three metal stairs Steele thought she looked like a costumed child on Halloween.

A pair of chem-bio troops guided her into the decon tent, and for another ten minutes she was sprayed from a series of pipe nozzles, rinsed, and doused once again like a Mini Cooper in a car wash. She came out the other end, wading through a pool of foam, where two more troops unlocked her helmet, handed it to her, and backed away.

Dr. Liang walked across the tarmac toward Steele, Hank, and Panther. She no longer had any respiratory protection, so they removed their masks too. She stopped ten feet away. Her glasses were fogged and her hair askew, but her comely features were calm.

"The hand was infected with Gantu-62," she said in English with a lilt of Hong Kong.

"Could you define that, Colonel?" Hank called to her.

"It is a gain-of-function novel corona virus, biochemically equivalent in terms of results to VX."

Panther whistled low. VX was one of the world's most deadly nerve agents. Just 8.6 milligrams of the substance could kill a 220-pound adult male merely by contact with the skin. Liang sighed and nodded at the three men.

"Yes, I take no pride in developing this strain myself, for the People's Liberation Army, in the laboratory which you know was destroyed. It was used on that ship in Africa as a test, to kill everyone on board. I am certain of it." She looked at Hank. "It was the ship you found, Mr. . . . ?"

"Wheelwright," Hank said. "Yes."

Steele looked at his father and thought, *Once a spook, always a spook, right, Dad?*

Liang put her helmet down on the macadam. She pulled off the silver tape sealing her gloves to her cuffs and dropped those as well. Some sort of liquid ran off her fingertips and dripped on her boots. Steele realized it was sweat. She looked directly at him now.

"I must tell you something," she said. She didn't use his name, because she didn't know his name, but she knew the tall bearded American with deeply green eyes was very capable and important. "During the Covid-19 crisis, one of your aircraft carriers was disabled by an infection on board. Do you recall?"

Steele nodded. The incident wasn't easy to forget for anyone in the American defense establishment. It had happened aboard the USS *Roosevelt* when numerous sailors had caught the virus while on shore leave in Southeast Asia. Subsequently, the ship's captain had appealed for emergency relief from Washington, and the *Roosevelt* had been temporarily taken out of action.

"The removal of that ship from the fleet was not due to carelessness on the part of the crew," Liang went on. "It was a direct attack by one of our female agents from the Ministry of State Security. She was infected, intentionally of course, with a heavy viral load of Covid-19. She then seduced a male sailor while the crew was on shore leave in the Philippines."

"Jesus," Steele hissed, and then he heard in his head Chinese expatriate Miles Guo singing, "Let's take down the CCP . . . Let the bullets fly a little longer." *Fuckers . . .*

"Afterward, the disease spread quickly throughout the ship," Liang continued, "but it was only removed from the fleet due to the sentimental weakness of the captain. Covid-19 was not effective as a tactical tool, only as an economic and political one. We knew then that it would take a more powerful bioweapon to eliminate such a behemoth of warfare. It would take something like Gantu-62."

"Does the CCP have its own cache of Gantu somewhere else?" Steele asked.

"No. The only specimens were at my laboratory, Toqui-13. We now know that the men who took them call themselves the Swords of Qing."

"*Suoyi ni shung chung,*" Panther growled to Liang. So you claim. Until Taiwan's National Security Bureau had a long conversation with her, he wasn't going to trust anything she said. But Liang understood and bowed her head, as if supplicating for his recommendations of mercy.

The rumble of an approaching vehicle turned their heads. It was an FMTV medium truck with a high cab in the front, and when it stopped and the passenger door opened, Steele was surprised to see Ralphy Persko climb down.

He was dressed like he'd grabbed half his clothes off the rack from Ranger Joe's, and the other half from Honolua Surf Co.— Moab boots, jungle safari pants, a Hawaiian shirt with parrots, big sunglasses, and an Australian bush hat with the side brim snapped up. He was dripping sweat from his bushy curls, had dark rings of it under his armpits, and was hauling his big Alienware laptop case and wearing a stuffed red backpack. Ralphy ambled toward Steele, panting, as two soldiers from the truck pulled a large black Pelican case out of the back and set it on the ground. Steele couldn't help but grin.

"Whatcha doing here, Ralphy? Had to use up your miles on United?"

"Very funny, Seven." Ralphy put his laptop down and tried sucking oxygen from the humid air. "The boss sent me out here to set up forward cyber and comms." He then noticed Panther staring at him. The dude was scary-looking and Ralphy unconsciously took a step back. "He also said to tell you that Pentagon's gone on a war footing, moving naval and air force assets this way. He says we better figure this one out, and fast."

"Great," Steele said. "Nothing too serious. Did you bring your Glock?"

"Oh, of course, dude . . . *not*." Ralphy rolled his eyes. "But I did bring some toys from S." He jerked a thumb toward the ominous-looking Pelican case. Then he looked up at the tall gray-haired man standing next to Steele. "Who's this gent?"

"My father," Steele said.

Hank dipped his head at Ralphy, whose mouth fell open like he'd seen a ghost. He and Eric were more than just colleagues—he knew the whole family history but had never raised it unless Steele did first.

"Holy mother of God," he whispered.

"No," Hank said, "just the father of an angry son."

Steele's jawline rippled, but he didn't respond. Ralphy went on.

"The boss says everyone in your crew, except for you and Blade, should pack their stuff and rotate back to D.C."

"Why's that?"

"Guess he doesn't think you're gonna live." Ralphy shrugged an apology. "And he needs to keep some assets."

"Yup," Hank Steele said. "*That's* the Program I remember."

Panther turned toward Dr. Liang. One of his commandos had given her a bottle of water and she was drinking and un-pinning her hair. He snapped something in Mandarin and the commando led her to the open back of a Humvee and helped her up to sit on the tailgate. The driver revved the engine.

"What should we do with the specimen, Colonel?" Steele called to her.

"Burn it," she said. "And the laboratory trailer as well, until it is no more than a puddle of metal."

"Wow," Ralphy whispered.

The Humvee drove away. Panther turned to Steele, fished a dangle of keys from his trouser pocket, and handed them over.

"Take my jeep," he said. "You and your father need time alone. Go to the monastery. It is a place that heals wounds."

It was evening in the Garden of Meditations atop a small hill at Fo Guang Shan. There were stone walkways circling around plain granite benches, smiling tubby statuettes of the deity, and can-dles on pedestals lit by the monks. The garden was surrounded by fifty-foot shoots of bamboo thick as horse thighs, with wispy green feathers on top. They knocked against one another in the breeze, making deep hollow sounds, like giants clucking their tongues.

Eric and Hank sat on a bench in the flickering light, but not close. A monk in a brown frock had brought them glasses of tea, but had wagged his finger at Hank's pipe, so he chewed on it empty but didn't smoke. The monk knew Panther Chun, which was why these foreigners could trespass during the meditative month when no other guests were allowed.

They hadn't said much. They both looked down past the edge

of the garden over a long dark pitch of cut grass. A train of five hundred monks in black robes was walking from their evening "medicine meal" to the doors of their large cenobium, heads bowed, hands clasped in front of their hemp belts, and silent.

So many years had passed for the Steeles without being in each other's lives, that neither knew where or how to begin. Eric had learned to bury his bitterness, Hank had learned to bank his guilt, and they both knew it would take another year of conversation for each to learn what the other had seen, and heard, and felt. Yet here they were, on the cusp of a mission. The Program had torn them apart, and now the Program had brought them together. Hank knew he had to take point, so he did.

"When you were small, and I was home," he said in a gravelly voice that would someday be Eric's, "I used to rock you in a big rocking chair before bedtime, and sing you songs."

"What did you sing?"

"Old folk tunes. 'Hang Down Your Head Tom Dooley.' 'Oh Susanna.'"

"Did I like it?"

"You liked that I was home."

Eric looked up at the clicking shoots of bamboo. He remembered every minute of every day he'd spent with his father, but he'd suppressed that long ago. He didn't trust himself to talk about that now.

"When I was in SF, in Afghanistan," he said, "and things were rough, I remembered stuff you said to me as a kid."

"What did I say?"

"Just keep putting one foot in front of the other."

"Did it help?"

"Well, I'm here."

Hank smiled at that and nodded. They were looking at every-thing but each other, at the trees and sky and stars. At the far end of the garden, a monk climbed onto a tree stand and swung a suspended log against the side of an enormous gong . . . *pong, pong, pong.* . . . At last Hank looked at Eric.

"I can't make up for what's gone," he said. "You know what happened, and why."

"I don't need you to fix anything."

"I'm gonna try."

Eric looked back at his father. Maybe Hank was planning on coming home, but he wasn't going to ask. If he said so, then he'd tell him about Rockford's promise, but not before.

"We can't cure the past," Eric said, though he was also think-ing about himself and the things he'd done.

"Nope. Not if I live to be a hundred."

"Maybe you will."

Hank smiled. "We're not in the longevity business, son."

Eric nodded at that, then looked away again.

"I'm going to be a father," he said.

Hank took a deep breath and sat back.

"I'm glad. You'll do better than I."

Some moments went by as the past swirled between them, then Eric said, "We should call her," and he took out his Program cell.

"Can you get cell service here with that thing?" Hank asked.

"I don't need cell service." He almost said Dad, but didn't. "It's a satcom."

"Call her."

It was thirteen hours earlier in the States. They woke Susan up. They moved closer together on the bench, bent their heads low, and put her on speaker. Hank slung an arm on the bench behind Eric's back, but thought better of touching his shoulder.

For just those few minutes, they were a family again, without her knowing where they were and not caring, happy only that they were all together. They laughed at a few things. She cried. No promises were made, except that they'd call her again when they could. But Susan knew what that meant with her kind of men, and she held them to nothing, told them she loved them, and both of them did the same, and then she hung up.

After that, they retreated from each other again, willing their swollen hearts to shrink. Hank spoke first again.

"Ever hear from your half sister?" he asked.

"Once in a while."

"I hear she's got a daughter," Hank said, thinking of the grandchild who, if things went well, he might at last meet.

"Yeah, Kristin. She's a lieutenant JG in the navy."

Hank looked at him and pulled the empty pipe from his mouth. "Where?"

"A carrier, I think—"

Their eyes locked. Then they both jumped up from the bench and ran to the jeep.

CHAPTER 36

It was the most dangerous four and a half acres on earth.

In the course of an eighteen-hour grueling shift on the flight deck, letting your mind wander for just one second could be the very last thought you had. Turn to the right, you could get cut in half by the huge propeller of an E-2C Hawkeye airborne early warning aircraft. Turn to the left, and the afterburner of one of forty-four F-18 Super Hornet strike fighters could burn you to a crisp. Lose focus and stick your head up too high while the carrier was pitching and rolling, and the rotors of an MH-60 Seahawk helo could remove it in a bloody froth.

Those mortal threats didn't include the four "spaghetti" arresting wires, the thick steel cables that landing airplanes grabbed with their tailhooks, but could snap without warning and amputate your foot. Or the leading edges of fighter wings that could crush your rib cage if you forgot to duck. Or the various FODs—foreign object damage—like some loose bolt getting sucked into a jet engine intake, igniting the tanks full of JP-5 fuel, setting off an AIM-9 Sidewinder missile, and blowing you all to Valhalla.

Working the flight deck was a choreographed dance of delivering death, while trying like hell to avoid it.

The deck was serviced by two hundred young men and women wearing color-coded jerseys and vests. Blue moved the aircraft, purple delivered fuel, red loaded bombs and missiles, green worked catapults and wires, brown handled aircraft maintenance and preflight inspections, and white ensured safe operations.

Yellow controlled all the chaos and launched the planes, and were considered the elite of the deck crews, having the most direct contact with the pilots and the triggerman that fired the catapults. Responding to yellow's signals—twirling fingers, cranking arms, low lunges, and dips—the pilots cranked up the engines, stood on their brakes, and watched their referees like sprinters cocked in their blocks, until they saw that straight-armed, go-for-it gesture and exploded off the end of the deck.

Those yellow-clad launchers had a big black SHOOTER stamped on their backs.

Lieutenant Junior Grade Kristin Fellows was a shooter, and she loved it.

Kristin had come aboard the *Roosevelt* after a midshipmen stint with the Sixth Fleet in the Med. The "Big Stick," as the sailors called the ship—from Teddy Roosevelt's famous phrase "Walk softly and carry a big stick"—was a floating city of five thousand souls, with amenities you'd find in any American town. There were gyms, movie theaters, classrooms, dining facilities, and hundreds of jobs, from engine maintainers to cooks, counselors, and radar geeks. But the flight deck was where all the action happened.

She was now OIC of the "Rough Riders," the very first all-female launch crew in the history of the U.S. Navy. She was a tall, slim, reddish brunette, easy on the eyes and hard on her girls. She was their shooter, and they were her ammunition.

The sun was sinking in the Philippine Sea and this was the last plane of her shift. The F-18/F in the breech had LT. COMMANDER ROY "PIKE" PORTNOY stenciled below the cockpit. Portnoy knew Kristin, she knew him, he worried about her safety and she worried about his. He'd shortly be launching on a mission to interdict potential CCP aggressors somewhere out there, and she'd be heading below to a shower, a quick meal in the mess, and her bunk. Maybe she'd read some Tolkien, but she usually fell asleep with the book on her chest.

Her head was pounding as it always did by the end of the day, her nostrils burning with jet fuel fumes, and she couldn't hear a damn thing. Everyone wore padded ear protectors and helmets with radio headsets, but with the din of the catapults spitting steam like dragons, the whines of the turbines, the *thwops* of helo rotors, and the screeches of landing gear slamming the deck, nobody used them except to take orders from the Air Boss high up on the bridge, where he managed the drama from a tower that looked like a Dairy Queen.

From his cockpit, Pike shot Kristin a grin, snapped on his oxygen mask, and gave her a snappy salute. In his backseat, his weapons and sensor officer, Margaret "Binky" Smith, showed Kristin three hand signals—Alpha, Mike, Foxtrot—for "Adios, motherfucker." Kristin smiled, flipped Binky the bird, and got down to business. She heard the same tune in her head she always heard when she launched a bird, "Two Steps from Hell—Protectors of the Earth."

She looked for a thumbs-up from under the jet where one of her greens had locked the tow bar to the catapult. She looked at the blast plate to make sure it was up, cleared everyone else as all the browns and greens scattered, then looked at Pike and whipped two gloved fingers in the air. His twin engines screamed, the nose dipped low, Kristin nodded at the firing officer in his deck hole, then she lunged like a fencer toward the prow, shot her arm straight out with a "bang bang" gesture, and the jet exploded from the blocks, went hurtling down the deck, dipped once toward the sea, and careened off into the sunset.

The deck was empty. Kristin took a long foul breath and sagged.

A first lieutenant appeared from somewhere, slapped her on her shoulder, showed her ten fingers three times, plus five more and yelled "Badass!" She'd launched thirty-five aircraft without a hitch. She grinned, saluted, and headed toward the superstructure.

She felt like she'd boxed ten rounds with a gorilla. She pulled off her helmet, shook out her hair, and headed down the stairwell past the "Ouija board," where officers moved toy airplanes around on a carrier model. She was craving something cold, so she walked into the "711" and straight to the dog machine—it squeezed out ice cream like poop—and made herself a cone. She was going to head straight for a shower, then remembered she'd promised to call her mom.

"Filthy Fellows! You look like you just pit crewed for Daytona 500."

She turned to find an officer colleague standing there with a Starbucks cup. They called him "Ramp" because he had an affinity for falling asleep on the cargo ramps of big airplanes.

"Ramp, shut up or I'll kiss you with my JP-5 tongue."

"*Eww.* Say, you wanna join my bunk later for some Texas Hold'em?"

"Maybe after I shower, get some chow, and call Mommy."

"You prolly didn't hear 'cause you were sunbathing out there," Ramp said, "but we just went full secure. No emails, no satcom calls either."

"Damn. You got a card on you?"

Ramp fished a telephone calling card from his pocket and handed it over.

"Don't use it all up," he said. "Girlfriend gets jealous if I don't report."

"I'll call her and tell her it's cool, but that you stink in the sack."

Ramp laughed and walked off. "Thanks!" Kristin called to his back, and she headed for another steel stairwell and down another level to a long slim corridor. On the port side was a rack of cubbyholes for stowing gear while you used what looked like old silver pay phones. They were actually digital and the lines ran through a secure communications bundle topside, but their keypads were totally retro and they had swipe slots for phone cards.

Kristin tossed her helmet in a cubbyhole, picked up a handset, swiped her card, and dialed. She leaned back on the opposite bulkhead, stretched the coiled black wire, and waited. After a few seconds it rang on the other end, and her mother, Marla Fellows, picked up the phone.

Marla was the biological daughter of a man Kristin had never met called Hank Steele. Kristin did, however, know Hank Steele's other progeny from his second marriage—her mother's half brother, Eric. She had no idea what Eric did for a living, and she rarely saw him, yet he was cool, cute, kind of spooky, and she liked him. But at the moment she wasn't thinking about any of that.

"Hello?" Marla said.

"Hi, Mom. How's it going?"

"Why are you calling me at midnight? What's wrong?"

"Nothing at all. I was free so I called."

"You scared me."

Kristin rolled her eyes. "Sorry, Mom, just the time difference, that's all."

"Where are you?"

"St. Croix."

"You're lying, honey."

"You know I can't tell you, Mom. How's Dad?"

"Sleeping."

"No, I meant *how*?"

"He's fine, he's fine." Marla paused for a moment as she tried not to be a paranoid military mommy, but she was chewing her lip in Virginia. "I worry about you being on that big ship, Kristie."

"I love you too, Mom." Kristin looked at her watch and chewed what was left of her cone. She was dying to pee, shower, and eat.

"No, I mean it," her mom said. "It scares me."

"Oh, Mom, seriously," Kristin said. "Listen, this boat is enormous, it's packed with five thousand people, it's got guns and airplanes and marines on board, and we're out in the middle of the freaking ocean."

"So? That's supposed to make me feel better?"

"*Yes*, Mom!" Kristin rolled her eyes again. "You can stop worrying. Believe me, it's the safest place on earth."

CHAPTER 37

SENKAKU ISLANDS, EAST CHINA SEA

The helicopters arrived at dawn, and for the Japanese fisherman of the small tuna vessel called *Fijimoru,* it was an unusual thing, and a bit worrisome. The Japanese men were not allowed to be on shore. No one was allowed to be there.

The Senkaku were a group of eight tiny islands in the middle of nowhere, set in crystal blue and green shallows exactly half-way between mainland China and the island of Okinawa, and 120 nautical miles northeast of Taiwan. They were uninhabited clumps of green bushy hills, caves and caverns, rocky beaches and sharp coral that could slice your feet raw. The only living creatures were black-footed albatross and terns, lizards, mosquitoes, and feral cats, with the surrounding seas full of marlin, tuna, and sharks. They were useless islands and no one really wanted them, although China, Taiwan, and Japan all claimed them as theirs.

The captain of *Fijimoru,* Taki Osawa, was a crusty old salt who had piloted his vessel for seven rough hours from the Japanese isle of Ishigaki. Once a month, he and his crew of eleven hardy men would make the trip at night to avoid the Japanese Coast Guard, then come ashore at the largest island, Uotsuri, and make camp for a few days between hooking and hauling fresh tuna. They set up their tents, made fires, cooked meals of fresh fish and rice, drank saki, smoked awful cigarettes, and sang. It was a joyful working vacation away from their mewling children and impatient wives.

"Trouble," Taki said to his first mate, Shingo, as he watched the three black Harbin Z-20s approaching just above the morning sea. Most of his men were donning their high boots and yellow slickers outside the tents, preparing to wade out to their anchored forty-foot diesel.

"Fucking Chinese." Shingo frowned as he tossed his cigarette into the foam at their feet. "I saw the red stars when they banked."

"Tell the men to hurry," Taki grunted. "If we're aboard the damn boat they can't do a thing."

He looked back at the three-hundred-meter-high crest that ran for two miles along the kidney-shaped island like the spine of some prehistoric beast. There was nowhere for the helicopters to land but the wide half circle of sloping stone beach where he stood. On the other side of the island the mountain sloped right down to the water, with nothing there but a slim strip of sand.

The first mate yelled "*Isogeh!*" and the men abandoned the tents and hustled with armfuls of whatever they could grab toward the waves and their boat. They were handsome, muscular, sunburned young men. A few had marlin hooks on pikes, a couple had machetes, and one had an old bolt-action Type 38 Arisaka rifle for shooting sharks—not very effective protection. Yet they were no more concerned than a pack of truant schoolboys. Naval patrols, whether Chinese, Taiwanese, or Japanese, usually just blew air horns and waved them off.

But today there would be no such diplomacy.

The first of the three helicopters swung in from the sea to Taki's right as he watched. It was large and black, pounding the air with its wide main rotor, and he saw that the side doors were open, and there were legs and black boots hanging down. The belly of the beast tipped up just ten meters in front of him and two off the deck, and the roaring windstorm plucked both of his tents from their stakes and sent them tumbling down the beach, along with his favorite straw fisherman's hat.

A man jumped to the ground. He wasn't large but dressed in all black and springy like a cat. He had a large pistol strapped to one thigh and also wore one of those black skull hoods that showed only his eyes and lips. He walked toward Taki as seven more men disgorged from the thundering machine and also dropped to the beach, although those held wicked-looking guns with strange black cans on their fronts. Taki wondered why Chinese commandos would be all the way out here in Senkaku, unless they were conducting some sort of exercise. The shark-like helicopter rose away and swung back out to sea.

The first man strode up to Taki and smiled. Taki was holding one of his marlin pikes, a six-foot pole with a large barbed spear on the end. He gripped the pole near the top, bowed his head once, and smiled back. This might turn out to be a friendly encounter after all.

Zaifeng drew his QSZ-92 pistol, shot Taki point-blank in the face and blew off the back of his skull. As Taki toppled backward, his fingers sprang open and Zaifeng reached out with his free left hand and caught the pike. He looked at it as he twirled it once, thinking this might make even a better weapon than his *bo,* and reminded himself to take it along in the helicopter, though they wouldn't be leaving for some time.

Meanwhile, Taki's men—almost all of them were still in the shallow waves and wading to *Fijimoru,* and had stopped momentarily to gawk at the helicopters and the Chinese commandos—jolted at the horrible sight of their captain being shot in the face, spun around, and started splashing like madmen toward their boat.

They weren't nearly fast enough.

Lieutenant Po barked at his six men, and they all waded into the water and opened fire. They were in no rush and there was no need to waste ammunition—these Japanese had nowhere to go. They sloshed through the water, the bolts of their QBZ-95 bullpup rifles clacked in double taps, blue smoke spewed from their coughing silencers, and the 5.8 × 42 mm bullets tore through the skulls and slickers of the wailing fishermen.

Taki's first mate, Shingo, chose to stand and fight. He tore the old bolt-action Arisaka rifle from the hands of his dying motorman and spun in the waves as he tried to work the rusty bolt. Just as he jerked up the rifle, Po was right there, gripping the barrel with his left glove and flipping it out of the way as it fired and just missed his ear. He shoved the mouth of his silencer into Shingo's chest, thumbed the weapon to full auto, and blew Shingo's sternum out through his spine. Shingo's corpse splashed in the water.

Another fisherman, whose father had taught him the art of the blade, also chose to die like a warrior. He screamed, yanked his machete from his belt, and charged his assaulters, whipping it over his head like a scythe. Two of Po's men watched him come at them, one of them smiled and quipped something cruel, and they both opened up and removed his legs.

The youngest and most spry of the fishermen, a seventeen-year-old boy from Hiroshima named Kenji, had thrown off his slicker and dived under the waves. He'd swum almost all the way to the boat in one breath, came up gasping and sputtering, and grabbed the rungs of the aluminum stern ladder and started scrambling up. But Po saw him out there, dropped his bullpup to hang from his neck, drew his pistol, and shot him offhand at fifty meters in the back of the head.

Two of Taki's fishermen had already been on *Fijimoru* when the helicopters arrived. Keening and crawling around on their hands and knees, they'd managed to fire up the diesel engine, made it into the wheelhouse, and were trying to work the throttles and old-fashioned wheel. But the boat only whined and sputtered as its props churned up water. In their panic they'd forgotten to pull in the anchor.

It didn't matter. Zaifeng's second helicopter was already hovering just off the bow. From its cargo bay, a door gunner with a Type 67 general purpose machine gun shattered the wheelhouse windshield, then blew the two men into clouds of blood and splintering bone.

The last surviving fisherman had fled from the carnage in the other direction, back toward the beach. He was an older man in his fifties and he was crying and completely spent. He collapsed in the shallows and crawled up onto the bed of sea-polished stones and sand, slinging tears and mucus.

Zaifeng holstered his pistol, took Taki's marlin pike, walked over to the exhausted man, drove the pike through his back and pinned him to the ground like a butterfly. He left the wooden handle twanging upright in the air.

The rest was silence. There were no more screams or gunfire, just the sounds of the breeze and the waves and the helicopters as they circled back in from the sea. Po emerged from the water and approached Zaifeng. There was blood and gobs of something like pink mayonnaise on his balaclava, and he pulled it off, soaked it in the salt water and wrung it out with his hands. Zaifeng nodded in approval at his work, and Po tapped the module of his headset, which was plugged in his ear.

"I have just heard from Miko," he said. "He has arrived in Taiwan."

"Very good. Now have the crews camouflage the aircraft," Zaifeng said, then he turned and pointed at the island's crest. "The main cave is there at the centerline. Have two men explore it to the end and see if there is an exit on the other side. If there is not, make one."

"Yes, *Xian Sheng*," Po said. Ziafeng had taught him that there must always be an exit. That's why they carried plenty of explosives.

"After that, post two men on top of that ridge with the QW-18s." He was referring to their pair of Chinese surface-to-air, shoulder-fired missiles. He traversed his finger from left to right, pointing out two formations of rock. "And they should set up the machine guns, there and there."

He took Po's elbow and locked his eyes to make sure he was focused. "The Gantu-62 canister must be moved, very carefully, into the cave. The men must suit up to do that. Am I clear?"

"Yes, sir."

"Good." Zaifeng turned him back toward the water and jutted his chin at the floundering *Fijimoru*. "Have Feng and one other swim out to the boat. The engine is still turning. They should take it out a kilometer or so, sink it, and swim back. I do not want to see any of its detritus."

"Of course."

"When all of that is done, make contact with Scarlet again. We need to know where the *Roosevelt* is."

Then Zaifeng looked at the water. The shallows were pink with blood and the corpses floated and turned in the waves.

"It is a shame," Zaifeng said.

Po was surprised at his commander's expression of pity.

"Perhaps we should have kept some alive?" Po asked. "Perhaps as hostages?"

Zaifeng looked at his lieutenant and his black eyes narrowed.

"They were Japanese, Po. Do you not remember the rape of Nanking? I meant it is a shame there weren't more of them to kill."

CHAPTER 38

At two o'clock in the morning, Central Intelligence Agency analyst Felicia Min should have been fast asleep. She was not.

Instead, she was perched on a cushy office chair in the dark spare bedroom of a luxury high-rise apartment, in one of the most coveted neighborhoods of Arlington, just across the river from the nation's capital. Crystal City was a tight sprawl of luxury residences, effete fashion stores, overpriced restaurants, and the offices of numerous government agencies, including the United States Marshals Service and the EPA. The city's twenty-two thousand spoiled residents enjoyed weather-protected underground passages to traverse from their homes to shopping or their places of work. The parking garages were packed with Audis and Volvos. You had to be a well-heeled senator, congressman, or defense establishment lobbyist to afford the ridiculous rents.

Tonight, Felicia, whose code name "Scarlet" was known only to Zaifeng and Po of the Swords of Qing, didn't look like the frumpy analyst who'd briefed President Rockford just days before. Her thick-framed glasses were gone, the tips of her bangs teased penciled eyebrows, her mouth was glossed in lipstick, and she was wearing an obscenely short sheer purple nightgown.

She hated the getup. She was much more comfortable in sweats or jeans, but the needs of the mission precluded good taste.

On the desk before her were two smartphones. One was her CIA issue, fully secure, which she wasn't going to touch—activity on that phone was always tracked by Langley, and likely the NSA. The other was her personal iPhone X. Just beyond the phones was an open MacBook Air laptop. That was also a secure device, but it wasn't hers. The laptop had a fingerprint reader, and since none of Felicia's fingertips would pass muster with its CCD detector, she wasn't going to try.

Instead, she pulled a tiny USB dongle from her Gucci purse, which contained a black hat program called PoisonTap, and plugged it into the laptop's Thunderbolt drive. She waited the prescribed two minutes, then removed the dongle, confident that PoisonTap had inserted a backdoor into the laptop's cache, creating undetectable access points to top secret files and real time government feeds. But the best part was full emulation with an injection of Reflector 3, turning her iPhone into the laptop's mirror image. She opened the PoisonTap app on her cell—disguised as a Bloomingdale's shopping icon—pressed her thumb down, and voilá, she was in.

What Felicia needed now was access to that morning's PDB, the intelligence community's presidential daily briefing. The document was highly classified but was shared with certain members of the House Permanent Select Committee on Intelligence. Somewhere within that daily tome was the current location of the U.S. Navy's Roosevelt strike group. As one of the CIA's top

Asia analysts, she could have simply searched for those details at her desk at Langley, but all of her keystrokes there were logged. Here, with PoisonTap and her iPhone, she could snoop like a wraith and no one would ever know. If later on by some chance her probing was discovered, the laptop's owner would be blamed.

It took another few minutes until she found the aircraft carrier's current location in the Philippine Sea, about 750 miles east-northeast of Manila. She memorized its latitude and longitude—18.21 x 130.17 on the World Geodetic System—then switched over on her iPhone to WhatsApp, where a friend named "Betty" had just texted her to ask about her upcoming plans for vacation.

Betty was Zaifeng's lieutenant, Po.

Felicia thought about the coordinates for a half a minute, then thumbed her return message.

"I'm thinking around the 18th. They're giving me three weeks, but I gotta lose some weight before I'll wear a bikini, lol. I'm up to 130, haven't been this fat since I was seventeen!"

"Okay, girlfriend!" Po tapped back. "Hit the gym and I'll see you then! xox."

It was done, at least for tonight. She might have to do it all again in a day or so, but she pushed that out of her mind. One day at a time was her mantra, though the days of this double life and its pressures were getting to be very long.

Just two days before, on the ride back to Langley from the White House, CIA director Tina Harcourt had indiscreetly shared her suspicion with Felicia that President Rockford had some sort of black operations program on the side. Harcourt's station chief in Taipei had reported American assets landing in Pingtung, and the director thought the president was mounting a "side bet" kinetic action to move against the Swords of Qing, in case they were real.

Felicia had feigned a stomach flu that afternoon, left her cubicle at Langley, and reported that intel to Po.

She was taking too many chances. She was drinking too much, and smoking cigarettes too. Langley didn't teach you how to be a coldblooded traitor at the Farm, although in fact she felt like an American patriot. Someone had to save this country from the megalomaniacal CCP.

She switched to the PoisonTap app and closed it down, making the program's worms dormant, for now. Then she stuffed both smartphones into her purse, sat back in the chair, blew her bangs off her forehead with an exasperated sigh, and thought about sneaking out of the flat and going home. But she knew she couldn't do that. Instead she got up, opened the bedroom door, leaned against the jamb with her arms folded, and stared at the mess in the living room.

Congressman Richard Stillwell was lying there on his back. Unfortunately, he wasn't dead. He was snoring, in fact, in the middle of a huge pullout couch. He was also naked except for half a sheet thrown across his thighs and crotch, arms askew to both sides, and the various bottles of beer and vodka and the empty pizza boxes on the coffee table seemed apt decor for his postcoital sloth. The air stank of alcohol, weed, and sex.

Felicia had never asked him why they always made love on the pullout and never in his bedroom, but she assumed it had something to do with his wife, who visited every couple of months from L.A. Maybe he thought Mrs. Stillwell would sense he was banging some young intern in his home away from home, or maybe he was just kinky that way—one bed for one woman, another for the other. In truth, Felicia didn't care.

He was one of the most egotistical, corrupt, and moronic politicians she'd ever met, and she'd met quite a few. She stood there with her back against the jamb and thought, *Maybe I have to act like a slut to get what I need, Richard, but you're the real whore.* He spent half his time being wooed by Communist assets from the CCP, turning a blind eye to their thefts of American intellectual property, and crying crocodile tears on TV whenever his political opponents called out Beijing. "Racists!" he'd scold them, then laugh about the whole thing an hour later while he dragged Felicia out for drinks at some showy saloon in D.C.

He was so dumb he didn't even realize she was CIA and believed she was a grad student at Georgetown. Once he'd even walked right past her workstation at Langley during one of those silly congressional tours. Probably didn't recognize her with her clothes on. *Pig.*

Stillwell stirred in the smoky dim light of the living room and snorted. He had strange blank eyes and a weird little mouth, as if he'd been hit in the face with a baseball bat as a kid—Felicia assumed that was the case, and probably justified. He raised his head and looked at her, gave her that creepy crooked smile, and patted the sheet.

"Come back to bed, *baby*," he crooned in a tenor slur that he probably thought was manly. "There's still time for one more ride!"

He pulled the sheet away from his crotch and Felicia's stomach turned, but she sauntered toward the bed. Very soon now, if everything worked according to plan, the Chinese Communist Party would be decimated from an all-out war. And then she'd secretly out Mr. Stillwell as one of their assets, and she'd do it anonymously through one of his "friends" in the mainstream media.

They'd turn on him in a flash.

As she crawled up onto the bed, she thought about the best part of it all. When this whole thing was over, she'd never have to kiss him again.

N O   A C K N O W L E D G E D   L O C A T I O N

EYES ONLY

SAP (Alphas/Support/OCO EAST) - FLASH

From: SAWTOOTH MAIN

To: All OCONUS EAST ASIA PAX

Subj: Displace

Source: Staff Ops/Duty Officer

Confidence: Highest

IMMEDIATE, all OCONUS EAST PAX, inc ALPHAS,
KEEPERS, SUPPORT, AIR: Withdraw SAWTOOTH
immediate, on site transport mode cleared.

Emphasis: Exceptions; Seven/Blade/Geek1.

STATUS: DEFCON Red.

Operational window: Immediate Execute

The sight of Panther's commandos smashing their foreheads into large slabs of brick made Ralphy Persko cover his eyes. It was the sound of it too, their wolflike karate screams, the impact of flesh and bone on stone, a horrid aural experience he knew he'd never forget. But he didn't have enough fingers to blind himself while also plugging his ears.

The commandos, in three rows of nine on the Pingtung parade ground, were dressed in snug black tactical utilities and kneeling before twenty-seven sets of upright cinder blocks, across which their red brick targets had been laid. All of those bricks were now cracked in half, and as the commandos stood up and snapped to parade rest, their faces were blank as if all they'd done was head-butt paper walls. Two had trickles of blood running off the tips of their noses, which they ignored.

"Those boys are hard," said Eric Steele.

"Hard?" Ralphy groaned. "They're insane."

Steele and Persko were sitting on a set of bleachers on the

north side of the training square, which was about half the size of a soccer field and bulldozed flat with gravel and crushed cement—the kind of thing that would never pass muster on a military base in the States because some troop's mommy would complain. Beyond that was the ASSC parachute training hangar and chute shed, braced by a low concrete barracks, the armory, motor pool, a comms shack bristling with antennas, and a TOC. With the rows of razor wire and the palm trees waving their lush fronds in the humid breeze, it looked like a Florida prison with an exercise yard.

"Are we supposed to clap?" Ralphy asked Steele.

"No. It isn't a show for us. They probably do this every day."

"Every day? They must all have TBIs," Ralphy said, meaning traumatic brain injuries.

"You don't need a lot of cerebrum for this kind of work," Steele said. "Just need to know where to shoot, and when, and who to kill, and how."

"Sorta like you."

"Yeah, like me."

The commandos had now cleared all their blocks and brick shards from the pitch, and were working through martial arts forms that appeared to be tae kwon do *katas* at third-degree black belt level. They were punching, kicking, and scything the air so fast with whipping knife hands that they looked like they could march straight into the elephant grass and mow it all down.

"Allie woulda loved this," Ralphy remarked. "She's always saying a hard man is good to find."

Steele smirked. She'd said that same thing to him a few times when they were back at Bagram doing things that were strictly nonregulation.

"Well, make a video for her," he said.

Ralphy pulled his smartphone from his cargo pocket, but Steele grabbed his wrist and said, "I was kidding, numb nuts. Want Panther to cut off your hand?"

Ralphy put the smartphone away.

Allie Whirly was no longer in Taiwan, nor were Slick, Shane Wiley, Miles Turner, or Tenzin the monk. They hadn't gone quietly and had made a fuss until Steele had shown them the flash from Sawtooth Main and said he supported Lansky's call. Orders were orders, and Lansky's disposition of assets made sense. The Progam was just getting back on its feet and it was his call to decide who was expendable, and who was not.

The only one who was happy to reboard the Gulfstream for Washington, D.C., was Tenzin. He'd dreamed his whole life about making it to the States someday, and more than anything wanted to have at least one last face-to-face with the man he called Hua Chang Mao, who, given his age at this point, might soon "kick the bucket" (another of Tenzin's quirky English expressions). Steele had lobbied for Tenzin with Lansky, claiming that without the monk's intervention, Colonel Dr. Liang would now be dead. Lansky had at last relented and said Tenzin could get on the plane. Lansky wasn't a people person, but he had a weakness for spies.

The commandos were now fetching training implements from two large rattan trunks, including nunchakus, polymer knives, *bo* staffs, and wooden Bokken swords.

"What are they gonna do now?" Ralphy asked Steele.

"They're going to hurt each other."

"Oh God, I can't watch this."

"Relax, Ralphy. They like it."

Steele heard low laughter coming from over his left shoulder, but he didn't turn. Up there on the last bench of the bleachers, his father and Dalton Goodhill, who hadn't seen each other in two and a half decades, were reliving events of the past. It felt strange having them both there while he was prepping a mission—sort of like having your parents watching while you were trying to impress a girl.

Steele and his father had raced back to Pingtung from the monastery the night before, ready to jump on a secure horn in Panther's HQ and shout at Lansky that the *Roosevelt* had to be turned around. But halfway back through the rice paddies, they'd both realized that they couldn't single out one vessel just because Kristin was aboard. Every ship in that carrier strike group was in peril, and there was no way to know which of them would be targeted by the Swords of Qing. All they could do was tell Lansky about Dr. Liang's revelation that Gantu-62 had been designed— and now successfully tested in Africa—to take out warships, and probably a lot more.

Lansky didn't tell them that a CIA subject matter expert on China had briefed the president that the whole thing might be a CCP ruse—a false flag op to cover for an invasion of Taiwan. Either way, he needed the Swords of Qing terminated.

The only problem was, nobody knew where they were.

At the top of the bleachers, Hank Steele was smoking his pipe and Dalton Goodhill chewed on a cigar. In their blue jeans, boots, and short-sleeved shirts, they looked like old stunt doubles for Lee Marvin and Bruce Willis.

"I remember when you made that cash drop in the Mog," Hank said. "That was all balls."

"I remember when you and Jerry Ginder dropped from that Huey skid in Cambodia," Goodhill said, "and nobody heard from either of you for half a friggin' year."

"Whatever happened to Ginder?" Hank asked.

"Covid," Goodhill said and shook his head.

"Seriously? Fifth group guy, two thousand jumps, three bronze stars, and he gets taken by the Chinese virus?"

"The world is a fine place and worth fighting for," Goodhill murmured, "and I hate very much to leave it."

Hank looked at him through a halo of smoke. "That's Hemingway."

"Yup." Goodhill examined the end of his burning cigar.

"Hell, I didn't even know you could read."

They both smiled at that, then Hank looked down at his son's wide back. "How's the kid doing?"

"Best operator I've ever seen. Don't tell him I said so."

"Your secret's safe," Hank said.

"He broke every Program protocol and tried to rescue your sorry ass from Siberia."

"So I heard."

"My kids barely talk to me," Goodhill complained.

"Maybe you need to go missing."

"If I stay in this game I probably will."

Panther arrived in his jeep with Ralphy's big black Pelican case in the back. He was followed by another jeep, empty except for its driver. He barked something at his squadron leader, who snapped an order to the twenty-seven commandos. They quickly packed up their training gear and marched off down toward the Pingtung firing range.

Panther summoned Steele with a downward wave of his slabby

hand. He was wearing his Ray-Bans, a black ball cap with the ROC special forces insignia, and had a cigarette tucked behind one ear.

"Colonel Liang has passed her debriefing with the NSB," he grunted. "She is clean."

"But is she still in one piece, Panther?" Steele asked.

"No one touched her. She talked freely for four hours."

"Good. My people back in the States will want to talk to her too."

Panther's smile curled. "She is worth her weight in gold."

"That won't be much. I've seen German shepherds that weigh more."

Panther laughed and called to the rest, "Okay, Yankees, get in. We do not know how much time we have."

"That sounds ominously existential," Ralphy mumbled, and Goodhill flicked him on the back of the head.

The firing range was half a klick past the end of the compound, with ten shooting stations facing a fifteen-foot berm and man-size targets at fifty yards. Steele noted that all the cardboard targets were caricatures of Mao Zedong—these people did not like Communists. To the left was a maze of plywood walls on stanchions, with doors and windows so Panther's men could practice close-quarters battle. They were peppered with bullet holes and grenade shrapnel.

The commandos had arrived first on the run and were already banging away with XT-105 assault rifles in 5.56 mm and a few nasty-looking XT-104 9 mm submachine guns. Spinning brass shell casings flew through the air, the smoke smelled like burnt hair, and all the men were wearing black caps like Panther's, Oakley sunglasses, and looked like killer clones from *The Matrix*.

Panther stopped his small convoy behind the stations, got out, jammed his big paw in a pail full of earplugs, and handed them out to his guests. Then he took Steele's elbow and walked him over to his squadron leader, who was punching a very tight grouping dead center at his distant target.

"You like to try a Taiwanese weapon, Steele?" he offered.

"Sure."

Panther's officer made the weapon safe and handed it over to Steele. Behind them, Ralphy nudged Hank and said, "Watch *this*, papa."

Steele raised the rifle, leaned forward, and before he'd settled his eye in the reflex site, punched three tight rounds in the target's upper left quadrant, three more in the upper right, then two nostril holes beneath the squadron leader's grouping, and beneath that a short curving burst, finishing a perfect smiley face.

The squadron leader retrieved his rifle and grunted something in Mandarin.

"What did he say?" Steele asked Panther.

"He said he is taking his weapon back before you write your name."

"Hope I didn't offend him."

"Jackson will not like you now, but it is important that he knows you can shoot."

"Jackson?"

"He attended Boston University. They could not pronounce Jae Ki Swon."

Panther's jeep drivers had pulled Ralphy's Pelican case out and set it down on the ground. Panther called a ceasefire, Jackson had his commandos clear and safe their weapons, and they all formed up in a semicircle to watch.

Ralphy punched a digital lock and opened the case. A pair of strange-looking handheld weapons were nestled in packing foam on the left. They were gunmetal blue and looked like fat semi-automatics, except their barrels were nine-inch-long tubes with open horizontal slots from the fore-end sights to the breech. To the right were "dishwasher" racks, holding two dozen five-inch-diameter disks that looked like razor-sharp buzz saw blades. In the center of each disk was a black golf ball. There were also two boxes of blank .44 magnum ammunition.

"What the hell's this?" Hank Steele muttered. "Looks like some *Star Trek* thing."

"Boomer," Goodhill snorted.

"These look like *shuriken*." Panther pointed at the disks, meaning the Japanese ninja throwing stars that could be hurled like mini Frisbees and impale human chests.

"Pretty much the same," Ralphy said as he picked up a pistol and one of the disks, "except this ball in the middle is packed with Semtex." He slid the wicked-looking disk into the pistol's front slot and pushed it back to the breech, where it locked into a revolving sprocket. "The magazine holds ten blanks for launching the disks, and the charge only arms when the thing reaches maximum velocity."

"You hope," Steele said.

"Well, that's what S said. I trust her."

"Good, then you can go first, Ralphy."

"I will try it," Panther volunteered, but Steele gripped his thick bicep and shook his head.

"You're our host, Panther. It might blow up."

"Okay, Steele, then who is expendable?"

Ralphy looked up at Dalton Goodhill.

"Shit, of course," Goodhill said.

Panther had his men suit Goodhill up with Kevlar. Then they gave him a helmet and ballistic goggles and walked him over to the CQB range. Everyone else stepped back, plugged their ears, and held their breaths.

Goodhill took aim at a thick wooden door at fifty yards. He squeezed the trigger, the blank charge boomed like a shotgun, the disk went spinning with a wicked whistle, chunked its blades in the door, then exploded like an M26 grenade that left nothing there but a piece of frame.

"Wicked!" Goodhill grinned as he walked back over to the crew. "What's this little shit called?"

"Whipsaw," Ralphy said. "Told ya it was cool."

"Hate to waste it on the Swords of Qing," Steele said. "There're so many deserving politicians."

Panther's commandos were thrilled with the deadly device and swarmed around Ralphy and the case, wanting to give it a go. Ralphy tried to wave them off, protesting that the Pelican's contents were all he had.

Someone tapped Steele's shoulder, and he turned to find Colonel Dr. Liang. He didn't know how she'd arrived, but she was dressed in civilian clothes—blue jeans, running shoes, and a loose white blouse—and he thought she looked pretty as an off-duty Singapore Airlines flight attendant. But her expression was troubled and she was holding three green plastic tubes that looked like military diazepam injectors. Panther walked over and pulled her and Steele aside.

"Will it work?" Panther said to Liang in English.

"Will what work?" Steele asked.

"The doctor's countermeasure to the Gantu-62," Panther said. "My men will not fight in MOPP suits, Steele. It is not honorable."

"Panther has been very helpful." Dr. Liang nodded at the colonel. "He had the biochemical battalion deliver materials, and I have been working on a temporary antidote."

"Temporary?" Steele said.

"Yes. I can modify these EpiPens, with shocks of adrenaline as well as rapid anticoagulants, plus their already inclusive anti-seizure properties. But if you and the commandos are exposed to Gantu-62, it will not save you."

"What will it do?" Steele said.

"It will only delay your deaths."

Steele raised an eyebrow at Dr. Liang. "If you're thinking about a career in advertising," he said, "you might want to reconsider."

CHAPTER 41

Zaifeng's assassin murdered Dr. Liang that night in her bed, and Steele wasn't fast enough to stop him.

It was Panther's tactical error, something the special forces commander would curse himself for and regret till his end of days. Panther had decided that his musky concrete barracks at Pingtung weren't fitting for honored guests, especially the petite and courageous PLA colonel, for whom he had growing respect and affection. So, in the evening he'd arranged for better accommodations. The monastery's labyrinth of structures included a small bed-and-breakfast for visiting tourists who wanted to experience deific devotion, and it so happened that Panther's sister was the bed-and-breakfast's bookkeeper and accountant. The reservations were easily made.

Panther's squadron leader, Jackson, who'd made his peace with Steele after challenging him to a pistol match—which Steele had intentionally lost—had escorted Steele and his small crew to the check-in desk. Jackson made it clear to the monk on duty that these were guests of Colonel Wi Lung Chun and the Airborne Special Service Company, and that he'd return for the five after breakfast.

No one imagined the worst of all nightmares, that in the morning they'd only be four.

Dinner at the monastery was stark and hardly a four-star repast. A brown-robed monk fetched the four Americans and the Chinese woman, escorted them through the Garden of Meditations, and before admitting them into a vast dining hall, smiled and crossed his lips with a finger, indicating absolute silence. Inside there were twenty tables, each forty feet long, where already five hundred monks in black vestments sat. They sipped tea and ate mounds of rice and vegetables using chopsticks, without uttering a word, reminding Steele of a punitive meal for plebes he'd once witnessed at West Point.

Steele, Hank, Ralphy, Goodhill, and Dr. Liang took their seats at a separate table reserved for guests. They were served by a pair of novice brothers, and they nodded thanks and pretended to enjoy their tasteless supper, having no inkling that Zaifeng's assassin, Miko, was also there.

Disguised as a student monk from the Nung Chan farming monastery outside Taipei, Miko had already been at Fo Guang Shan for more than a day. His commander, Zaifeng, had received an encrypted message from Scarlet that an American strike team had arrived at Pingtung, and had concluded that these were likely the very same commandos who'd rescued the PLA colonel in Mongolia and had slaughtered so many of his Swords. These operators were a mortal danger to Zaifeng's plans, so he'd dispatched Miko to Taiwan to blunt their spear with murder.

Miko was a compact beast and an expert killer with knives and barehanded kuntao kung fu, but he'd shaved his head, bought wire-rimmed glasses, and affected a studious hunch in his baggy robes. The special operations base at Pingtung was only three kilometers away, but it wouldn't be easy to infiltrate. He knew he'd have to find a way, quickly, yet suddenly he was saved the trouble by a remarkable turn of fortune.

Sitting among a row of monks, he was bobbing in silent prayer and eating his meal, when he glanced up, saw the foreign guests arrive, and his killer instincts raised the hairs on his neck. He knew right away who they were. These three large muscular Americans didn't look anything like religious tourists, except perhaps for the small fat one. They were clearly men on a mission, and he instantly recognized the female Chinese colonel who he'd chased through Toqui-13—the one he'd failed to kill.

He took it as a dharmic blessing upon Zaifeng's imperial designs. He would not fail again. He would terminate all of them, but she would be first.

Dinner was brief. Without conversation there was no reason to dawdle, and there was also no dessert. Steele and his crew walked back toward the bed-and-breakfast. The day had been long and hot, they exchanged a few comments about the cooler evening weather and how they wished there was a hotel bar, but they really didn't have much to say. Dr. Liang tripped over a stone in the dark, Goodhill grabbed her elbow to steady her, and she smiled at him and he blushed.

When they arrived at the bed-and-breakfast's front desk, each was given a key, and they parted for their sparse single rooms, which were all in a row like dorm rooms in a low-budget college. Each room had one wooden bed with a slim foam mattress and pillow, one headboard lamp, one latched window that looked out on the grounds, and a television that broadcast only prayers from the monastery's great shrine.

Separately, they all folded their clothes, lay down on their beds, and looked at the blank stucco walls until the lights were extinguished by automated curfew. Ralphy had his Alienware laptop, but there was no Wi-Fi, so instead he thought about Frankie, and missed her. Hank lay there ruminating about his reunion with Eric and the pride he felt for his son. Goodhill thought about a woman in Virginia, then fell asleep snoring. Steele thought about his reunion with his father, with conflicting emotions about whether he should be glad about that, or forever angry, and he drifted off with the words of an old Harry Chapin tune in his head.

When you comin' home, Dad? I don't know when, but we'll get together then, son. We'll get together then. . . .

Dr. Liang lay awake for a while, torn with guilt about all the things she'd done for the Party, yet hopeful that she might make a good life for herself in America, atone for all of it, and someday be happy again. At last she fell asleep.

Hers was the first window that Miko pried open.

At midnight he slipped out of the monks' dormitory, taking his clothing satchel, and in the garden shed his robes and donned a hooded black track suit. He was barefoot and carried a wicked *tanto* blade. He didn't know which of the guest rooms was hers, but he slinked along the outside wall, pulled himself up to the first windowsill, peered inside, saw only a large male form, and dropped back down. At the next window he spotted her small white feet poking up from the end of a blanket. He whispered *"shehsheh"* to the gods of war, and with a twist of his blade in the simple lock, he was in.

Liang's scream was muffled when something like a giant nightmare spider straddled her small body, crushed down onto her chest, and a hand slammed over her mouth. Another hand gripped her throat, and she arched her back and scrambled for something, anything, and her fingers found the lamp behind her head and she smashed it into that awful face and the bulb exploded. She twisted and choked as she kicked, and with everything left in her burning lungs tried to throw him off. Then her eyes went horribly wide when she saw the blade in his upraised fist, and when he plunged it right through her ribs and into her heart, Steele heard it.

He was in the room next to Liang's and sprang to his feet, wearing only his jeans, and he grabbed his father's 1911 and flew out into the hallway. The door to her room was locked and without thinking he angle fired, split the lock and the wood, kicked it open with the ball of his bare foot, and charged inside into blackness. The pistol was instantly kicked from his fist and clanged off a wall, and a bullet-shaped head rammed him in his solar plexus.

Steele slammed backward into the doorjamb, saw a gleaming blade lancing straight for his throat, jerked to the left, smashed the knife hand with a right sudo strike, and kicked Miko into the television set with a whipping left roundhouse. The old TV's cathode ray tube burst in a flash and he saw Liang's bloody corpse on the bed, and the rage burst in his brain like typhoon lightning.

Miko charged him again. Steele punched his face, first with his left, cracking his cheekbone, then with his right, straight on, and saw black blood gush from his nose. He broke Miko's left knee with a stomping side kick, making him scream, then arm barred his knife hand and wrenched the blade away. He grabbed the front of Miko's track suit with his left hand, hurled him right off his feet into the wall under the window, and he was raising the knife and just about to flay the bastard in half, when his father grabbed his arm, spun him around, and said, "Dead men don't talk, son."

Goodhill burst into the room. He saw Dr. Liang sprawled on her back, went right over to her, sat on the edge of the bed, touched her throat with his fingers, then dropped his big bald head and whispered, "Mother*fucker.*"

Ralphy arrived at the room, panting, and he wheezed, "I just called Panther." Then a light flicked on in the hallway behind him and he saw what had happened inside. He staggered over to the wall by the foot of the bed, slid to the floor, covered his eyes, and wept.

No one said a word while they waited for Panther. Miko sat there where he'd fallen, his broken leg twisted like a rag doll's, snorting through his smashed nose, and staring at Steele, who was still gripping his bloody blade. Miko didn't dare move because this man wanted only to kill him. It took Panther ten minutes.

He stormed into the room with Jackson and pushed Steele and his father aside. The Taiwanese commandos were in untucked uniforms and breathing hard. Panther saw Dr. Liang's corpse, made a sound like a wolverine who'd just lost a pup to a heartless hunter, then saw her killer slumped in the corner and stabbed a sausage finger at Miko's wild feral eyes.

"We will take this bastard back to Pingtung," he snarled. "And we will soon know *everything* he knows. This is not Washington."

CHAPTER 42

Meg Harden felt the first jab at one o'clock in the morning, and it was premature.

She figured at first it was indigestion. She was a healthy woman of average height, and had been in excellent shape and fighting weight prior to the arrival of this human bowling ball distending her belly. It wasn't the first time that something she'd craved and succumbed to, like the pepperoni pizza and can of Coke she'd consumed tonight, reminded her and the baby in the middle of slumber that such indulgence came with a price.

But something about this pain was different. During her army career, and then further missions and adventures with the Program, Meg had given it physically as good as she got. She'd been knocked out cold, and had done the same to men half again her size. She'd been blown up downrange, grazed by bullets that drew blood, and had lived to tell about it, and even laugh.

But this one hurt.

It felt like something tearing inside. A sharp contraction, yes, but it was too early for that. It felt like the baby needed his toenails cut and was starting to kick at her way low down, except that's where his head was supposed to be. No, that wasn't right. That would only come later when she was in labor, right? She couldn't remember.

Something in the back of her mind told her to get dressed. She usually slept in a button-down old-fashioned nightshirt, or if it was cold, one of Eric's big red flannel lumberjack shirts that he'd left behind. Tonight it was cold, so she left Eric's shirt on and struggled into a pair of panties and a set of gray sweatpants. But she wasn't going to bother, just yet, with a bra or shoes. No sense in getting paranoid and crazy.

Another jab doubled her over. She put a hand on the end table next to the bed and stopped to just breathe, and she saw her handgun lying there and decided to lock it up. It was a Ruger SP101 .357 revolver—perfect house gun when you wanted to be sure nothing could jam. She managed to get it into the digital safe in her closet, but it was hard.

She sat down on the couch in the living room, drank a full glass of water, and tried not to think too much about all the stupid stuff she'd read online—preterm labor, placenta previa, placental abruption, uterine rupture, preeclampsia—all dangerous conditions that could strike without warning and kill the mother, or the baby, or both. She'd asked her doctor, a cranky old Brooklyn-born physician named Goldstein, about all these things, and he'd said, "Meg, stay off the goddamn internet." But she couldn't ask him now because he was away on vacation. Or at least that's what she remembered he'd said. Or was that last month?

She stared at the wall next to her flat-screen TV and a framed photo of her and Eric that his old keeper, Demo, had taken when they were all out at Smith Mountain Lake on leave. She and Eric were sitting in a small wooden boat, holding fishing rods and laughing. He was kissing her temple and she was grinning at Demo, who'd just made a remark about public displays of affection being strictly *verboten* in the Program. The original photo had been in color, but she'd had it printed in black and white, as if that could permanently engrave a sweeter past. But Demo was dead, Eric was gone, and it wasn't sweet anymore.

She liked things black and white, but she and Eric had never been that. She'd driven him off, told him she was going to keep the baby, but that he'd be nothing more than a passing figure in their child's life. Now, all at once, she regretted that and wanted to change it. She wanted a father for her son. She wanted him around as part of their lives, every day, for all time, or as long as he lived. She'd been a coward and needed to confess it, one of the hardest things for a tough girl to do.

Another stab, this one much longer, took her breath away and arched her back. When she was able to breathe again, and had both her small hands on her belly, trying to feel for some movement, she looked down at the couch and saw blood.

She called an ambulance. She grabbed her purse and threw her wallet and cell phone in it and made it downstairs in the elevator, barefoot, through the lobby and all the way out the front door. But then the two EMTs rushing toward her were just in time to get her onto the gurney before she collapsed.

Her blood pressure soared as the siren wailed and they rocketed over to the Virginia Hospital Center just a few miles away in

Arlington. They put an oxygen mask on her face, and the female EMT gripped her hand and said meaningless things about all the odds being in Meg's favor. Meg asked for her cell phone and they gave it to her, but she wasn't sure who to call. Her parents? No. Her father, General "Black Jack" Harden, had made it pointedly clear that he was no fan of her out-of-wedlock choices, and her mother, Meredith, was too meek to defy the old army man. There was only one person on earth she wanted to talk to, so she called Ted Lansky.

She wasn't concerned about waking him up. Lansky was one of those government vampires who never slept. He'd been President Rockford's chief of staff, but she knew from indiscreet occasional phone calls with Ralphy Persko that he was now top dog at the revitalized Program, and that Eric was again operational. She couldn't call Eric directly, but if anyone could put her in touch with him, Lansky could.

"I'm sorry, Meg," he said in that annoying slur that meant he was chewing his cold dead pipe, "but he's out of pocket."

"I know, Mr. Lansky." She was breathing hard and had pulled the mask off for the moment, which upset her fretting EMTs in the back of the truck. "But it's an emergency and I need to tell him something important, just for a minute."

"I don't even know where he is at the moment," Lansky lied.

"Yes you do, and even if you didn't I know you could arrange for a comms relay. Please, just do it."

"You know the rules, Meg," he said. "I'm sorry, good luck." And he hung up.

The EMTs put her mask back on, looked at each other across her distended belly, and she thought one said something about a valium injection while the other shook his head, but she wasn't sure because her pulse was pounding in her ears and those stabs were coming faster, like she was wearing some medieval iron chastity belt and someone was turning the screw, and under her hips she felt soaking wet.

The ambulance arrived at the emergency entrance. The EMTs jumped from the tailgate, pulled her out on the gurney, and rushed her through the big glass sliding doors, just as she looked up at the sky and saw a million winking stars. A nurse appeared and might have been smiling down at her, except everyone was still wearing those stupid Covid masks, as if the frontline hospital workers knew something that everyone else had long since eschewed.

"Hello, hon," the nurse said in her kind, immutable, everything's-gonna-be-okay voice. "Who's the dad?"

"Eric Steele," Meg panted. She was cold, and the tips of her fingers were trembling and blue.

"Where is he?" the nurse asked.

"I don't know."

And then she felt a wash of enormous relief. From somewhere, somehow, Dr. Goldstein had appeared. You couldn't mistake that face or that head, with his spiky gray hair, thick black-framed glasses, and ears like the handles of coffee mugs. But he wasn't smiling. Even with his mask on she could tell that.

He leaned over her, put a big hand on her belly, touched the pulse on her neck with his sandpaper rough fingers, then smeared his palm on her glistening forehead.

"How ya doin', kid?" he asked, though he didn't expect an accurate answer or care about her self-assessment.

"Not so good, Doc," she whispered.

"We'll see," he said.

Then he reached down and pulled up the bottom hem of Steele's big flannel shirt.

"Jesus *Christ*," he hissed, and then he shouted at someone across the emergency room. "Code Blue. Get me a goddamn crash cart."

CHAPTER 43

It didn't take much to make Miko talk.

The Airborne Special Service Company had its own miniversion of a SERE school, a training phase during which the commandos learned the techniques of survival, evasion, resistance, and escape. The resistance module was conducted in a blockhouse building next to the classrooms and the comm shack, where the trainees were subjected to interrogation techniques that broke every rule in the Hague Convention. However, as Panther had said, Pingtung was not Washington, D.C., or the Netherlands.

Miko had been trussed, thrown in the back of a truck, and delivered straight to the blockhouse from the monastery. Panther knew he didn't have much time to produce results, because he'd already had to report the incident to HQ at Kaohsiung, and "big army" investigators would soon arrive.

As his men roped Miko to a metal chair inside, Panther stood outside the door in the early morning sun, seething, smoking, and swollen with guilt and fury. Steele and Goodhill, Hank and

Ralphy, were standing there with him when they watched Jackson arrive and hand Panther a long-handled, heavy steel bolt cutter and a blowtorch.

Steele put a hand on Panther's big shoulder.

"Panther, think it over. We all want him dead as much as you do."

"I do not want him dead, Steele," Panther said, though his eyes looked crazy. "I want him to suffer."

Goodhill pulled Steele off. It wasn't their business, and they watched Panther take the tools, kick the heavy iron door open, and storm inside.

With his shattered knee, smashed nose, and cracked cheekbone, Miko was in substantial pain, yet he was silent and defiant. Then Panther placed the tools on a metal table, slowly unbuttoned his uniform tunic and took it off. In the dim light of a single overhead bulb, Miko saw Panther's huge naked chest and rippling stomach, the vicious pink welts of bullet holes and blade scars, and a pectoral tattoo in Chinese characters that said "Your Death Is My Honor." Then Panther picked up the bolt cutter, lit the blowtorch, turned the faucet handle so the flame spit long and blue and orange, and said in Cantonese, "*Ching buyao shuo hua.*"

Please, *don't* talk.

Miko told him everything he knew about the Swords of Qing. Everything. He babbled details about Zaifeng, SOQ's disposition, their helicopters, their weapons. He told Panther things the commando leader didn't even need to know. It was very productive, but to Panther, a disappointment. . . .

Soon after that, they escorted Colonel Dr. Ai Liang to her final rest. The National Security Bureau had ordered Panther not to acquire a casket from a civilian funeral home outside the base. Technically speaking, the PLA biowarfare officer had never arrived in Taiwan, and the agents said the CCP should never know of her death. She might still be useful someday, as a ghost.

And so, her body had been washed, per tradition, by Panther's sister and niece, who then dressed her again in a black monk's sheath for her journey, and placed her in a long wooden ammunition crate that had been used for ground-to-air rockets. Panther, Jackson, and four more commandos carried her makeshift coffin on their shoulders, followed by the rest of the squadron and their American comrades. They walked down to the end of the airstrip and out to a small hill on the parachute landing zone, and placed her on a crisscrossed construct of timbers the men had ripped down from an old outdoor latrine and soaked with aircraft fuel.

The ceremony was brief. They didn't have much time, but in the Buddhist tenets, grace took precedence over warfare.

They did not have the traditional bouquets of flowers, but they spread a few lotus blossoms picked from the field. They did not have piles of fruit, but they'd stuffed their pockets with oranges, and those joined the blossoms. They did not have bells to ring, but each man carried an empty rifle magazine and a bullet, and they clanged the bullets on the magazines and it sounded like a chorus of wind chimes.

Panther faced west, with Steele at his side, and performed the Dana. Steele had rescued this courageous woman and felt no less responsible than Panther for her death, and he stared at the distant sea and clenched his fists as Panther proffered a prayer. He prayed that of the Six Realms, Ai Lang should be reborn into the Manusya-gati, the human realm where one escapes Samsara and becomes enlightened. Then he recited the Vajracchedika.

"The Buddha said, life is a journey. Death is a return to earth. The universe is like an inn. The passing years are like dust.

"Regard this phantom world as a star at dawn, a bubble in a stream, a flash of lightning in a summer cloud, a flickering lamp—a phantom—and a dream."

The men bowed their heads. Panther lit a match and the pyre burst into orange flames. They all turned away from Ai Liang's immolation, and returned to the TOC to prepare for war.

Panther's tactical operations center was nothing like the elaborate Program setup back at Q Street. It was more like the special forces TOCs that Steele had encountered at FOBs in Afghanistan.

It was a cinder block bunker, with one large flat screen on the western wall, a ten-foot-wide briefing space, and two rows of scuffed wooden desks piled with tactical radios, all of them linked to the comm shack and its antenna forest by twists and tangles of wires slung from the drop-down ceiling. Six young male and female communications specialists wearing starched uniforms and headsets were perched at the desks, fielding updates from all branches of the ROC armed forces. They chattered in Chinese and tore incoming printouts from old-style teletype machines, while the echoes of gunfire boomed from the ranges outside.

Ralphy had been given an empty desk, had opened his Alienware, and was firing encrypted messages back and forth with Frankie in Washington. Goodhill had another desk, where he'd opened a comm link directly to Ted Lansky. But he couldn't sit still and was pacing back and forth with a handset at the end of a coiled wire, chewing an unlit cigar, awaiting instructions and cursing under his breath.

Panther's interrogation session with Miko had been recorded and quickly transcribed by an ASSC intel analyst. Jackson had a copy in hand, and therefore the flat-screen monitor already displayed an overhead view of Uotsuri Island. A squad of Jackson's men had set up a long wooden folding table in the briefing space, brought buckets of mud inside, and were finishing a six-foot primitive model of the kidney-shaped island so the ASSC could plan their raid.

Panther, Jackson, three of their element leaders, Steele, and his father surrounded the table and looked at the mud pile model. Panther was holding a long wooden pointer and was just about to start issuing orders when one of his radiomen called him to his station and gave the commander a handset. Panther listened, grunted a series of "yessirs," flushed deeply red in the face, and gave the module back.

He walked over to Steele, handed him the pointer, and said, "That was the minister of defense. He is displeased with the careless death of Dr. Liang. I have been dishonored. The mission is yours to command."

Steele shook his head. "I'm not going without you, Panther."

"He did not say that I could not go. He said that I could not lead."

"Fuck the minister of defense," Steele said. "We'll do this together."

Panther grinned. "You are a thief and a renegade, Steele."

"Thank you." Steele nodded back, then he turned to Jackson and tapped the model's muddy ridgeline with the pointer. "What have they got, Jackson?"

"They have at least two heavy machine guns, likely W85s in 12.7 mm, and some type 67s. The men carry QBZ-95 bullpup assault rifles in 5.8 mm. All have pistols, type 86 ball grenades, and some RPG-7s."

"Standard stuff," said Steele. "Tell me about the helos."

"Three Chinese Harbin Z-20s. Like your Black Hawks."

"Where the hell did they get those?"

"Purchased from the manufacturer," Panther said. "Painted them to look like CCP aircraft."

"That's a lot of money from somewhere," Steele said.

"Seven," Ralphy called out to Steele. "I've got a feed from the NRO. They picked up another burn in northwest Manchuria."

"That was their base," Panther said. "They destroyed it."

"So they've got no plans to go home," Steele said.

"They're not going home, kid," Goodhill said from where he was pacing and waiting for a green light from Lansky. "They're going to freaking Valhalla."

"Jackson, tell us about the Gantu-62," Steele said.

Jackson perused the interrogation transcript.

"The prisoner said they have one vacuum-type canister, but also two kinds of sprayers. They are backpacks, like those tools you Americans use in your yards."

"Leafblowers?"

"Yes, like that."

"That's what they used on the *Windhoek*," Hank said.

Steele scratched his beard for a moment and then said to Panther, "Have you got a flamethrower?"

"A flamethrower? Maybe. We have one old one from the 1980s in the armory, but we have never used it."

"Can you crank it up?"

Panther snapped something in Chinese to one of his element leaders, who hustled out of the TOC.

"Hank," Goodhill called over. He had a strange smirk on his face. "Lansky says when you get back, the boss wants to see you."

"Which boss?" Hank asked.

"POTUS."

Hank frowned. "Tell him I'll check my calendar."

"What is this potus?" Panther asked.

"The president of the United States," Steele said.

Panther looked at both Steeles. "You are a very insubordinate family."

"You can stop with the compliments, Colonel," Hank said, and Panther laughed.

Steele peered at the model of the island, then dropped the pointer to the half-circle of beach on the southern side.

"This is the only spot they could have landed those helos."

"Yes," Panther said, "which leaves us no room to land ours."

"What do you guys have?" Steele asked him.

"UH-60s."

"We're not going to land then. We'll fast rope." Steele tapped the pointer at three spots below the model's ridgeline. "We'll do it here, here, and here, and take them from the high ground. Agreed?"

"Yes, very good," Panther said.

"We'll hit them tonight," Steele said, "which means we've got time for a dry run."

"Yes." Panther snapped out more orders, and his other two element leaders hurried from the TOC.

"Lansky says you're not going anywhere," Goodhill called over, "till he gets a green light from 1600."

"Seven?" Ralphy said as he tapped like a madman on his Alienware. "I've got the Roosevelt strike group at a hundred and thirty-two nautical miles south southeast of Uotsuri and closing. Looks like they're heading for the gap between the Jimas."

Steele and his father exchanged looks. They were both thinking about Kristin, but said nothing.

"Goddammit," Goodhill spat. "Lansky just ordered me to stay here on station."

"Well," Steele said, "somebody's got to write the obituaries and the AAR."

Goodhill shot him the finger.

"Houston, we have a problem," Jackson said.

"You really *did* go to BU," Steele said, but then he saw Jackson's grim expression.

Jackson said something to Panther in Chinese, and Panther nodded, reached up behind his ear, pulled out a cigarette, and lit it.

"I am afraid I missed something in the interrogation," he said, "perhaps during my enthusiasm."

"What is it, Panther?" Steele asked.

"They have surface-to-air missiles. Chinese QW-18s. They will shoot us out of the sky before the first man ropes to the ground."

"Jesus," Ralphy moaned from his workstation.

"Well, Panther," Steele said, "guess you'd better call the minister of defense back."

"You want to stand down?"

"No. I want a submarine. That's how we're going in."

Panther blinked at Steele, then grinned broadly through a stream of smoke.

"A submarine. Yes!" He stomped over to a comm station and snatched up a handset.

Hank smirked and muttered, "Zodiacs from a sub. Haven't done that in a long, long time."

"And you won't be doing it now," Steele snapped. "This isn't *The Rock* and you're not Sean Connery."

Hank cocked his head at his progeny.

"What's your Alpha designator again?"

"Seven," Steele said.

"That's right. And as you might remember, we code from the top down. Technically, I never left the Program. No retirement papers, no pension, no black DD214. And my designator is Forty-four, which means I outrank you times six." Hank fired a finger at his son's green eyes. "So, shut up and let's draw some gear."

CHAPTER 44

It was a long way to drive for a midnight rendezvous, and the president's Secret Service detail didn't like it.

But you didn't argue with Hammer. You could advise, implore, point out the exigencies of security measures, and then you just had to go with the flow. In most cases, Rockford would at least acquiesce to the drama of what he called "the circus," the long train of armored vehicles with whipping pennants and flashing lights, packed with agents armed to the teeth. Yet tonight he was driving them all crazy.

He'd insisted on not taking the Beast, so they had him in one of those armored limousines reserved for picking up visiting guests, like his in-laws. He'd also limited the follow car to just one nondescript Suburban, and no air cover of any kind. He'd told Jack to not even log it. It was these kinds of things that were making Jack carry a roll of Tums in his pocket and consider early retirement. He really liked Rockford, but sometimes the guy still acted like a pulp fiction spook.

It was pouring rain when they pulled off a slim roadway and drove through the woods into a wide muddy clearing. The clearing was bordered on three sides by pointy black pines, with a firing range berm on the far perimeter and some shooting benches with primitive roofs closer by. The president had spent the ride using two secure phones in the back, having curt conversations with Pentagon generals, the CIA, and the secretary of state. Now he was off comms, pulling a dark raincoat on over his suit, and unsheathing a large umbrella.

Sitting in the front right shotgun position, Jack saw something flash under one of the shooting bench shelters. It looked like an old Zippo lighter.

"All right, Jack," Rockford said.

Jack got out, ignoring the mud that instantly creamed over his shoes, scanned the surroundings, and opened the president's door. Then, in a flash of lightning, he saw the distant figure—a man in a heavy raincoat, with a hat and some sort of walking stick.

"Can I at least frisk him, Mr. President?" he asked as Rockford got out and opened his own umbrella.

"You can try, Jack. But he'll probably break your legs."

He walked off into the rain while the agents in the follow car started to get out, and Jack waved them back and thought, *Helluva spot to end my career.*

"Evening, Thorn," Rockford said as they shook hands beneath the shelter and he folded the dripping umbrella.

"A pleasure, as always, Mr. President." Thorn McHugh, per the norm, was impeccably dressed, in a Burberry coat, tweed jacket, and pearl pinned tie.

The bench under the shelter was dry, so they both leaned back against it, facing the vehicles and Rockford's edgy agents, who were standing there getting pummeled with rain, swiveling their heads, and ignoring the discomfort.

"Apologies for the short notice," Rockford said. "I needed a nonpolitical assessment."

"And you shall have it, of course," McHugh said. "And my apologies for the venue, but your neighborhood is fraught with surveillance."

"Tell me about it." Rockford looked around for another vehicle. "How'd you get here?"

"Horseback." McHugh smiled and Rockford wasn't sure if he was joking.

"I assume you've heard about Colonel Liang," Rockford said.

"Terrible shame, particularly after all that effort to extract her." McHugh looked wistfully at the cloud-swollen sky. "Just think what we might have gleaned from that brain."

Rockford looked at him and thought, *Heart like an ice cube,* and he knew right then that he'd chosen the right consigliere.

"I've got a decision to make, Thorn," the president said, "and it has to be fast."

"Yes, it's your Bay of Pigs moment."

"You could have used a softer analogy," Rockford snorted.

"Well, I am nothing if not blunt," McHugh said. "In sum, Mr. President, if I may. You've got your primary Alpha in place, with appropriate supporting foreign allied operators, prepared to eliminate the Swords of Qing, if that is in fact who they are. However, the precipitous threat against our Pacific forces may be a CCP ruse designed to ignite open warfare, and provide them an excuse to invade Taiwan. It's a conundrum."

"It's a fucking shit show is what it is, Thorn."

"Indeed. And what are your advisors saying?"

"Pentagon wants me to strike first, on multiple fronts."

"Naturally. That's what they do for a living. And the IC?" McHugh asked, meaning the intelligence community.

"Tina just called me in the car. She says we should let the SOQ attack, whether it's Beijing's trickery or not, then hit the Chinese with a massive counterstrike. Like Golda Meir did with the Egyptians in '73."

"Quite a gamble, I'd say. Mrs. Meir nearly lost her entire country with that misadventure. Frankly, I think you should have fired Ms. Harcourt on your first day in office. She's as deep as the deep state goes."

Rockford laughed without mirth. "If I fired every deep state holdover, I'd have nothing left but a driver and a servant."

"Spot on." McHugh raised a finger. "Well, you can clean house next term."

"If I have one."

Neither man spoke for a long moment. They stood there listening to the rain hammer the wooden roof till McHugh's expression grew pensive and dark.

"Would you like my assessment, Mr. President?"

"No, Thorn. I came here 'cause I missed your historical humor." McHugh didn't smile.

"Regardless of whether or not these Chinese imperial revolutionary miscreants are genuine, or in fact a CCP false flag . . . and regardless of whether the Communists are wholly ignorant of what's about to transpire, or have in fact planned the entire venture, or are simply drooling at the prospects, one thing is clear. You cannot permit an attack on the fleet. You must ignore the geopolitical ramifications and think of nothing more than your sailors." He turned his head and fixed Rockford with an iron squint. "You have a very fine scalpel out there in your Stalker Seven, John. Let the surgeon cut."

Rockford looked at McHugh. He was a renowned warrior, a fearless spy and a patriot, but he was also the most officious and formal creature that Rockford had ever met. McHugh had just called him by his Christian name, which was the ultimate coda on his pronouncement. It was like hearing a judge's gavel ringing the bench. Rockford reached out and shook his hand.

"Thank you. That's what I needed to hear."

"A pleasure."

Rockford opened his umbrella and stepped out in the rain.

"Come down to Camp David for dinner," he said, "after all this is over."

"I shan't, ever. Yet the invitation is treasured."

"When you finally retire, then," Rockford said.

McHugh smiled and tipped his hat brim.

"They shall have to carry me from the field."

Rockford waved over his shoulder as he walked off through the mud and the pelting rain and returned to the limousine. Jack opened the door and the president turned and looked back as he got in the car.

But McHugh was already gone.

N O   A C K N O W L E D G E D   L O C A T I O N

EYES ONLY

SAP (Alphas/Support/OCO EAST) - FLASH

From: SAWTOOTH MAIN

To: All OCONUS EAST ASIA PAX

Subj: Ops Order

Source: Command/Primary

Confidence: Highest

IMMEDIATE, all OCONUS EAST PAX, inc ALPHA,
CYBER, KEEPER, FORN SUPPORT: Initiate Op BLUE
HERON per Hammer green, all TTPs cleared.

Emphasis: Exceptions; None

STATUS: DEFCON Purple.

Operational window: Execute, Execute, Execute.

CHAPTER 46

Eric Steele leaped into the night from a UH-60 Black Hawk, straight into the roaring wind, and as the helo jerked sideways in the turbulence he almost fell to his death.

But his gloves found the three-inch-thick dangling fast rope, his ankles locked to its slippery hemp, and he looked down into a cauldron of swirling mist and roiling waves and went twisting downward, fast. He was burdened with a Taiwanese assault rifle, his father's 1911, his Gerber combat blade, MICH helmet, and forty more pounds of ammunition and grenades, and when he slammed onto the sea-slickened deck of the submarine, it sounded like a sack full of kettlebells.

He cranked himself to his feet, spread his legs on the pitching deck, grabbed the whipping rope, and stomped on its tail with a boot. He was just aft of the black conning tower, which he could barely see, but in a flash of white wave foam its stenciled letters, 793, showed bright and clear.

At least he was at the correct address.

The Taiwanese had only four submarines, all ancient diesels, because due to pressure from the red Chinese, no nation would sell them anything better. This one was an old Dutch-made Chien Lung class attack boat, the Hai Lung, or Sea Dragon. It was a modest 66.9 meters long and 8 meters abeam, and had twenty-eight torpedoes aboard, but no other armaments of any kind, except for the small crew's rifles and pistols. It didn't even have a deck gun, but it could do twenty knots per hour, submerged.

Steele heard a deck hatch *thwang* open behind him, looked up at the Black Hawk's thrumming belly, waved his arm in a wide circle, and the next man came down. *Bang*, he tumbled onto the deck. Steele grabbed his combat harness, hauled him up, shoved him astern toward the hatch, and saw the operator disappear into the hold. Another man corkscrewed down, then five more, then the large canvas case of a packed-up fifteen-foot FC 470 Zodiac rubber assault boat, which the last two men dragged to the hatch, and the Black Hawk pulled pitch and roared away.

Steele stayed where he was, with the boat making five knots on the surface and the wave foam soaking his boots, and he anchored the ropes and shepherded the operators into the sub until two more birds had disgorged their men. In the onyx darkness and a typhoon of sea mist, and with the commandos all wearing helmets and balaclavas, he couldn't tell who was who—not Panther, Jackson, his father, or anyone else—but he'd counted twenty-four including himself, plus the flamethrower, LAW rockets, and three Zodiac boats. With the Black Hawks gone it was suddenly quiet, except for the waves slapping the hull, and the sky above was packed with stars. He walked to the hatch and slid down the steel ladder into something that looked like an old World War II "pig."

The sub's claustrophobic interior was like a plumber's wet

dream. It was packed with long silver and blue pipes, black faucets and wheels, orange iron brackets and steam gauges, old-style flip switches, and green and red on-and-off lights. Taiwanese sailors in blue dungarees and chambray shirts chattered through their headsets in Mandarin, while officers in khakis with blue submariner patches on their shoulders barked orders into handheld mikes that looked like surplus from NYPD squad cars. All of their faces were shiny, their armpits and uniform backs were soaked with sweat, and the air was rank with diesel fuel, *jitang* chicken broth, and recycled breaths.

Panther's commandos had already squeezed into every available space they could find, standing between fire control stations, steel stanchions and ventilation pipes, doffing their helmets and balaclavas and dripping puddles on the dimpled steel floor.

Steele saw a young sailor charge up the ladder to close the hatch, so he quickly tapped his Program ear transceiver, which was linked to his vest's MBITR.

"Blue Heron Bench, Blue Heron Quarterback here. How copy?"

"Lima Charlie, Quarterback," Ralphy's tinny voice said.

"All aboard for Hollywood," Steele advised.

"Roger, QB," Ralphy said. "Now don't forget to come back."

"Is that a recall order?" Steele asked, not that he intended to comply if it was.

"Negative, QB," Ralphy said. "It's a life wish. Good luck."

The transmission went dead as the hatch was secured, a dive klaxon honked through the sub, the ballast tanks blew like the spouts of breaching whales, and they submerged and the big screws churned ocean.

For three hours, the Sea Dragon cruised at a depth of six fathoms and twenty knots. It was a respectable speed for the old diesel vessel, but not fast enough. Steele's strike team had boarded the sub at sixty-seven miles southwest of Uotsuri, but the tides were against them and the night was crawling away.

Steele, Panther, and Jackson had shucked their gear and weapons, squeezed their way throughout the vessel to check on the men, and had ordered them to do the same with their loads to conserve muscle strength. Yet there was nowhere to sit but the cold hard deck, and those who did were packed boots to ass like calves in a slaughterhouse chute. They chewed biscuits and dried seaweed crisps, drank water and pungent submariner tea, and a few somehow managed to make it to the head, which was about the size of an upright coffin.

Many of them had found breathing spaces in the forward torpedo room, where Steele finally spotted his father at the very tip of the bow. Hank was standing between two enormous silver torpedo tubes, with his arms draped over the tubes and his empty pipe gripped in his grin like he'd just rediscovered Disneyland. He didn't look like some broken old ancient Alpha. He looked like a warrior king who belonged there. Even so, Steele shook his head, his mouth turned down in disapproval.

"You shouldn't be here," he said. "You should be smoking that thing on a porch in a rocker."

"You shouldn't be here either," Hank retorted, "but you had a shitty upbringing."

"Can't argue that."

"However," Hank said as he jabbed his pipe stem at his son, "you're going to be a father. So somebody's got to watch your ass."

Steele turned away and moved on, as images of Meg and her pregnant belly swirled in his head. But he couldn't think about any of that now. There was nothing so dangerous to a man on a mission as images of hearth and home, nothing so deadly as caring about anything other than the impending kill zone. And as often on the cusp of a kinetic strike, he summoned a tune in his head. This one was Dave Ralston's "I Don't Care," a pounding R&B ode of indifference to lesser mortals, a favorite of special forces.

I don't care about your Ugg boots, or one-night stands . . . And I don't care about your favorite show, or boyfriend's band. . . .

The Sea Dragon's captain came down from his bridge in the conning tower. He was in his forties with gray hair and a crush cap pushed back on his head. He called Panther and Steele over to a plotting table in the sub's dive control room. He'd studied at Norfolk on a navy exchange and had good English.

"We are short," he said as he tapped a telescopic pointer on the table's nautical map, "but we must surface."

"What's the range, Captain?" Steele asked.

"Seven miles, but it will take you time to build your rubber boats."

"That is correct." Panther grunted. "They are beasts to make ready."

"We will continue to cruise on the surface, half speed ahead," the captain said, "but we have coral reefs at three miles, so no farther than that."

"Let's go," Steele said, "and thanks for the ride." He saluted smartly from his eyebrow.

"Godspeed." The captain returned the salute, handed Panther a microphone, and Panther barked an order to his men to gear up, and it boomed throughout the sub.

Five minutes later, the commandos were back in all their kit, stacked up in two lines running fore and aft from the control room, and the three large Zodiac carriers and the clumsy flame-thrower had been maneuvered below the stern hatch. The klaxon sounded again, the compressors hissed and blew ballast, and the interior lights went dark, then flipped over to combat orange.

Steele gripped a vent pipe and looked up as the Sea Dragon breached the surface. It bounced and shuddered and settled, and then a sailor undogged the stern hatch, got soaked head to foot in seawater, and rocketed back down the ladder. Up above, Steele saw a circle of paling night sky. The stars were dimming. He looked at his Rolex watch, then at Panther and Jackson and said, "Tell the men they can leave their NVGs. This is gonna be hell in living color."

Steele took the lead while behind him the men shouldered, pushed, and hauled the Zodiac cases up through the hatchway and onto the deck. The Sea Dragon was still making seven knots, the air was joint-cracking cold, and the waves curled over the gunwales and sloshed across the plates in slithering, slippery black pools. They laid the fat cases out line astern behind the conning tower, unzipped them and disgorged the contents, folded the cases up and tossed them back down the hatch to be used again—they were optimistic men, and young. Then they unfurled the boats and hooked up the battery-powered air pumps. The pumps hissed air into the rubber hulls, but the deck was pitching and rolling, and the men were so burdened with weapons and ammo that they fell and tumbled and scrambled upright again, like helpless children on some sort of Tilt-A-Whirl.

One of the commandos lost his footing, fell on his ass, and slid right over a gunwale. Hank Steele saw it, slammed himself prone on the deck, grabbed the man's drag handle on the back of his load-bearing vest, and was almost pulled overboard with him, except two more of Panther's men crashed onto Hank's legs and hauled him and their comrade back onto the deck.

No one said a word. They just went right back to work.

Steele, Panther, and Jackson were each commanding a boat crew of seven. They helped the men slot in the tongue-and-groove floorboards, lock in the side rails, and assemble the small black aluminum oars. The flamethrower went into Panther's last boat, each of the Zodiacs held two LAW rockets, and Steele and Jackson each had one of Ralphy's Whipsaw pistols with a slung canvas case of *shuriken* blades.

They all had plenty of guns, grenades, and ammunition, but none were wearing body armor. If the Zodiacs flipped, the plates would drown them. And they hadn't been issued luck. The only quartermaster for that piece of gear was God.

Steele stalked the rolling deck and ordered the commandos to straddle the Zodiac hulls, four on each side of each boat, weapons slung from their necks, balaclavas and helmets on, oars at the ready. Then he mounted the prow of the first boat, looked up to see the captain peering down at him from the conning tower, and shot him a thumbs-up. The captain waved and disappeared, the stern hatch clanged closed, the Sea Dragon hissed, and a mass of bursting air bubbles roiled the black waters on both flanks of the sub.

And all at once it was gone, with nothing but the periscope and snorkel gleaming above the waves, and then those disappeared as well.

Jackson's Zodiac crawled up along Steele's port side, then Panther's appeared to starboard. Steele peered due north as his eyes adjusted to the nothingness left in the submarine's wake, and there in the distance, at about three miles, the black hump of

Uotsuri came into focus against a feather of pale pink sky. Steele nodded at Panther, then Jackson, and then looked to his left at the man across from him on his boat.

He saw the green eyes in the early light, nodded at his father, and they rowed.

CHAPTER 47

SENKAKU ISLANDS, EAST CHINA SEA

"You will kill everyone on deck."

Zaifeng stood on a slab of granite, gripping his Chinese *bo* as he issued his final briefing to the Swords of Qing. The slimmest sliver of pink was breaching the eastern horizon, but the island of Uotsuri and the sea were still dark, and the air was windless and cold.

He was dressed for combat, wearing his black tactical trousers, tunic, and boots, with a load-bearing vest packed with ammunition. A QBZ-95 bullpup rifle was slung across his chest and his QSZ-92 pistol was tucked in his thigh rig. But neither of the weapons was fixed with suppressors, nor were those of any of his men. He was no longer concerned about the thunder of gunfire. In fact, he wanted it.

The more horror, the better.

Next to Zaifeng was an artist's easel pinned with a four-foot-long laminated overhead photo of the USS *Roosevelt* aircraft carrier. It had been sent to Zaifeng by a Shanghai contact who'd purchased it from the Smithsonian Air and Space Museum in

Washington, D.C. The photo was illuminated by chemlights hung from the ends of Japanese fishing poles jammed into the sand. The chemlights were eerily green phosphorescent, and more than sufficient.

"That is your primary mission, above all else," Zaifeng continued. "There will be aircraft, air crews, and ground crews on deck, and you must eliminate all threats so that the Gantu-62 team can enter the superstructure and the bridge. You will use your machine guns, sidearms, rockets, and grenades, set the aircraft ablaze and show no mercy. Am I clear?"

"Yes, *Xian Sheng*," his commandos said in unison, but they did not shout.

Before Zaifeng on the beach below, thirty-two men stood in a semicircle of three ranks. Their assault rifles were slung from their necks, some carried Chinese RPG-7 antitank tubes and quivers of rockets, and two had Type 67 light machine guns resting on bipods in the stony sand beside their Gore-Tex boots. They were dressed and kitted like Zaifeng, except for the six helo pilots in flight overalls, and six more men dressed in Level IV chem-bio suits. Those six spacemen stood to one side, sweating under their oxygen rigs, holding their helmets under their arms and staying well clear of the other men's bristling weapons. Rips or tears in their suits could result in their deaths before they'd accomplished their tasks.

Off to Zaifeng's right as he faced the sea, the three Harbin Z-20s had been stripped of their camouflage netting and their Red Chinese stars had been groomed and refreshed. Their crew chiefs had switched on their APUs, and the massive blades were starting to turn, like hulking athletes warming their muscles.

Until just fifteen minutes before, only Zaifeng and Po had

known the exact nature of the mission. Yet when Zaifeng had tapped his *bo* on the photograph and said, "Gentlemen, this is your target, the United States Navy aircraft carrier *Roosevelt*," there hadn't been a single murmur or swallow. The Swords were believers, and disciplined.

"We will be executing a raid on this ship," he'd begun, "much like the trial run on the *Windhoek*. Our tactical objective is mass casualties. Our strategic objective is that the Americans will fault Beijing, and therefore strike back in fury at the CCP. Thus we'll begin our historical reclamation of the Empire."

The men had cheered at that, and Zaifeng couldn't help but smile. Now he delved deeper into operational details.

"And so, here is the plan, and your orders. The Roosevelt strike group is currently sixty-four nautical miles east of this island, steaming for the Jima gap. We will approach the carrier off the starboard stern, as if in a provocative flyby. To date, although many PLA aircraft have harassed the Americans this way, they have never opened fire, nor will they today. Their rules of engagement are determined by attorneys in Washington, rather than admirals."

Some of Zaifeng's men smiled. He jabbed his *bo* at the spinning-up Harbin Z-20s.

"Helicopter number one will have no one aboard but the pilots." He nodded respectfully at two of his air crews. "You pilots will pass the ship a hundred meters off the starboard side and proceed past the bow for half a kilometer. You will then call Mayday over the international emergency net, and ditch your craft in the ocean. . . . I suggest you be wearing your life vests."

No one raised an eyebrow or an objection, though it was obvious that even if the pilots survived the ditching, a rescue would be unlikely. Zaifeng carried on.

"Helicopter number two, with twelve warriors aboard, will then call the ship and announce its intention to rescue. The Americans will not forbid the act, in accordance with international law. In fact they may slow their speed to observe, or assist, but that is of no matter."

Zaifeng moved his *bo* tip to the stern of the ship.

"Here on the port side aft is a Phalanx antiaircraft system on a recessed platform three meters below the main deck. At this juncture, helicopter number two will change course and land on the deck to the right of the Phalanx. The left-door gunner will open fire on the Phalanx, which cannot return fire from its defilade position or it will strike the carrier's bridge. The right-door gunner will open fire on the aircraft and fuel pumps. You twelve assaulters will disembark and kill all personnel between helicopter number two and the superstructure on the carrier's starboard side."

"*Xian Sheng,*" Lieutenant Po whispered. He was standing to Zaifeng's left and touched his commander's elbow, an impertinence he'd never before dared. Zaifeng stopped talking and followed Po's gaze. He was staring at a point in the distant sea beyond the men's heads. The waves were still black yet the sky was pewter, and there seemed to be a small object floating out there.

"Dolphins," Zaifeng muttered. "They were here yesterday. Don't interrupt me again."

"Yes, *Xian Sheng.*" Po nodded, but he gripped his rifle, stepped from the granite slab, and started walking down to the beach, just to be sure. Zaifeng looked at his watch and pushed through the rest of his briefing.

"And finally, gentlemen." He tapped the *bo* on a spot of empty deck to the left of the carrier's multistory bridge. "Helicopter number three, with our six Gantu-62 warriors aboard, and six more assaulters, will land here just beside the superstructure. You assaulters will kill any remaining opposition and lead the Gantu team to the superstructure hatches, here. Inside, the Gantu team will split into two elements. Gantu one will deploy its dispenser, work its way up the stairwells to the bridge, and kill all the command staff. Gantu two will descend belowdecks, work toward the bow, and infect all the air ducts and the ventilation systems."

Zaifeng pulled his *bo* back from the photograph and stabbed one end down on his boot in the manner of a kung fu Wushu practitioner.

"That is our plan. Simple, yet effective. It is my assumption that when the first effects of the Gantu occur, there will be panic and little resistance. I expect that the Americans will sound their alarms, retreat belowdecks, and seal themselves inside their own coffin. Once all the Gantu is deployed, we will then withdraw."

He didn't mention his intention to abandon the Gantu-62 operators inside the carrier. They'd all be contaminated and some would likely be wounded by desperate American gunfire. They couldn't be allowed back on the helicopters.

"Questions?" Zaifeng offered.

One courageous young commando raised his gloved hand.

"Respectfully, *Xian Sheng* . . . Where will you be?" he asked.

Zaifeng smiled. "Aboard helicopter number two, with *you*. Did you think I would stay here and watch this on YouTube?"

The men laughed and some slapped the impertinent one on his back.

Zaifeng raised his *bo* high over his head.

"To the aircraft," he ordered, then shouted, "for the sake of the Empire and Honor!"

They all raised their weapons and echoed Zaifeng's war cry, "For the sake of the Empire and Honor!" And because of that, no one heard Po's shout from the beach.

Then something like a screaming steel Frisbee whipped through the air, and the first helicopter exploded.

CHAPTER 48

Eric Steele opened fire first.

Jackson and his men were the first to die.

Steele and his commandos were paddling hell-bent for leather. They were hunched forward, gripping the Zodiac's fat rubber hulls with their thighs, and slicing the cold dark waves with their blurring black oars like insane Ivy League scullers. But they couldn't hold back the light. The dawn was starting to halo the island and they were still two hundred meters from shore. Steele's Taiwanese commandos didn't speak English, but they understood that the hiss from his lips meant *faster*.

In the distance on the beachhead he saw the glow of chemlights, the sheen of some sort of briefing board, and a small dark figure, who had to be Zaifeng, their leader, commanding the high ground. He saw the assembly of men bristling with weapons, and over on the left flank where Jackson was supposed to come ashore, the glossy black helicopters with their bright red stars and their thick black rotors spinning faster and faster.

He had to stop those helos. Not a single one of them could get off the ground.

No one had spotted them yet. The whines of the spinning-up helos were covering the sounds of their oars in the water and the panting breaths from their lungs. But then Steele saw a figure break from the briefing. He was heading down the beach, gripping a rifle. He'd smelled something, or seen something, or he just had that hunter's instinct. Then Steele saw his eyes and knew he was out of time.

He tossed his paddle in the boat and ripped the Whipsaw pistol from his front vest Velcro pocket. To his left, Hank felt the Zodiac skew to the right and back sliced his paddle to turn it about, because he knew what Eric was doing. Steele pulled a saw-toothed disk from his pouch, rammed it into the Whipsaw's slot, rose up on his haunches, twisted left, sighted one-handed on the closest helicopter, and fired.

The .44 caliber blank round felt like the kick of a mule. The spinning projectile screamed in the air like a Stuka siren, chunked into the tail boom of the nearest Harbin Z-20, and a split second later blew the whole thing off in a ball of detonating aircraft fuel and a column of orange fire.

The party was on. The surprise was over.

Jackson's Zodiac, with his commando's paddles furiously churning the water, rose on the curl of a wave, crashed down onto a wide reef of coral spines and was instantly grounded. Directly before him at fifty meters, Jackson saw the closest helicopter burst into flames as its tail rotor went cartwheeling down the beach like a blender blade, whipping up gouts of sand. But to the left of that burning helo there were still two more, completely intact. He yelled *"Gong keh!,"* jumped from the rubber boat, and pounded toward the beach through the surf, and his seven men echoed his battle cry and went hurdling after him.

A thundering burst of machine gun gunfire flashed from the shore, scythed through Jackson's Zodiac and shredded it into scraps of rubber. The machine gun was joined by rifles, and the bullets found Jackson's intrepid seven and cut them down one after the other. They tried to return fire, but they were staggering through the surf, and they twisted and fell and their twitching fingers sent wild red tracers sparking off rocks and into the air.

Jackson was almost there. He was ankle deep, with the loaded Whipsaw in his right glove and his XT-105 grasped in his left, when a rifle round fractured his pelvis. He fell to his knees in the water, gasping, then somehow cranked himself up again. Six of the Swords of Qing were marching toward him from his right flank, methodically raining gunfire.

He fired the rifle one-handed and sent one flipping backward. Then a bullet splintered his rifle and broke his left wrist, and another punched through his chest. He staggered forward, raised the trembling Whipsaw, and fired it at the point man's chest. The bladed *shuriken* screamed, *thunked* into breast bone, and exploded in white light and a hundred shrapnels, killing that man and the rest.

Jackson fell on his face in the surf. He wasn't dead yet, but he drowned.

Eric Steele's battle was hand to hand, and murderous chaos.

His Zodiac had almost made the shoreline when a squad of Zaifeng's men charged from the high ground, screaming and firing their weapons. With his left boot, Steele kicked his father into the water, spun off the hull into the surf, threw the empty Whipsaw away, and opened fire with his rifle. His six ASSC commandos yelled curses in Mandarin and joined him as the Zodiac flipped over and a LAW rocket exploded from the incoming rounds. The orange sun had breached the horizon, there was no cover, and as he'd predicted, it was hell in living color.

Steele shot one man in the face, then another in both knees. A bullet cracked his helmet in half, and as he tore it off he saw one of his men on his right hurling a baseball grenade, and that man disappeared in a burst of bloody mist from close range automatic fire, and the grenade exploded somewhere and its shrapnel pinged off weapons and sliced into skulls.

He saw Chinese killing Chinese, ugly and close. They didn't duck or go prone on the stony beach but charged at one another like duelers, firing point-blank at each other's faces and chests, unsheathing their knives and tumbling together to die in tangles.

Farther up on the beach, he saw two men in pilot's coveralls sprinting to the left toward the helos. At a hundred meters he shot one in the back of the skull, but missed the other, and he spun to the right as he sensed another Sword charging.

It was Po, though Steele didn't know that. The man screamed something at him, as if Steele were his cheating wife's lover. At a flat-out sprint, Po fired his QBZ-95 and shattered Steele's rifle. Steele yanked his father's 1911 from his holster, and at five meters, shot Po twice in the face just as Po shot him in his left shoulder.

The impact spun Steele around and he fell to his knees, spewing hot breath, facing the ocean. He was half deaf from the close-quarters gunfire. The sea looked placid now, silver and pretty, but it was swirled in blood and rolled with corpses like Normandy.

To his left he saw Panther's Zodiac, ruined and wallowing in the surf. The bodies of Panther's men and those they'd killed were impossible to discern from each other. Then he saw Panther, with the hulk of the flamethrower strapped to his back, the heavy iron torch in his hammy fists, and Panther ran by him and saw him and grunted, "The helicopters, Steele . . . the *helicopters.*"

Steele pushed himself to his feet and turned to see Panther making his end zone dash. The colonel was pounding toward the flank of the second Harbin just as Steele saw six men in chem-bio suits piling into the cargo door of the first. He raised the 1911 and gunned one down at the lip, but the others scrambled aboard.

Panther opened up with the roaring flamethrower just meters away from the second helicopter, and the jellied napalm immolated the fuselage in a torrent of orange fire. Then a screaming crew chief appeared in the cargo door with a weapon, shot Panther point-blank with a burst of bullets, and his flamethrower tank exploded.

Steele stood there in shock, stunned by the vision. Pain seared his lungs with every breath and his gun-smoke-ravaged eyes were blurred and streaming. He watched the first helicopter as it lifted off from the beach, flew straightaway, then banked to the right, as if swinging around to the other side of the island. He heard a shout and spun to his right.

He saw a man running from the beach toward the island's forested hump. He was carrying a long bamboo pole and a pistol. It was the man who'd been giving the briefing, Zaifeng, and he disappeared into the dark mouth of something that looked like a cave. There was another man chasing Zaifeng in a flat-out sprint, one of Steele's men, but he had no helmet on, as if he'd torn it off in the heat. He had spiky gray hair.

No, Dad . . . No!

Steele jerked forward to chase him, then he skidded to a stop, twisting in circles, his eyes madly searching the wrecked guns and corpses. He spotted an RPG-7 tube, holstered his 1911, snatched it up, and yanked one rocket from a dead man's quiver.

He ran with everything he had left. Po's bullet had ricocheted somewhere inside his body and he tasted frothy blood in his mouth. His soaked boots slammed over sand and rock and scree, the maw of the cave grew larger in his vision, then he heard a gunshot, and another, and he cursed and ran faster.

There was a hazy circle of light at the end of that rock-strewn tunnel. He heard the helo's rotors surging. In special forces he'd trained with every enemy weapon they had at the JFK Warfare Center and School, and he slammed the RPG rocket into the tube, seated its nipple in the barrel slot, and yanked the arming ring and cap from the green phallic tip of the warhead.

He burst from the end of the cave onto a slope of soft brown beach. Zaifeng was nowhere, but his father was sprawled on his face to his left, with a slither of black blood crawling down toward the sea. And right there, at a hundred meters out over the water, the last Harbin Z-20 was thundering toward him. In a moment, it was going to blur right past him.

He shouldered the RPG, cocked the hammer down with his thumb, and tried to remember the anomalies of the weapon. The rocket would deploy spring-loaded guide fins, but the wind would turn it on its axis, so in flight it would turn *into* the wind, not away from it. *Right?*

A breeze was slapping his blood-spattered face from the right. He followed the Harbin dead center with the iron sights, but he didn't lead it.

He fired. The explosion banged his head like a hammer, the backblast singed his eyebrows, and the warhead went rocketing straight for the Harbin. Then it slowly skewed like a curveball, right along with it, and detonated in the cockpit. The helo's shattered smoking nose jerked skyward, then it rolled over and crashed in a huge plume of water.

Steele dropped the RPG in the sand.

Zaifeng stabbed him deep in the back with the blade of his *bo*.

Steele fell to his knees. His left arm was useless. He reached behind with his right, yanked the *bo* from his rib cage, and Zaifeng kicked it out of his hand and then kicked him in his solar plexus. Steele grunted, got to his feet, turned to Zaifeng, and said, "I'm not fucking interested."

But the man was like a cat. He had raging fire in his eyes. He spun his entire body in the air and kicked Steele's pistol out of his fist before he could fully draw it, then continued his spin and kicked him in the face. Steele felt his jaw crack, and he knew he had nothing left of any of the hundreds of hand-to-hand skills he knew, so he charged Zaifeng like a bull and took every knife hand to his forearms and the kicks to his knees, until he got his right hand on that muscled throat, just above Zaifeng's embroidered Swords of Qing emblem, and choked him one-handed, digging his fingers into every sinew and bone, until Zaifeng's face turned purple and his eyes rolled back and Steele dropped him on his back in the sand.

Steele collapsed on his hands and knees. He crawled to the *bo*. It was lying there smeared in his own slick blood. He used the staff to help himself up, staggered over to Zaifeng, and raised it.

Zaifeng looked up at him, and in perfect Shanghai English,

rasped, "You should have welcomed this war with China . . . I was your only hope."

Steele rammed the blade down into Zaifeng's heart and said, "Thanks for the advice, asshole."

He picked up his 1911 and staggered over to his father. He sat down next to him and leaned back against a slab of stone. Then he reached out, turned Hank over, and dragged him onto his lap. His father's eyes were shut, but he was still breathing. His gray hair fluttered in the breeze.

Steele looked out at the sea. It was shimmering blue and silver now, gentle and calm. The helicopter was gone, but the shape of some sort of small warship was out there. It wasn't an American ship. It was closing.

He laid his head back against the rock, and closed his eyes. . . .

In the TOC at Pingtung, Ralphy was desperately trying to raise him. There was nothing but static.

Dalton Goodhill had Ted Lansky on comms. He was shouting at Lansky that he had to spin up a QRF from the fleet and order a rescue. Lansky told him there were Chinese warships in the area. He told him to stand down.

Goodhill staggered from the TOC and out into the burning morning sun.

He fell to his knees and threw up.

Susan Steele stepped out of Eric's house. The morning was young, cold and clear, and for a while after locking the door, she just stood there on the landing and breathed. The tops of the tall black pines were waving their feathers in the wind from the river, hungry starlings were flitting and chirping, and high above in the pale azure sky, she thought she saw an eagle wheeling.

Susan didn't really believe in omens, neither good nor bad, but she'd take her comforts where she could.

She was wearing her fashionable boots and jeans, her hands in the pockets of her thick plaid car coat and her sunglasses perched in her hair. She was dressed for work, but lately she'd been dragging herself to the office. Showing all those houses to happy families wasn't something she cared much about these days.

For the first two weeks when she hadn't heard anything from Eric, she had reminded herself that it wasn't unusual and had often happened before. After all, when he'd deployed on multiple tours to Afghanistan, or God knew where, at times a whole month would go by before he could email or text or call. But then another week had passed, and another, and she knew that something was different. Eric and Hank had been together, they knew how much she would worry, and she kept hearing their precious voices over and over in that last, tinny, far-away call.

No. She told herself that it would be all right. And then that man had appeared at her office.

She'd never met him before. Eric had never talked about him, and as far as she remembered, he wasn't someone from Hank's past either. Yet he'd introduced himself warmly, saying he knew them both well. He looked and talked like someone from one of those old Cary Grant films, with his Burberry coat and bow tie, and a fedora with a feather. He had a very nice walking stick that it didn't seem like he was using as a cane.

Thorn was his name, and it seemed to match his demeanor. His facial features were soft and pinkish but his blue eyes were sharp as razors. He removed his hat, sat down in front of Susan's desk, and told her she'd need to be patient. Eric and Hank were away on a very important government project, something he couldn't really describe, and Susan told him she understood, because for years she'd been a guardian of secrets. He handed her a business card. It was thick and white with gold embossed letters, with only his name and a phone number. But she was already feeling weak in her ankles and sick to her stomach, when he then reached across her desk and squeezed her hand.

"I shan't lie to you, Susan," he said. "There is the possibility that they shall not return."

He told her he'd be in touch on a regular basis, but that if she needed anything at all, she should call. When he left she didn't escort him out to his car. She couldn't stand.

After that, she hadn't eaten at all for three whole days. This morning had been her first eggs and a cup of coffee. It felt almost like a betrayal, but she reminded herself she was a military spouse and mother.

We must keep ourselves going, and suffer in patience and silence.

She took a deep breath, jangled her keys, and was about to walk past Eric's fugly red hybrid and get in her Jeep, when a car rolled out of the woods and up the gravel. It was a cream-colored Kia with Uber and Lyft stickers on the windshield. It stopped next to her Jeep, and she frowned.

The rear door opened and Meg Harden got out. Susan touched her chest and almost gasped. Meg looked as beautiful as Susan remembered, maybe more so, with her mink-black hair and her crystal blue eyes gleaming. And she was hugging a very small blue bundle, and inside Susan could see a tiny baby. The Uber backed up, made a K turn, and drove away, leaving Meg and the baby there alone.

"He's not here, is he?" Meg said. Her blue eyes were rimmed in liquid.

"No, hon," Susan said as she walked down to Meg. She gently tipped the baby's blanket away from his little bald head. He had striking green eyes.

"I brought him a son," Meg said.

Susan smiled and tipped her chin at the homely Toyota. "That's fair. He left you a car."

"My parents . . ." Meg's voice was liquid, and a tear rolled down her cheek. "They're hardly speaking to me, Susan. They're not big fans of unwed mothers."

Susan nodded and kissed the baby on his head. Then she touched Meg's cheek, slipped one arm around her shoulders, and walked her back toward the house.

"That's all right," she said. "We'll do fine. I know how to raise good men."

ACKNOWLEDGMENTS

Left for Dead would not have been possible without the hard work and dedication of several people. David Highfill, my editor, is flat-out incredible. I've worked with him for more than nine years now and he's become more than an editor. He's a friend. Dan Conaway is my agent. He took a chance on me and I'm thankful for it. Dan, thank you for your time and attention.

Next up is my good friend Steve Hartov. Thank you for advice, counsel, and mentorship. *Left for Dead* is the best Eric Steele thriller yet and that is because of you.

Melanie is my much, much better half. Thank you for reading all of my books and giving me feedback before anyone else. Thank you for always being there for me.

Ethan, Emma, and Evan. My three children. I love you all! Being your Dad and watching you grow has been the privilege of a lifetime. You are the reason for all of this!